THE NOVELS OF SH...

"Sizzling...

...ling author

"Scorchi...

...ling author

"Wickedly seductive from start to finish."

—Jaci Burton, *New York Times* bestselling author

"The perfect combination of excitement, adventure, romance, and really hot sex." —Smexy Books

THE NOVELS OF LEXI BLAKE ARE . . .

"A book to enjoy again and again . . . Captivating."

—Guilty Pleasures Book Reviews

"A satisfying snack of love, romance, and hot, steamy sex."

—Sizzling Hot Books

"Hot and emotional." —Two Lips Reviews

continued . . .

PRAISE FOR THE MASTERS OF MÉNAGE SERIES
BY SHAYLA BLACK AND LEXI BLAKE

"Smoking hot! Blake and Black know just when to turn up the burner to scorching."
—Under the Covers Book Blog

"Well done . . . full of spicy sex, and a quick read."
—Smart Bitches, Trashy Books

"Steamy, poignant, and captivating . . . A funny, touching, lively story that will capture the reader from page one and have them wishing for more when it ends."
—Guilty Pleasures Book Reviews

"Very well written. With just the right amount of love, sex, danger, and adventure . . . A fun, sexy, exciting, hot read."
—Girly Girl Book Reviews

BIG EASY
TEMPTATION

SHAYLA BLACK
AND LEXI BLAKE

BERKLEY BOOKS, NEW YORK

BERKLEY

An imprint of Penguin Random House LLC
375 Hudson Street, New York, New York 10014

Library of Congress Cataloging-in-Publication Data

Names: Black, Shayla, author. | Blake, Lexi, author.
Title: Big Easy temptation : the perfect gentlemen / Shayla Black and Lexi Blake.
Description: Berkley trade paperback edition. | New York : Berkley Books,
2016. | Series: The perfect gentlemen ; 3
Identifiers: LCCN 2016001370 (print) | LCCN 2016005064 (ebook) | ISBN
9780425275344 (softcover) | ISBN 9780698163034 ()
Subjects: LCSH: Man-woman relationships—Fiction. | BISAC: FICTION / Romance /
Contemporary. | FICTION / Romance / General. | GSAFD: Romantic suspense
fiction. | Erotic fiction.
Classification: LCC PS3602.L325245 B54 2016 (print) | LCC PS3602.L325245
(ebook) | DDC 813/.6—dc23
LC record available at http://lccn.loc.gov/2016001370

PUBLISHING HISTORY
Berkley trade paperback edition / May 2016

PRINTED IN THE UNITED STATES OF AMERICA

10 9 8 7 6 5 4 3 2 1

Cover photograph © Westend61 / Corbis.
Cover design by Alana Colucci.
Interior text design by Laura K. Corless.

Penguin
Random
House

BIG EASY
TEMPTATION

PROLOGUE

San Diego, California
Nine years ago

Dax Spencer peered down over the elegant reception and wondered where the time had gone. Wasn't it just yesterday that he and his friends were attending Creighton Academy, where their biggest worry was passing calculus and sneaking out to the girls' school down the road?

Now Zack, one of his pack, was married. In fact, Zack was the first to fall on the matrimonial sword. He was also a senator about to make a run for the White House, but somehow the idea of Scooter being a husband seemed weirder.

And the political world had come to watch the nuptials. *People* magazine had even sent a photographer. The wedding was the bash of the year for America's elite and had all the pomp of a royal affair, complete with a few foreign dignitaries who had come hedging their bets that Zack and Joy Hayes would one day occupy the White House.

Dax nodded as Connor Sparks and Gabe Bond approached, drinks in hand. In the distance he could see his own parents among the crowd lining the dance floor. A simple glance proved this was the wedding of a Naval daughter, since the place was a sea of dress whites.

"I can't believe he really tied the knot." Connor, his best friend, put a hand on his shoulder as they watched the bride and groom begin their first dance.

Dax was sure they all felt that way. "After the year they spent planning this shindig, I think Joy's parents would have had Zack's head if he hadn't gone through with it."

"True." Connor smirked. "I hope he'll be happy. I like Joy but I worry she's too . . . I don't know, nice for Zack."

Gabe sighed. "Yeah. I would have thought he'd want someone with a little more attitude."

"To survive Zack's future, she'll definitely need backbone." Campaigning and politics seemed like a nasty business to Dax. Zack's senatorial campaign had been peppered with negativity about everything from his youth to his family ties. How would Joy weather the media scrutiny on a larger scale?

"Bitchiness would even be better, though that word will probably get me slapped," Connor said with a chuckle. "But yeah, I worry she's a bit fragile."

"Joy is the perfect first lady—pretty, gracious, kind. She'll be a true benefit to him politically," Gabe said. "I guess I wanted something more for him."

"He's been with her for two years. He seems happy." At least Dax hoped he was. Since the day he'd met Zack Hayes, when they'd been gangly, pimply-faced kids, Zack had been on a path, one his father had set for him long ago.

Dax couldn't exactly complain. His own father had set a path for him as well. Spencer sons went into the Navy. There had been a Spencer in every war fought since the Revolution. Only days before, he'd been promoted. He would become captain of his own ship in the next few years and eventually follow in his father's footsteps to become an admiral. Dax saw his path clearly—and he couldn't wait.

Then why did he feel so restless? There were at least a hundred gorgeous women roaming the reception. The likelihood of him getting lucky tonight was supremely high.

Yet Dax only sought one woman.

"You seem anxious tonight. What's up with you?" Connor tipped back his beer.

"You seem to know everything, Mr. Spy," he shot back. His best friend worked for the Central Intelligence Agency as an analyst. It fit Connor actually. He'd always been good at chess and strategy.

Connor rolled his eyes. "You know it's really more boring than you would think. And I don't have to be a spy to know that you're looking for one pretty blond law enforcement officer. Tell me something, has she shown you her handcuffs?"

No, she hadn't shown him anything at all. Holland Kirk was proving damned elusive. Her father was a Naval officer stationed here in San Diego under Dax's own dad. He'd met her shortly after Joy and Zack started dating. Zack had invited him over to meet some of Joy's college friends and Dax hadn't been able to take his eyes off the beauty.

The admiration was not mutual. Holland Kirk had been perfectly pleasant with him on every occasion they'd met. They had intelligent conversation, spent fun times together in groups, and enjoyed each other's company. But she'd turned him down flat every time he asked her out. She would smile politely and murmur some excuse before she turned the conversation to something she obviously found more pleasant.

"She's not interested." And that hurt. Besides being gorgeous, Holland was smart and funny. He'd never been so into a woman. They had chemistry. Heat. Well, he'd thought they had.

"Oh, she's interested. But I think your reputation has preceded you. Or maybe all of our reputations. I overheard her talking to Joy about how brave she was to be marrying into scandal central." Connor shrugged. "But we haven't had any scandals lately."

"We also haven't been choir boys." Gabe winced. "I got caught boning one of the Swedish princesses at that UN reception. In my own defense, she swore that broom closet was locked."

Dax remembered the episode fondly. "You looked good in those tabloid pics, bro. You've really kept up the ab routine. But seriously, we've all matured. I don't think that *Vanity Fair* article chronicling our love lives was really fair."

"Sexcapades," Gabe corrected. "It was a massive article detailing our sexcapades, complete with a detailed relationship map that proves we're all six sexual degrees away from Kevin Bacon. I blame Mad. He slept with the entire cast of that *Little Women* remake."

"C'mon, wasn't that fluff piece more tongue-in-cheek?" Dax argued hopefully.

"They managed to keep me out of it but, you guys . . . that was a double foldout." Connor sighed. "Which is probably enough to make any woman think twice. Well, any sane one. Especially someone like Holland. She's being recruited for NCIS. Another thing I heard her talking to Joy about."

Connor apparently listened in a lot. Dax looked over the dance floor again. He'd caught glimpses of Holland during the ceremony, but he hadn't seen her since. Instead, he'd been playing the good groomsman, ensuring all the parents were happy and comfortable. They'd all come except Connor's mother. In that respect, not much had changed since their Creighton days.

He needed to show Holland that he'd matured. Yes, he'd had a somewhat salacious youth, but he was older now. Even his friends were starting to settle down. Except Gabe, who was still screwing every princess, model, or Hollywood starlet he could. And Mad, who would apparently do any woman with a skirt and a pulse.

But he, Connor, and Roman were discerning and mature. Mostly.

Damn, he wanted to dance with Holland, see if he could talk to her.

"Even if she takes an NCIS job, she wouldn't be under my command. She's not enlisted so there's no problem. You really think she's turned off by the fact that I've dated a lot?"

"I think she's turned off by your status as a major manwhore," Gabe offered helpfully.

"Oooo, are we talking about who I think we are?" Maddox Crawford sauntered over with a smile. He'd already ditched his bow tie and looked as if he'd found the Scotch. He was carrying a crystal decanter of booze and several glasses. Mad was the very picture of decadence. "Because that girl is hot. That fine ass of hers nearly made the front seat of the Bentley smoke when I picked her up earlier."

Dax froze. "You picked her up?"

Mad flashed him a grin full of teeth. "She's my date."

Connor shook his head. "Yeah, we weren't going to tell him that."

Dax had never actually seen red before, but a dark swath of crimson coated his vision now.

"Uh, Dax, I was joking." Mad stepped back, his eyes wide. "She needed a ride. That's all. Joy wanted her here early, so Zack called me. Dude, you look like you're about to kill someone and I'm a little afraid it's me."

Dax took a deep breath. For a moment, he'd actually seen himself murdering one of his best friends over a woman, so maybe he had to accept that, to him, she was more. "If you touch her . . ."

Mad nodded. "I'll die a really horrible death. Got it. You called dibs. I respect the dibs, man. I also did you a solid. She's waiting downstairs in the lounge. I told her I had to talk to her about something important."

The red haze was threatening to come back. "Why were you trying to get her alone?"

"For you, buddy. All for you. Why do you think I'm up here while she's slipping into the library down there?" He pointed vaguely over the landing, to the first level below.

But Holland had agreed to meet Mad alone. That sat bitter in his gut. "She wants you."

Gabe snorted. "Dax, I heard her call Mad a festering disease pit on two legs."

"Walking syphilis is how I heard it," Connor added.

Mad nodded. "Actually, she called me stuff even worse. So go down there and talk to her. I made you look good earlier today. Mostly by making myself look like a complete shit. It's easy. I've got a lot of ammo in that gun, if you know what I mean. Gabe, my man, I've lined up twins for us. I'm going to warn you. They're very open minded and free spirited, and their father might have access to nuclear weapons so if we have to run, we're going to have to be fast."

"I'm totally in." Gabe grinned as he took a glass and looked down at the wedding. "God, I'm never getting married."

"For the right woman, I might consider it." Dax smiled in anticipation, then headed down the stairs before the elusive Holland could slip away again.

One shot. That's all he really had. If he couldn't convince her that he wasn't the same sort of skirt chaser as Mad or Gabe, she might cut him cold for good.

He headed for the library and eased the door open, stepping inside. Clearly, the room belonged to Joy's father. It was a masculine space and filled from floor to ceiling with books. The room was stunning, but nothing made his breath catch like the woman standing in the center.

The late afternoon light streamed through the windows, catching her honey-blond hair until it glowed. Her very tasteful bridesmaid dress showed off the curve of her breasts and her slender waist. Holland was fit and graceful and steely on the outside. But something about her seemed delicate under the surface. That vulnerability called to the protector in him.

At the sound of his footsteps, she turned. Her lips curled up in a wry grin. "So Mad betrayed me. Big shock. I should have known he didn't have a huge surprise planned for Zack and Joy that he needed my help with."

Dax closed the door behind him. Even though nerves attacked him like a swarm of buzzing bees, simply being alone with her calmed something inside him. He'd never realized how restless he felt until he'd met this woman.

He sent her a smile. "I wouldn't say that. I'm almost certain he changed out the cans we tied to the limo for good luck with neon butt plugs. Luckily, Roman usually manages to clean up everything Mad defiles. Seriously, Roman even hired a man to seek and destroy all of the 'adult' presents Mad snuck into the gifts."

An actual smile crossed her face and she lit up the room. "He's an interesting friend. I think the press is going to love him on the campaign trail."

"Oh, Roman has protocols in place for that, too," Dax admitted. "Mad is not allowed in the same state where Zack is campaigning. If he comes too close, Gabe will kidnap Mad and they'll hunt up a pair of supermodels. Win-win. Do you think Zack and Joy will really do it?"

This was a safe topic. Politics normally wasn't, but he wasn't discussing political opinions, just their friends.

Holland glanced toward the window. "You mean run for the White House? Oh, I think that's a given. I wish they wouldn't. I don't know how that particular scrutiny makes anyone happy. I love Joy. Hell, I love Zack. He's an amazing man, which is why I worry about both of them in that den of snakes slithering around D.C."

"Zack is more ruthless than you know. He was bred for this and he'll protect Joy. Roman will, too. He seems to really like her, which is a feat since Roman doesn't like many people. I swear, we'll all do our best to watch out for her."

"I'm sure she'll appreciate it." Holland sighed. "Well, I should get back to the reception."

God, his one chance was slipping through his fingers. "Why are you afraid to be alone with me?"

She arched an elegant brow over her blue eyes. "Commander, I could take you in a fight. I'm not afraid of you."

There it was, that crackling energy he felt every time she challenged him. It made his heart speed up, his head buzz, his dick get hard. He always felt this heady desire around her. "I don't want to fight with you, Holland. I just want to talk. I want to understand why you won't go out with me. I'm going to lay it on the line here and now. I'm crazy about you."

She hesitated. "I like you, too, Dax. I won't lie and say I'm not attracted to you, but we can't work."

"What do you mean? I'm not asking for a commitment, just dinner. Maybe a movie. I want to spend time with you."

Holland shook her head and brushed past him to open the door. Dax scrambled back and blocked her.

She sighed at him. "Look, your lifestyle is not one I would choose."

"What lifestyle? I'm a sailor. I know you've heard some crazy stories about me, but they're not true."

That judgmental brow rose again. "Really? So you didn't nearly cause an international incident because you slept with the daughter of a South American dictator."

The things he did in Vegas. "I didn't know who she was, but I was also twenty-three at the time and I didn't really care. Besides, that whole thing was really exaggerated by the press."

"Sure it was. Spencer, I'm the daughter of an enlisted man. The rest of my family are cops. I'm blue collar. You're American royalty."

"Do you know what I like about the Navy? I'm not royalty there. No one gives a crap that my family has money. No one cares what my last name is. I work hard and I'll continue to do so."

"You're naive if you think your last name doesn't open doors," she said almost sadly. "I admit I'm attracted. Absolutely one hundred percent drawn to you. I also really crave chocolate. That doesn't mean I'm going to indulge."

She didn't wait for his reply, just shouldered her way past him. If he let her leave now, Dax feared he wouldn't get another chance. He couldn't let her walk out the door without a fight.

Dax wrapped gentle but firm fingers around her wrist. "So you'll never even try a taste?"

She looked down at her wrist until he released her, holding up his hands. "I'm fairly sure that a taste will only make me want more. Besides, I'm leaving San Diego in a few weeks. NCIS made me an offer, so I'll be working in New Orleans. I still have family there. Since my father passed, I've decided I'd like to be with them."

New Orleans. His family lived in New Orleans. "Give me a chance. Kiss me once and see if you can walk away, because I don't think I'll be able to. Distance doesn't mean anything if two people want to be together. Give me a shot to prove I'm not the man you think I am."

They stood so close and yet weren't touching at all. Still, he could practically feel her skin against his.

Holland looked torn. "I don't want to be another conquest for you."

That was easy. Honesty, in this case, was definitely his friend. "I haven't slept with anyone in almost a year. I've been on assignment. Then I met you. I had a colorful youth; I won't deny that. But now I want something more, something deeper. The man you've read about, he isn't real. I am. Kiss me and let me show you."

God, he wanted to. Ached to. He wished like hell he could wrap his arms around her and show her everything he had to offer, but rushing her would be a mistake. He had to wait for Holland. Whatever happened between them needed be her choice.

She hesitated and for a moment, Dax thought she would leave for good. She met his stare as though taking his measure. After a moment's silent perusal, she stepped closer, her skirt gently swishing against her graceful legs, bringing her so near. His heart revved.

She skimmed her fingertips along his jawline. "You want me to kiss you, Commander? That might be dangerous."

He knew it was, because there was no way they'd end up in bed tonight. Dax would be in a world of hurt no matter which way this went. He was startled to realize he didn't want to be just another conquest for her, either.

"It could be," he admitted. "I'm willing to take the chance. I know you won't believe me, but I like you. Really like you. I enjoy talking to you, being around you, hearing you laugh. I'm not looking for a one-night stand or some easy hookup. I'm pretty sure I'm looking for something more."

She stared at him as if she tried to memorize his face. An openness, almost an intimacy, in her expression gave the moment gravity. The way she looked at him went beyond anything sexual. Dax set about memorizing her, too. He drank in the delicate angles of her face, the tiny scar that ran across her cheekbone, the way her bottom lip plumped out. A light dusting of freckles sprinkled across her nose. She was beautiful, yes, but Holland was way more than a pretty face.

"I think that's the most dangerous thing you've ever said to me, Commander. I am going to kiss you—once—but when it's over I'll still vote to save my sanity and walk away." She rose onto her toes and lightly pressed her lips against his.

Damn, she felt soft and warm and sweet—all the things he loved about women. But he savored her so much more. This simple kiss packed heat. It flashed through his system, sizzled down his spine. He wanted to revel in this moment and make it last.

When she circled her arms around his waist and her lips brushed sensually over his, Dax couldn't hold back anymore. He cupped her face in his hands and deepened the connection. He explored her lips, slowly, deeply. Restlessly, she slid against him, coming even closer. He could feel her breasts crushed against his chest. His head spun. He went in for more, filtering his fingers through her hair and groaning into their kiss.

She pulled away, her breathing not quite steady.

"Holland . . ." That couldn't be it. That taste had only made him hunger for more. His whole body felt alive, every nerve focused on her.

"That's what I was afraid of." She crashed against him once more. This time when she kissed him, her mouth flowered open, inviting him inside.

His tongue slid against hers in a velvet caress as she moved in, sliding her hands up his chest until she wrapped them around his neck.

Dax devoured her. So hungry. She was the source of his every craving and, until he'd taken her in his arms, he'd only suspected how utterly she could thrill and satisfy him. Now he knew.

Holland felt perfect against him as their tongues mated. The rest of the world fell away as he lost himself in her teasing scent and silken touch. He gripped her tightly, wishing he could strip her dress off. He definitely had to rethink not wooing her into bed.

He drew her closer still, needing her in a way he'd never needed a woman before.

Then the door swung open behind him, banging against the wall, startling them apart.

"Please, Admiral. You're the only one who can help me," a woman tearfully implored.

Fuck. He held on to Holland, terrified she would walk out if he didn't. He looked over his shoulder to find his father following Zack's mother into the room.

"Oh, no." Holland sounded anxious. "Joy and Zack worried about this. Constance has been drinking all day."

His father caught sight of him and Holland. His eyes flared wide for a brief moment. "I'm sorry. She was creating a scene. I wasn't sure what to do."

"I'll go get Zack." Holland pulled away, then spared him one last glance. "I'm leaving for New Orleans soon. Have a good life, Commander."

Dax didn't want to let her go, but Zack's mom burst into noisy tears, and he knew he had to get this situation under control. Frustrated and feeling helpless, he watched Holland stride out of his life.

If he looked her up next time he visited home, would she speak to him?

"They're going to kill me," Constance shrieked. "And that poor girl.

She doesn't know the truth. How can I tell her? How can I tell anyone? It was an accident. I didn't mean to do it." She fell on the couch and wrapped her arms around her knees, sobbing.

Dax zipped a confused stare over to his dad.

The older Spencer shrugged. "She's been talking like that for ten minutes, son."

With a sigh, Dax sat beside his buddy's mom and tried his best to calm her.

He didn't see Holland again for years.

Washington, D.C.
Present Day

"You're sure you want to do this?"

Connor's question brought Dax out of his memories. He'd been thinking of that day with Holland, the day he'd first kissed her. He liked that memory much better than the later ones. A chill went through him. The wind in D.C. was cold this time of year. He stood outside the condo Connor shared with Lara, his wife, and prepared for the long ride home.

"I have to find out whatever I can." Dax set his helmet on the seat of his bike and pulled his gloves on. "My father's name was on that list."

Only days before they'd tracked down the mysterious Natalia Kuilikov. She was a Russian woman connected to the Hayes family when Zack's father had been the U.S. ambassador to the Soviet Union, before the fall of the Wall. She'd written a diary people had died for, including his dear friend Maddox Crawford. All clues led to the *Bratva*, the Russian mob, being responsible for the murder. Connor and Lara had recently spoken to the older woman. Moments after a bullet ripped through her forehead, they'd discovered Kuilikov's handwritten notes in Cyrillic.

The translation had come back as a dead pool—a list of assassination targets.

Joy Hayes had been on that list, as had Constance, Zack's mother.

Admiral Harold Spencer had been on that list, as well. They were all dead. Dax damn sure wanted answers.

His father had been gone for three years. His death had been declared a suicide. Dax hated to think about any of it—not the scandal that had come before his father's death, nor the horrible time after it, and definitely not the investigation that ended with him losing Holland Kirk forever.

Until he'd seen that translation, he'd never intended to set eyes on her again. She'd betrayed him in the cruelest fashion possible by closing her investigation after giving it as much thought as someone opening an umbrella on a rainy day. In the blink of an eye, she'd made a judgment call that gave the press free license to vilify his father. Hell, she'd even had him believing his father was guilty at one point. She'd torn down his family to further her career. Oh, he'd paid her back. Now nothing lay between them but anger and regret.

But he couldn't let this case rest in peace anymore. Things had changed. *He* had changed. Armed with new evidence, Dax intended to personally make sure Holland opened the investigation again—and gave the facts the due process they deserved.

"Yes, his name was on the list," Connor agreed in that tone that let Dax know he was being handled with care. "I'll look into it. Lara will help. You know we can do a lot. You don't have to go back to New Orleans. Zack pulled strings and got you placed on a special assignment here in D.C. When we're done, you can decide if you want to go back to the Navy or not. You can spend the next couple of months with me and I'll help you sort it all out."

Connor knew damn well what was waiting for him in New Orleans. Or rather, who. "Thanks, buddy. But I think I'll spend the time I have left with her."

Connor grimaced. "Yes, that's exactly what I'm trying to avoid. You two will only tear each other up. You've done some stupid shit over that woman."

Like waking up after a bender to find himself married to someone else? Connor had a point; some of the worst moments of his life had been because of Holland Kirk.

Dax shook that reality off. "I'll be fine. I'm certainly not going to drink myself into oblivion and marry whatever woman happens to be next to me."

"Her best friend. You married her best friend," Connor pointed out. "Don't expect her to be helpful. Hell, I half expect her to bite your head off."

"Yeah? Well, I expect her to finally give me the truth." He picked up the helmet before pulling his best friend into a manly hug. "I'll call you if I need anything. I'm going to get to the bottom of this. For my dad. For Mad. For Zack."

Someone was playing a dangerous game with his friend, the president. Unfortunately for whoever it was, Zack was one of Dax's inner circle. They'd already lost Mad to this nasty business. Dax refused to lose anyone else.

Holland Kirk was either a pawn or a power player. He would damn sure find out which.

With a nod to Lara on the balcony above, he hopped on his bike and revved the engine. He headed southwest, toward New Orleans and the only woman he'd ever loved. As the miles rolled, the past flowed over him like a tidal wave . . .

PART ONE

THEN

ONE

New Orleans, Louisiana
Three years ago

Holland Kirk sighed as she packed up her laptop. Another case closed. She liked the simple ones. Two enlisted sailors had gotten into a bar fight over a local and one of them had waited two days before deciding to jump his opponent back on base. He'd nearly gutted the other man. Luckily, she'd found a witness and now the seaman was sitting in a jail cell.

If only all her cases were so easy.

She stood and stretched, trying not to think about the news she'd heard earlier today. Courtney had waltzed in with two chicken salad sandwiches and the latest gossip.

Captain Dax Spencer had taken a one-month training assignment right here in New Orleans. Could Holland believe it? One of the Perfect Gentlemen here in their backyard. Courtney had been star struck.

Holland kind of wanted to hide.

Her cell phone trilled and she looked down to find a text from Courtney.

He's even hotter than I imagined. I'm the writer assigned to him for this project! Squee! I need an entirely new wardrobe. And a mani pedi.

A flurry of emoticons followed, all conveying her excitement. Holland wasn't sure what a couple of them were, but they definitely looked happy. Courtney knew she'd met Spencer at some point, but had no idea he was basically the man of her dreams. And now she meant to avoid him at all costs.

Sounds good! Hope you two have fun.

She sent the text, trying not to admit that her stomach dropped at the thought of pretty, curvy Courtney with Dax. Courtney looked like a swimsuit model. She was exactly the type of woman Holland would expect on the arm of one of the infamous Perfect Gentlemen.

Absolutely not her. Never Holland.

It had been years since she'd spoken to the gorgeous Dax Spencer, but she dreamed of him often. It wasn't like she hadn't dated, but she ended up comparing every single man who came into her life to Dax, and they always came up short.

She'd seen him at his father's funeral. She'd shown up quietly and sat in the back. It had been a travesty how few people had been in attendance. Admiral Harold Spencer's exemplary reputation had been washed away with one indiscretion.

"Hey, I've heard we're going to have trouble." Jim Kellison leaned against the door to her office, his dark eyes grim. "Your friend was telling everyone Captain Spencer has come back to town for a while."

She was certain that had a couple of special agents thinking about early retirement, including the one in front of her. "Apparently he's agreed to help write the documentation on the new training procedures. He's been testing them on his ship."

"Sure. That's what every captain dreams of," Jim shot back. "Spending several weeks writing training manuals. I've heard a rumor you run in his circle."

She shook her head. "God, no. I'm friends with his sister. I was very close to the wife of one of his friends."

Joy Hayes. It was hard to believe she was really gone, the victim of a single bullet from a lone shooter. Tears threatened. They did every single time she thought about the day Joy died. How could she ever forget it? Some TV news show rolled the video of her friend dying at least once a week.

Joy had been killed by a man who'd wanted to assassinate her husband. The news stories claimed the assassin was a mentally ill man who hated Zack and couldn't stand the thought of him in the White House. Three days later, Zack Hayes had been elected president.

Six weeks after that, the terrible scandal involving Admiral Spencer had blown up. In the thick of the gossip and media speculation, he'd killed himself. Holland could only imagine how dark those days had been for Dax.

So much pain in a short amount of time.

She would love Zack Hayes to the end of her days because while everyone else had abandoned the Spencer family, the man with the most political capital to lose had sat beside Dax in the church for the admiral's funeral that day. All of the Perfect Gentlemen had been there—Crawford, Bond, the scary one, Hayes, and Calder. They'd deflected the press from Dax and protected their friend.

She might not always understand the ties that bound those men together, but she sometimes envied them.

Jim nodded sympathetically. "Yes, Mrs. Hayes was a gracious lady. We all mourn her loss."

More tears burned her eyes. She blinked them back. "Has Captain Spencer been in touch with you? You and Bill closed the case on his father, if I recall."

That was an understatement. She knew exactly who had worked the case, but she'd tried to stay far from it. Being close to Augustine Spencer, Dax's sister, meant recusing herself from participating in the admiral's open investigation. She hadn't even read the file. She couldn't bring herself to do it.

Harold Spencer, upright family man and Naval officer, a beacon of New Orleans society, had been caught on camera in bed with an underage prostitute. She'd heard that a witnesses close to the admiral told NCIS the man had been a pedophile for a very long time. Rumors had spread like a bad virus and the jackals had shown up to drag the Spencer family through the mud.

And then, before he could be court-martialed, he'd been found with a bullet in his brain.

"We closed the case, but the captain made it very clear how unhappy he was about it." Jim huffed. "We did a thorough investigation."

Jim was one of the finest investigators she knew. He'd been a special agent for more than fifteen years. "I'm sure you did your best. These kinds of cases are always hard. There was a lot of media scrutiny."

The press had been like a pack of wolves. The office had been inundated with their calls. Once the salacious story hit the tabloids, reporters had written article after article speculating on the lurid details of the admiral's organized sex parties and the supposed ways in which he'd defrauded taxpayers to host them.

NCIS had been forced to investigate each and every rumor. All of them had been proven false, except the original allegation.

God, she hoped the admiral hadn't known the girl's true age. Amber Taylor had been fifteen, but on camera she'd looked at least a half dozen years older.

"I have gray hair from that case," Jim acknowledged. "And I swear Bill went bald after that last press conference. I've never seen a man look so terrified on camera. There's a reason he didn't go into the entertainment field."

It was probably for the best since Bill had a brilliant mind but a potbelly that wouldn't look great on screen. "I remember. So I guess you're afraid Captain Spencer's return will mean more media attention? If it's any consolation, I don't think he liked the press coverage any more than we did."

"I'm not worried about the press." Jim ran a hand over his hair. "I'm worried about *him*. I don't need his harassment again. He was like a dog with a bone, Kirk. He called ten times a day, sent so many e-mails I couldn't keep up with them, and I won't even go into all the times I could have arrested him for interfering with an investigation. I didn't, because I like his mother and sister. I thought they'd been through enough, but I won't put up with that crap again."

Holland had stayed away. She'd actually taken a couple of weeks off and gone to visit some friends because the temptation to interfere had been so great. But she'd heard stories of Captain Spencer causing trouble. He'd apparently been particularly angry when his father's death had been ruled a suicide.

It would be a hard truth for a man like Dax to take.

Still, according to Gus, her brother was trying to move on. Holland liked Augustine Spencer. She was wild and smart and larger than life. She also worked at the White House and had been close to Joy. The three had formed a special friendship, and she still cherished the time Gus spent in New Orleans.

"Maybe the captain simply took the assignment to be close to his mother for a while," Holland suggested. "I know this mess has been hard on her."

Gus had offered to turn down the job with the Hayes administration and Dax had offered to leave the Navy, but Judith Spencer had insisted her children continue with their lives. Their mother had been adamant. Still, Holland checked in on her from time to time. She had to be lonely in that huge house.

"I don't buy it." Jim shook his head. "He's been in the Gulf for six months. Lots of action there."

"Maybe he's ready for a change." Holland shrugged.

"Does Captain Spencer strike you as a desk-job sort of man?"

She frowned and bit her lip.

"You know I'm right. He's not a man who likes peace and quiet. And he didn't choose a New Orleans training post for the gumbo."

"You think he's here to try to get the case reopened?" She really hoped not.

"I think he's a son who loved his father and can't handle knowing that the man who raised him wasn't who he thought. I wouldn't want to believe it of my own father. It's got to be doubly hard on a man like the captain, who's used to getting his way. All that money must have made his life pretty cushy up until now."

In an instant, Holland remembered him, so handsome and earnest, that day in the library.

Do you know what I like about the Navy? I'm not royalty there. No one gives a crap that my family has money. No one cares what my last name is. I work hard and I'll continue to do so.

At the time she'd thought he was naive. Having worked NCIS for the last few years, she'd figured out that for all of the captain's connections, his father had been as much of a negative as a positive. He'd had to work twice as hard to prove he wasn't moving up the ranks due to nepotism. During the war, he'd served his country valiantly in the Persian Gulf. She'd read reports of his bravery and knew he'd earned his captaincy.

"The Spencer I knew was a hard worker despite the fact that he could have coasted through," she argued. "He's honest and loyal. Just because he's rich doesn't make him soft. He's a good man, and you should treat him with respect when he shows up."

"I'm glad to hear you say that, Holland."

She stopped, her focus narrowing to that deep voice dredged up from the depths of her memory. Dax Spencer had the sexiest accent, having been raised right here in New Orleans. His father had been career Navy, but Judith Spencer had insisted on a somewhat normal childhood for Dax and Gus. They spent time with their father, but also lived in a big mansion in the Garden District. Dax had gone off to Creighton Academy at the age of twelve, but he'd never lost that thick, molasses-rich NOLA drawl. When he spoke, his tones deep and dark, it did something to Holland she couldn't explain.

"Speak of the devil. You could have knocked, Captain Spencer." She turned, and the sight of him was like a punch to the solar plexus. She breathed through the reaction, trying to hide the fact that being this close to him already had her heart pounding.

Damn, but he looked good. The years had been kind to him, turning a beautiful boy into a gorgeous, powerful man. He filled out his khakis in a way most sailors couldn't. Tall and broad and powerfully built, he was a glorious hunk of masculinity.

He gave her a lopsided grin that threatened to stop her heart. "I didn't want to interrupt."

Jim had gone a nice shade of red. "Captain Spencer, it's good to see you again."

Dax didn't seem fazed at all that he'd overheard them talking about him, but then he was likely used to it. He simply gave Jim a friendly grin. "Now I'm absolutely sure that's a lie. I'm sure I was a pain in the ass and the last couple of months without me have likely been pleasant. How about I promise to be respectful this time around. I wasn't in a good place the last time we talked."

"That's understandable," Jim allowed, holding out a hand. "Let me know if I can help you, and welcome back to New Orleans."

Dax shook his hand with a nod. "Thank you, Agent Kellison. I promise I'm not going to make your life hell." Jim left with a friendly wave, and Dax turned his attention to Holland. "I called him a lowlife cocksucker who deserved to have his entrails eaten by a gator. I might have been in a bad mood at the time."

"It seems so." Why did she sound so breathy? She wasn't the vampy type.

"You look good, Holland," he said. "Did I ever thank you for coming to my father's funeral?"

She shot him a startled glance. "I didn't realize you'd seen me there."

"Sweetheart, there were so few people I couldn't have missed you. I truly appreciate it. I know my momma and Gus did as well."

As Holland's heart continued to race, she thanked goodness the office door stood open and she could see people moving out in the hallway. She wasn't sure she could handle being alone with him, knowing the last time she had been she'd kissed him. The press of their bodies and lips had been the single most erotic moment of her life. She'd slept with men and not felt as close to them as she had to Dax Spencer in that one moment.

Sometimes she could still feel the way his tongue had moved against hers, sliding in a silky dance. She could feel his hands on her body. He'd been subtle, but she'd felt the possession in his grip. If Admiral Spencer and Constance Hayes hadn't barged in, she'd likely have found herself on top of that desk with her legs spread and clinging to Dax Spencer as he drove into her.

"Why are you here, Captain?"

"Can't you call me Dax? You have dinner with my mother twice a month. You see my sister every time she's in town. Can't we at least be on a first-name basis?"

Her reticence sounded ridiculous when he put it that way. They actually did run in the same small circle. She simply avoided him at all costs and had since the moment she realized she wanted him in a way she'd never wanted any man. "All right. Dax, welcome back to New Orleans. What are you doing here?"

He cast her a sidelong glance. "Well, Holland. I'm in the Navy and I was recently stationed at the Joint Reserve Base New Orleans in a training capacity. I've been involved in new training methods on modern ships."

"Yes, because Captain Awesome really wants to spend a month writing training manuals." That was the moniker the sailors had given him after his wartime bravery. He'd been creative and smart and he'd stood by his men. They loved him. They would lay their lives on the line for him. He was everything the Navy looked for in a captain.

Dax's eyes widened in surprise. "Captain Awesome? Are you serious?"

As a heart attack. "It's what everyone calls you. After what you did in Operation Iraqi Freedom, can you doubt it?" In the middle of unexpected enemy fire, he had devised and implemented a battle plan on the fly. He'd used his ship in a way that had shortened the skirmish and saved lives.

His gorgeous mouth turned down. "That was supposed to be classified."

He wasn't that naive. "Nothing that cool is classified, Captain. Dax."

"Captain Awesome might be the worst call sign I've ever heard." He shook his head woefully. "I'm back in New Orleans because I was asked to spend the month providing insight on the new training procedures. Since I implemented them on my ship, I decided to help out."

She didn't believe that for a second. "And that's the only reason you're here?"

He sent her an unreadable smile. "I have some other things to accomplish while I'm here."

"You want us to look into your father's case again." Nothing else made sense to her.

"I'm here for numerous reasons. One, my mother's birthday is soon. Two, Gus is taking a little time off. So I came to be with my family. After everything that happened, family is my priority."

She understood. "I'm glad. I think your mom is lonely. I'm pretty sure Gus isn't."

Dax shuddered, proving he'd heard about Gus's proclivities. "I do not need to know what my sister is doing. Or who. I came back to make sure my mother is all right . . . and to take care of a few other loose ends."

Finally they were getting to the point. "Did you come to see Jim or Bill?"

His eyes pinned her. "I came to see you, sweetheart."

Damn, but she was in trouble. "Why? I can't help you."

"Oh, I think you can. Holland, have dinner with me. Give me a chance."

She shook her head because even if the Spencer name wasn't as shiny as it had once been, they still came from different worlds. "I don't think that's a good idea."

Besides, Holland wasn't entirely sure what he was after. He might be asking for her to reopen his father's case. Or he might be asking her for a date. Either would be a bad freaking idea.

"Holland, listen. Please. You're the only one who might give me a shot, the only one who might hear what I have to say." His jaw hardened to a stubborn line. "Have dinner with me. Let me plead my case."

"Or?" There was always an "or" in these types of conversations.

"I spend the rest of my life knowing I didn't do everything I could to honor my father."

Shit. What was she supposed to do with that plea? He'd given her the one argument that guaranteed she wouldn't turn him away. "All right. My place. Eight o'clock. Don't be late."

He flashed dimples, sending her into a tailspin. "I'll bring the wine."

He turned and strode out, leaving her watching his amazingly hot backside and wondering what the hell she'd agreed to. She'd known she couldn't handle him when he'd done his best to persuade her to give him a shot during Joy and Zack's reception years ago. Not much had changed. Besides, she'd wanted a career of her own then. She still did. Certainly, she didn't want to be like her mother, following her father from base to base, always having to make new friends and find a way to fit in. If she'd allowed herself to date Spencer back then, she would be his wife now and she would have had his children, watching him as he rose through the ranks and left her further and further behind.

She wanted more for herself.

Yes, she was stronger now. More mature. She'd had more experience with the opposite sex. Could she handle him? Ready or not, it seemed she was going to find out.

TWO

Dax tried not to stare at Holland as she set a steaming plate in front of him. He was so hungry. Not for the food. Oh, it smelled delicious and he wasn't surprised that, despite being a tough NCIS investigator, she could also produce what looked like a gourmet meal. Holland Kirk was the kind of woman who would master anything she put her mind to.

Yeah, he wanted the food, but he craved her far more. She was still the most beautiful woman to him. Her blond hair cascaded around her shoulders in waves. When he'd seen her earlier, she'd had it tucked up in a tidy bun that matched her neat but utilitarian clothes. But when she'd opened the door to him not fifteen minutes earlier, she'd looked so pretty and feminine in jeans and a pink shirt that hugged her slender curves.

Years, miles, war, and death stood between their kiss in the library and now. He'd never gotten this woman out of his head.

"This looks amazing. Thank you. You have no idea how long it's been since someone cooked for me. Well, someone who didn't learn his skills from the Navy," Dax admitted. Captaining his own ship had its privileges, but made-from-scratch Cajun food wasn't one of them.

She sat across from him and lifted her wineglass with an elegant hand. "My mother was a good cook, but after she passed, my dad was still at sea. So I ended up here in New Orleans with my uncle. Now, that man can cook. This is his gumbo recipe. Sorry it's nothing more exciting."

"This is the most excitement I've had in a while, Holland." He took a spoonful. The dish was perfectly made with just the right bite of heat. "It's excellent. And I really do thank you for hearing me out."

He was going to do his damnedest to be polite with her. He needed her on his side. If this investigation wasn't between them, he would have walked into her office and finished what they'd started almost seven years before.

The only times he'd seen her since that kiss had all been at funerals. First Zack's mother had perished in a car accident about a year after the wedding. He'd glimpsed Holland there from a distance. She'd certainly been at Joy's funeral, but that had been a clusterfuck. So many reporters, so many people mourning the woman who would have been first lady. Then Holland had attended his father's services. Even though Dax had viewed the whole thing through a filter of disbelief and rage, the one sweet moment had been when he'd scanned the sparsely attended event and seen her sitting in the back pew, silently honoring his father.

Besides his family and best friends, she'd been the only person he knew to show up. Everyone else had run from the scandal and abandoned the Spencer family during their time of tragedy.

Now she was his only hope of seeing any kind of justice done. He'd spent the last week before his return to New Orleans plotting and planning ways to persuade her to do what he needed. He couldn't get emotional no matter how much she moved him.

"You can't behave the way you did before," Holland said, her mouth turned down. "My coworkers gave you a pass because they knew you were hurting. They won't do it again."

He'd been a righteous prick and a pain in the ass. He'd battled with

anyone who got in his way. NCIS had definitely seemed like one obsta-
cle after another. "I understand. I was running on emotion at the time.
I've cooled off and I'm coming at the problem logically now."

Well, with as much logic as he could. It wasn't easy watching others
sling mud and tarnish his father's reputation. Hell, they'd ripped a
dead man to shreds and fed what had been left of his good name to the
dogs of the press.

"You've been conducting your own investigation?" Holland asked,
passing him the cornbread.

He accepted it gratefully. He hadn't been joking about his last
decent meal. It had been months ago, right before Joy Hayes had died.
He and the other Perfect Gentlemen had come together for Labor Day
in the Hamptons. They'd had a cookout and laughed and joked around
about what perverted things they would all do in the White House
once Zack was elected.

That had been less than a year ago. Why did he feel a decade
older now?

"I hired a couple of private investigators and had some friends look
into a few things for me." It didn't hurt that his best friend was an
analyst with the Central Intelligence Agency. Though Gabe and Mad
thought Connor was in deeper than that. Dax often wondered if they
were right. "They found some information I thought was disturbing."

"Do you think Jim and Bill didn't do their jobs?"

She asked the question politely, her voice soft, but Dax knew a
landmine when he heard one.

He shook his head. "I think NCIS did the best they could with the
information and resources available at the time. No one was ready for
the way the story exploded in the press."

"No, we weren't. Any media relations training we have is cursory.
I think even the feds would have had trouble with a story of that mag-
nitude," she admitted. "Normally it would have lasted one news cycle
and been over."

"My father wasn't news for what he did but because I'm his son and I have powerful friends." Guilt still twisted his gut over that fact.

Holland was correct. The news would definitely have run the story about the admiral's disgrace, but the tabloids wouldn't have covered it. His father hadn't been a rock star or a celebrity. He'd been old school money serving in a position of prestige.

Dax was the celebrity. It didn't matter how hard he tried to stay out of the press, the media associated him with two of the most self-avowed playboys of the Western world, along with the White House chief of staff and the president of the United States. Somehow, Connor managed to duck the news coverage. Probably because he never allowed anyone to take a full-frontal picture of him. And the CIA kept him out of the public eye. Being dragged into the news had never bothered Dax much. It had been fine. He was used to it. But his parents had not been.

"I wish I could have kept them off the story. We tried to keep it quiet." She reached out, her hand almost touching his before she abruptly pulled back.

Damn it. He wanted her hand in his, wanted any touch she would give him. It had been so long since he'd felt any kind of affection for a woman. From a woman. "I know. They were always going to find the story and they were always going to spin it to sound as salacious as possible. It's their job."

She settled back in her chair. "So you think you have new information?"

She seemed determined to keep things professional. Maybe that was for the best. He'd come for a mission, not a woman. "I'm approaching the investigation from a new angle. It wasn't hard to do. There was really only about a week of actual fieldwork put into the case. I was surprised at how thin the file was."

She put a hand up. "I don't want to know how you got a copy of that file."

He was resourceful. He was also good at flirting with secretaries.

"I'll keep that to myself. Anyway, NCIS closed the investigation into my father's case after his death was ruled a suicide."

"There was no one to prosecute. It didn't seem right to drag his name further through the mud. I actually had some say in making that call. I asked Bill and Jim to stop looking into it because they would have had to question your mother. I didn't want to put her through that."

He could understand her decision. "I appreciate that, but I think there's more going on here than the report suggests. Did you know the girl my father was accused of sleeping with had disappeared?"

He used that bland euphemism. What his father had been accused of could be construed as anything from statutory rape to sexual assault of a minor.

"No. I wasn't aware of that." She took a sip of the wine he'd brought. "But she was a teenage prostitute with a history of running away. It's not so surprising that she would go missing."

"But Amber Taylor went missing before the investigation was closed. No one on your staff ever spoke to her. There's no record on file to indicate they even attempted to contact her."

She raised an elegant brow in surprise. "Really?"

Dax nodded. "The only evidence against my father is that videotape and the testimony of two of his aides." For Dax, those clues made an awfully thin reason to tear a man's reputation apart. Even if he'd been proven innocent, the damage would have been done. His father's career had ended the minute he'd been called a pedophile in public.

"Maybe they didn't need to talk to Amber Taylor. Those two aides of your father's gave very in-depth interviews," Holland explained. "They were good witnesses from everything I understand. I know Jim felt like they were solid and so did JAG."

The Navy's legal arm had been all for prosecuting his father. They would have a much harder time if they tried to prosecute him today since all their evidence was rapidly vanishing. "Did you know that one of those two aides was recently murdered?"

"What?" Holland reared back. "No."

He'd been fairly certain she was out of the loop. "He was transferred out of NOLA about a week after my father died. He was killed in Puerto Rico during a mugging."

"I will admit it's odd, but it doesn't prove anything." Even as she spoke, her brow furrowed, a sure sign that her thinking cap was on.

Making her think was exactly what he'd hoped for. "I don't have to prove anything. I simply have to prod your curiosity enough to look."

"You think you know me?"

"I do know you, Holland. You're smart and quick and you like to see justice done. You also liked my father." In fact, Dax was counting on it.

That's why he'd come back to New Orleans in the first place. He'd asked for the training assignment. Hell, he'd practically begged for it because he needed to be here if he was going to convince Holland to reopen his father's case. He didn't trust anyone else to look at it with a fresh, fair approach.

"I can't deny that," she murmured.

"In fact, you like my whole family and you hate what happened to us. If you could give us any respite at all, you would work day and night for it."

"Now you're playing to my ego." A hint of an amused smile crossed her lips.

"Is it working?"

"You know it is," she replied. "I'll look over what you have tonight, but I can't promise you anything."

"All I want is a shot at convincing you."

"Like I said, I'll read your file. I really was sorry about your dad. I'm also sorry I didn't reach out to you. I should have. We were friends once."

"Why didn't you? You've stayed in touch with Gus and Mom."

She sighed. "I got buried in work. They were here and you weren't.

It seemed easier to let it go. And you were so angry. I'll be honest, I was afraid you would tear me up. Sometimes people lash out when they're in as much pain as you were. Your world had crumbled under your feet. I didn't want to be collateral damage."

"You were right to stay away. I was so angry I couldn't think straight. When the allegations came to light, I learned some things about my father I didn't want to know."

"But you don't believe he raped a fifteen-year-old girl." It sounded like a statement of fact rather than a question.

Dax nodded. "I think my father was set up. There are too many coincidences, and I question how so many people with critical information about the case suddenly disappeared when they were no longer needed."

"Be careful, Captain. You're starting to sound like a conspiracy theorist. Why would anyone want to ruin your father? No one came after his money from what I can tell."

No, they'd come after his reputation. "I don't know why someone would do this." Dax sucked in a deep breath. Now he had to drop the hammer. Holland wasn't going to like this part, but he couldn't hold off any longer. Either she would help him . . . or kick him out. "I also don't understand why, after all of that, they felt the need to murder him."

She closed her eyes briefly but seemed calm when she opened them again. "I was wondering if we would get there. Your father was found with a single gunshot wound to the head from a pistol registered to him. His fingerprints were the only set we found on the weapon."

"But you know that sometimes evidence lies."

"Very rarely."

"But it can, and sometimes you have to rely on instinct, even when the evidence points to something else. You handled a case a few years back concerning the murder of an ensign. Your partner wanted to close it because all the evidence suggested his girlfriend attacked him in a fit of rage. She'd been drunk and blacked out."

"Again, I probably don't want to know how you learned about that. And yes, I should have closed the file. It seemed open and shut, but there was something about the girl. At the end of the day, I didn't believe she was truly capable of violence, even when she was drunk. I dug further and found out the ensign had been brutally hazed by a superior and he intended to go to command the day after his murder. His CO was brought up on charges and is serving a life sentence."

"You listened to your gut and you were right. I know my father was incapable of committing suicide." Now Dax had proof. "Before he died, Dad left me a letter—not a suicide note."

She frowned. "I didn't see anything about that in the file."

"Because I didn't find it until right before I had to rejoin my ship. My dad didn't like e-mail. He felt it was impersonal. He wrote a note asking me not to make any judgments until we talked. He told me he had something important he wanted to tell me and asked me to please come home so we could talk. After I really thought about it, I realized my father wouldn't have been contemplating suicide if he'd written that note."

He'd found the letter while cleaning out his father's desk. His mother couldn't stand to go into the room, so it sat untouched, right down to the glass half full of Scotch his father had been drinking. Another clue. That ridiculously expensive Scotch had been a gift from a friend. If his father had been planning on killing himself, he would have at least finished his damn drink. But he didn't use that logic on Holland. He hoped the letter would be enough.

She shrugged. "Dax, he didn't mail it."

At least she wasn't calling him by his rank or last name. He would take every little victory he could. "It was stamped and ready to go. My father didn't make decisions on a whim. He wouldn't have written asking me to come home and later that night blow his brains out. My father was a fighter."

"The vile crime he was accused of could make anyone want to die."

He leaned forward, looking her right in the eyes. "Holland, I want you to take everything you know about my father and listen to your instincts. Think about who he was when you read that file. If you can still tell me you believe one hundred percent that he was guilty and that he killed himself, I won't bother you again."

Dax would find another way to clear his father's name. He wouldn't stop, but he prayed she was still the same woman he'd known before, the woman Gus and his mother believed in.

"All right. I'll look through it. Then we can talk. Eat your gumbo. I made a chess pie for dessert. So tell me how the boys are doing. I haven't talked to Zack in a while."

It was his cue to back off. She was going to read his file and make a judgment call.

He found it very interesting that she'd just happened to bake his favorite pie. Maybe she hadn't forgotten him, either. "He's drowning himself in work, but Roman is watching out for him. Now, if we want to change the subject to something more pleasant, I could tell you about how Mad got his ass kicked by a Parisian prostitute last month."

Her eyes lit up. "Oh, please do."

He smiled as he started his tale, happy to make her laugh for once.

Holland eased out onto her balcony, closing the door behind her as silently as possible since she had an unexpected overnight guest. After dessert, Dax had helped her do dishes. Afterward she'd told him to wait in the living room while she put on a pot of coffee. She should have shown him the door because it had been almost ten, but she'd enjoyed the evening with him. After they'd gotten the business out of the way, he'd told her stories about his friends and talked about some of the antics of his crew. She'd laughed and laughed.

It was the nicest evening she'd had in a long time. When she'd walked out with his coffee, the captain had been asleep on her couch. She hadn't had the heart to wake him. He was likely jet-lagged as hell and probably hadn't slept much. So she'd eased off his shoes and covered him with a blanket.

Then she'd sat at her kitchen table with the cup of coffee and his file. And she'd read.

Now as morning dawned, she looked out over the city. Even the Quarter was quiet. She liked this time, right before the sun came up. The streets had been cleaned from the nightly debauchery, and just for a moment everything seemed fresh and new again.

The sky was beginning to light with pinks and oranges as she thought about the man sleeping on her sofa. From what she could tell, he hadn't moved an inch. He must have been exhausted. After reading his file, she'd tried to get some sleep herself. Instead, she'd dreamed of him and of what might have been if she hadn't walked away.

Holland didn't regret it exactly. She liked her life. It was filled with good work and good people, so why did she feel restless the minute she thought of Daxton Spencer? Why did she want more simply because he walked through her door?

"Do you ever think about it?" he asked behind her suddenly.

It was as though her thoughts had awakened him. Holland hadn't heard him open the door, but now she could sense him behind her. She didn't need to turn around to know he would look adorable slightly rumpled. It wouldn't make him any less sexy.

"Yes." She knew what he was asking and she didn't bother to prevaricate.

He moved in behind her, cupping her shoulders with his warm, solid hands. She wanted nothing more than to lean back into the strength of his body. "I think about it all the time, Holland. Why did you run away from me?"

"I wasn't ready for anything serious," she replied honestly. "I also wasn't sure I could handle your lifestyle."

"The military lifestyle? You grew up in it."

She didn't turn to look at him because this conversation had grown so intimate so quickly. "Yes. I watched my mom pine for my father every day until she died. I then watched my father turn bitter and angry because he didn't get the life he'd been promised. He was supposed to work hard and then one day he could come home and be with her. But she wasn't around for the good part. Regardless, she never complained. I guess some women are built for life as a military wife. I'm not."

Dax turned her to face him. He'd taken off his dress shirt and stood there wearing a tight tee that clung to his every bulging muscle, along with his khaki pants from the night before. She'd been right. He looked rumpled and adorable and delicious all at once. He'd definitely filled out, and she couldn't help but sneak a peek at his sculpted, bronzed shoulders. He practically made her mouth water.

"That's ridiculous," he shot back with a shake of his head. "When two people want each other, they work it out. Holland, I've never stopped wanting you."

She had to smile. "Even when you were dating that supermodel?"

He sighed. "She needed a date to an awards show. Mad and Gabe were escorting her friends. I happened to be in town so I agreed to help out."

He'd looked gorgeous in his dress whites escorting the stunning model to the Oscars. The pictures had been everywhere, and she'd felt a truly illogical tug of jealousy. "So it was just a favor and you didn't sleep with her or anything."

Even in the low light of dawn, she could see the way he flushed. "I haven't been a saint, but then, you walked away from me."

And he'd walked into the arms of god only knew how many women. This was another facet of his life she wasn't sure she could handle. He would always have women hitting on him, trying to tempt him. The fact that he had a girlfriend or a wife would simply make them try harder.

"I wasn't judging you, Spencer. I was simply pointing out that our lifestyles couldn't be more different. You date supermodels and actresses. I date cops."

When she dated at all.

He shook his head. "Yes, you date cops. Many of whom used to be military. I find it funny that seven years have passed and we're right back to where we started. Except this time, there's nowhere to run. I'm going to be around, Holland."

Oh, but she was still safe from him. "Yes. You're going to be around and I'm going to be investigating your father's death, so now we have a conflict of interest. We're not going to date and I'm not going to kiss you again."

She knew what that would lead to and she wasn't sure she could afford the price to her heart. He might stay around for a while, but he would ship out again and she would be alone. That arrangement might work with another man. She might be able to live in the moment and enjoy the time they had together. But she would always want more from Dax Spencer.

His eyes lit up. "You read the file."

"I did and I'm not promising anything except that I'll ask a few questions and see what I can come up with."

Dax was right. No one had put much work into the case. Holland tended to think it was because the whole office had been sidetracked by the whirlwind of the press at the time. When the thick of the story had blown over, there had been no reason to further investigate. Admiral Spencer had been dead, and dragging his family through more mud seemed both unnecessary and unkind.

But so many loose threads and coincidences made her uneasy. Too many skirted this case. One of the two main witnesses was dead. The second had been shipped out almost immediately following the admiral's suicide. And the girl at the center of everything was missing—and had been since almost the beginning.

How could she not be suspicious?

And when she'd really thought about the admiral, truly listened to her instincts, she had to agree that he hadn't seemed like a man capable of killing himself in that manner.

"You're making the right call."

She could practically feel the satisfaction pouring off him. "I thought about everything you said and it stirred up something I'd forgotten. Something Gus told me afterward."

His jaw tightened. "Gus found him. I wish she hadn't seen that."

"But he would have known that Gus would be the one to find him," she pointed out. "His office was set back far enough that it's possible no one would have heard the gunshot."

Dax nodded. "Dad often worked late at night. Mom can be a light sleeper. He had the office insulated so he could play music, regardless of the hour. He preferred Chopin and Liszt. He didn't like quiet. I think he spent too much time on ships. The quiet bugged him."

"Gus told me that was why she'd found the scene so eerie before she even stepped into the room. His office had been quiet. She told me that she'd taken to bringing him coffee and beignets after her morning run, at around nine. She said he and your mother were arguing a lot so he'd been spending more time in the office. Gus had been trying to ease him into a routine to help steady him. She was the first person he saw every morning. And he knew that."

"My father would never have willingly allowed his baby girl to find his body. He loved Gus with all his heart," Dax said passionately. "He wouldn't hurt her like that."

Holland agreed with him. With some cases, the devil was in the details. A good investigator had to know how to ask the right questions of the right people, how to filter through their emotions to find the truth. "I'm going to talk to some people I know on the civilian side. See what they know."

All she could really do was shake a few trees and see what fell out of them.

Dax eased toward her. "I can't thank you enough. I knew you would listen to me."

He was moving in too close. She stepped back, holding up a hand. "I said I would look into it. That means we're working together, and I don't date where I work."

He stopped, holding up his hands to signal that he wouldn't push the issue. "We don't really work together and there's absolutely no reason not to explore this chemistry we have. I've thought about you for years. Tell me you don't feel the same and I'll back off."

She couldn't make herself lie to him. It would be worse than admitting the truth. "I think about you, too. But that's my rule. You want me to look into this, I do it my way."

"So I get justice or you?"

So arrogant. "No. Even if I wasn't investigating your father's case, I probably wouldn't date you."

He stared at her for a minute before the sexiest smile crossed his face. "Yeah, you would. You wouldn't be able to help yourself."

"You think a lot of yourself, Spencer."

When he grinned, he lit up the world. "That's Captain Awesome to you, sweetheart, and I'll take your rules. But you should understand that I'm famous for bending the rules from time to time."

"And you should know I enforce them." It was pretty much her job.

"We'll have to agree to disagree about where we stand. For now I'll make us some coffee." He stopped, his hand on the doorknob. "Did I say thank you for letting me sleep? I haven't slept that well in months."

"I don't see how you did it. You're too big for my couch." His feet had hung off the side. She wasn't about to admit that she'd thought about waking him up and taking him to her bed. Deeming it too dangerous a prospect, she'd forced herself to walk away.

"I think it was the company," he replied, his face softening. "I knew I was right to come to you, Holland. I knew you would be a safe haven. I might joke with you, but thank you. No one else is willing to listen to me. I knew you would."

"Because of that kiss?" Did he really think he had that much of a hold over her?

He shook his head. "No. Because I've always known you were the best woman I've ever met."

He slipped back into the apartment, and she was left with the beauty of the sun rising over the French Quarter and his words ringing in her ears.

She could resist the "Perfect Gentlemen" part of Dax Spencer. Even if it might be a bit tougher, she could also refuse Captain Awesome. She wasn't so sure about the man who'd just shown her his vulnerable, sincere side.

With a sigh, Holland stared out at the city and prayed for strength, because if she intended to resist that man, she was going to need it.

THREE

Dax was feeling unaccountably optimistic as he hopped off the Saint Charles Avenue streetcar and began to make his way home. Well, his parents' place. He wasn't truly certain he could call anywhere home. Since the time he'd shipped off to Creighton Academy, home had become a collection of people rather than a place. Home meant his friends, his family.

Seeing Holland again had put him in a reflective mood. Or maybe it was coming back to New Orleans. The last time he'd been in town had been for his father's funeral. He'd been so angry he couldn't see or think straight. Time and distance had made him calmer, more rational.

But there was nothing calm or rational about the way he felt when he looked at Holland Kirk. A part of him had hoped that his hunger for her had been a memory, embellished by time and his lingering fondness until the feeling had become too big to be true. Nope. Instead, Dax was more convinced than ever that she was the one. Holland made him want more from life, made him want to be better. She was the one woman for whom he would fold his six-foot-four body in two and sleep on that god-awful couch just to be close to her.

He strolled past tourists staring up at the gorgeous antebellum mansions that made the Garden District an attraction. They came in pairs and trios. Later, the large, guided groups would follow, eager to see a slice of New Orleans history and the beauty of the neighborhood his mother had lived in all her life.

Dax ducked his head and meandered to the other side of the street to give the tourists a wide berth. The last thing he needed was for someone to recognize him. He'd really tried to keep a low profile . . . until his friends dragged him into stupid crap like that date with the anorexic supermodel.

His cell phone trilled and he smiled as he answered it. He'd been on assignment for months without talking to his friends or family. He'd exchanged some e-mails with them, but hearing a friendly voice was a different thing. "My man. What's going on, super spy?"

"Seriously? You know that would get me killed if I really was a spy?" Connor shot back, though he was chuckling. "How was your flight?"

"Long and rough." He'd hitched a ride on a transport plane. It was a long way from the private jets his buddies took. If he'd called Gabe, Bond Aeronautics would have sent a plane for him, but he'd wanted to move as quickly as possible. Mad would have sent him a Crawford jet, but it also would have been filled with Mad, three hookers, and more liquor than anyone should ever drink. And herpes. He was pretty sure Mad's jet had herpes.

"Ah, you have to love the military. Well, I suppose you'll have some comfort now that you're in New Orleans. Tell me you're staying with your mother and not in some barracks."

He was kind of hoping that after a while he'd be staying with Holland. Despite what she'd said, he had no intentions of playing fair. If she didn't think she could handle his lifestyle, he would show her differently.

"I'm staying with Mom. Gus is on a short vacation, too. It'll be nice to spend some time with them." He let out another breath. "And I've convinced NCIS to take another look."

Connor paused. "Don't you mean you convinced Holland Kirk to take another look?"

He hadn't mentioned that he would be seeing her again, but he should have known Connor would figure it out. "Yes."

"Good. I just want you to be careful with her. She's not a good-time girl."

He'd never once thought she was. "You're right. She's an intriguing woman and I've been serious about her for years. You know, I wish just once someone would warn her about hurting my tender feelings. She's the one who walked away."

"I'll be sure to tell everyone," Connor said, sounding terribly amused. "Now, I've got good news and bad news. Which do you want to hear first?"

His mother's house was another block down, but Dax slowed his pace. He wasn't talking about his father's death in front of his mother or Gus unless he had a reason. As far as they knew, he was in town to work on the new training manuals and spend some time with family. He didn't want to get their hopes up. "Give me the bad news."

"The girl is a ghost. I can't find a trace of her anywhere. Amber Taylor dropped off the face of the earth roughly three weeks after your father was killed." Connor was one hundred percent on Dax's side. None of his friends referred to his father's death as a suicide. "She never went back to her high school after winter break. Her mother apparently told the administrators she would be home schooling after the new year. I'm trying to track the woman down. The house they lived in has been rented to someone else. The landlord said the mom and her daughter walked away one day and left everything behind. He hasn't seen her since."

Another dead end. "Keep trying."

"I will, but I have to put this on the back burner for a little bit. I've been asked to look into another matter. It's important, Dax. You know I wouldn't let this lie unless it was."

If Connor said it was important, then it likely had something to do with national security, and Dax couldn't argue with that. "I do. Don't worry about it. I'm here now and I've got Holland. We'll work it from this angle. Do what you need to do. Are you going to be out of touch?"

"Yes. It could be a while. I'm sorry," Connor said over the line.

"Don't be, buddy. You have a job to do. Go and get it done."

"And now the good news . . . I hope. I didn't leave you to your own devices," Connor continued. "I wasn't sure you should look into this by yourself and I didn't know you would recruit Holland. I thought you needed some backup."

Dax stopped in front of the massive house that had been in his family since before the Civil War. "What do you mean, backup?"

The front door opened and his jaw dropped.

Maddox Crawford held a bottle of champagne in one hand and waved at the tourists shuffling behind him with the other. "Hello, lovely ladies. Welcome to New Orleans. The first drink's on me." Mad glanced at a group of older women, who started fluttering like teenagers when he winked their way. Mad flirted regardless of age, beauty, and in some cases sanity. He gave Dax a broad smile. "My brother, welcome back! We expected you in hours ago. I guess someone got lucky last night. By the way, your mother is still as hot as she was when we were teenagers. And she's making us breakfast. Well, she told the housekeeper to make us breakfast which is totally the same thing."

"Don't hate me," Connor said in his ear. "I'm sure they'll be helpful. Well, one of them will. Mad will be fun. Gabe, however, has a file for you, which should help. I've spent weeks putting that together. It's everything we know about the case including my thoughts on where we should continue the investigation."

It was a good thing he'd left it in Gabe's hands. Mad would likely use it for writing down the phone numbers of women he would never actually call. Still, Connor had meant well. "Thank you for everything. And stay safe wherever you are."

"Later, brother."

"Sooner, I hope," Dax said as he hung up.

Life had been so much easier when they all shared a house while attending Yale. Most of them could have afforded their own places, but it had been so much more fun to live together. They'd all grown up since then, gone about their own lives. It would be good to spend some time with a couple of his best buddies.

Still, having Mad around for anything other than a party seemed like a bad idea now.

Gabe strolled onto the front porch, a sheepish smile on his face. "Sorry. I tried to come alone, but Mad stowed away on the plane. The good news is I tossed off the three strippers he tried to bring."

"He's lost all sense of humor since he started working at Bond Aeronautics. Does anyone have orange juice we could borrow?" Mad shook his head. "Screw it. I never liked orange juice anyway. I need something stronger. Bloody Marys all around."

"Yeah, he's going to be a ton of fun. Your mother is a gracious hostess, by the way. She gave us each rooms in the east wing. I hope it's all right. Connor didn't think you should be alone. He also sent this." Gabe held out a file.

Mad strode back toward the house. "Hey, Spencer, when is your sister getting in?"

"Leave my sister alone, Mad." Like that was going to happen. He was well aware that Mad wasn't the only problem. Gus tended to have a mind of her own and she wasn't shy about what she wanted.

"I promise only to not make the first move but I never like to let a lady down, you know. God, that bacon smells good." Mad disappeared behind the door as it swung closed.

"Don't mind him. Since his dad died, he's been at Crawford pretty much twenty-four seven. This is the first time he's taken off since, well . . ."

He knew where Gabe was going. "Since Dad's funeral." He was going to cut Mad some slack. Mad had always been there when Dax needed him. "How are things at Crawford?"

"Good as far as I can tell." Gabe walked next to him up to the house. "The stock is doing surprisingly well. Despite all his bad behavior, Mad has a business degree from Yale. He knows what he's doing. But there's a lot at stake. I think he needs to be out of New York for a couple of weeks. I could use the time away, too. I need to be in the boardroom but I'd rather concentrate on research and development. I've got all these ideas on how to streamline the new luxury choppers. Sometimes I think I should have followed you into the Navy. At least I would be in the air."

He likely would have been. Gabe had been flying planes since it was slightly legal for him to do so. He would have made a great fighter pilot.

"I would have loved to see you deal with the training." Dax slapped his friend on the back.

"Yes, there's a reason I only think of it from time to time," Gabe admitted. "So tell me everything that's been going on."

He stopped Gabe before they made it inside. "First, you should know I'm trying to keep my mother out of this as much as possible."

Gabe nodded. "I haven't said a word, but she's going to figure it out. And honestly, she's got information you need."

"I will cross that bridge when I come to it. I'm trying to walk delicately around her and Gus. Is she really taking that new position at the White House?"

Gabe grinned. "Oh, I think Roman's insisting on it. Liz is an amazing press secretary, but she's got to have someone who can run the office so she can worry about Zack and stop playing two roles."

"It's hard for me to imagine Gus running something so important. I remember when she couldn't keep Kool-Aid in a cup."

Gabe shook his head. "That's because you still see her as your little sister and not the man-mangling, tear-inducing, mega shark with a perfect blowout she's become. Everyone at the White House is afraid of her. She'll keep those damn reporters in line. I heard she made the head of ABC News cry last week."

"My sister is a sweetheart."

"She is to you and her family," Gabe agreed. "She's a man-eating T. rex to everyone else. But you should know Roman swears he stopped sleeping with her when they started working together."

"Jeez, I don't need to know that." He took the file from Gabe's hand.

"Yeah, well, you should also know Mad's hot to see her again. I swear, I'm so happy my sister has zero interest in my friends. Sara thinks you're walking venereal diseases. Take a look at the notes in the back. Everything else you can go over in your leisure time."

He flipped to the back and found Connor's list of recommendations for how to proceed. One name stood out.

"Beau Kirk? I've never heard his name mentioned in conjunction with my father's case."

"Because you've only been working it from the Navy's perspective. Connor found out the case was largely handled in the civilian world. They only relinquished control to NCIS when it became clear the news was going to explode," Gabe explained. "Holland's uncle works for NOLA PD and he handled the civilian side of the investigation. If anyone is going to know how to look into this, it will be him."

Dax had a name. It was really all he could ask for right now. Though at some point he intended to sit down with Holland and ask why she'd never mentioned her uncle had kicked off the investigation. "Let's go get some breakfast. I'm starving."

For the first time in months, he meant that.

Holland sighed gratefully as the bartender passed her an ice-cold beer. It had been a shitty day. She'd had to arrest a lieutenant junior grade for beating the crap out of his wife. The whole time the wife had pleaded with her not to take her husband, crying and begging and trying to say the whole thing had been her fault.

The Threat Management Unit usually handled cases like this, but the agent's partner had called in sick and agents didn't go in without backup. Holland had agreed to assist, even though she hated cases like this. She hoped the lieutenant's wife got the help she needed, but the likelihood was she would follow her abusive husband right out of the military.

"Yay! Margarita!" Courtney's eyes widened as the bartender placed the fishbowl-sized cocktail in front of her. "This afternoon was so pleasant. I swear I could look at that man all day. We were supposed to go over how we'll lay out the training materials, but mostly I just looked at his arms. Do you think I could convince him to work without his shirt? I mean, writing training manuals is a really hard job. Oh, I'll tell him the air conditioner is broken and see if I can fast-talk him down to his underwear."

Courtney's antics usually amused her. They'd become fast friends right after Holland had taken the New Orleans job. It was good to have a girly friend. Most of her work colleagues were male. The lone exception was Berta, who looked as if she'd been a former pro wrestler in a past life. She was a nice lady, but she didn't give a damn about mani pedis or where to get her hair done. Courtney was smart and funny, if a little shallow when it came to men.

The problem was Courtney was talking about *her* man.

Stop. Halt. Do not go there, Holland. He is not yours and he never will be.

It had been a whole ten hours since Dax had made her coffee and then left to go back to his mother's house. He'd slept on her couch and she'd let him. What had she been thinking? She'd taken a shower and hustled into work after he'd left this morning, but all she could concentrate on was the file he'd given her. And how masculine he'd looked standing there wearing nothing but a thin T-shirt and a pair of khaki pants. They'd rode low on his hips, and that white, almost transparent tee had shown off how well shaped his body was.

"Earth to Holland?"

She shook her head. "Sorry. I was thinking about something else."

"Yeah, I can tell. What's his name?"

Holland stared down at her beer, wondering how much to tell her friend.

Courtney put a hand on her shoulder. "Hey, seriously, what's wrong? Did I say something?"

"I know Captain Spencer personally."

Courtney sat back. "I was wondering about that. You don't like to talk about it, but I know you were friends with Joy Hayes. That means you probably knew the PGs."

She hated that nickname. The Perfect Gentlemen. The press used it all the time. Somehow Captain Awesome was a better fit for Dax Spencer. "I wasn't his girlfriend or anything. We've never been anything but friends."

Courtney stared at her with disbelieving eyes. "Really? That's good because I've got a date with him tonight."

She felt herself flush. Well, she'd told him flat out she wouldn't date him. She'd said it in no uncertain terms. Somehow she hadn't expected him to give up so easily. But she'd also thought that maybe he'd give it a few days before he moved on to the next woman. This underscored one of the main reasons she refused to get involved with him.

"There it is." Courtney sat back with a shake of her head. "Damn. I was hoping that was all one sided, but it's plain to see you like him, too. I don't have a date with him. I just wanted to see your reaction."

"What are you talking about?"

"I'm talking about the fact that once the man found out you and I are friends, he very subtly tried to get as much information out of me as possible. Give me the scoop because if you don't want Captain Spencer, I'll go after him."

The idea of Courtney—gorgeous, fun Courtney—with Dax made her flush all over again and it wasn't with embarrassment. She was angry. Holland forced herself to calm down, but Courtney was making her think. She wouldn't be so irrationally angry if she didn't care at least a little. "We never had a relationship, but I do have some feelings for him. I can't seem to help it."

"I think he likes you, too. Otherwise, he wouldn't have been able to resist the girls." She thrust her chest out. "They were on full display today and I got nothing out of him. Not even a lingering glance, just questions about how I met you and what we do in New Orleans. So he got to hear about our hairdresser and our favorite spa. No man listens to spa stories if he isn't interested."

Holland sipped her beer. He'd left her a message today, asking for a meeting to discuss the case when she had the time. She'd called back and gotten his voice mail. It wasn't so surprising. They were both busy professionals. The next few days were fairly packed, and so she'd offered him a meeting on Friday. In her office. In the morning after breakfast, but not so close to lunch that he could persuade her to join him.

She was feeling weak where Dax was concerned and she didn't dare tempt fate.

"I walked away from him once before," Holland admitted. "He wanted to move past friendship, but I couldn't do it."

Her friend blinked. "You know you're insane, right? That is the hottest man I've ever seen. How could you sleep with him and not want to be with him?"

"I didn't sleep with him. Like I said, we didn't move past being friends."

Courtney waved her off. "I sleep with lots of my friends. How am I supposed to figure out if I want to be more than friends if I don't take a test drive, so to speak? The last thing I want to do is get all emotionally invested in some dude who can't find my clitoris."

"Dax Spencer? Bad in bed?"

"He could be," Courtney said with a shrug. "I mean some guys who are that good looking and have that much money don't even need to try. Women fall into their beds. They get lazy."

"Somehow I doubt a man whose penis has its own Twitter account is bad in bed."

Courtney snorted. "That's not Dax. That's Maddox Crawford."

"Well, I'm sure they'll all have them soon. He kisses like he would be good in bed."

"So you've kissed him. What was that like? Too much tongue? Not enough?"

"There was exactly the right amount of tongue. Why are we talking about this?"

"Because we're girls and that's what we do. Also because you haven't slept with anyone interesting in the last couple of years, so I'm all kinds of on board for you jumping into bed with the captain. I have the biggest crush on him, but I know the girl code. Thou shalt not sink your well-manicured claws into your best friend's dream guy."

Holland opened her mouth to dispute that claim and then sighed. "I like him a lot. But his lifestyle . . . God only knows how many women that man has gone through."

"It's a lot according to *Star*. They have a timeline and everything," Courtney supplied helpfully. "They also tend to exaggerate. He's a Naval officer. He's working most of the time. I think you're damning him for his misspent youth. The last few years the man has been doing his best to protect his country. That should count for something."

It did. "Any woman who dates him is going to have to deal with his past and the press."

"You've dealt with shit before. Listen, if you're seriously not interested I would like to take a shot with the guy. He's gorgeous and kind and really smart and funny. I know this might make me a bitch, but I'm not going to stand back and let him go if you're too scared to even try."

Once again hot anger filled her. "Can I have a couple of days to settle into seeing him again before you jump him?"

Courtney nodded. "You may. And again, I point out that I've never seen you get this emotional about a guy you were actually dating, so maybe you should think about taking a chance for once in your life. I know you think I take too many of them."

She thought Courtney might jump into bed with guys way too soon, but it didn't make her a bad person. "I think you get hurt a lot."

"But one day it's going to pay off. One day the right guy is going to make me an offer and I won't refuse it. I won't stand back because I'm scared I'll get hurt or it won't work out. I'll jump in with both feet and never look back. It looks like I won't be doing that with Captain Awesome. The good news is he's got two friends in town."

She shuddered to think about who was here. She prayed it was Connor. Connor was levelheaded, if a bit dark. Gabe Bond was nice. If Maddox Crawford was in town, then she should really alert the authorities because that man was trouble. "I've got more problems than his lifestyle. He wants me to reopen his dad's case."

"That's why you didn't join the watercooler chat." Courtney took another drink. "I always wondered. Everyone else was gossiping up a storm and there you were with the scoop. I thought you were being all stoic and NCIS we-don't-talk-about-our-cases girl. You were protecting the man you loved. That's really romantic."

Courtney could go way out there. She was the very definition of over-drama at times. "I knew the admiral. I liked him and his family. I wasn't going to gossip. But now I'm faced with the dilemma of working on a case where I have feelings for a person directly involved in the outcome."

"It's not an official thing, right? It's off the books. You've done that before. You found Mrs. McCallahan's granddaughter when she ran away. And you found George's cat."

Mrs. McCallahan lived in her building. She was a nice older lady raising her wild grandchild. It hadn't been hard to find the girl and bring her home. As for the cat, it had been up a tree. No real investigative work there. She'd simply followed the meows.

"This feels different. I didn't start the investigation, so I'm at a bit of a loss about where to begin. I've read the case file a hundred times. I've talked to the NCIS investigators." She'd tried to avoid thinking about this all day, but she wanted to have something to tell Dax when she saw him on Friday. Something beyond "I read over the reports again."

"You should do what we do in tech writing. Start at the beginning of the process and work your way through. You already know everything NCIS does, so start outside your group."

"I have to talk to my uncle." Her uncle had advised her against touching this case. He'd called her after some gossip rag had reported that Dax was in town and warned her away from it. He wasn't going to be happy that she was diving in now.

"I think you do. Tell Beau hi for me. Now, let's talk about potential double dates. You and Dax and me and whoever he has with him."

Courtney chattered on, but Holland was already thinking about how to approach her uncle. It would not be a pleasant meeting.

But her friend was right. It was time to start over, at the beginning.

FOUR

"Why are you doing this, honey? This case is closed and all you can possibly do now is kick up a mess of trouble. What did I teach you about a hornet's nest?"

Holland had to give it to her uncle. Beau Kirk could likely make anyone feel as if they were twelve years old again. Even though she was a grown woman with a career and responsibilities, when her uncle looked at her, his eyes narrowed ever so slightly and that Cajun drawl deepening, she would almost swear she was sitting in his big office at the house along the bayou, hoping she didn't get grounded.

After her mother had died, she'd lived with her aunt and uncle. She'd seen her dad when he came home on leave, but her aunt had been the steady influence in her life and her uncle the authority figure.

"You taught me not to kick one," Holland replied. "I'm not trying to cause trouble, Uncle Beau. I'm simply trying to give a friend some peace of mind."

Her uncle frowned, sitting back in his massive chair. He'd moved up the ranks of the NOLA PD and now occupied a large office and headed a division of men who handled some of the city's worst cases. "You're talking about the son, right? Daxton? Isn't he some sort of war hero?"

Her uncle knew exactly who she was talking about, but she played along. "Yes, Captain Spencer is considered one of the Navy's finest."

"I'm sure he was on track to follow in his daddy's footsteps." Commander Beauregard Kirk was in his mid-fifties, but he was still a powerfully built man. He wasn't one to slide into middle age gracefully. He still trained with his men on a daily basis. "I doubt he'll make it past captain now."

Holland frowned. Dax was meant for bigger and better things. He was certainly capable of them. The minute she'd met him, she'd known he would go far in the Navy. "What is that supposed to mean? He's great at his job."

"Oh, the Navy will certainly move him around and give him bigger ships, but they won't want the Spencer name to ever again come anywhere near the rank of admiral. Too much bad press." Uncle Beau shook his head. "That story took forever to die. The Spencer boy has to know his career in the Navy has an invisible wall he'll never scale now."

"He's not pursuing this investigation because he wants a higher rank," Holland tried to explain. "He's doing this because he loved his father."

Her uncle sat back, scanning the office. He left the blinds open as though he was watching and waiting for something to happen. "I'm sure he does. That's the problem with parents and children, though. As a child, you tend to see your parents in the best possible light. It's hard to understand that they're human like the rest of us. Some people can't handle it. I remember how disappointed I was when I realized my father was a drunk. Growing up, I always thought he was the life of the party. A truly happy man. Then I realized he was happy because he didn't have to face a thing. Momma did all the work and it wore her out in the end. I had to face two facts: my father was an irresponsible asshole and my mother let herself become a doormat."

Her uncle had always been terribly good at giving lectures.

"I think his case is different," she argued.

He sent her a cool stare. "Yes, it's much worse. He thought his father was a hero. It turns out the man was a criminal. Which is precisely why I told you to stay away from this investigation in the first place. You did the right thing by recusing yourself. Why would you go back and screw things up now?"

She'd known she would have to endure this lecture. That's why she'd put off seeing her uncle until this afternoon. But she planned to meet with Dax tomorrow and she wanted to have something to tell him. Otherwise, she might never have forced herself to come here. "This isn't a formal investigation. This is me looking into a few questions for a friend."

"A friend or a lover?" He managed to make the question sound like an accusation.

Holland sat up straighter, fingers curling around the arms of her chair. "Uncle Beau, I love you, but I'm an adult. My relationship with Captain Spencer is none of your business."

"It damn straight is if he's causing trouble for you at work."

"There won't be any trouble." Sometimes, like now, Holland really missed her aunt Dixie. She'd divorced her uncle a few years back and moved to Texas with her sister. If her aunt was still here, Dixie could have reasoned with her stubborn uncle. Of course, his stubbornness had been one of the major causes of the divorce in the first place. "Uncle Beau, I'm asking as a favor. You'll save me some legwork if you'll let me read the file. Think of it as a professional courtesy."

"I'm sure NCIS has the file somewhere," he replied with a sour expression.

"Again, I'm not doing this on the clock. It's why I came to you and not my colleagues. I want to peruse the file, maybe close some of those open-ended questions and make Dax feel more comfortable." She wasn't about to mention that she thought Dax could have a point. She didn't want her uncle to think she was seriously considering building a case to bring to her superiors.

Uncle Beau ran a frustrated hand across his almost nonexistent hair and cursed under his breath. "Fine." He picked up his phone and asked his assistant to get a hard copy of the file. "I still don't understand what that boy thinks he's going to prove. That his father wasn't guilty? Because he was, Holland. I wouldn't have sent the accusation to NCIS if I hadn't found it to be credible. I didn't like ruining the life of a man so many people admired."

Finally they were getting somewhere. "I know you didn't."

"If I'd found even a hint that it might be false, I would have tried harder to disprove it before the press got hold of the story. I knew the minute I found out the admiral was involved that the incident would blow up in everyone's faces. There are days I wished that call had never come in. Not on my watch."

Yes, she had some questions about the call that had led her uncle to that seedy motel. "So the original tip came from an anonymous source?"

"Yes, we didn't realize the tip involved a high-ranking Naval officer at the time." Beau seemed to settle in as though he realized she wasn't going away.

She could be stubborn, too. She'd learned through the years that she had to be if she was going to survive her uncle. He'd taught her to be like a dog with a bone. "So you got a call?"

"Yes, to this very precinct, shortly after midnight on the day in question. I've attempted to ID the caller, but it's impossible. The caller reached out via a landline from somewhere inside the motel the admiral had taken that girl to."

"But he was gone by the time you arrived?" She wanted to get the timeline down. "I've heard surveillance cameras caught him going into the motel but not coming out of it."

"Yes. The cameras in the motel are stationary. Cheap security, nothing that you couldn't buy at a local electronics store, so they don't swing." Her uncle rolled his eyes. "There were only a few cameras in high-traffic areas. Apparently the admiral left through a different door than he entered. Besides being captured by the security camera in the hall, the motel employee I spoke to identified him. As far as I can tell, the caller was most likely another guest of the motel. She didn't leave her name because she was probably a working girl."

The motel that had become the scene of the crime was well known for its hourly rates. A prostitute likely wouldn't want to deal with the police on any level. It was surprising that anyone who frequented the place would call in at all. "I can hardly imagine the admiral going to a rattrap like that."

"Men have their secrets, Holland. I believe I taught you that, too," he said with a sad sigh. "What men present to the women they love tends to be a shiny, happy surface they don't ever want their wives and daughters to scratch past. We're dark creatures, especially someone like the admiral. You know he'd cheated on his wife for years."

"I heard that rumor." There had been any number of salacious bits of gossip floating around after the story broke. The tabloids had speculated about everything from numerous mistresses to orgies in the name of Satan.

Her uncle's voice softened in sympathy. "No, honey. That was what his wife told us after his death. She accepted who her husband was, though she didn't know about the underage girls. I think that's what broke her. She thought she was the only one Hal Spencer was hurting."

Holland's stomach took a nosedive. She definitely didn't want to be the one who had to tell Dax that his mother believed the accusations. "Why don't you start at the beginning and tell me everything you know. I'd also like any and all information you have on the victim."

She didn't say alleged victim. One way or another that girl had been victimized. She'd been fifteen. Holland had seen Amber Taylor's picture on the evening news, watched as she'd been escorted into the police station by two burly officers at her side. She'd been a pretty girl who, with a little makeup, could definitely have passed for much older. She had the body of an adult, but Holland had been haunted by her eyes. They'd been what truly made the girl look older. She'd had the blank stare of someone who had seen far too much and no longer cared.

Had Admiral Harold Spencer put that look on the girl's face? She didn't want to believe it, but then she knew enough about criminals to know the smart ones could fool the people closest to them. The most successful pedophiles, rapists, and killers came with nice faces and demeanors that hoodwinked those around them.

Holland started taking notes as her uncle ran through the basics of the case with her.

Almost an hour had passed when she stood and stretched. "I know you're against me looking into this. So thank you for sharing your information with me."

Her uncle approached from behind his desk and enveloped her in a bear hug. "Now, honey, you know I'd do anything for you. I love you like you were my own. That's why I'm going to tell you to be careful with that Spencer boy."

She gave him a squeeze and then pulled away. "I'm not dating him."

"But you'd like to." He gave her a little shake. "Hell, if I was female I'd want that boy, too. He's handsome and rich and charming. Apparently he's got a very large—"

"Uncle Beau!"

"Heart." He laughed out loud. "You didn't let me finish. I was going to say that he must have a big heart since he's done so much charity work. You hush that nasty mind now, girl. All I'm saying is I understand the impulse to be around the boy. But he's asking something of you that you might not be able to give and I don't know how he'll handle it if you tell him something he doesn't want to hear."

If she had to tell him all the evidence pointed to his father's guilt, he would be so angry. He could possibly turn that anger on her. No one liked to hear bad things about their loved ones. Yes, cops got to hand out bad news all the time. It was part of the job. Still, she couldn't stand the thought of Dax Spencer hating her. Even though they weren't together, knowing they liked each other was somehow a comfort.

"I'm sure it won't cause any trouble. I'll be professional and he will, too. He's given this over to me, so you shouldn't have to deal with him at all."

Her uncle raised his brows. "Really? Not even once? Because it looks like I'm about to deal with him right now."

She turned and sure enough Captain Spencer was standing in the middle of the precinct, staring at her with his eyes narrowed. He wore civilian clothes, slacks and a dress shirt. No tie. He didn't need one. He looked cool and in charge. And fairly angry, if she read the set of his shoulders right.

He stormed over. She could practically hear the clomping of his probably ridiculously overpriced loafers as he made his way toward her.

"So it's all professional?" Her uncle sounded entirely amused.

"It is on my side." But something about Dax's expression looked as if he had other ideas.

He strode up to them, his stare never leaving her face. "Hello, Holland. I thought we were meeting tomorrow."

"I did as well."

"I thought we were going over the case tomorrow at lunch."

"No. I never said anything about lunch."

His face turned a bit pink. "Holland, I thought we were partners. Tell me you're not here talking to your uncle about my case."

Was he serious? They had some misconceptions she needed to clear up. "No, we're not partners. I'm looking into your father's case. And why, pray tell, are you here, Dax? Do you have some parking tickets? Because those should really be dealt with at the parish courthouse."

He fell quiet for a moment, but that didn't mean she couldn't feel his anger. "We had a long talk about this yesterday. I thought we'd been clear."

"Then why the hell are you here, Spencer?"

She was pleased when he went a more brilliant shade of red.

Her uncle leaned against the doorjamb. "You two seem to be completely on the same page. I'm utterly sure this is going to work out for the best."

Dax exhaled, looking as if he tried to relax. "You never told me your uncle ran the civilian investigation."

"I didn't think it mattered. I told you I would look into it. And I made plans to keep you up to date. You never intended to let me investigate, did you? You thought you'd be with me every step of the way."

Her uncle let out a long sigh. "Y'all obviously have more to work out than you thought. I don't think this is the place to do it. You might not mind some gossip, Captain Spencer, but I don't like men flapping their gums about my niece, not even the ones I work with."

Sure enough when she looked around, all eyes were on them. Every cop in the precinct was watching. She wasn't afraid they would go to the press, but she knew damn well they would talk amongst themselves. That would be uncomfortable for her uncle. "I'm sorry. We'll leave. I need to make a few things clear to the captain."

Dax nodded. "Yes, I think we need to talk."

Uncle Beau waved his arm as though shooing away a couple of unwanted cats. "Go on, then. Holland, honey, why don't you take him on over to Antoine's? It's quiet there this time of day and the staff is discreet."

And her uncle had a standing dinner reservation there. He didn't often use it, but Antoine's had been serving NOLA's power players for as long as it had been open. She could get a drink and maybe cool the situation down. "What do you say, Captain Awesome?"

He rolled his eyes, but it was obvious she'd managed to deflate his anger. "All right. I could use a drink. Commander, I apologize. I didn't mean to cause a scene."

"See that you don't get my niece in trouble, now. You hear?"

Yes, she was right back to feeling like a teenager and her uncle was vetting her boyfriends. It was obvious he didn't like this one. She sighed and led Dax out into the late afternoon sunlight.

He followed Holland and the hostess into the cool back room of Antoine's. They'd walked past the sunny environs of the front dining room. That was for tourists and families celebrating special occasions. The real politics of New Orleans happened in the back of the establishment, the room where the sunlight didn't reach.

Once they'd arrived at a corner table, Dax sat across from her and pondered what to say.

He'd fucked up. He'd known she expected to shake a few trees and report back to him. But he'd been itching to do some fact finding of his own and talk to her uncle so he'd have something to bring to the table at their meeting tomorrow. Maybe then she'd see that they could work together. And a part of him hoped that if she could partner with him in the investigation, she'd see that they could partner in other ways.

"I'm sorry about the scene at the police station." He needed to calm her and talk that horrible cop frown off her face. She wore it like a mask, and Dax wanted to talk to the woman.

"Why were you there?" And she was using her cop voice on him, too. It was bland and impersonal. He was sure she used that voice when she was questioning a suspect.

"You know why I was there." He wasn't going to lie. Honesty was his only way out of the mess he'd plopped himself in. "I found out your uncle led the initial civilian investigation and I wanted to ask him a few questions."

"You didn't think I could manage that all on my own?" Her frown turned right side up, into a friendly grin, as the waiter approached. "Thanks, I don't need a menu. I'll have a Sazerac and for dinner the *Poulet sauce Rochambeau* with *asperges au Beurre*."

Show-off. Her accent was perfect and she had the menu memorized like a good NOLA daughter would. Well, he was a son and he could play that game, too. "I'll have a Sazerac as well and let's start with the *Huitres Bienville* for the table. For my entrée I'll have the *Crabes mous frits* and *pommes de terre. Merci.*"

The waiter nodded and went off to put their orders in.

Holland finally smiled just enough to let him know she was amused. "Really? Oysters?"

Sure they were an aphrodisiac, but they were also quite good. "If you don't want any, *chère*, I'll eat them all myself."

She pulled the white napkin out, settling it over her lap. "I'll have a few. I don't know that you should eat a dozen oysters. God only knows what it will do for your libido."

He was glad she was finally relaxing after their tense trek to the restaurant. "Your French is excellent."

"I spent most of my teen years here. My aunt and uncle spoke a lot of French in their home. It was a survival skill. It's also one of the reasons I got the job here. There are still a lot of people around here who speak Creole or some form of it. Even I can get confused out on the bayou."

Because some communities out there cut themselves off from the world. They spoke the old languages and didn't like authorities nosing into their business. "You shouldn't have to go out there often."

"More than you'd think. Navy boys can be very adventurous. Now, what exactly did you think you could accomplish with my uncle that I couldn't?" She was right back to formal, though she accepted her drink from the passing waiter with a gracious smile.

Maybe a Sazerac or two could break through her chilly reserve. And maybe so could honesty. "I wanted to walk into tomorrow's meeting with something solid to show you."

"That's supposed to be my job, Captain." She took a healthy sip of the whiskey and absinthe cocktail. "I'm the investigator. You asked me to look into it."

He had to tread carefully here. "Not exactly. I asked you to help me look into it."

"Then we have a problem, because I'm not taking you everywhere with me. Your presence will do more harm than good. Can't you see that?"

"All I see is that my family was destroyed and I don't think I can sit on my hands while someone else finds out why."

"They don't seem destroyed, Dax." She softened and leaned forward. "Your mother is finally getting out again. She's seeing her friends."

"The ones who didn't turn their backs on her."

"Yes, her real friends. She's playing bridge again and she's planning a cruise with some of her old sorority sisters."

"She told you about that, huh?"

"I have dinner with her from time to time. As for Gus, she's smiling again. She's back to being Gus. And I heard she's about to start a big new job for the White House. They're not destroyed, Dax. They're starting to live again, and this could bring it all back."

Did she think he hadn't considered that? "That's why I'm trying to keep quiet. But I can't let it go when I know someone did something terrible to my father. I can't allow it to pass simply because my mother and sister are getting over it."

"The bigger issue is, you're not getting over it."

"Don't turn this into something selfish, Holland."

"I'm sorry if it sounded like that. That wasn't my intention. You need closure to move forward. And you deserve that. What you're saying is that you won't find that closure unless you're active in this investigation, right?"

He shook his head. "I can't sit on the sidelines this time."

"You didn't sit on the sidelines last time. You marched out onto the field and told the other players how awful they were."

Put like that, he had been an ass. "I'm sorry. I wasn't thinking logically at the time."

"No one can under those circumstances." She swirled her drink around. "Tell me something. Are you going to be able to handle it if this investigation doesn't go your way?"

It wasn't going to end up like that. He was one hundred percent certain, so he could easily answer her. "Yes. Though I don't think I'll be able to believe it if I don't see it with my own two eyes."

"That's what I was afraid of." She sat back. "All right. I'll let you know what's going on, and where it's appropriate, you can come with me. The first time you cause trouble, I stop investigating."

That was all he could hope for. "I won't cause trouble. I know I did last time. But I'm ready to find the truth now. What did you learn from your uncle? Scary guy, by the way."

Beauregard Kirk was built like a linebacker and looked twice as mean.

"You should have seen the way he liked to scare off my prospective dates in high school. He would greet them with a shotgun. I didn't really date much until I went off to college. But on to the topic at hand," she said as a segue. "I learned a little something new. Have you ever been to the Raven Motel?"

The name made his stomach turn. He took another drink. "I hadn't been there before the incident. I know its reputation, though. It's a place where hookers take their johns. Did anyone uncover the name of the woman who called in the tip?"

"I've got a copy of the call. It was never released to the press for obvious reasons."

He knew exactly the reason. "If the woman was a prostitute, it would have made the police's narrative seem a little less substantial."

"Yes. Besides, the woman was trying to do a good deed. If she didn't want to be identified, that's her business. We want to keep anonymous tips anonymous or no one will call in."

He understood the reasoning behind it, but damn he wanted to talk to that woman. "I'd like to listen to it. Her accent alone might tell us something."

Holland nodded. "Agreed, but I don't know that finding out who made the call will change anything. We've still got the issue of the security tape."

He remembered that footage well. That fifteen seconds of tape had been played over and over on the news. Something about that seemed fishy as well. "It never shows my father's face, only the girl's."

"Yes, but your father was in uniform. He's identified by the insignia and there's the moment when the girl looks up at him. We had our best lip-readers figure out what she was saying."

Where are you taking me, Admiral Hal?

She'd asked the question as they walked down the hall toward the rooms. There hadn't been any audio.

"How stupid do you think my father would have to be to take the risk that someone would notice an officer in full uniform?"

"I wouldn't say stupid. I would say reckless, and that does fit your father's profile. He was a smart man, but he liked adrenaline. After he left his command and began working behind a desk, what did he like to do in his off time?"

His father had jumped out of planes, raced cars, and engaged in anything dangerous. "I understand your point, but I can't see him being this reckless."

"He was identified by four different people."

"Three of whom are missing, Holland."

"Okay, I admit that gives me pause as well. I've got a call in to his old aide-de-camp. He's overseas on assignment, so it could take a while for him to get back to me. We'll see what he has to say."

Waiting really was the hardest part. "What does your uncle think about the girl?"

"She had a history of running away from home. A few juvenile arrests for petty theft. She served a few months in juvie and went home to an alcoholic mother and absentee father. It's not surprising that she left after the scandal."

"What I find surprising is that no one has seen her since."

She shook her head sadly. "Dax, no one cares anymore. The press has moved on to the next scandal. The girl likely ran and didn't look back."

As much as he hated to admit it, Holland was right. No one outside of his family and friends cared anymore. His father was dead and buried and there were new salacious stories for the press to devour. Hell, half of them were about Mad and Gabe. "Still, someone somewhere has to have seen her."

"I've got a list of everyone involved in the case. I'm making a timeline. Then I intend to track every single witness down. The victim's mother is no longer at her old residence, so I'll head over there in the morning to ask some questions, see if I can find out where she's moved. I don't know if she'll be helpful, but she's the best lead I've got."

Then that was where they would start. The waiter brought out the oysters, placing them on the fine linen in between them.

Dax switched seats. He wanted to be closer to her. He'd scored a major victory. She was discussing the case with him. If he was a smart man, he would accept that as enough. He'd never been particularly smart when it came to Holland Kirk.

Her eyes widened.

"I can hear you better here," he claimed as innocently as he could. "And you know a nice bottle of wine would really complement the meals we have coming up. I think I saw a proper sauvignon blanc on the menu. It pairs with your chicken and my crab."

Hopefully. He wasn't exactly a sommelier, but white went with chicken and seafood, and it definitely loosened Holland up. She was finally smiling, and he wasn't about to let that stop.

"Fine, since neither one of us is driving," she allowed and asked the waiter to bring a bottle with dinner.

She ate one of the oysters with the relish and gusto of a woman who'd been eating them all her life. When she set the shell back down, she leaned in. "So which one of your walking penis friends is in town?"

"How did you . . . Courtney. Of course. She's a nice girl." She was exactly the kind of woman he used to go after. Sweet, a little funny, open sexually. She'd pretty much offered herself up on a silver platter the day they'd met, but she'd been less aggressive since she discovered he had a connection to her best friend. Slightly less. "Gabe is here. I know he'd love to see you."

"And? Oh, god. If Gabe's here that means Mad is, too," she said with a laugh. "I'll call the local hospital and tell them they're going to need a rush shipment of penicillin. Wait, didn't Gus come in last night? Gus can handle Mad. Though the prostitutes of New Orleans will weep." She blushed. "I'm so sorry. I wasn't saying something mean about your sister. I adore her."

But Gus was kind of the female equivalent of Mad. "I'm sure she's handling Mad as we speak." He shuddered. "Let's talk about something more pleasant. Don't you have a murder or something that's nicer to think about than my sister sleeping with my friend?"

"Oh, I've had some great murders," she said with relish. She was smiling as she started to talk.

And he had her right where he wanted her.

An hour and a half and one shared *Cerises jubilee* later, Dax was a happy man. They'd spent the entire time talking about their work and friends. She'd discussed a few cases she'd worked and what it had been like growing up as the niece of one of the biggest, baddest cops in the parish. He'd told her a few stories about his friends—the ones that made him look like a choirboy, of course. And he'd talked about what it meant for him to have his own ship, to lead his men. It had been everything he'd thought a date with her would be. Fun and satisfying on a level he hadn't known with a woman before. Yes, he wanted her sexually. No doubt about that. He'd been tamping down his arousal most of the night. And when she really laughed . . . well, that throaty sound fired his blood. But the desire went beyond sex. He wanted her company. He wanted her near him.

He wanted her always.

He'd only checked his phone once. She'd gotten a call she couldn't avoid and stepped away to talk. That was when he'd seen the alert pop up. Connor had rigged a system that alerted Dax when his name came up in the tabloids. Dax had clicked through to find a picture of him and Holland entering Antoine's, his hand on the small of her back.

Three Internet gossip sites had already picked up the story. It was possible the bigger rags would run with the story, too.

God, he was going to have to tell her, but he wanted to wait a little while longer before reminding her of all the reasons she refused to date him.

"I haven't eaten that much in forever," she admitted. "After work, I usually heat up something in the microwave."

"Why would you do that when you're such an amazing cook?"

She blushed sweetly. "I like to cook, but I rarely do it. Cooking for one isn't much fun. I don't like to waste all that food. My uncle's recipes usually feed a dozen men. Though you ate almost everything I made the other night."

He would have eaten more if it kept her talking to him. "So what was the special occasion that night? You made gumbo and pie. Did I interrupt something?"

"No, not at all. I was experimenting." She huffed a little and set her wineglass down. "That's a lie. I made it for you. I remembered how much you love chess pie and the fact that you can't get it outside of the south. I wanted to impress you."

He wanted to reach out and pull her into his lap, to cuddle her and thank her properly. He settled for a smile. "Consider me impressed, sweetheart. It was amazing. I haven't had anyone give a damn about me in so long I think I've forgotten what it felt like."

"I can hardly imagine that's true. You're Captain Awesome."

He rolled his eyes. "Apparently the men call me that. I'm sure it's because I turn a blind eye to some of the stupid stuff they do. It can be hard to be stuck on a ship for months at a time. If they want to start a broom hockey league when they're off duty, who am I to stop them? No, I was talking about women, Holland. It's been a long time since a woman cooked for me. I think it was my college girlfriend. And she majored in ramen noodles, so I'm not sure that counts." There was something deeply intimate about a woman cooking a meal. There was something special because it hadn't been any woman. It had been Holland.

"How can that be true?" She shook her head as she stared at him, as though trying to figure him out. "You have women chasing after you constantly."

She assumed so many things about him. He could clear up a few misconceptions. "They chase after me a lot, but most women aren't actually interested in *me*. They like being seen with me. If they're into politics and power, they're hoping to get close to Zack or Roman. If they want money and glitz, then Gabe or Mad. They want me to take them out and show them off so they'll get their pictures in the tabloids. They don't know the real me and they don't want to. They certainly couldn't care less that I love gumbo and chess pie."

"I hadn't thought about it that way," she mused. "That sounds like a lonely way to live."

"It's starting to feel that way." When he was younger, he hadn't been looking for anything serious. Good-time girls had seemed like the perfect solution. He'd just wanted to have fun and hang with his friends. Then Zack had gotten married and the things he'd once sought seemed pointless. "Hell, most of the men under me are married with children. At some point the playboy thing becomes less a way of life and more like a joke."

"You could get married tomorrow if you wanted to."

"I don't want to just get married. I want to be in love. Everyone looks at marriage like it's the prize to be had. It should be the inevitable outcome of the real prize."

"Being in love?"

"Loving a woman so much that I know I won't ever want another one the way I want her. Knowing she completes me in some inexplicable way and I do the same for her. Marriage, children, the house in the suburbs, they don't mean a damn thing without that foundation."

She sat up suddenly and wiped a hand across her eyes. "I must be allergic to something. I'm going to visit the ladies' room, Captain. I'll be right back."

She picked up her purse and scurried off like a scared little rabbit. So he'd gotten to her with the truth. He called over the waiter and took care of the bill.

What he hadn't told her was that the whole time he'd been on his last deployment, he'd thought about her. There hadn't been some nameless, faceless wife who would magically round out his world. He'd pictured Holland. He knew what he wanted and it wasn't some sweet thing who would look at him like he was the king of the world because every now and then he remembered to bring her flowers or help with the dishes. No, he wanted a woman who would chew his ass out when he forgot. He wanted a woman who demanded respect, who earned it with her smarts and quick wit and passion.

He wanted Holland.

He damn sure intended his marriage to be stronger and have more substance than his parents'. Maybe he was being naive, but he intended to get it right with Holland. Starting now.

Dax stood, refusing to waste any opportunity. If he had any chance of a future with Holland, he would grab it every single time.

He strode into the hallway that led to the restrooms. Antoine's was larger than it looked and it could be a bit labyrinthine to the casual diner, but despite the cool, dark interior, he knew exactly where he was going.

Outside it would be twilight, the air hot and muggy, but here he could feel the air conditioner over his skin. It did nothing to cool him down.

She emerged from the bathroom as he approached. Her eyes widened when she caught sight of him, but she settled back into her calm and collected persona. "Are you ready to go?"

So polite. He wanted to get past that genteel surface and find the passionate woman he knew lay underneath. "I'm ready for a lot of things, Holland. Most of all, I'm ready to finish what we started all those years ago."

She backed up, her body hitting the wall behind her. "What are you talking about?"

Oh, she knew exactly what he was talking about, but he could make it clear to her. "I never got to finish that kiss. My father interrupted us."

Holland shook her head, but she was looking at his mouth. Her breath had gone shallow. "We finished. And I walked away."

He moved closer, crowding her. "I definitely didn't get my fill, sweetheart. Maybe if I had, you wouldn't have left. I think it's time we fixed that problem."

Dax leaned in slowly, giving her the opportunity to protest. He'd never force her . . . but persuasion was something else entirely.

"Tell me you don't want me to kiss you right here, right now."

"You know I can't," she whispered.

That was what he wanted to hear. He braced his hand against the wall above her head and hovered close, breathing in her scent. She smelled like ripe peaches and something so her. It thrilled his senses.

Slowly, he reached for the soft skin of her face and cupped it. "I never stopped thinking about you. Not once, Holland. I don't think I'm capable of forgetting you."

"This is a mistake." She breathed the words onto his lips, their mouths drawing ever closer. "It can't end well."

He closed the remaining distance between them and brushed his lips over hers, giving her a taste of what was to come. "It can if we make it. We choose our fates."

He would make his marriage work. Together, they would have children who always felt loved and never worried that their parents didn't put them and each other first.

Dax deepened the kiss, sliding his tongue over her plump bottom lip and thrilling when she shuddered. Her trembling hands skated up his torso as she pressed their bodies closer and kissed him harder. Then she opened her mouth and he felt the slide of her tongue against his.

Pure fire threatened to consume him. Usually, he took his time and worked up to sex, but the feel of this woman in his arms made him rough and ready in a heartbeat. He wanted to shove her against the wall and thrust his cock deep. Take her. His whole being screamed out to claim her once and for all.

He pinned her to the wall, covering her body with his as he prolonged the kiss. With greedy palms, he hugged her curves, then settled on her waist and pulled her hard against him. He hated the clothing between them, wanted nothing more than to feel her silky flesh.

"Dax, we shouldn't," she breathed against his mouth.

"Stop thinking. Feel. Feel how much I want you, Holland." He pressed his pelvis against hers. It wasn't a gentlemanly thing to do, but he couldn't be polite with her. She brought out the caveman in him. He wanted to mark her, to let everyone else know this one woman was his.

He silenced her with his kiss, delving deep again. Her fingers clung to his shoulders as her body molded to his, fitting together. Chest to chest. Belly to belly. His erection nestled against her pussy.

Could he take her in the bathroom? He had a condom. All he needed was a few minutes of privacy to ease the ache they were both suffering. But as much as he wanted her, Dax couldn't fathom that his first time with Holland would be in a public john. She deserved better. So did they.

As he forced himself to ease back, an unfamiliar voice drifted down the hall. "If you'll come this way, we'll take a peek into the private dining room."

Holland gasped at the intrusion and shoved at him. Dax stared at her flushed cheeks and swollen lips, a ribbon of satisfaction winding through him.

"As you can plainly see, Antoine's is noted for its romantic environment. Like everything here in New Orleans, we keep it spicy," the male voice said again.

Dax grimaced when he noticed a group of tourists taking one of the food and wine tours conducted daily throughout the city. As the group passed, Holland looked even more flustered. Obviously, she hadn't been caught in many compromising positions before. Luckily he had.

Dax stepped in front of her and nodded to the guide as he walked past.

"Y'all have a nice night in the Quarter," he said with a smile, taking all of the attention off Holland.

A few eyes widened and some whispers followed, as if someone recognized him, but the tour walked on.

"I can't believe I did that." Holland still panted behind him, her chest rising and falling when he turned back to her.

"That was nothing to be ashamed of, sweetheart. I bet we're not the first couple caught kissing in a hallway." He smoothed back her hair. "I'm sorry. I should have waited until we got home."

Her blond hair shook. "No, you shouldn't have done it at all. I told you, if we're going to investigate together, we can't be involved."

"Why? We're adults. We don't actually work together. Neither of our jobs have rules that prohibit a relationship between us. If you're still worried about my lifestyle, I assure you it's quiet. I only want you. I want to settle down. No more parties. No more craziness. Let's pursue this thing between us that's been building since the day I met you."

She blinked up at him. For a moment, he thought she would acquiesce. "I can't. If you want to look into your father's case, you have to put aside any romantic relationship with me."

Frustration welled up inside him. She'd told him she wanted him. She'd responded to his touch like she'd been made for him. So why was she pushing him away? The only reason he could see were her illogical fears. "Is this an either/or proposition? I can investigate my father's case or I can have you?"

She wouldn't quite meet his gaze. "No. I'm not saying that. I'm saying I'm not ready. I need some space. You knew you were coming back into my life. You've been thinking about this and planning it for months, but this is all a shock to me, Dax. Everything has been neat and tidy in my life and you're the hurricane that could blow it all away."

Her words kicked him squarely in the gut. She was right. He'd been plotting for months, and not once had he reached out to talk to her. He'd done that on purpose so he could surprise her, keep the upper hand . . . see if he could glean her real feelings. Holland didn't work like that. She wasn't a leap-then-look-later girl. She needed to think about things. She wouldn't feel safe until she'd mulled the options and possibilities completely. As much as her answer frustrated him, Dax knew Holland wasn't trying to force him to her will. She was simply being who she was. She was smart and methodical, but once she made a decision she stuck with it.

He cupped her chin and forced her gaze up to him. "Holland, I'm sorry. I pushed you when I promised I wouldn't. Can you forgive me?"

Tears shimmered in her clear blue eyes as she nodded. "It wasn't like I didn't respond."

"But you weren't ready," he replied. "Let me be plain with you. I want you, and not for some one-night stand. I want to try something lasting. I think we could be spectacular together, but I want you to feel the same way. So take the time you need. Ask me any question you want to. Test me out. I'm not going anywhere."

He pulled her into his arms but kept the touch light, comforting.

"We've always been friends," she said as she sighed and held on to him.

Friendship was important to her. She'd lost one of her best friends. While he wanted to be more than pals with her, the fact that she was including him in her circle was meaningful, and he would take it. "We'll always be friends, Holland. No matter what happens."

"I'll hold you to that, Spencer."

FIVE

Dax breathed in the humid air as they stepped outside the restaurant. Night had fallen, which brought out the crowds in the Quarter. The streets were always crowded, but after the sun went down . . . the real party began.

He glanced up and down the avenue, scanning for any hint of the paparazzi. Traffic congested the street in front of them, the cars traveling from south to north. The east/west streets were closed in the Quarter for foot traffic, and that seemed to agitate the people who'd been foolish enough to drive. Honking and revving of engines filled the air.

"You said it was only the one picture. That means one photographer," Holland pointed out. "We were in there for a long time. He's probably moved on. I've heard Brad and Angelina are in town. They're way more interesting than you, buddy."

She had a way of bringing him back down to earth.

"Well, I'm sorry to drag you into it anyway." Perhaps she was right. It had only been the one picture. That didn't mean a horde was waiting to descend, especially since Mad and Gabe weren't with him.

Holland smiled his way. Feeding her seemed to have vastly improved her mood. "It's all right. I looked really good in that pic."

He couldn't argue with that. She looked gorgeous always.

Jazz music, loud and heavy, blared from the various clubs and bars that dotted the street.

"Looks like a crazy night," Holland said with a shake of her head. "You're the one who actually lives here. How do you manage it?"

She gave him a breezy little shrug. "My grandmother left me her apartment. I couldn't possibly sell it. Who doesn't want to live over a real New Orleans voodoo store?"

He could think of many people. Including himself. "Anyone who doesn't want to listen to tours every hour of every day."

He happened to know that the voodoo store she lived above was rumored to have been frequented by one Marie Laveau, queen of NOLA voodoo. Informational tours stopped by several times a day.

She simply waved off that nuisance. "The good news is my grandmother had the place soundproofed. All the glory and fun of the French Quarter. None of the retching sounds. Or daily tourist information. It's a great place to live. Everything I could possibly need is right here. You're just a rich boy from the Garden. You can't handle a real party."

Had she forgotten who the hell he was? "Oh, I assure you, some of the parties I've been to would curl your toes, little girl. I went to Maddox Crawford's twenty-first birthday party. I have no idea how we ended up in Tijuana. We started out at a nice restaurant in Soho. It's a mystery."

She shook her head and settled the strap of her laptop bag on her shoulder. "The rich are truly different. We're three blocks from my place. Are you heading home?"

"Not until I see you to your door." He was going to take every damn minute he had with her. He refused to leave her side until he absolutely had to, especially after finding out the press was on to him. He wouldn't leave her to face that by herself.

"I would point out that I'm carrying a gun, but I think the gentlemanly thing is nice."

"Hell, sweetheart. I'm not being a gentleman. I can catch a cab over at your place. I'm expecting you to protect me." He winked.

But she could do it. Holland was more competent than anyone he knew with the singular exception of Connor. Instead, he grinned her way and decided not to tell her that he would walk her home because he didn't want the evening to end.

St. Louis Street was a crowded mess, but then it was every night. Even during the dog days of summer, the Quarter was jammed with tourists and students, all trying to out-party the next guy.

Dax grabbed her hand so he wouldn't lose her in the throng as he headed for her apartment. Maybe he could convince her to fix him some coffee and they could talk a little more. Not about the case. He wanted to forget about that for one night. He wouldn't kiss her again. He would show her they could be friends and when she was comfortable, he would move them to something more physical.

A woman bumped into him, their shoulders banging together. "Excuse me."

"Sorry. So sorry. Hey, do you know where Bourbon Street is?" Given the way she slurred her words, it sounded as if she'd already had enough for the night. She also looked like she couldn't be much past nineteen. She pushed her unruly hair out of her eyes, which weren't quite focused.

"Where are your parents?" Holland asked, obviously seeing what he did.

"Fucking cops." The girl rolled her eyes and stumbled on.

"Par for the course." Holland sighed. "I could follow her, but I don't have jurisdiction here. I hope she's got a good fake ID because those boys on Bourbon Street know they're being watched. When we get home, I'll call and have the street cops look for her. At least we know where she's going."

A group of women decked out for a bachelorette party rambled through, causing him to separate slightly from her.

She stepped out of the way of the drunk women. Unfortunately, that caused Holland to step into a part of the street that hadn't been blocked off to traffic. A long line of cars waited, their drivers impatient. He turned in her direction when a man on a bicycle wove through the cars.

That bike was on a collision course for Holland. Dax's eyes widened.

"Holland!" He tried to push his way through. Only feet separated them, but he couldn't reach her fast enough. "Watch your twelve!"

She seemed to hear him and looked up just in time to see the bike plowing toward her. Horns honked and the world suddenly seemed louder than before. Holland didn't panic. She simply stepped back up onto the curb and balanced herself.

He breathed a sigh of relief as the bike started to zoom past her, its rider thrusting out a muscled arm. He snatched the bag right off Holland's shoulder.

She whirled around and fell to one knee, knocking it hard against the pavement.

Dax finally managed to push his way through to her. He knelt and lifted her.

Holland clutched his hand as she struggled to her feet. "He took my computer. That asswipe took my computer."

Now that he knew she wasn't hurt, Dax spun around and gave chase. If she wanted her computer, he would get it for her.

He took off running, his feet pounding on the uneven pavement. He had to fight his way through the crowd, keeping his eyes on that bike. As he wove through the nasty tangle of traffic, he heard someone shouting behind him. He thought it might have been Holland, but if he took his eyes off the man for even a second, he might lose the thief.

Damn it, he hated not having control—over the press from following them, over his past, and definitely over this stealing motherfucker. But he intended to hunt the thug down and get her computer back.

Then it hit him: someone had targeted Holland, specifically went out of his way to take her computer. The Quarter was filled with tourists who'd imbibed too much dangling purses from their shoulders and tucking fat wallets in their back pocket. But the guy on the bike had gone straight for his girl. She'd just started the investigation and already someone wanted whatever notes or evidence she had, so they'd taken her laptop.

Just like they'd taken the life from his father.

He shoved the suspicion aside in favor of running, of giving into his predatory instincts.

The bike turned, gliding down a side street.

Traffic was moving, but that didn't matter to Dax. He heard the horns blare but ran anyway. He slammed his hand on the hood of a car that stopped suddenly and dashed around it, across the street, his chest heaving.

He managed to sprint onto that street and his way opened up. Then he picked up the pace. If he let the thief sneak out of these tight streets, Dax would surely lose him.

The guy on the bike pedaled hard, but the streets were uneven and riddled with potholes that could trip up a person walking—much less some asshat pedaling hard to flee the scene of his crime. Dax watched as the guy hit a big divot in the road, his body flying forward before finally giving in to gravity.

Fucking hell, yes. This was the break he needed.

He sped up, even though his heart was threatening to pound out of his chest. He saw Holland's laptop bag go flying. It had been hanging from the handlebars and now flung upward before falling once more and hitting the street.

Dax headed for it but he watched the groaning man writhe on the ground. Nondescript besides being tall and well built, the criminal wore sweatpants and a black light jacket.

He cursed loudly and twisted to his feet. When he spun around, Dax could see the guy wore sunglasses under his helmet. He couldn't tell much more than that except that the man was tan and either Caucasian or Hispanic.

"I'm taking that bag back," Dax yelled as he moved down the alley.

"Fuck you," the man said in a deep voice and reached for his bike.

Darkness had fallen and very little light penetrated the bodies and buildings from the main streets. Shadow encroached on all sides, but Dax was determined. He went for the bag.

The man's foot kicked out, catching him on the forearm. Dax gritted his teeth and whirled around, attempting to stay on his feet. The asshole was stronger than he looked and Dax found himself taking a hard punch that landed him on the ground, his knees hitting the bricks with a jaw-jarring strike.

Pain flared through him, but he tried to shove that aside and reach for the laptop bag.

Just as he grabbed it, Dax realized the asshole on the bike had brought along more than a helmet for protection.

"Let go." The man stood over him, gripping a gun in his hand.

Unfortunately, Dax knew what kind of damage a SIG Sauer could do, and the thug looked pretty competent with the damn thing. He was forced to drop the leather satchel.

Damn it, he was in the inferior position, never thinking that his pleasant evening with Holland could turn dangerous so quickly. He calculated his odds of distracting the other man, but his knee had taken a nice hit, the right one bleeding. Jarring pain swept through his thigh and gripped his kneecap. He might be able to use his martial arts training and catch the criminal off guard with a well-aimed kick using his uninjured leg, but if he couldn't sprint away, Dax knew he'd have a big, fatal hole in his body.

"I'm serious, fucker," the man ground out. "Move another inch and I'll blow your head off."

Dax believed him. Humiliation flashed hot through his blood. He should be able to take down a lone assailant and retrieve Holland's bag. He was a damn Naval officer. He'd had years of training, but that didn't make him Superman. He was defenseless against a speeding bullet.

"Dax!"

Shit. Holland. She'd followed him. She would have a gun, but might not see that this fucker also did until it was too late. The thug could turn and shoot her before she could even defend herself.

Never taking his eyes off Dax, the criminal stooped down and nabbed the bag, looping it over his head and across his chest. The gun never wavered as he shouted down the narrow alley, "Don't make a move or I'll blow his head off."

"Take the bag and go. I'm not making any kind of move." Holland halted near the street, her hands in the air. "You don't have to make this worse. Right now, all you've managed is some petty theft. We'll file a report and move on. You shoot him and the cops won't ever stop looking for you."

The man used his free hand to lift his bike, but he didn't turn his back to either of them. The alley was narrow, letting out to the next street west. He could easily lose himself in more tourists.

"Go on. I won't stop you," Holland promised, her voice calm and easy.

The man backed down the alley and took off.

Dax rose to his feet, eyeing the distance between himself and the assailant.

"Don't you dare," Holland warned, racing down the alley, her gun in hand. She carried it with the competency of a woman who had been around firearms all her life. She got to the end of the alley and holstered her weapon.

"We can still catch him," Dax insisted.

She pulled her phone from her purse and started to dial. "You're not going anywhere. Chasing him down was a crazy thing to do."

Dax had to stop her from making that call. "Holland, if you call the police, the press will follow. They'll be everywhere. It's why I took off after him in the first place."

She hesitated, sighed, then tucked the phone way. "I have to file a report, but you're right. Are you okay?"

The night had gone to shit. "I'll clean up at home."

"Absolutely not. We're a block from my place. Let's go."

"How can you let him get away with that?"

She frowned. "You know how? Because if I chased him down and started shooting, someone would get hurt. You're looking at me like I should have been more of a cop. You know what? I was being a cop, Dax. My job is to protect and I didn't act any differently than I would want someone else to in my situation. That computer is a thing. It can be replaced. People can't."

Dax studied her stony expression, her tight jaw. She was more upset than she was letting on.

"I'm sorry. I thought I was helping." He'd thought he could be her hero. He'd done it a hundred times over the course of his career, but he'd failed with his woman.

"I know. Let's get you cleaned up."

So he could head home. Gabe and Mad were probably somewhere partying it up. He would sit with his mother and have a quiet, lonely chat over a glass of brandy, see if he could catch a glimpse of the laughing, happy woman he remembered from his childhood.

He followed Holland toward her place and wished they'd never left the restaurant.

This is going to hurt." Holland winced as she dabbed the antiseptic on his elbow.

Dax hissed slightly but didn't flinch. More proof that he was completely insane. Instead, he stared at a stationary point above her head.

"You really should have let me call the paramedics so they could take a look at you."

He shrugged as she placed the bandage over his wound. "I didn't want to deal with the press. It's better if we just quietly file a report on the theft and leave the rest out of it. Have you wondered why he didn't take your purse?"

She moved on to the angry red scrape across his knee. He'd hit the pavement so hard he'd torn through his slacks, but it didn't look as if he needed stitches. The bleeding had thankfully stopped. "I have no idea. He wasn't very smart, though. He got the cheaper of the two bags I was carrying. This purse is actually vintage Versace. Joy bought it for me as her maid of honor. It's worth a small fortune, much more than the laptop itself."

"Was that the only thing in the bag?" His low voice sounded monotone. He'd been distant, almost removed ever since the asshole had gotten away.

Holland wondered if he was angry or embarrassed that he hadn't brought the bad guy down. There was nothing more Dax could have done. "My laptop, an extra battery, wireless mouse. That's all. My phone was in my purse, thank god."

"Was it a particularly expensive laptop?"

"It's government issued, so what do you think?" she asked with an acidic little grin. "It sucked. And don't worry. I already called the office. They shut down any access from that system and changed every one of my passwords. It's really more of a hassle than anything. I bet he was actually trying to get my purse and missed."

Dax finally cast his gaze on her, his eyes chilly. "He wasn't. I watched him. He knew exactly what he wanted."

A tinge of disquiet rolled through her. "Are you saying someone followed us? How would they even have known where we were?"

His mouth tightened. "Don't forget, someone took a picture of us going into Antoine's. It was up about five minutes after we entered the restaurant. We were there for two hours. Unfortunately, it's not hard to follow someone like me around. All you have to do is watch the gossip sites." He glanced at his phone. "I'm glad no one snapped pictures of me fighting that asshole. That would have made for awesome press."

With a wry nod, Holland closed up the first aid kit and sat back on her couch, trying to figure Dax out. He'd been so heroic and intent on saving her. Now he seemed all but shut down and she couldn't stand it. She needed to come at the problem from a different angle.

"I was scared for you," she murmured.

He stared her way through narrowed eyes. "I know you like to think of me as a spoiled rich kid, but I am a captain in the Navy. I know how to handle myself in a fight."

As the truth behind his mood hit her, she softened. He was still feeling the adrenaline. She'd seen this time and time again after a battle or fight, felt it herself a few times when she'd gotten into dangerous situations. He needed calm and she was going to give it to him.

"Yes, but that doesn't mean he couldn't have shot you. My laptop wasn't worth your life. I back everything up. Every note I had, every file I've gathered is saved to an alternate storage system. Even the notes I took during the interview with my uncle are saved there. I'll pull it all onto my home system tonight, so it's not a big deal. You were amazing, Dax. I appreciate you for trying to come to my rescue but I never want you to put yourself in that position for me again."

His body language softened slightly. "Didn't like watching him pull a gun on me, huh?"

Her heart had nearly stopped when she'd caught up to them. "If I never see it again, it will be too soon."

She'd stood at the entrance of the alley helplessly, knowing she couldn't get to him or her own weapon in time. If the assailant had wanted to pull the trigger, she couldn't have saved Dax. In that moment, she'd realized she could lose him. And something had shifted inside her. Yes, she was afraid that a relationship with him could end in heartache, but was she willing to go her whole life without knowing what it felt like to wake up beside him? To wrap her arms around him and know he belonged to her? To surrender utterly to the one man she knew would make everything else worthwhile?

As if their kiss at Antoine's had taken place mere moments ago, she could still feel his lips on hers, tempting her as his big body had pressed her, hot and hard, to the wall. She'd almost been willing to do anything to have him right then and there.

"He got lucky. If I'd been closer, I would have gotten that gun out of his hand and grabbed your laptop," Dax vowed. "If I ever see that asshole again, I'm going to wipe the floor with him."

She gave him a placating smile, intending to make sure they stayed far away from the guy. "Like I said, there's nothing important on that laptop that I can't get back. So if this was some nefarious plot to steal my secrets, they failed."

He fell quiet for a moment. "I find it interesting that you start investigating my father's case and someone immediately assaults you."

He sounded a bit suspicious, like he was looking for conspiracy theories all around him. She had a few theories of her own. "It was very likely a random street crime. It's the season, and we happened to be on the perfect street and at the right time of day. Or if they were targeting me, it was because of your media attention. If a reporter thinks we're dating, they likely want the laptop to get information on me. Or in case we have stuff stored on it."

"Stuff?"

She felt herself blush. She really shouldn't have to tell him what she could potentially have on her computer that a tabloid might pay tons of money to own.

His lips curled up into a broad, male grin. "You think someone hoped that you had a sex tape of us?"

"I've heard that there's a bounty out on any of the president's friends. Well, except for Mad. He practically has a YouTube channel devoted to his sex life. If we've already hit the tabloid pages, it makes sense that some asshole reporter would try to get a scoop. He did have a camera bag on his bike."

"Stupid bicycles should have license plates. I didn't get that great a look at the asshole once we turned down that alley. It was too dark and he was wearing that douchebag helmet. I don't like that someone is already stalking us. Holland, I should go."

"Leave?" She blinked at him and resisted the urge to pull him close.

"I think I should," he said grimly. "Maybe you should stop investigating and we shouldn't see each other anymore. It's too soon after the giant shit storm of my father's scandal. Whoever wanted him dead doesn't want the truth uncovered. I can't risk you."

Yesterday, she would have started singing hallelujah at the thought of Dax not dangling his tempting self in front of her anymore. Now she couldn't stand the thought of not seeing him every day. She'd been a coward where he was concerned for nearly ten years, always running from this amazing man because she wanted him too much and she'd long feared he would leave her broken. Yes, he came with baggage. Granted, some phenomenally wretched baggage, but she couldn't stop thinking about the loneliness on his face when he'd admitted that no woman he dated had cared about him enough to know his favorite foods. She knew far more about him and they'd barely flirted with anything beyond friendship.

But now Holland had found something she was more afraid of losing than her heart. She feared losing Dax Spencer forever.

"You're not risking me. I agreed to help you. And you can't let a random street thief derail you from getting the answers you deserve. I'm fine. Let me do my job. And don't worry about the press, either. The truth is you're a lesser Gentleman," she joked. "You and Connor are the boring ones. You have a good job and you're excellent at it. You don't dance drunk in Italian fountains."

"In Mad's defense, it's not just Italian fountains. He'll swim naked in any public body of water."

She laughed. His friends were crazy, but they were loyal to the bone. Would Dax be as loyal to the woman who snared his heart? Would he stand by her the way he did his friends? Would he forgive her even if she couldn't give him the answers he wanted most in the world? "Dax, I don't want you to go."

"I don't want to, either, but it might be for the best. I moved too fast earlier. I meant what I said. I'm not going to push you again. Our relationship—in whatever form it comes—is too important to me to lose. I'll take you any way I can get you."

Had he been this sweet all those years ago? Maybe he had been and she hadn't wanted to hear it. Her younger self had been afraid of being another notch in his bedpost, but she couldn't find the will to turn him away now.

She wanted more than a kiss. She wanted more than to have her body hum just being near him. Now she wanted to follow him down the hall and to find where that hum led, to finally know what it meant to be Dax Spencer's lover.

The trouble was she'd convinced him that she didn't. She might regret this tomorrow . . . but tonight had underscored the fact that life could be cut short in an instant. She'd rather regret what she did do, not what she hadn't.

"Our friendship is important to me, too. That's one of the reasons I walked away at the wedding."

"I thought that was all about your career and my fast-lane life."

"It was in part." She'd held the truth in all these years. She hadn't told anyone, not even Joy. She'd joked about flirting with Dax and made the easy excuse of not wanting to be in the spotlight, but there had been more behind her decision. "I knew I wanted to go into law enforcement. I've known since I was a kid. Other girls were playing princess and I was taking down the bad guys. Maybe I looked up to my uncle too much." She shrugged. "Eventually, I realized that I wanted to venture more into the investigative part of the job. I like the mental challenge of solving crime. But it's a tough role for a woman."

He winced a bit as he sat up, but his gaze remained steady on her. "I can imagine. Especially down here. It's still a good old boys' network in the South."

"Yes. Oddly, my last name buys me some goodwill. It's one reason I wanted to come to New Orleans. Well, and because it feels like home. When you approached me at Joy and Zack's wedding, I worried that being your girlfriend would negatively impact my coworkers' perceptions of me. After all, if I was dating a playboy, how serious could I be?" She sighed, reluctant to carry on, but she owed him. "At worst, being in a relationship with you would have softened me. You always got me right here." She laid a hand over her heart. "That vulnerability would have been a chink in my mental toughness. It was another hurdle I wasn't prepared to jump."

She hated how self-centered that sounded, but at that point in her life her career had seemed like all she had. She'd been driven to establish herself before she dove into a relationship.

His jaw tightened. "I understand that, but you dated other men. Why did you always refuse me?"

"I dated men I could never be serious about. I kept it casual. I never had pictures of them on my desk or called them my boyfriend. I compartmentalized my life. I kept my dates out of my professional life and vice versa. I wouldn't have been able to do that with you. I knew it then. I know it now."

A slight frown marred his dark brow. "I never meant to disrupt your life."

"You're not a man I can take or leave or have a good time with one night and totally forget the next."

"You're the woman for me. I've never forgotten you, not once since the moment we met. I've dated other women because I couldn't have you, but I never forgot and I never really gave up hope that we would meet again."

Deep down, she hadn't, either. She'd always known he was the one man who could make her want more than her career. "I think if I'd stayed with you that day, I would be following you around from base to base now, waiting on you to come home. I know many couples do it. It's honorable and sweet in a way, but I watched that life nearly kill my mother. She waited through her best years for my dad to retire but she died before he could. I feared living like I'm always waiting for something that never comes. I don't know that I could be happy. And yet your service to your country is a part of who you are and what you do."

"Do we have to make decisions today, Holland? Do we have zero chance unless I leave the Navy?"

She shook her head. "Of course not. I'm simply telling you how I felt. How I still feel from time to time. I'm also worried that if I don't find a way to restore your father's reputation, you'll hate me."

He moved to sit beside her. "I could never hate you."

The heat of his body surrounded her, and it took all she had not to lean into his strength. She wanted more than anything to let go of all her worries for a night, to see where it could lead. "Never say never, Captain."

He shook his head and gently turned her face his way. "Don't distance yourself from me. I don't want to be a captain tonight. I don't want to be a fucking Perfect Gentleman or tabloid fodder. I want to be Dax, the guy who wants so badly to be with Holland. Just the two of us, with no outside influences."

"Those influences will still be around come morning, Dax." She spoke his name because he was right. She had been trying to keep her distance. But if they spent the night together, there would be nothing between them for those beautiful hours. No investigation. No worries about the future. Just one glorious night with the man of her dreams.

"We'll deal with them then." His gaze had heated, but he made no move to kiss her. "But I won't touch you unless I hear you say exactly what you want."

She wasn't going to pretend to misunderstand. She heard the need in his voice and it touched her. He probably craved hearing her say the words out loud because she'd pushed him away for almost a decade. Had she convinced him that he meant nothing to her? "I want to make love with you, Dax."

He must have known the words were coming, but even so his body tensed. "I've never wanted a woman the way I want you. Be sure, sweetheart. I don't want a one-night stand. If we spend the night together, it's because we're going to give us a chance. That means you'll be in the press. Unless we never leave this apartment again, they'll snap pictures of us. But you're right. Since I'm the boring Perfect Gentleman, after a few weeks, it will calm down. Everyone in your family and in your office will know about us, though. No getting around that."

She would take some serious ribbing from her peers and with her uncle, but she could handle it. "Kiss me again and see if I run this time."

His lips curled up in a sexy, dangerous smile. "We're at your place. There's nowhere to run. The first time I approached you, I should have locked the door and thrown away the key." He sobered a bit as he met her gaze with a stare so hot and intent, her pulse jumped. "I wonder what would have happened between us that day if my father hadn't interrupted. I sometimes wish I could go back and make sure Zack's mom didn't dive headfirst into a vat of Chardonnay."

Like Dax's father, Constance Hayes was dead, too. She'd perished on a road in England, years of alcoholism and poor decision-making finally taking their toll.

So much loss all around her, yet Holland had never reached out to grab life. She'd let the loss and the potential for pain frighten her, but now she was realizing how little life meant without some risk—and someone to share it with. "Are you going to kiss me?"

"The funny thing is, I'm nervous. I've waited all these years . . . You know?"

She was nervous, too. How long had it been since she had butterflies in her belly, her skin warming to a hot sting of a flush? And he'd barely touched her. She'd certainly had sex, and some of it had been good. But she hadn't wanted any other man like this. "You've kissed hundreds of women."

He brushed his fingers along her jawline, watching her as if he intended to memorize this moment. "None who mattered besides you."

"You didn't have a problem with shyness earlier today when you nearly showed those little old ladies on the food tour how Naval captains make babies." Somehow his nervousness eased her own. Despite the ridiculous amount of experience he had, she would be new to him. They would make their own memories, their own rules and rituals.

He chuckled and leaned in, his arm curling around her back and over her shoulders. "It wasn't that racy." As their laughter fell silent, he fused his gaze to hers. Hunger filled his dark eyes, tightened his big body. "I'm going to kiss you now and I won't stop unless you tell me to."

"I won't say a word," she breathed.

He lifted his free hand to her hair, sliding out the elastic band holding the low ponytail she typically wore. He gripped the strands. "Soft as silk. Just like you."

"I'm not soft, Dax." She didn't want him to think she was like the other women he'd been with. They likely had been sweet, feminine creatures. Holland couldn't afford to be.

"Yes, you are. You can be strong and soft and silky all at the same time. That's who you are and one of the reasons I find you interesting. I want to know every single facet of Holland Kirk. I want to be the man you explore with, experiment with, be true with."

She had the feeling he wasn't merely talking about sex. This was why she'd always hesitated. Dax wanted all of her, even the parts of herself she'd shut down and hidden and told herself didn't matter. He wouldn't accept anything less than the whole of her soul.

But if he gave her back the whole of his, wasn't that worth it? If they were both vulnerable, they could learn to trust.

She leaned in and his lips finally met hers. Slow and steady. He took her mouth like a man indulging in decadence, as though knowing they would share the pleasure of sex made him willing to stretch this moment out to something rich and sinful.

Gently, he fisted a hand in her hair, lighting up her scalp with sensation as he took her lips more fully, clasping her body against his own. She softened, giving in to the demand of his mouth, his hands. And when his tongue slid over her lower lip, demanding entry, she couldn't stop herself from flowering open for him.

Dax pulled her up and onto his lap. She clasped her arms around his neck, bringing him closer. She could feel his erection pressing against her, thick and hard. So big. She couldn't help but wriggle a little, trying to get closer to him.

His arms tightened on her. "Stop it, sweetheart, or we're going to have a problem. I want this to last. After waiting this long, I want to savor tonight."

But she was already on the edge, dying for him to be on top of her, inside of her. "We should go to my bedroom."

"We should set some ground rules first," he growled against her neck. "Holland, I'm crazy about you, but you're going to let me control sex. I'm not foolish enough to think I could control anything else in our relationship but I need you to let me handle this."

"Why does anyone have to be in control?" She'd always been in the power position with the men in her bed. Ceding it to Dax both excited and scared her.

"Because, as you pointed out, I have more experience. And I'm wired to take control. We're not going to go at it like two teenagers. Not this first time. Maybe later, when I know exactly how to touch you to get you hot." Heat melted his dark eyes like chocolate. "But right now I have to figure out how to handle you, how to steer you the right way."

"I'm not a boat, Captain."

"Aren't you?" He brushed a big hand over one of her breasts, cupping her flesh in his broad palm and making her gasp. "Everything that's worth doing is worth doing right. Making love to you is definitely worth my best effort. See, this little nipple is begging for attention." He dragged his thumb across the sensitive bud so slowly she bit her lip to hold in a moan. "Take off your shirt and your bra so I can give it the proper attention."

His voice had dropped an octave and gone velvety. Holland found herself obeying him. Her fingers shook as she reached for the buttons of her shirt, twisting each and releasing it before moving to the next. She didn't leave the comfort of his lap, but he sat back like a king watching the show, mentally undressing her with those eyes. There was something a bit forbidden about baring herself while his erection pressed so intimately against her.

Holland unfastened the last button and let her shirt fall away before she unhooked the front clasp of her bra. Her breasts were nothing special. She hit the gym three or four times a week to stay in shape. She considered herself more athletic than sexy, but the way Dax's breath hitched and he affixed his stare to her bare mounds, as if he'd never seen anything sexier, made her rethink all that.

He dragged his heated palm down the valley between her breasts. "Sweetheart . . . I always knew you would be gorgeous without all those clothes. So beautiful."

Until him, she hadn't felt that way. Her body had been a tool to use in service of her job, a way to move about each day. When she'd had sex, she preferred to go to the bedroom, get the deed done, and get to sleep. Her few longer-term boyfriends hadn't seemed to mind, but she got the feeling Dax would take exception to that routine.

With him, it meant far more to her than a rote activity, too.

He kissed her again, their tongues tangling as he explored her breasts, caressing her nipples, plying them with his touch. Fire licked through her system. She could feel herself getting wet and ready.

"Lean back for me. I'll hold you and keep you safe." His words rumbled over the sensitive flesh of her neck as he gently leaned her back, resting her over his arm until she arched and thrust her chest up to him like an offering.

"Yes, these little pearls need affection." He tongued one, laving and sucking it.

She had to bite her lip to hold in a cry. She'd never thought her nipples were particularly sensitive, but that was because they'd never experienced Dax's clever mouth.

She heard herself whimper as he sucked one bud deeper between his lips. He didn't satisfy himself with a little lick, a short few seconds of suckling. Not Captain Dax Spencer. He indulged. He reveled. He caressed her with his tongue, tracing her areola before he sucked the tip back into his mouth and gave her the bare edge of his teeth. A tiny bite of pain flared before he soothed the bud with a soft laving. Her body balled into an ache, her sex throbbed as he shifted his attention to her left breast and gave it the same loving treatment.

"I want to kiss and lick and taste every inch of you, Holland. Do you know how long I've waited to be here? Years. Fuck, sweetheart, even before I met you, I dreamed about you. I've always known you're the one woman who could make me feel, make me want forever." He nuzzled her, the stubble of his hard jaw gently abrading her skin. "Stand up and take off your pants. I don't want anything to stop me from touching you."

God, she wasn't the girl who simply obeyed, but she found herself sliding off his lap and standing in front of him. Breathless, the moment full of gravity, she peered down at the man who had tried so hard to be her hero. None of her boyfriends had fought for her like that. Most had considered her more competent than they were. Not one of them had made her feel soft and feminine or so desired. Her father had wanted a boy, so he'd raised her to be tough. Maybe Dax was right that she didn't have to be a stereotypical tough girl. Maybe here with him it was safe to be open, to express all her facets—strong and soft and terribly weak where he was concerned.

Holland lowered her guard and opened her heart as she unhooked the fastening of her slacks and let them slide down her hips. For a night, she could be Dax Spencer's woman. That made her feel beautiful and feminine for once. And whole.

She watched as his hot stare followed the trail of her slacks as they fell slowly to the floor. He was right. They didn't have to rush. After waiting for so long, they should savor every kiss and touch. After all, they'd never have a first time together again. Why hurry when she had no intention of moving on? Dax was the destination.

Every inch of him looked so masculine, his face all hard planes and angles that somehow formed a perfect definition of male beauty.

Dax sat, still fully dressed while he studied her. She stood a heartbeat away wearing nothing more than her panties. Being so exposed should make her feel vulnerable. Instead, Holland felt every bit as beautiful as he'd told her she was even as the fear of being so emotionally exposed cut through her. But she took a deep breath and remembered his sweet words. God, when he told her how much he wanted her, that he wouldn't leave her, she believed him.

Flirting with something lasting was uncharted territory for her and perhaps a bit dangerous with Dax, but she couldn't turn back now. She was finally ready to see if they could have something like forever.

She stepped out of the slacks, having kicked aside her shoes long ago. He sat forward, his stare unwavering as he cupped her hips. There was nothing between those hot hands and her aching flesh but a tiny scrap of cotton. Her bikini panties weren't as sexy as she'd like, but Dax didn't seem to mind. He leaned in and nuzzled his nose against her sex, breathing in her scent.

Normally, she would shy away from such intimacy, but he gave a low groan. The sound rumbled and vibrated along her sensitive flesh.

"Fuck, I can smell how aroused you are. Your panties are damp. You're wet, aren't you, sweetheart?"

She closed her eyes and sank her fingers into his hair. "Yes. I'm not usually like this, Dax. What are you doing to me?"

"Showing you how good we are together. Give over and let me take you somewhere only the two of us can find. This isn't normal for me, either. Something this amazing can only happen with you." His fingers slid under the straps of her panties and dragged them down her thighs, baring her feminine flesh to him. "You smell so fucking good to me."

His words were like drugs, clouding her mind and turning her whole world soft and hazy. He nosed her, rubbing against her labia as he dragged her scent in with an audible breath again. And when he nudged her folds with his tongue, gliding between to taste her, she couldn't help crying out in a strangled scream.

Her body trembled as she closed her eyes and sank into the moment. "Oh, Dax. Oh . . . That feels so good."

"You taste good, just like I knew you would. Honey and sunshine." He wrapped his arms around her waist and lifted her onto the couch. "Lie back and spread your legs for me."

She did, and he followed her, settling on top of her. Holland's sofa was apartment-sized and Dax was a big man, but the awkward tangle of arms and legs still made her shiver with a pleasure that went beyond the physical. She enjoyed being close to him and feeling like a woman in his arms. She loved feeling as if he was all hers.

After a lingering kiss, he stood again. She watched as he unbuttoned his shirt and tugged it off. That spectacular chest of his came into view. The sight almost had her gaping. Powerfully built, muscle and bronzed skin covered his arms, shoulders, and torso. His slacks rode low on his hips, showing off the notches there. Now she understood perfectly what he'd meant about wanting to lick every inch of her, run his nose over her flesh. She wanted to learn his touch, his taste, his scent. Wanted to surround herself with him until nothing and no one else existed. Only Dax.

He knelt on the floor and turned her to face him as he settled in, his big body twisting until he wedged his shoulders between her thighs and found a place for himself at her core. "I want to make you fly, sweetheart. I want to be the only man you come for ever again, the only man who gets to see and taste and touch you."

He lowered his head and licked his way through her wet flesh to her clitoris.

Holland groaned, reached for him. Need pounded through her. She let her head fall back as he parted her flesh even more and licked her again, spearing her with his tongue. Another flash of lightning heat sizzled her, scorching along her skin until all that mattered was the pleasure he gave her and the intimacy they shared. He unwound her polite façade, obliterated her protective walls, and reduced her to a trembling bundle of need. And she knew that he alone could put out this fire and save her.

He slid his tongue deeper inside her before replacing it with one of his thick fingers.

"You want more?" His husky murmur taunted her just the slightest bit.

When she looked down her naked body to find him staring up at her with a decadent grin, he tantalized her by rotating his finger deeper inside.

She nodded.

"No, you have to ask me," he chided gently. "Ask me to make you come, Holland."

He was a bastard to make her beg, but she was too far gone to fight him. "Please. Dax, please make me come."

"My pleasure," he growled against her needy flesh.

He picked up the pace, adding another finger as his lips closed around her clitoris and began to work the little button hard. His fingers curled up inside her, rubbing and exploring while his tongue worried her sensitive nub. Holland clutched at the pillows around her as her head thrashed. Dax's big body held her down or she might have come off the couch as he found some magical place inside her body that had her gasping with a growing ecstasy she could barely fathom. Between his fingers inside her and his mouth all over her, she couldn't fight orgasm a second longer.

Pleasure swamped her, hard and fast, and as she splintered, she cried out his name. Her body shook and stiffened as the orgasm became her everything. He didn't let up, forcing her higher and higher. She could have sworn her peripheral vision began to fade, narrowing her whole world to just Dax.

Finally, he let her go and she relaxed, limp and satisfied. Her blood flowed through her system in a pleasurable thrum. He scooped her up and stood, cradling her to his body. And she felt both delicate and adored in his arms.

Holland let her head roll onto his chest and she listened to the speeding gait of his heart with a punch-drunk smile. "Now I know why they call you Captain Awesome."

His eyes flared as he marched toward her bedroom. "Oh, sweetheart, I haven't even started showing you how awesome I can be."

Holland sighed. If the last few minutes hadn't been the peak of her day, then she just might have found heaven. She should have known Dax would be the one to take her there.

SIX

Dax was fairly certain his libido was running on a short fuse. He was set to explode at any moment, and he would be damned if he came all over Holland like a seventeen-year-old kid with his first woman. He'd had to apologize profusely to Gabi Webber, a pretty senior at the girls' school near his prep school alma mater, Creighton Academy, because he'd ruined her uniform. Not happening tonight. He would give Holland the best he had. His past, his thoughts, his heart . . . they all led him right to this woman. He belonged with her.

He forgave her for refusing him all those years ago. She'd been young. Hell, he probably hadn't been ready, either. He would have expected her to be a good Naval wife, to stay home and have their children. But Holland needed a career every bit as engrossing as his own, and asking her to live alone and eventually single parent wasn't entirely fair. He understood that now. She was driven and needed to achieve outside the home, and he would do everything he could to make that possible for her. This time, they were both ready for something more, something lasting. Nothing was going to tear them apart. He would make sure of it.

He stepped into her bedroom and eased her down to the bed. The room was functional, the furnishings comfortable and feminine without the frilliness of other women's bedrooms. All grays and creams with a hint of peacock blue. He liked it. He felt at home in her tidy apartment.

He'd definitely felt at home when he'd been between her legs, his mouth on her pussy. She'd been so hot, the feel of her around his fingers had singed him. He'd tasted her sweetness as she shattered against his tongue. It had been everything he'd fantasized about and so much more because Holland was real—stubborn and smart—and she'd chosen him. She'd spread her legs and welcomed him inside.

Now he intended to brand her with pleasure so profound that she'd ache deep inside whenever they were apart. He would feel it, too. Neither of them would be complete unless they were together in every way possible.

She turned over, bracing her head in her hand, that glorious body of hers laid out. "Do you know how much I want to see you naked, Captain Awesome?"

He didn't want to get into that shit. "Just Dax."

She sighed. "Dax, could I please see you naked? I've wanted to for so long. Unlike some of your friends, you've been careful about not getting caught by the press with your pants down."

He had to grin at the thought. He'd been lucky, especially after that wild weekend in Vegas with Harry and strip pool. He'd been a much better pool player than the English prince. "Did you watch for me?"

Her smile dimmed the slightest bit. "Always. I suspect you're going to be gorgeous."

Hearing her say that made him feel about ten feet tall. She wouldn't believe it, but he rarely had a woman look at him with such open and honest desire. The fact that she knew and wanted him—and that her feelings had nothing to do with his friends, money, or position—did something for him.

He reached for the fly of his slacks and he undid them, letting the garment slide to the floor.

He didn't wear underwear, and when her eyes widened and she gasped, he just smiled.

Holland sat up, staring, her breath hitching. He groaned inwardly, his cock harder than he ever remembered. When had he desired a woman more than his next meal, his next sunrise, his next breath? Dax knew the answer.

He couldn't believe he was finally about to have the woman he'd always wanted. A part of him ached to simply jump on her and find some blessed relief, but he wasn't going to rush this or her.

When she scooted to the edge of her bed and touched a soft hand to his chest, it was the sweetest torture. Her palm glided over his torso, her fingers tracing every line and muscle that defined his body. Soon, she raised her other hand. It joined the first in her exploration like twin butterflies brushing a soft, aching path across his skin.

Then she leaned forward and pressed her mouth right over his heart.

He clenched his fists at his sides so he didn't toss her to the bed and penetrate her in the next five seconds. "You're going to make me crazy."

She gave him a Mona Lisa smile. "I'm going to explore you the way you explored me."

Holland bowed her head and ran her tongue over his nipple. A pleasant shiver went up his spine. He bit back a groan as he sank his hands into her gloriously soft hair. "Bite me. Just a little nip. I want to feel your teeth."

Her lips curled against his skin and he tensed, waiting. Then she nipped him. It was blissful torment, exactly enough to drag him back from the edge. It made his dick jump, too. But now he could stand still and give her what she wanted.

She shifted to the other nipple, giving it the same treatment. He looked down, watching her golden hair brush across his skin. It was like a web he could get lost in. Holland was usually so tidy in her appearance—sleek suits, neat skirts, never a hair out of its perfect and functional swept-back do. But now she looked a little primal. With her hair mussed from his hands and those gorgeous lips bruised from his kisses, she was the most tempting woman he'd ever seen.

She dropped to her knees in front of him and he held his breath, praying he would outlast what she planned next.

"You're beautiful, Dax." Her eyes fell to his cock as she brushed her hand up the length of his erection. She looked at him as if he was everything she'd wanted for Christmas.

"Grip me, Holland. Tight."

She closed her hand around his rock hard flesh and Dax's eyes nearly rolled into the back of his head. She pumped his shaft, finding a rhythm that started a slow build in his system. Her grip felt both soft and firm, and he forced himself to look down, take in the sight of her giving him pleasure. Her nipples were hard, and he rolled his tongue around his mouth, remembering the feel of them. Then—dear god—she inched closer and spread her knees, bracing herself. The pose put her sex on display. That had been the sweetest pussy he'd ever put his mouth on.

She stared at his rigid length for a moment, held him in her hand, her blue eyes glazing over just before she leaned in, lips parted. Her pretty pink tongue peeked out and he nearly came right then and there.

Dax sucked in a breath, his entire body tensing with the grip of pleasure. *Oh . . . hell.*

He had to take back control. The way he felt now, he'd never last if she licked every inch of him.

His fingers tightened. "Stop. I want to feel you all around me. I want to make you come again before I do."

"Yes," she breathed. "I want that, Dax. I want that so much."

He was going to have her. Finally. After all these years, he was going to make love to Holland Kirk. Then she would be his.

Somewhere in the back of his head, he worried that he was being selfish. He was committed to finding out the truth about his father's scandal and death. He understood now that it would be dangerous.

While he'd been fighting the asshole who'd taken her laptop, he'd practically sworn he would walk away from her. He'd even tried to leave her. For her sake.

But lost in her sweet scent and silky skin, he could barely remember now why that had seemed like a good idea. She was a capable woman, and he would do everything in his power to keep her safe. He would worship her and make any unpleasant part of the investigation worth her while. No one in the world mattered to him the way she did. She was the be-all, end-all of his existence. He'd done without her for nearly a decade. He couldn't live without her anymore.

He hauled her up, his passion cresting as he lowered his mouth toward hers. Lust churned his blood as he kissed her, crushing her body against his. Finally, he could feel her bare flesh. Chest to chest, heart to heart. Hips met. Thighs touched. When he gripped her waist and pulled her closer, forcing her softest flesh against his cock, she felt soft and wet.

God, she was perfect.

He slanted his mouth over hers, tangling their tongues. He could spend hours kissing her. Later, he would. But he needed her now—so fucking badly.

He pressed her back against the bed before realizing he'd forgotten something. Damn it. He bent and fished out his wallet, happy that he'd started carrying an emergency condom there decades before.

One day he wouldn't need it. Even as he opened the packet and began rolling it over his cock, Dax realized he didn't want to wear one with her. He would for now. They needed time together to solidify what he knew in his heart. But one day he wouldn't need that thin piece of latex to separate them. She would welcome him as he planted his seed. She would carry his babies. Together, they would have a family.

First, he had to convince her that they would work.

He wasn't stupid. He knew that tonight wouldn't solve their problems. They would still exist tomorrow. So he had work to do if he wanted to make her believe in them the way he did.

And he had decisions to make. After hearing about her mother's sad life and Holland's fears, maybe the time had come to exit the Navy. He would work in the private sector. Sure, he'd always believed he would retire as a Naval officer, but the idea of leaving Holland behind to keep the home fires burning for months on end didn't sit well with him. He couldn't imagine not spending time with her, not being here to protect her.

Maybe it should surprise him that she'd become more important to him than any career. It didn't.

He secured the condom and climbed over her, spreading her legs and settling himself between her thighs. "I'm crazy about you, Holland." He couldn't divulge the true extent of his feelings. She wasn't ready to hear them.

Her smile was lazy and sexy as she reached up for him. "Back at you, Spencer." She touched his face and seemed to sober a bit. "I'm crazy about you, Dax. Have been since the day I met you."

He pressed his stiff flesh against her soft opening, remembering the day. Joy had been dating Zack for a few months before Dax had gone out to San Diego for some R&R. The gang had been there, everyone meeting Zack's girl for the first time, but all he'd been able to see was Holland. He couldn't remember if the sky had been full of gloomy rain or brilliant sunshine. All he remembered was the yellow sundress she'd worn and the way her smile had lit up the room.

After tonight all he would be able to remember was how delicate she felt in his arms and how her eyes looked sleepy after she came even as she still welcomed him into her body.

Dax eased inside her hot, slick channel. Damn, she was so tight around him. He worked his way in, inch by inch, joining their bodies together. She wrapped her arms around his neck. When he pressed in deeper still, her eyes flared wide.

He froze. "I don't want to hurt you."

Those nails of hers dug in slightly. "Don't you dare stop. It feels good. So good. I'm not fragile, either. Don't treat me like I am."

She wasn't weak, nor would she break if he was a little rough. She'd been built to take him, his need, his passion, then give it all back.

With a savage groan, he pushed inside her.

Fuck. It felt so perfect. So fucking right. He held himself still inside her, moving in to take her lips again. He slid his tongue against hers, showing her the rhythm he intended to use when he took her body. He thrust in and out of her mouth, just as he would the rest of her until he made a home for himself deep inside her soul.

He ground his hips against her as he started to thrust in sync with his kisses. Instantly, sensations swamped him. This was beyond anything he'd felt before. He was connected to her—and not just by their bodies. He could feel her all around him, her quiet reserve, her feminine strength, her intelligence, that sass she often hid.

Holland gasped and tightened her legs around him. She clung to him, her nails not so gentle on his back as he withdrew then sank deeper than before.

God, he loved it. He liked the little bite of pain from her nails as he ramped up the pace, shifting to hit the sensitive spot he'd found inside her. Her breath caught. She looked at him, stunned and needy, before she closed her eyes and cried out. She dug her fingers into his shoulders as she went over the edge. She couldn't seem to help herself. And he'd done that to her, given her that pleasure. That jerked him off the leash. Dax let go of his restraint and pounded inside her.

She tightened again around him, her body tensing. She screamed his name.

His spine tingled and his whole body tensed. His heart slammed into his chest. Pleasure brewed, bubbled and rose, engulfing him in a torrent. It morphed into a consuming ecstasy that burst free and had him moaning with a guttural roar as he came. He gripped her as if he'd never let go and gave her everything he had, the bliss drowning him as it dragged him under in waves.

Timeless moments later, he dropped against her, completely spent.

She held him tight, panting from one breath to the next. "Are you sure that's not why they call you Captain Awesome?"

Dax laughed. "Nope. That was all for you, sweetheart. And don't think there isn't more where that came from."

He rolled to his side and kissed her again, determined to prove his point.

Dax's mood was contemplative as he walked up the flower-lined path to his mother's house. Earlier, Holland had headed into work, but he had the day off. He'd planned to ask some questions, poke around a bit, shake some trees. But he and Holland now had a deal. She would be leading the investigation. He would follow. It wasn't comfortable exactly, but she was right. She had more experience with crime. And he trusted her to do the right thing.

Especially after last night. He'd made love to her over and over again. She'd felt perfectly right in his arms. In the morning light, he had to think about the repercussions.

Could he ask her to give up her career? Or give up his? It was naive to think that a long distance relationship could work for them. She wouldn't know where he was most of the time and he wouldn't be able to call or talk. That wasn't a life she wanted. It wouldn't make her happy. More than anything, that's what Dax wanted to give her.

Their relationship was just starting out and despite the fact that they'd obviously wanted each other for years, he had to accept that sharing their feelings was new and what lay in their hearts was fragile. It could be easily broken.

"Good morning, son."

His mother's familiar voice jolted him out of his thoughts. Dax smiled and jogged up the big wraparound porch to join her. She sat in a rocker, a cup of coffee in her hands. Despite the earliness of the morning, she was already perfectly dressed in slacks and a silk blouse, her hair and makeup done with an expert hand.

"Were you waiting for me?"

She set the cup down on the saucer and placed them on the table beside her. "It wouldn't be the first time I waited up for you. I have to admit, sending you to boarding school saved my sanity. I can't imagine how I would have worried during your high school years."

He grinned and took the adjoining seat. "It was for the best. How are you this morning?"

The smile on her face didn't reach her eyes. "Lovely. Your friends are fun companions. Augustine arrived last night and the four of us had a very nice dinner before she adjourned upstairs to unpack. Gabriel and I played backgammon. He's such a nice young man."

"And Mad? Did he go out?"

His mother sighed. "No. I believe he turned in early."

He was going to beat the shit out of Maddox, who was very likely not sleeping in his own fucking bed. "I'll handle the situation, Momma."

"Don't you dare. Augustine has always been a spirited young lady. She's smart. She knows what she's doing."

So did he. Gus was doing Mad. "She should have a little more respect."

His mother frowned, chiding him with soft brown eyes. "Respect for what? For my tender feelings? I'm not an idiot, son. I know that Augustine has run through most of the men in this town, and god only knows what she's been doing in D.C. Maddox is a lively young man who looks as if he knows what he's about. I'm not upset with Gus, just a little envious. She has a career she loves and she's good at it. She does what and who she likes, when she likes, and she doesn't answer to anyone. I wish I'd had that freedom when I was younger."

He hadn't thought of it that way. "I'll ask them to keep it down."

His mother waved a hand. "Gus will likely tell me all about it when she gets up this morning. We're quite close, you know. I listen with a good ear. Would you like to talk about your night? Did you finally properly make love to Holland? You better have treated her right, Dax.

She's a dear friend and I don't believe she's had any sexual relations lately."

His jaw dropped and he couldn't help but stare at his very genteel mother.

She reached for her porcelain cup once more. "Oh, wipe that shocked expression from your face. I'm not a prude. And I'm not foolish. I know why you're really here. I was hoping Holland would distract you, but you've brought her into your little investigation, haven't you?"

He forced his mouth closed and whispered a curse. "How did you know about that?"

She sighed. "I always knew you wouldn't let it lie. It's not in your nature. I doubt Gus has, either, though she'll go about it differently. I don't like to think about it much myself. I wish you would concentrate on your relationship with Holland. She's such a nice woman. She would make a perfect wife for you."

He agreed Holland would make a perfect wife if they could figure out their issues, but he had a job to do, too. He'd never meant to discuss this with his mother. Not until he'd cleared his father's name. "You think he was guilty, don't you?"

He couldn't not ask the question. He needed to know. They'd sidestepped the issue so many times he couldn't count anymore. It was finally time for the truth.

She looked away for a quiet moment, and Dax wondered if she'd go silent on the subject again. Finally, she set her cup aside and turned to him. She patted his hand with her own. "I loved your father. We were so in love in the beginning. But sustaining love can be difficult, son. Years go by, and one day you realize that you've changed. Your spouse has changed. You've grown apart." She sighed. "Do I believe your father raped that girl? No. He didn't need power over someone else to feel big and he didn't have that sort of violent streak. Do I believe he could have been mistaken about her age and gotten into a situation he shouldn't have? Yes. I do believe that because he'd done it many times before."

Dax felt his gut twist. His father?

"Dax, I'm not trying to disillusion you or make you think less of your father," his mother said quietly. "This is something I wish you never had to know. He was human. I know he seemed like he was larger than life and so heroic, but he was flawed like the rest of us."

"Are you saying he cheated on you? And you knew it?" He could barely fathom that. His father had been a good man. Dax had built his whole life on the fact that his parents had been good people who loved each other and their children.

"Not at first. At least I don't think so. But sometime after he hit forty, things changed. He had an eye for the younger ladies. He had several affairs, though they never lasted very long. I found out because one of the women contacted me. It was the only time I nearly divorced your father. He was careful, you see. He usually chose women who didn't want more than a good time and some nice gifts. But this particular woman decided she wanted more. She wrote me and explained the situation. I sought a lawyer and threatened divorce. Your father talked me out of it. You were in college at the time. Gus had just started graduate studies at Harvard. A divorce could have derailed you both, so I stayed. I often wonder if that incident was what sent him to prostitutes."

He felt as if he'd been kicked in the gut. He scrubbed a hand over his face. "You can't know that or blame yourself."

"If I'd ignored it or perhaps if I'd followed through, he might be alive today. He might not have walked into that seedy motel with that girl."

He gripped his mother's hand. "Momma, none of this is your fault. He was the one with the problem."

Obviously more problems than Dax had imagined.

"I wish everything had been different," she murmured, and sipped her coffee again.

Yeah, him, too.

They fell silent until a Benz pulled up, stopping in front of their house.

His mother patted his hand. "That's my friend Gloria. We're going to have a nice brunch and then go to afternoon bridge club. I'm so sorry I had to tell you that, Dax. I simply don't want you to chase after some vindication only to get your heart broken. I love you very much." She stood and he watched her school her face as she waved. "I'll be back this evening. We're having a lovely roast and the housekeeper made pecan pie. You bring Holland if you like. I know Gus would love to see her."

Dax watched his mother stride down the walk to join her friend. He sat there, his whole world shaken.

The glow with which he'd started the day seemed a bit dimmer than before.

Had he really been so blind and naive? How had he never known his father had cheated? His father had lied, broken his vows, and left his own wife crushed.

Dax stood, feeling inexcusably weary. He needed a drink. God, it wasn't even nine o'clock and he was going to have a Scotch.

He stepped inside. He could hear the housekeeper humming to herself in the kitchen. He avoided her. That wasn't where they kept the good stuff anyway. The expensive Scotch was in his father's office, that shrine to a man he now wondered if he'd ever really known.

Well, at least the booze had been stored there until his friends had shown up.

When he sauntered in, Gabe was sitting in the dining room, a cup of coffee beside him, tapping away on his laptop. He looked up, his tawny brows rising. "Welcome home, Captain. Did you visit a new port last night?"

He flipped his friend off and continued to the stairs.

"Wow, touchy. I wouldn't go up there if I were you. Sorry, but Gus couldn't be convinced it was a bad idea. Believe me, I tried."

"Does Mad have the Scotch?" That was all he cared about at the moment.

"Yeah, but . . . Whoa. Scotch at this hour? What the hell happened?"

Dax didn't know how to answer so he kept walking up the stairs and right to the room his mom had given Mad. The door was closed. It was almost too quiet at first but then he heard whispering. "I know you're in there, Augustine. I don't give a damn. I want the Scotch. Mad, you better not have drank it all or I'll expect that replaced. This morning."

After a bit of shuffling, the portal opened and Mad poked his head around the door, looking somewhere between wide eyed and worried as he passed over the crystal decanter and what looked like a clean glass. Not that it mattered at that point. "Uh, Dax, it's early."

"Like that matters."

"It doesn't to me. It does to my very staid and buttoned-up Naval captain friend. He doesn't drink at inappropriate times anymore. He also very politely ignores the fact that I'm sleeping with his sister."

"Hooking up." Gus yelled from inside the room. "*Sleeping with* makes it sound important, Crawford."

"She wounds me," Mad said with a pout. "Give me a minute and I'll get dressed."

"Don't bother." He grabbed the Scotch and glass and strode off again. He knew exactly where he wanted to go and now he wished his friends hadn't come. He needed to be alone, and there was no way they'd let that happen.

But they didn't know about the balcony off the upstairs library. It was hidden by heavy curtains that no one opened because in the afternoon the sun heated everything up to a broil. At this time of the day, he could hide away and drink and think about the bombshell his mother had dropped.

He made his way to his hidey-hole and shut the curtains behind him before pouring himself that much-needed drink. He swallowed it down as he looked over the back gardens. He'd romped there as a child. He and Gus had played hide-and-seek and when their father had been home, he would chase them all over, calling them his little monkeys. He would catch Dax and his sister in huge hugs. He'd always felt safe in his father's arms.

Had everything been a lie?

Had his mother and father begun their marriage with all the good intentions in the world only to see everything crumble? Would that happen to him and Holland?

He took a drink and slumped into one of two chairs that graced the balcony. This had been his quiet place as a child. When he would come home for the summer, he'd often hidden here when he needed to be alone.

He heard a rustling behind him and sighed because he should have remembered even back then, a certain sister of his had rarely left him in peace.

"Hey." Augustine stepped out. She'd donned pajama bottoms and a tank top, sans bra, her feet bare and her hair all kinds of sexed up. From Maddox Crawford's hands.

"Shouldn't you go play with my friends? Gabe looked like he hadn't fucked anyone today." Dax was feeling mean.

Gus simply chuckled. "Wow. That was low, especially for you. What happened? Usually that sort of hypocrisy takes time. I at least get a 'how's it going, Gus' before you start in on me."

What was she talking about? He turned, watching as she sat in the opposite chair. "Hypocrisy?"

"Yes, Scotch-at-nine-in-the-morning guy. I called you a hypocrite. How many of my friends have you slept with? I'm betting given the fact that you're still in last night's clothes you slept with one very recently. What's up with the tear in your slacks? Holland get a little rough with you?"

"It's not the same. I'm serious about Holland."

"Were you serious about my sorority sisters? Because you plowed through them." Her voice dropped. "I'm sorry I called you a hypocrite, Dax. My feelings got hurt and I lashed out. You're right. I'm not serious about Mad. The only people who should be serious about that boy are doctors who should try to solve the mystery of how he hasn't con-tracted a sexually transmitted disease yet. We used protection, by the way. He's not touching me without a glove. The trouble is, he's really good in bed. And he doesn't fall in love with me. All the rest of them do. That's what I like about your friends. They're realists."

God, he hadn't meant to make his sister feel bad. "I'm sorry, Gus. Though I would like to point out I've been way more circumspect about sleeping with your friends. I think Momma knows what you were doing."

"Of course she does. I told her. She's my mother, not some dried-up prude. Dax, I'm not married. I have a healthy sex drive. Well, I have a raging sex drive and I like it that way."

"Just like dear old dad." The words came out in a bitter huff. He hadn't meant to say them out loud.

"Whoa, I can't believe she told you about that."

"You knew?" He shook his head.

"I figured it out a long time ago. I was here more than you were." Gus hadn't gone to boarding school. She'd put her foot down and told their parents she wanted to stay home, so she'd attended a nice private day school instead.

Sometimes he'd envied his sister. Mostly in the beginning because after he'd found his friends, he'd been happy to go back to Creighton every term.

"What gave Dad's cheating away?" he asked.

"Dad would come home on leave and sometimes he and Mom would fight. He started sleeping in his office more often than not. Oh, he would tell me it was because he was working. That's how I got used to bringing him his coffee there when I was home." Her jaw tightened and there was no way she wasn't remembering that last morning she'd brought their father his coffee.

"Did you know about the woman who wrote Mom?"

"After the fact," Gus explained. "She told me later about that. And obviously we talked after Dad died."

"But no one thought to mention it to me?"

"Mom didn't want you to think poorly of Dad. You worshipped

him . . . and you can be a little judgmental, as proven by your very dicklike actions this morning. You really think I'm like Dad? You think that because I like sex I'm hurting everyone around me?"

He turned to her, reaching for her hand. "No, you're not hurting anyone. I'm being a dick, Gus. I'm sorry. I kind of got gut punched. I know what you're doing with Mad. I've just seen how he can treat women."

She raised a pale brow. "Quite well. I like Mad because he gives a damn about what a woman wants in bed. He has a reputation as a playboy, but he never lies about it. He's up-front about what he wants and what he's willing to give. All of your friends are. It's what I like about them."

"All of them?"

She didn't even blush, simply reached over and poured him another drink. "Not all. Connor turned me down because he couldn't sleep with his best friend's sister. He's a good egg. Do you have any idea how hard it was for a seventeen-year-old boy to turn all of this down?" She gestured vaguely toward her curves. "Gabe is too lean for me. Roman was fun. I actually liked him. We hooked up but that was a lifetime ago."

"Not Zack, though." Dax willed it to be true. "Definitely not Zack."

"How do you think he got the nickname Scooter?"

"Oh, god." He dropped his face in his hands. "So many things have gone wrong today."

"Fine, not Zack. I was joking about that. He earned that nickname with a friend of mine, but I did hear about the incident." She stared, her intelligent eyes boring into him. "Does it make you think differently of me? I've had about as many sexual partners as you. Why is it all right for you but not me?"

"Because you're my sister."

"Will you hate Dad now? Because he was your father and the people in your life aren't allowed to be human?"

Dax felt tears stinging his eyes and fought not to shed the damn things. He hated seeing himself through his sister's eyes. Maybe his mother had been right to keep the truth from him. He'd been viewing the world in black and white. A man was either a hero or a villain. Why could he be tolerant of his friends' foibles but not his father's? "I came back to clear his name."

"I know."

"How?"

"I work with Roman and I'm ridiculously good at eavesdropping. Also, I'm good at spying. Mad sleeps like a log. I got out of bed last night and couldn't sleep. I thought I'd peruse some of the porn on his laptop but I found the files. Then he and Gabe were talking earlier this morning. I think they've found a couple of things they want to share with you."

His sister was kind of an evil genius. And she was the only person he could really talk to about this. And she was the one person in the world besides himself who knew what it meant to be Admiral Harold Spencer's kid. "Should I give the investigation up? Am I just hurting Mom more?"

Gus leaned forward, her stare serious. "Do you think he deserves less because he cheated? I don't love him less, Dax. I was angry for a while. Still am. But he was my father. He loved us. He sacrificed for us. Whatever he was like as a husband, he was a good dad. I can't let his mistakes take that from me."

Dax squeezed her hand, emotion rolling through him. He remembered all the times his father had shown up at Creighton unannounced. He would get some leave and drag the family up to spend a single afternoon, taking Dax and his friends out to lunch, to the movies. He would say he missed his boy.

His boy. He'd been his father's son. What did he owe his dad? His father had obviously hurt his mom terribly, but did that negate everything else in his life? His mother hadn't wanted a rift between them.

"Do you think he raped that girl?" It didn't matter that the sex might have been consensual. Legally, the girl wasn't old enough to consent. It was still rape.

"No, I do not." His sister stood and walked to the railing, her shoulders straight. "I don't believe he's the man who appears on that video. I know it looked like him, but the camera never captured his face. Mom says he was into younger women. So I did some digging of my own after he was murdered. None of his mistresses—and let me be plain, I could only find three—not a one of them was under thirty-five."

Then why had his dad suddenly chosen fifteen-year-old Amber Taylor? Unless, like Gus suspected, his father hadn't actually been the man on that footage.

"Our mother has a skewed perspective about age," Gus went on. "I know why and I'm not going to correct her. She's entitled to what she believes, but I know the truth. Dad got lonely. I'm not saying it was Mom's fault, but there are always, always two points of view, two sides to any relationship. I know she threw herself into being a mom after she had us." Gus let out a long breath. "Each of those three women looked like her."

Tears rolled down his sister's golden cheeks. Damn, he hated to see Gus crying. He hated even more that he'd been the one to upset her.

Dax stood and wrapped his arms around his older sister. She was larger than life and so strong willed that sometimes he forgot she was fragile, too.

"I'm sorry. And I apologize for what I said earlier. You aren't like Dad. Hell, I don't even know what to think anymore. I only know I don't believe the reports. I think NCIS covered something up or they missed key facts."

"No matter what he did, he was our dad. Dax, we can't let this stand. I need to help you. We need to find out who killed him because the father I knew would never commit suicide. Ever. He simply wouldn't have done it." She turned and cried against his shoulder.

He heard someone moving behind them. The curtains fluttered and Mad emerged, his face red from his fight with the voluminous fabric. "Damn it. I knew it was hiding something. Fucking curtains. Hey. Shit. I'm sorry. I didn't mean to interrupt."

Gus lifted her head and sniffled. "Of course you did, Mad. Interrupting is what you do best."

"That's not what you said last . . . Never mind." Mad knew better than to finish that sentence.

His sister held on to him even as she rolled her eyes. "Give it a rest, Mad."

His sister could handle his crazy, lovably douchy friend. She would take what Mad had to offer without needing more. He had to admit, Gus was a woman who knew what she wanted and at this point, she wanted to have fun.

One day some guy would set Gus's world on its ear, and he was really looking forward to that day. But for now, he could have fun, too.

"Hey, sis, who's better in bed? Mad or Roman? You see, I've always heard women say Mad was a little immature. I wondered if that wasn't referring to his . . . technique."

Mad scowled, his face turning beet red. "That is so untrue. In the old days, that would lead to a duel, sir. In fact, I think it should now. You have impugned my manhood. My dick is like the Energizer Bunny. Except more manly. And bigger. And without ears. The point is, I got stamina. And technique."

Gus snorted and shook her head. "I'll never tell. Well, not until I need the cash and then I've got notes for a book that will shock everyone. I'm going to get some breakfast. I seem to have worked up an appetite. Ta-ta, dearies."

Mad pointed her way. "See. She worked up an appetite because I'm awesome."

And humble. Dax hauled back and punched him right on the nose. Not enough to actually break the fucker, but Mad would feel it for a while.

"Shit!" Mad hunched over, covering his nose. His shoulders shook, but he stood up again and started laughing. "Okay. I probably deserved that."

The burst of anger had left Dax's system. He still had unresolved feelings but none of that was Mad's fault—or anyone else's. "Just keep it to yourself. I don't want to hear you bragging about bagging my sister."

Mad shook his head. "Never. Ever. Seriously, I'm more scared of Gus than I am you. She's mean. Like seriously mean. And I won't see her anymore if it really bugs you. I like Gus. There's nothing serious there, but she's cool."

"That's Gus's business," Dax allowed. He looked down, but suddenly he didn't need the Scotch anymore. "And I think I'll join her for breakfast. I worked up an appetite, too."

"So you bagged NCIS last night. Nice."

"I'm going to punch you again."

"Let me rephrase. I'm very happy that you were finally able to profess all your man feelings to the lovely and proper NCIS special agent in a physical fashion. Should I have brought glitter so we could throw it around and show the world how happy and shiny you are now?"

"Fuck you, Mad." But he said it with a laugh.

"I'm really happy for you, man. We're going to lose you the way we lost . . ." Mad frowned suddenly. "Sorry. I was going to say Zack. It's hard to believe Joy is dead."

"Yeah. I don't know how Zack deals with it." If he lost Holland . . .

"Zack buries himself in work. He works from the minute he gets up until way past time any sane person would go to bed. I'm worried about him."

"Really?"

"What? I can worry. I know I'm an irresponsible party boy, but I care about my friends. You guys . . . you're my real family. My parents didn't give a shit. I felt more comfortable here and at Gabe's penthouse than I ever did at home. I'm living in the place where my dad kept his mistresses. I can redo the fucker all I like, but it's not home. This is a real home. No matter what your dad did, at least he gave you love inside these four walls."

"You were listening?"

"It was hard to avoid overhearing as I was being slowly digested by three hundred pounds of brocade. I think you're doing the right thing. Gabe and I have been looking into it. Well, Gabe has been looking into it while I play solitaire, but he's certain something's going on. Do you ever find it odd that Joy died and your father was killed six weeks later?"

"Joy was killed by someone who was trying to assassinate Zack. I don't see the connection."

"That's the funny thing about connections, isn't it? You don't always see them at first. I just have to wonder what the odds are that you and Zack would lose immediate family so close together." Mad shook his head as if clearing it. "But don't listen to me. My brain is twelve kinds of fucked-up at this time of the morning. Come on. Let's eat something. Gabe uncovered some stuff about the investigation. He's got some leads we can follow."

"Sure. I think my drinking is done for now."

Mad waggled his brows and picked up the Scotch. "Thank god. I thought you would drink it all. Come to Papa. And don't sweat the stuff with your dad. God knows mine was far worse. I shudder to think of all the damage that man did. It's certainly not my place to clean it all up. But I will help with yours." Mad frowned as he stared at the gaping doors. "Don't let the curtains kill me this time."

Dax followed Mad in. No matter what happened, he had his family. And Holland. She belonged to him now. Just because his parents had struggled didn't mean he and Holland would. They would be honest and open with each other. They would not make the same mistakes.

No way. No how.

SEVEN

H olland swept her finger across the screen to accept the call. Dax. Her guy. She was becoming that chick who grinned way too much and lost IQ points when her boyfriend walked into a room. Even her coworkers had started to rib her about it. She was more relaxed, definitely happier, and all because she had Captain Awesome in her bed—not to mention on her couch and over the dining room table. Over the last few weeks they'd pretty much made love on every surface of her apartment. And the night they'd had dinner at his mother's place, he'd snuck her up into his old bedroom for a quickie. Not that they'd fooled anyone. His friends and Gus had been relentless in their teasing. And Judith Spencer had simply smiled and patted Holland's hand and told her how happy she was.

"Hey, you," she said into her phone, leaning against her car. She didn't drive often when she was in the city, but the streetcars didn't run out this far. She wouldn't have taken one even if it did since she was standing in front of a prison.

"Hey, sweetheart. Did you make it all right?" Dax's deep voice resounded over the line, every drawled syllable a reminder of the man's slow, Southern sensuality.

All she had to do was hear his voice and she shivered on the inside. "I'm here. My appointment is in a half hour. I'm going to talk to the prison officials first. It's strictly a courtesy. They're used to dealing with locals. My team doesn't come out this way often."

Most of the prisons she dealt with were military.

"I wish you would wait until I can be there with you."

They'd been over this more than once. "Dax, if you'd come along, I'd have to explain why. It's easier this way, and if anyone dangerous really is watching us, it will look much less suspicious."

Not that anything frightening or out of the ordinary had happened since the asshole on the bike. But something about this case was starting to give her a bad feeling.

"I'm the one who brought you the lead," Dax argued.

"No, Gabe did. You don't see him here with me." She sighed. "Babe, I explained all of this. It's one of those times I should go in alone. Besides, aren't you working today?"

There was a lull on his end of the line. "Yes. Apparently they're serious about getting this manual done, and soon. They want the new protocols in place in the next couple of weeks. Courtney is working her butt off, but there's only so much she can do without me."

Courtney likely stared at his butt most of the day. Jealously flared, but she tamped it down. He had a really amazing backside. She would have stared at it, too.

"I understand. You've already done your part. Your guys found Amber Taylor's mom. This woman's used so many aliases I'm not surprised we couldn't find her. Connor has connections most law enforcement would pay a lot for. So relax and let me handle this. Did Gabe and Mad get off okay?"

"Mad surely did. My sister made sure of that," he said grumpily.

Holland smothered a laugh. The last couple of weeks had been a revelation. Dax had spent every night at her place with the excuse that he didn't want to hear his sister and Mad Crawford going at it. Holland kind of thought he just liked sleeping beside her. He'd practically moved in. She didn't see him leaving because his friends had gotten on a plane to New York. "I'm glad he enjoyed his stay. I'm sure he made Gus's pleasant as well."

"I'm joking about Gus. She leaves for D.C. tomorrow, and I'm going to miss her." He cleared his throat. She'd learned he did that a lot when he got emotional. "Anyway, I hope this means we have enough to really reopen the case."

She didn't want to give him false hope, but she was feeling optimistic. "I'm asking for the complete files. I'm going to tell my boss what I'm doing and why. Even though I can't make it official, I think I have enough to put some of the team's resources into it. My boss liked your father quite a bit. I think he'll be open to a discussion. If I get NCIS involved again, I should be able to request access to your father's former aide. He's the one I really want to talk to."

"But naturally he's on assignment and his whereabouts are classified," Dax said with a cynical bite to his tone.

Naturally. Everywhere they turned they encountered another roadblock or another detour that led to nowhere. "I think I can talk them into it if all goes well today. Especially when I show them the money trail Connor and Gabe found."

Once they'd located Amber Taylor's mother, finding her financial information had been simple. She'd never actually been married to Amber's father, though Sue Carlyle used his surname as an alias for years. The woman was a known con artist and roughly three days before her daughter had been caught with the admiral on tape, Sue Carlyle deposited five thousand dollars in cash to her bank account.

Holland wanted to know where that money had come from.

"Be careful," Dax said over the line.

"I will. Hey, it's a prison. I'm fairly safe here." She glanced up at the dour-looking building in front of her. It was a medium-security women's facility. Unlike the land around it, it was gray and gloomy. "I'll see you tonight."

"I'll be late, but I'll pick us up some supper. Bye, sweetheart."

She hung up with a sigh and turned to the task at hand. She might be able to give him the testimony or peace of mind he needed. They'd stayed up a few nights earlier making love and talking. He'd told her what he'd learned about his father. Clearly, Dax was hurt, and if she could be a balm to that ache, she would. Finding out his father hadn't been a pedophile would definitely help ease his heavy heart.

Gathering herself, Holland entered the prison. Half an hour later, she found herself in a small interrogation room used for interviews with law enforcement and attorneys. Nothing of interest lay inside the room. Like everything about the prison, it looked stark and seemingly hopeless. The table was stainless steel, the chairs bolted to the floor. A two-way mirror lined the back, but she didn't see why anyone would use it on her. She'd explained she was simply following up with a potential witness on a cold case.

The door opened and a slight woman entered, hauled in by a burly guard. Sue Carlyle's face was the after photo on a poster of why not to try meth. Lined and wrinkled, cheeks sagging, she had aged far beyond her forty-eight years. The few teeth she had were black. According to the information Holland had obtained, this woman hadn't lived an easy life. But what the hell had happened to her in the months since her daughter had become the center of a huge case?

"You going to be all right?" the guard asked Holland.

Sue shook almost uncontrollably as she sat.

Yes, she could handle the drug addict. She looked like she weighed all of ninety pounds. "I'll be fine. Thank you."

The door closed and she was left with one of the only people alive who could tell her anything about what had happened the night Admiral Spencer had fallen from grace.

"They said you wanted to see me. What's this about?" Her gaze didn't meet Holland's but darted around as though scanning furiously for some kind of threat.

"I need to talk to you about your daughter."

"She's gone. Ain't coming back. Ain't none of us coming back."

"She ran away from home."

A snort came out of Sue's mouth. "Sure. She ran away. Is that what you want? I already told everyone she ran."

"Who did you tell?"

"Everyone I was supposed to, damn it. I'm tired of this shit. You got everything you wanted. Everything! But you keep sending in people to make sure you get more."

A chill cut through Holland, clear to her bones. "Ms. Carlyle, I'm not who you think I am. I'm here to help you. I want to help find your daughter."

A brittle laugh erupted from her chest, and she coughed as though the action hurt her in some way. "Bastards. You can't find my daughter. Unless you remember where you buried her."

Sue's words shocked her. Holland leaned in. "You believe your daughter is dead?"

"I know it. Am I not supposed to say that, either? Is this some kind of test? I'm tired of you people fucking with me. I did what you asked. I took the money, and you know what? It wasn't enough. Not even close. Do you know what that girl was worth? She could have worked and made more than that measly five thousand."

Holland froze. She and the woman were having a definite misunderstanding and she wasn't exactly sure how to calm Amber's mother down enough to get a coherent story. Holland had to talk her off the ledge, convince Sue she was here to help, and hope she didn't clam up.

"You took the money," Holland reminded in a cold, factual tone. "You could have negotiated for more."

Sue's eyes narrowed before she shook her head and looked away. "I'm not talking anymore, especially to your kind. I saw what you people did to my girl. My baby. She did you a favor."

A favor? Holland went with her gut on this hunch. "Yes, she set up the admiral nicely."

"Don't know nothing about that." Sue's lips formed a grim line. "Nothing at all. All I know now is my girl's gone and you people sent me here."

How did she get Sue to explain who "you people" were?

"Perhaps we could also get you out of here if you cooperate with us."

"I don't do nothing but cooperate."

Holland knew she was walking a thin line now. She tried to sound as reasonable and non-threatening as possible. "I'm trying to clean up a few issues within the organization I work for. Some overly enthusiastic associates worked the front end of this operation. I need to make sure I have all the facts. Who was your contact?"

Sue stared blankly for a moment before her eyes came back into focus. Then she shook her head. "I ain't saying nothing. I ain't got no contact." Tears started running down her face. "I hate you Russians. I hate you all."

Russians? "I'm going to have to insist that we have this debrief, Carlyle. My boss wants to know all the facts before he makes a decision."

"About what?"

"About whether or not to help you get out of this prison." Guilt twisted her gut, but she had to have the information. "Who was your contact?"

Her gaze glazed over. "What does it matter now? I hate you all for what you did to my girl. Especially the Navy man. I hate that fucking Navy man."

"The admiral?"

"Short little shit. Hate him." Suddenly, she pounded her fists on the table. "Hate you all!"

She screamed then, a sound that seemed to come from deep in her soul. Then she burst into tears.

The door flew open and the guard hurried in. Sue Carlyle struggled, her eyes wild as she spewed curses, looking both angry and terrified.

The guard had her cuffed in record time. "Look who gets to visit the SHU. You're a regular guest there, Carlyle." The guard looked up. "Sorry. She's very unstable. I hope you got what you wanted because she'll be like this for days."

A female guard came in and hauled the prisoner out.

"What's wrong with her? Besides the obvious?"

The guard frowned. They could hear Carlyle shouting all the way down the hall. "She's delusional. Likely due to the insane amount of drugs she's done. She's here for dealing, but that woman was way too interested in her own product."

So her brain had been damaged because she'd done too much meth. Paranoia was one of the by-products of the drug. "Does she talk much?"

"Oh, Carlyle likes to tell anyone and everyone who will listen about how some Russian guy killed her baby girl and he's coming for her, too. I don't suppose you represent the Russian mob? Because that's who she's blaming."

Holland managed a little laugh, but she was already thinking.

As she exited the prison, she was still ruminating on her bizarre conversation with Sue Carlyle and the implications. The woman wasn't a good witness, and most lawyers would say that anything she'd uttered was unreliable and inadmissible in court. Holland sighed. It was unlikely her boss would reopen the admiral's case based on the ramblings of an obviously insane woman. So she needed to figure out where that money had come from and why Sue thought the Russian mob was after her.

Had the admiral's death been the result of a shakedown gone wrong? Had the plan been to blackmail him? Control him by dangling his indiscretions in his face? If so, why would Russians have targeted him, of all people? And how would a Navy man be involved? Sue couldn't have been talking about the admiral. She'd called him a short shit. Admiral Spencer had been somewhere around six foot two.

None of this made sense. Then again, neither had Sue. Holland frowned. Maybe she was putting too much stock in the woman's drug-riddled words.

She pulled out her keys but stopped short of her vehicle because someone stood, blocking her car door.

"Hello, Special Agent Kirk." A nondescript man in a perfectly pressed suit nodded her way.

"Do I know you?"

"Not at all, and my name is irrelevant."

She tucked her purse—which held her gun—closer. "It's pretty relevant to me."

"I merely represent another party. I know you'll spend an inordinate amount of time and effort trying to find me, but I promise it's useless. I'm merely here to reason with you. You're getting involved in something that no longer matters."

She wasn't going to pretend to misunderstand. The longer she kept him talking, the more likely the security cameras dotting the parking lot and slowly sweeping every inch would pick up his face so recognition software could identify him. "It matters to the admiral's family."

"I'm sure it does, but they need to move on or they'll face more loss. Greater loss. You don't want to lose anyone, do you?" As she reached into her purse for her weapon, he shook his head. "Don't pull that gun on me, Special Agent. I'm just here to talk, but I'm not alone."

She turned and saw he was right. Two other big guys stood sentry on either side of the parking lot, both with their stares locked on her. They also wore impeccable suit jackets that likely concealed the weapons they were carrying.

She was outgunned. "What do you want?"

"I merely wish to explain to you that if you don't stop this investigation, someone will get hurt. No one wants that. The admiral got into a bad situation, and while my employers regret the eventual outcome, they would prefer that the past remain there."

"You work for the Russian mob?"

His expression never changed. He was damn good at his job. "I work for a group of people who had prior dealings with the admiral. This one went wrong."

"You're saying the admiral was dirty."

"The admiral had proclivities he kept hidden. My employer indulged said proclivities from time to time. If you continue down this path, not only will you further harm the Spencer family name, but we might decide to deal with the real problem."

"The real problem?" She wasn't sure she wanted the answer to that question.

"You wouldn't be kicking up this dust if it weren't for Captain Spencer. He's the one behind everything. He will be disappointed when embarrassing photographs of his father surface. That would prove detrimental to his career. If you continue to create problems, it may be detrimental to his health."

Holland tried to hold her fear in. "If you have those photos, why not release them?"

"We never intended to release them, merely keep the images to ensure the admiral couldn't turn on us. Someone else turned him in. I believe it was his aide. He proved to have a stronger moral code than the admiral would have liked. Do you understand?"

She understood this man was threatening Dax and she didn't like it. "The Spencers have a right to know who killed the admiral."

He sighed. "We had no reason to kill him. Why are you looking for zebras when you hear hoofbeats? I thought they taught you Occam's razor in school."

"The simplest explanation is almost always correct." Yes, that was something investigators learned. "But you're here threatening to kill a Naval officer if I don't back down. What's the simplest explanation for that?"

"That my boss doesn't wish to be exposed for his part in this situation and he's prepared to do anything he must to stop it. Now, you can choose to go home and tell your boyfriend everything I've told you. He'll be brave. He'll stand firm and eventually he'll have some accident that you won't be able to pin on anyone in my organization. Or you can do the smart thing and tell him you found proof that his father committed suicide. He'll be depressed, but somehow I think you'll find a way to bring him out of it."

Anger flared inside her. This asshole wanted to corrupt justice. He wanted Dax kept in the dark . . . or dead. She had to get out of here without getting shot. The minute she could get away from these assholes, she would arrange to view the parking lot's security tapes and ID these men. "I'll take it under advisement."

"See that you do." He nodded to his henchmen and backed toward a black SUV. "And, Special Agent, I believe you'll find the cameras have mysteriously malfunctioned. It's a shame that technology doesn't always work."

She gritted her teeth, fearing the power he must have. "I can still figure out who you are."

"Then I'll have some sort of 'accident' and they'll replace me. I know how these things work. My boss will simply hire someone else and the business will continue." He paused, regarding her with a shrewd stare. "You're not convinced, so I'll prove my point. If you don't shut down the investigation, we'll start small. Maybe simply scare the captain. After that he will receive the photos of his father. If that doesn't convince him he's on a witch hunt and the investigation still doesn't cease . . . then we'll start eliminating the problems. You'll be last so that you can watch them all fall. How will you live with that, I wonder? Will that 'justice' you're seeking have been worth the price? Think about it. Good evening, Special Agent Kirk."

He slipped into his vehicle and was gone. She memorized the plate number but wondered if it would mean anything. After a quick call to the prison, she learned the cameras had indeed been shut down briefly for a software issue.

So whoever this man represented was powerful enough to have someone on the inside.

Shock rolled over Holland as she climbed into her car and sped away, trembling fingers gripping the wheel. She had no idea what to do now, what to say to Dax. But maybe she knew one person she could trust who would give her straight talk.

Flipping a U-turn, she headed to her uncle's office.

Dax glanced at the clock. Almost lunchtime. He hated the fact that Holland was investigating the case alone while he was stuck in the office talking about procedure and processes.

"I think this wording really works," Courtney said, peering at her computer screen.

"Good."

She looked at him, a frown on her pretty face. "You're really distracted. Is there anything I can help you with, Dax? Your brain has been somewhere else all morning."

Courtney was an attractive girl with a waterfall of dark hair and hazel eyes. If he didn't have Holland, he might have been interested. She was sweet and funny, but she didn't have Holland's grit or acerbic wit.

His brain had been on Holland. All day. All week. Ever since the day he'd come back into town, he'd been able to think of little but her. "Sorry. I'll be better this afternoon."

After he knew Holland was out of that prison and back at her office. Though her job was always dangerous. Somehow it was easier not knowing exactly where she was. He could pretend she was comfy and cozy in her office and not tracking down some crazed bitch who'd likely sold her daughter for cash.

Courtney's eyes narrowed. "So everything is going well? I know the answer to that question since I haven't heard from Holland. We usually have lunch a couple of times a week but I've barely heard from her."

Because he'd consumed her every spare moment. His lunches were all scheduled here. If she could, she met him. Twice she'd been called away on assignment, but he understood that. "Sorry. We're a new couple. I'm sure we'll hate each other soon."

Not if he had his way. They would be one of those couples that couldn't get enough of each other, the sort who annoyed everyone around them because they were so deeply entwined.

"I don't know about that." Courtney looked back at her computer with a sigh. "I think I've pretty much lost my best friend."

Damn. He hadn't meant to come between Holland and her friends, especially one with whom she was so close. Dax knew well how important it was to have people he trusted. After Joy's death, Holland needed friends more than ever. Courtney seemed a little frivolous for Holland. The girl was smart, no doubt. And funny. But she spent an awful lot of time talking about her nails. Still, maybe Holland had needed someone lighter in the wake of her grief.

"She's not ignoring you. I'm just a possessive bastard and I've stolen all her time for myself." He tried to give her a reassuring smile. "She's talked about you, but I don't know how the two of you met."

Courtney smiled with the memory. "She was working a case involving some serious procedural problems during a training exercise. I'm kind of the expert, so she talked to me to make sure she fully understood what was expected. I deal with NCIS on a regular basis. About half of them are non-military based, so I'm a fairly good translator."

The military had its own language and sometimes civvies got a little lost. Sailors tended to speak in an odd mixture of acronyms and slang only other sailors understood. He could definitely see where someone like Courtney could be an asset. She'd grown up in the military but had her schooling in the civilian world. "You two hit it off?"

"We're both civilian females in a military world. No offense, but this is still a man's turf."

The landscape was changing, slowly. "I can understand that." Though they seemed like opposites, the women were apparently fast friends. "Holland really likes you."

Courtney smiled, her eyes lighting up. "I like her, too. She can be so serious sometimes. She needs someone to pull her out of herself. Her job can be a little grim, you know. She needs to be reminded that there's fun in the world, too. I force her to go out a couple of times a week. Well, I did until the last few weeks." She shot him a wry grin.

He'd been greedy about his time with Holland and he didn't intend to change. While he was here, he intended to have Holland to himself as often as he could. "I don't suppose you could tell your superiors we need another six months or so to get this manual done, huh?"

She leaned forward, a sympathetic expression softening her face. "You don't want to go back to your ship, do you?"

"I don't want to leave her." But he had responsibilities. No matter how much he wanted to stay, he owed his ship and his men another year. He was due to report back in two weeks.

The thought of leaving Holland kicked him in the gut.

"She'll be fine. I'll be here and she'll have her work. The time will fly by. When you get leave, you'll come back."

"Do you think she can be happy in that kind of relationship?" It was a question he'd been asking himself nonstop.

"I think she's capable of handling anything she wants to."

There was something about the way she phrased that answer that set him on edge. "If she wants to?"

Courtney paused, looking thoughtful for a moment. "I think she's never seen herself as a military wife. Her mom was, and from what I can tell, it didn't work out so great for her. I was actually surprised she gave you a chance. And I can't see Holland dealing well with all the press you get."

"I don't get too much." After those first photos of them entering Antoine's weeks ago, they hadn't encountered any more press. The paparazzi had moved on to more interesting prey, including his friends. Mad and Gabe were back on a supermodel kick, and it seemed to satisfy the tabloids. He was fairly certain they were doing it to give him a little cover.

"You will as time goes by. I can't imagine the president isn't going to give you some high-profile job."

Zack knew better. He'd already told his friend he refused to be turned into some kind of politician. If he left the military, he would go into private security or some other field. He was not about to get stuck in D.C. No way. No how. "I won't be taking any high-profile jobs. That's not for me."

"Really?" Courtney asked, one brow raised. "Because having the president as a childhood friend usually means a career in politics at some point. I'm sure he needs people around him he can trust."

Zack needed that badly, and Dax felt a bit guilty for refusing his buddy. He knew Zack had intended for his father to sit on the Joint Chiefs. Dax was lucky he wasn't eligible due to his rank or Zack and Roman might have browbeaten him into it. Still, maybe he should think about taking a position with Zack. If he couldn't get a more stationary position with the Navy.

God, he'd just decided. He would leave the Navy for Holland so they could build a life together. He didn't want to spend years away from her, never sure of when he might see her again. He was at the tail end of his contract. If he didn't re-up, he could be in D.C. by this time next year. Holland could apply for a transfer and never have to leave NCIS. They could get married, buy a house, start a normal life.

Somehow that didn't sound so scary anymore.

Courtney was wrong about one thing, though. "If I decide to work for Zack, that will likely be the end of my paparazzi days. No one cares about old married people."

"Married?" Courtney's eyes had gone wide.

He nodded. "Yeah. If I take a job with Zack, it's because I'm going to get married and start a family, and I don't want to miss out on my kids' childhoods. My dad did. He got back as often as he could, but he still missed things. I want to be there for every minute. I can find a way to serve my country and still have my family the way I want it."

He could do it. He and Holland could make it work.

Courtney sat back. "Wow. I didn't expect that so fast. You've only been with her for a few weeks."

"But I've known her for years. We've been circling each other the whole time. This is finally the right time for us."

"Well, I hope so. She's not big on marriage. I hope she says yes."

He was going to make sure she did. He wouldn't take no for an answer.

Dax sat back with a smile. He was going to change his whole life for her—for the better. "She will. She doesn't know it yet, but she loves me."

Courtney stood up. "You're a good man, Dax. I hope she realizes what she has in you. I'm going to go and file this."

Her eyes were suspiciously red as she walked out.

Dax frowned. He did not understand most women. The good news was he did get Holland. And only she mattered.

He picked up the phone to call his mother. He had an engagement to plan.

D o you have a description of this man?" Her uncle had gone utterly still the minute she told him about the man who'd been waiting for her in the prison's parking lot.

She nodded. "I talked to him for probably ten minutes. I can definitely describe him. He had two other goons with him, but I didn't see them as clearly."

"He didn't disguise himself? Didn't wear sunglasses or a hat?"

"No." She understood why that disturbed her uncle. The guy in the suit had behaved like a man who didn't have anything to worry about, as if he was above anything she could do to him. She'd worked law enforcement long enough to know that was a possible scenario. There were places she couldn't go, things that were classified. She wasn't naive and she certainly understood that powerful people sometimes went to very long lengths to keep secrets hidden.

With a deep sigh, her uncle walked to the window on his left. His office had windows on three sides. He'd always told her he liked to be able to intimidate his men at all times. Now he slowly approached each window, closing the blinds and sealing them in.

"What haven't you told me?" she blurted. Her uncle would never have closed those blinds unless he was about to say something he didn't want other people to witness.

"As a result of my investigation, I found some pictures I didn't release to the press. Pictures that came to me after Admiral Spencer killed himself."

"Of what?"

"Images taken from a hidden camera on Amber Taylor's purse."

Holland blinked in shock, cold washing through her. "Why didn't you tell me before?"

"Honey, because you're in love with that man's son and seeing those photos could hurt his family. From what I've been able to piece together, the entire thing was a blackmail scheme gone wrong."

"You believe the Russian mob used Amber Taylor to blackmail Admiral Spencer?" Dax had never said a thing about a blackmail threat. "Why would the Russian mob give a shit about an admiral? I know the Spencer family has money, but surely they've got bigger fish to fry."

"Maybe it wasn't about the money. Maybe it was about his connections."

"But who? The admiral had run with the same friends for years, so why now?"

Her uncle sat forward. "Because someone figured out his weakness and decided to exploit it shortly after the admiral made a brand-new connection, thanks to his son. A lot of ruthless people wouldn't hesitate to use that relationship to their advantage."

"What . . . Oh, god. Zack. I mean President Hayes. You think they were trying to use him to get to President Hayes?"

Beau sat back, shaking his head. "It's still hard for me to believe you can legitimately call the president of the United States by his first name, but yes. The admiral died six weeks after the election. You can't tell me the timing isn't interesting?"

No, she couldn't. Holland swallowed and sank into her seat.

"Those are some serious people you're involved with, honey. And they come with serious enemies. In my opinion, someone connected to the Russian mob wanted dirt on Admiral Spencer. It would have come in handy later when he almost certainly would have been appointed to the Joint Chiefs of Staff."

She closed her eyes, the gravity of the implications crushing her. The Joint Chiefs of Staff advised the president, senate, and congress on all matters military. They had enormous influence.

"But wouldn't it have all come out when the White House vetted him? Surely they would have discovered his penchant for teenaged girls?"

"If these people are powerful enough to hold a man like Admiral Spencer in the palm of their hand, it stands to reason that they can coerce other powerful people to keep their secrets," her uncle reasoned.

True. "So why kill him even before Zack's inauguration?"

Her uncle approached and wrapped a hand around hers. "They had no reason to since he hadn't had the opportunity to prove himself useful yet. I think they blackmailed him but didn't have anything to do with his death. After all, they lost a big fish when the admiral's aide turned him in. I also believe that's why the Navy shipped Peter Morgan out and put him on a classified mission. They were protecting their informant."

"I don't have any record of that." She shook her head at the statement. "Which naturally I wouldn't because it's classified."

It connected a whole lot of dots. It explained why she couldn't contact Admiral Spencer's aide. The Russian mob's role and motive was enough to make her gut churn, but it made sense.

"You saw the pictures?"

Her uncle closed his eyes briefly. "I did. I hoped you wouldn't have to. Do you need to? I can have them retrieved. I kept them out of the public eye because there was no need to hurt the Spencer family further."

"You're sure Dax's father killed himself?"

He nodded. "I can't see another scenario, Holland. We never found a note, but I think the old boy couldn't take it anymore. All that press. His whole life's work thrown down the toilet. His wife filing for divorce."

"What?"

"She hadn't filed, but she had visited a divorce lawyer the day before he died. You can't know the true measure of a man until he's placed under pressure. I can't say I wouldn't do the same thing."

"But Dax is so sure. I know the admiral loved his children."

"Yes, but he was still just a man. And at some point I'm sure ending his life seemed like an act of mercy to spare them what would have been a horrible trial that would have kept the sordid affair all over the media. The Spencer family would have been dragged through the spotlight at the exact moment President Hayes was appointing his cabinet. His friendship with Dax would have come under some nasty scrutiny. Hell, if anyone had a reason to kill the admiral, it wasn't the Russians. It was the White House."

She stood abruptly. "He would never. I know Zack."

"Sometimes the president doesn't call all the shots. And I'm speculating. I don't believe for a second that the admiral did anything except honorably fall on his sword. He spared his family and the Navy an enormous amount of pain."

Holland absorbed another shock for the day. "You think he did the right thing?"

"I saw those terrible pictures, honey, so I know he did."

"What the hell do I do now? Dax won't give up. I can try to talk to him, but I don't think I'll be able to persuade him to stop. I think I have to at least prove that his father was set up."

Her uncle hesitated, then let loose a reluctant sigh. "I'm going to give you a file. It's my personal investigation. The pictures will be inside. If you want to stop Dax, show him these images. Otherwise, you're trying to take on something you have zero jurisdiction over."

"But there's something sinister and wrong here. Why haven't you continued looking for the truth?"

"Because I like breathing. And the Russian mob is something bigger than local law enforcement. If the FBI wants to investigate, I'll help them out, but I'm not putting any of my men in the line of fire when it isn't their responsibility and it would only ruffle feathers. We have other crimes to fight and solve every single day."

Uncle Beau lacked the funds and manpower to fight every battle. It was a sad truth of law enforcement. Like doctors, police officers were often forced to triage a situation rather than fix it.

She waited quietly while her uncle unlocked his file cabinet and retrieved the pictures that would prove Dax's father's guilt.

EIGHT

Dax opened the door to Holland's place with a sigh, thankful the long day was over. All he wanted was to eat a little something before he crawled into bed with her—and not necessarily in that order. Food could really wait. He needed her love and affection.

What a freaking day.

He set the pizza down on the counter. "Sweetheart? You home?"

For a moment he thought he was alone. He was about to pick up his phone and give her a call when he saw her hair blowing out on the balcony. He watched her for a moment, her slender form graceful, before he joined her. Dusk had nearly arrived and her shadow moved along the window, past the little bistro table and chairs, as if she'd begun pacing.

He opened the door and immediately found himself with an armful of Holland. She threw herself against his chest, wrapping that body around him. "Hey, if I'd known I was going to get this kind of welcome, I would have snuck out of work and found you hours ago."

She turned her face up. "It was a long day. That prison is depressing."

He studied her and smoothed her hair back. "I'm sorry about that, sweetheart. I wish I could have been with you. Did you learn any-thing new?"

"I found out that Sue Carlyle is a raging drug addict with serious mental problems. All that getting high affected her memory. She can't tell us anything. It was another dead end. I'm so sorry."

Clearly, Holland was upset about that. He hugged her tight. "It's not your fault. This investigation was cold. We knew it would be hard."

She squeezed him back. After the day he'd had, he winced.

"Are you all right?" She eased away, staring up at him with con-cerned blue eyes.

"It's nothing," he assured her. "I just damn near got mowed down near Jackson Square today. I'm fairly certain that drunk asshole started hitting the bottle way too early."

Holland gasped. "What happened? Tell me."

He kissed her forehead, doing his best to soothe her. "Just some of the usual rowdiness in the city."

She took a step back, looking him over. Her stare immediately fell to the nasty spot on his arm where he'd crashed to the concrete in order to avoid the oncoming SUV. Luckily, he moved fast or he would have been in serious trouble. He'd had a few nasty words for that ine-briated prick who naturally hadn't stopped so he could say them.

"Tell me everything." Her eyes had flared wide with fear, tears shimmering. She ran her hands over him as though trying to seek out the damage and heal it with her touch.

Dax sighed because worrying her wasn't how he wanted to spend his evening, but maybe the whole story would set her at ease. She looked genuinely upset. "Yeah, the fucker never even put his foot on the brakes. I don't know if he even realized what he'd almost done. Idiot. You want to explain to me why there are never any cops around when I need one, but at least three ready to write me a ticket when I go five miles over the speed limit?"

"Did you get the plate?" Her voice trembled.

He frowned. "No. I was trying to scrape myself off the concrete. I guess I should have asked if anyone else had, but I doubt it. Everything happened so fast." The people around him had been concerned with helping him up and making sure he was all right. No one had offered him information about the car or driver.

"Dax . . ." She threw her arms around him and held tight.

What the devil? He appreciated her concern but didn't need it.

Easing back, he cupped her face and studied her for a moment. "Holland, I'm fine."

"That's the second time since you've been in town that someone's nearly killed you."

What was her point? "Well, I promise not to run after street thieves again and I'll stay away from Jackson Square. I really am fine, sweetheart. After the incident, I picked up lunch for the office and went back. No harm, no foul."

She hugged him again, trailing her fingers down his face. She stared at him as if nothing was more precious to her. "I can't stand the thought of you being hurt. I would do just about anything to make sure you're all right. You know that, don't you?"

That prison must have really rattled her. "I would do the same for you. Stop looking like you lost your best friend. I'm right here and I'm not going anywhere."

"Really? And if I can't solve this case?"

He didn't want to think about that tonight. Besides, she would. He knew Holland. She was brilliant and had tenacity. She wouldn't stop searching. So Amber Taylor's mom had turned out to be a bust. If the woman's drug-addled memory couldn't be trusted, it was a setback but not Holland's fault. Maybe he should talk to Sue Carlyle's cellmates. Sometimes crazy people told kernels of truth in their tales.

He would ring some contacts and call in a few favors, maybe set up an interview or two. Talking to the guards might shed some light, too. But if the prison had disturbed Holland that much, he'd leave her out of it. He'd do everything he could to save her from more distress.

But now he intended to make her feel so much better.

Dax tangled his fingers in her silky waves as he lowered his mouth to hers. Kissing Holland was so different. Before her, pressing his lips to another woman's had merely been the beginning of the seduction, an eventual means to an end. It was something he'd done to get both he and his partner ready for sex.

With Holland, kissing was a thrill to savor, a destination he could enjoy for long hours. He devoured her mouth, dragging his tongue over her lower lip until she sighed and melted against him, winding her arms around his torso. Dax felt her start to relax.

That was good, because she didn't need to think here. When they were alone, together, that was their safe haven. They had no room here for anything beyond the two of them.

In the distance, Dax heard the music from nearby clubs starting up. As darkness fell, the party would be starting, but he was only interested in the good times he could share with Holland. Though he rather liked the idea of enjoying their "privacy" in the middle of a crowd.

He skimmed his palms down her back before finding her backside and filling his hands with her as he drew her closer. She gave him the sweetest little whimper. The overhead light of her balcony wasn't illuminated. Up here, the neon signs flashing below seemed hazy, almost soft as the earthy plants in their clay pots all around filtered their garish colors.

She kissed him once more, then heaved a weighty sigh before turning away again to lean against the wrought-iron railing. She looked pensive, her shoulders clustered around her ears.

"What's wrong?"

"It's just hard. My job can get me down from time to time. There are some things I can't fix and it really makes me crazy."

Dax wrapped his arms around her from behind and was satisfied when she let her head fall back against him. "There's only so much you can do."

"It makes me angry."

"I know you. If you say you're unable to do more, then I know you've done everything you could. Now you need to let it go." He kissed along the shell of her ear, satisfied when she shuddered. "You need to relax, sweetheart. Let me take over."

She paused, then let out a little groan. "I shouldn't, but I can't help it. I need you, Dax. I need you so badly."

"Tell me about it. Tell me about your day." His hand cupped her breast.

She shook her head. "I want to forget it."

He thumbed her nipple, feeling it stiffen against his thumb. He could give her pleasure and a respite from the day. "I can help you with that."

"Let's go inside." Her voice sounded slightly husky.

"Hmm," he murmured in her ear. "The party is just getting started out here, sweetheart. Hush, no one can see you. No one has any idea what we're doing up here. We're just a couple looking out over the Quarter, enjoying a romantic evening."

He slid his hand down to the waistband of her slacks, aware of her frozen and staring down at the people on the street, as if gauging who might be able to see them. A trellis of climbing ivy concealed his movements, but they still had full view of the action below. Couples milled about, holding hands and kissing. Groups of friends strolled through the Quarter. People began to fill up the restaurants and bars.

"Look out there. Tell me what you see." He would use both mental and physical tactics to slip past her defenses so he could take her mind off her problems. So as he spoke, he slipped his hand just under her waistband and down to the silk of her undies.

Her breath caught. "Dax, what are you doing?"

With his other hand, he pinched her nipple lightly, just enough to make her gasp. He also reminded her who was in charge for now. "I'm having a nice time with the most beautiful woman in the world and she's going to let me. Aren't you, sweetheart? Because you know I'll take you somewhere wonderful, someplace where you don't have to think about anything but your next orgasm. So give over and let me do my job."

"Your job?"

"Taking care of you. I've decided it's my primary job in life." He whispered the words against her ear. "So hush unless I ask you a question. No one can see us. They're too busy with their own pleasures. Now look at that couple on the street below and tell me what you see."

They were standing in line, waiting to be seated. The woman wore a white sundress and the man slacks with a collared shirt. Occasionally, she looked up at him as if they shared a secret. He always gave her a sly smile back.

"They've been together for a while. You can see it in the way he holds her hand, the way they look at each other," she murmured.

"Yes." He nipped her ear and she moaned.

Emboldened, Dax slipped his hand a bit lower, well under the band of her bikini underwear, skimming the pad of her sex with his fingertips and intentionally missing her clitoris. She was already heating up for him.

"God, Dax, please touch me there. Please." Holland arched her back, grinding her firm backside against his stiff cock.

She wasn't playing fair, but then two minutes ago she'd told him she hadn't wanted to play at all, so he was calling this a win.

He smiled as he soothed the little bite he'd given her with his tongue, tracing it along the shell of her ear. "I'll get there, but not until you give me what I want. So tell me what makes you think they've been together for a while."

"You're going to kill me, Spencer. Fine. They're comfortable holding hands. She leans into him. She smiles at him differently than she does at everyone else. Watch her. She's polite to others, but when he talks, she lights up."

He teased down farther, brushing the little jewel that brought them both so much pleasure. He let the pad of his finger rub against it, starting the slow roll to her orgasm. His erection jumped when he realized she was already wet. "Where do you think they're at in their relationship?"

"They're in love." Her voice had taken on a breathless quality as she watched the couple take their seats. The restaurant doors were glass with big bay windows. The couple was seated in the front. The man moved quickly, not allowing the waiter to seat his date. He pulled out the chair for her, held a hand out to ease her down.

"I think you're right," he whispered as he rubbed her sensitive nub in little circles.

He dipped his fingers lower, slipping into her labia where he found all the evidence of her arousal he needed. She was so wet. All he had to do was touch her. No woman had ever responded to him the way Holland did. It was as if she was made for him.

"He treats her like you treat me." Her head fell back against his chest, a sure sign of her surrender.

They hadn't exchanged words of love, not exactly. He didn't say them now, either. He wanted to save it. He had plans for his girl.

"Yes, he treats her the way I treat you. I'll bet he's always thinking of her. She's the last thought he has before he goes to sleep at night and the first when he wakes up in the morning. He can't work sometimes because she's taking over all his thoughts. And when he's around her? Oh, he's useless for anything but touching her, being close to her. She's his home."

"Dax," she said, her voice breaking.

"Shh, let it happen, sweetheart. I won't say another word." She wasn't ready for undying declarations tonight. They needed a little more time. He had a bit left to give her.

He picked up the pace, her arousal making her melt even more quickly. Over and over, he circled her clitoris, her body beginning to move in time to his. She thrust her pelvis against his hand, offering herself up to him. They weren't watching the street below anymore. He was watching her. And with her head thrown back and her eyes closed, she gave herself over to him.

Her body shuddered, and he caught her mouth in a kiss to cover her cries. He was fairly certain no one would hear those sweet whimpers over the raucous racket on the street below, but she would be mortified if they did.

When he'd finally wrung every last second of ecstasy from her, he gently pulled his hand back and sucked his fingers into his mouth, tasting the sweetness of her arousal. She was honey on his lips.

"How do you do that to me?" Holland turned in his arms. "How do you make me forget everything except you? I'm not a wild sort of girl."

"Of course not. You enjoy sex, as you should. You're not only a woman, you're a lady."

She frowned. "I'm also not the sort who needs help to sit in a chair or someone to open the door."

"I know, but I need to do things for you. Don't make my wanting to ensure you're protected and cared for into some mark against your strength. I need for you to know how special you are to me. That's why I do those things for you."

She sniffled a little and rolled those gorgeous eyes of hers. "Naturally. You know exactly what to say to me. God, you're too good to be true, Dax. This is all going to fall apart."

What was going on with her? He drew her closer, hugging her tight. "Everything falls apart at one point in time. The key is making sure you put it back together."

"I love you, Dax. Don't ever forget it." She kissed him, cupping his face in her hands and pressing her whole body against his.

He lit up like a kid at Christmas. Clearly, he'd read her wrong. She was ready. He was damn sure ready. Finally, their timing was right. "I love you, too. God, you have no idea how much I love you."

He picked her up, filling his palms with that luscious ass of hers. Holland wound her legs around his waist. He loved the weight of her in his arms. If she let him, he would carry her everywhere, holding her close.

Now he fumbled his way to the balcony door because what he was about to do did require privacy. He wasn't going to quiet her this time. He wanted to hear her scream for him.

Somehow he managed to get the door open, managed to get them inside. All the while their tongues mated, sliding against each other in a frenzy of love and euphoria. He let his every sense be inundated by her. Her sweet scent, peaches and arousal. Fuck, all he had to do now was smell damn peaches and he would get hard. The feel of her curves pressed to his, her breasts against his chest. The sound of her mewling cries. He loved it when his badass woman turned into a sweet kitten in his arms.

He moved to the bedroom, his cock jumping every single time he took a step. The friction of his erection against her core threatened to undo him.

Her fingers slid against his scalp. She wasn't even trying to hold on to him, just explore. She trusted him. The knowledge flared through his system, arousing him as surely as the feel of her bare skin against his. She knew he would never drop her, never let her be hurt.

When his knees made contact with the side of the bed, he let himself tip forward, sending her down gently. He straightened and ripped his shirt over his head. He didn't have time for a slow strip tease. He needed to be inside her now.

With shaky hands, she fumbled with the button of her slacks. A sweet desperation marked her expression, very likely mirroring his own. They needed each other, needed this act of passion to place the stamp on their words. *I love you.* They'd said it with their mouths, and now their bodies wanted to put an exclamation point on the confession.

His hands trembled, too, as he undid his belt and the fly of his khakis. He toed out of his shoes because he was not making love to her with shoes on and his pants around his knees. This was too important. Besides, once he got her into bed, he was keeping her there.

"Let me do it." Holland scrambled off the bed, chucking her slacks to the side. She was down to her pretty bra and panties, which sported a wet spot. Yeah, he'd done that to her.

She dropped to her knees and finished dragging down his zipper. "I don't think it's Naval policy to go commando, Captain."

He took a shuddering breath as she pulled his khakis down, freeing his cock. "Good thing I don't have to pass inspection, then, isn't it?"

"Oh, you pass inspection." She leaned forward and took the head of his cock in her mouth.

He watched it disappear behind her plump lips with a groan.

Dax loved how she went after what she wanted. He'd been with women who played shy. Maybe some actually had been, but for the most part it had been a game to get him hot. They would pretend to be innocent and sweet, like they'd never sucked a cock before. Not Holland. She dove in with gusto, minus the silly games.

"Fuck, that feels good." He slid his fingers around the crown of her head, guiding her to take more. Her mouth was like hot silk, encasing him. He wanted to feel the back of her throat.

She whirled her tongue around, then eased back. "I love how you taste. I want every part of you, Dax. Everything you have to give me."

He was fairly certain they were talking about more than simple oral sex, but that was part of the mix. He'd never let her bring him to climax this way, simply let her play and increase his arousal before climbing between her thighs.

"Sweetheart . . ."

"Please, Dax. I want to do this. I want to feel you come in my mouth."

He damn near did right then and there. Even more, he couldn't refuse her. "All right, but it's my way the rest of the night. Now take more. Take it all."

He gently fucked her mouth, in and out, forcing his way in inch by solid inch. As he did, she cupped his balls. Pleasure radiated up his spine, making his eyes roll back. So good. She felt so damn good. And when she dropped to her knees, it felt like he'd earned her. Holland wouldn't get intimate with anyone for fame or money. She would only do it because she wanted to. That was the best rush of all, knowing he'd made her want him.

Made her love him.

Even as her mouth worked him, his blood heating to a boil, all he could think about was how much he worshipped her and would forever. Yeah, she was good at giving head—but that was part of the love, along with sex and comfort. She was all that to him, wrapped up in one beautifully strong package.

They would be better than his parents. He would be a better man. He would be the best husband in the world for this precious woman.

Her tongue worked the underside of his dick, sending a crazy thrill up his spine. When she gave him the barest edge of her teeth he hissed, the sensation elevating his pleasure.

"More." He tightened his grip on her hair.

She rewarded him with a groan that played along his skin and vibrated up his flesh, urging him to shove his cock deeper into her mouth.

She sucked him hard, working his dick to the back of her mouth with pliant lips and an active tongue. She swallowed around him and he couldn't hold back another second. He gave her what she'd asked for. He let go and came with a hard moan, thrusting into her mouth and releasing everything he had. Through a haze of ecstasy, he watched as she sucked him down.

Electricity sizzled over his skin. His whole body felt alive. She did that for him. No other woman could. But it was more than mere desire. He ought to know, because he'd felt it a million times. It was more than just pleasure. He'd experienced that, too. This . . . only love could feel this big and life changing.

Dax smiled as she pulled back and stared up at him, wearing the sweetest smile, like a cat that had stolen all the cream.

He grinned back, then lifted her up and tossed her on the bed.

He wasn't done with her. Not even close.

Holland woke hours later and couldn't help but stare at Dax. He was spread out on his back, the sheet clinging to his hips. Even in the moonlight she could see all the muscular cuts of his torso. His face appeared so peaceful in repose.

She felt as if she struggled against a storm of anxiety.

She'd almost lost him again. After he'd made love to her for the second time, he'd fallen asleep. Holland had risen and paced. That was when she'd noticed the text on her phone from an unknown number, likely an untraceable burner phone. Whoever had sent the terrible message had probably already dumped the phone.

Next time it's for real.

Simple message. Nothing that pointed to any particular incident. Hell, if she were another woman in another situation, she might convince herself someone had texted her by mistake.

But she knew the truth. The Russian mob or whoever the admiral's enemies had been could get to Dax. They could kill him.

She'd thought about it all afternoon. After visiting her uncle, she'd considered going straight to her bosses. She'd actually started driving to work before she realized she would be putting all her coworkers at risk. Yes, they were law enforcement and risk was part of the job, but first she would have to convince them she wasn't simply love struck or paranoid. She would have to sell her murky conspiracy theory.

If she did, they'd all be ass-deep in something dangerous—and whoever had threatened Dax would only come for him harder. Even if she couldn't convince her peers that she was onto something, every one of them would be vulnerable to a threat they wouldn't see coming simply because they'd heard the truth.

As her uncle had shown her the incriminating pictures of the admiral with Amber Taylor, all Holland could think of was how disillusioned Dax would be if he saw how rough Hal Spencer had been with the girl, the way in which he'd left her bruised and battered. What was the point of putting him through that now? His dad was gone.

If she told him everything she'd seen and learned today, he'd be hurt and angry but he still wouldn't believe his father had killed himself, at least not when and where he had. And Dax would never stop looking for the admiral's killer.

What was she going to do? How could she distract him from this case and keep him safe? If she didn't find a way, the violence that had taken the admiral could also take Dax. Even the thought made her crazy. She couldn't lose him like that. Not when they'd finally come together.

What did she owe justice? Certainly not the life of the man she loved. Her uncle seemed to think that Admiral Spencer's death had been a suicide. Should she risk Dax's life to go after the people who might have driven his father to it?

She leaned over and kissed Dax's forehead. How could such a good man come from such a flawed and selfish one?

"Hey, we never ate." He chuckled as he turned over and dragged her into his arms. "Well, we never ate the pizza I brought."

"I put it in the fridge a little while ago." She hadn't been at all hungry since she'd realized the Russian mob could make good on their threat. "Do you want me to heat up a slice for you?"

Holland wanted to make him comfortable and happy before she told him   somehow—that she would no longer be investigating any further and that he shouldn't, either. Not tonight, but tomorrow. He had to work tomorrow, and she would do everything possible to make sure whoever was watching believed that she had dropped the case.

Tomorrow night, she would make him see that not digging up these old bones was for the best—for everyone. They needed to let the past rest so they could have a future.

He gave her a sleepy smile. "Nah. I just want to lie here with you. How late is it?"

"A little past midnight. Dax, I love you."

"I love you, too. I like saying it. I've never said those words to any woman but my momma and sister." He turned on his side, propping his head on his hand. "You're the one for me, Holland. You're the one I want to keep safe, the one I trust."

God, she prayed he still trusted her tomorrow. "I feel the same way."

But she had to put his life first. Even if he got angry with her and they had a horrible argument, she would make sure he stayed safe. She couldn't do any less.

They would make it through this.

He leaned over and kissed her with a groan, his big body rubbing against hers.

She had to smile despite the dark thoughts in her head. "How on earth are you hard again?"

It didn't seem possible but the man had the stamina of a rutting bull. Thank god.

He kissed her again, deeper this time. "This is all for you, sweetheart. I'm always hard around you. I don't need to eat or drink or sleep. I just need you."

She wrapped her arms around him and kissed him back, reveling in the way his big hands felt on her body. She understood. She'd never gotten so hot so fast for anyone before Dax. It was like the man knew how to touch her, to kiss her, to arouse her like no other.

The minute he touched her, she softened, her heart beating faster. When he lowered his head and sucked a nipple in his mouth, Holland let all the bad stuff drift away. She would convince him somehow that dropping the investigation was all for the best and they would move on together. She would be good for him, and when he had to go back to his ship, she would wait for him to come home again.

She'd already waited years for him. At least this time she'd know he was coming home to her.

Holland rolled over, covering his body with hers. "My turn."

"We're taking turns?"

She could hear the smile in his voice and grinned. "You've had most of the turns tonight, babe. You've kept me on my back all night. I want to be on top."

He watched as she straddled him. He was already hard. Such a beautiful beast. She reached down and took his shaft in her hand.

He liked a firm grip. She knew because he'd told her so. Her man liked to talk during sex. He liked to tell her how beautiful she was. It was time to pay him back for that, too.

"Do you have any idea how hot you are, Captain?"

His lips curled up. "I do not, Special Agent. You should tell me."

"It's easy to see you're suffering from low self-esteem because no one ever told you how gorgeous you really are." He'd had whole magazine articles devoted to his body, but he needed to hear it from her. The compliment would mean more to him because it was coming from the woman who saw deeper than his surface and still loved him.

She saw past the glorious abs and handsome face and knew what an amazing man he was on the inside. Loyal and brave and good. God, she hoped he was forgiving, too.

"Gee, Kirk. No one has ever once told me I'm attractive." He clasped his hands around her thighs and playfully leered her way. "No one who mattered, anyway."

They were in sync. She pumped his cock in her hand. "You are simply stunning, Captain, and I can't think of another man I could possibly want in my bed."

"Now, that's a good thing because no other man is ever going to get into this bed. Not without crawling over my dead body."

She fought off a shiver and tried to focus on the positive. "Possessive, huh? Well, it so happens I like your body alive. I like your body hot, too. And I definitely love this part of you."

Holland was already damp and aching and ready for him.

"Sweetheart, I need to go grab a new box of condoms. We've worked our way through the last one."

If she was in, she was going all in. "Dax, I've had my birth control shot so unless you're hiding something from your last physical, I think we can agree we're planning on being monogamous."

His eyes flared and she felt his dick pulse in her hand. "I've only had sex with you since my last physical. I don't want to ever have sex with anyone except you again, Holland. You're the only woman for me."

She rubbed her aching flesh over his cock, loving the way his erection teased her clit. Even after making her scream his name over and over just hours before, she still felt the flare of awareness zing through her body. "I liked what you did earlier."

He skimmed his hands over her hips. "I did a lot of things. You're going to have to be more specific. Was it how long I ate your pussy? Or the way I sucked on your sweet nipples?"

He liked to talk dirty. How would he like to hear it from her? "I liked being out in the open, watching everyone walk around the Quarter and not a one of them knew that you were fucking me with your fingers and I was coming all over your hand."

His eyes slid shut briefly as arousal overtook his face. "Sweetheart, I'm more than willing to fuck you anytime and anyplace. I'm ready now. I want to watch you ride me and those gorgeous breasts bounce. I definitely want to feel you all around my cock. I've never had sex without a condom before."

That surprised Holland. He seemed like a man who could have had sex any way he chose with anyone he wanted, but since she'd really come to know him, she believed him. He took care of his partners and himself. But they didn't need those barriers between them anymore. And one day, they wouldn't need a chemical, either. One day, they would start a family.

For the first time in her life, she truly believed she could have a family of her own. Yes, the prospect terrified her, but the idea of never holding a baby who looked like Dax was even worse. She would sacrifice the past so they could have a future together.

She slowly lowered herself down his steely erection, loving every inch of the sensation. He was so big as he filled her up, stretched her. Even after all the times they'd made love, she still felt her eyes widen when he started to press in.

She lowered herself down slowly, wanting to draw it out. Up and down, taking him a little deeper with each pass.

"Tease." He growled the words but did nothing to rush her.

"That's because it's my turn."

Like he could talk. Dax was king of teasing. He could make sex last for hours. He would push her almost to the edge and then bring her right back. He'd repeat the process over and over again until she thought she couldn't take another second. Then he would slide over her sweet spot and send her whirling.

She took him slowly, finally bringing them completely together only to stop and let herself savor every inch of him inside her.

His big, hot hands roamed up to cup her breasts and he sighed. "I love being inside you. You feel so right."

Everything about him was right.

Holland rolled her hips. Dax filled her up so deliciously. Up and down, she rode his cock while his hands explored her body. There wasn't a place he didn't touch as though he wanted to mark her as his for all time.

She was. She couldn't imagine another man putting his hands on her. She leaned over, never letting up on the rhythm of her hips. Lowering her mouth to his, she kissed him long and slow, tangling their tongues together.

He thrust up from beneath her, hips surging, while his hands tightened on her, forcing her down.

"Ride me, sweetheart. Ride me hard."

Holland intended to give the man what he needed, so she rocked up and thrust down harder, finding a deeper rhythm. With a groan, he settled his fingers between their joined bodies and worked her swollen bundle of nerves, moaning as he rubbed her hard. Then she was the one who couldn't wait. She quickened her pace. Pleasure rising, her head swimming, heart drumming, Holland gasped. This hot, quick ride felt like the beginning of forever. Even if it was sexy as hell, she felt his love. All the sensations converged with her emotions and splintered her apart. She came an instant later, ecstasy sweeping over her wild and fast.

Before she could begin to enjoy the languor of her orgasm, Holland found herself on her back, Dax staring down at her as he spread her legs wide and thrust in deep. He was obviously through playing around, and she nearly shouted when he hit some magical place that detonated a new flurry of tingles. Orgasm began to build again.

"Give me one more, sweetheart. I want to feel your pussy clamp me tight. You feel so fucking good."

She moved with him, lifting to him and feeling the rise of need. She clutched his shoulders, cried out when he nipped at her neck and plunged deep.

Then she went over the edge again. This time he was with her. He held himself hard and high inside her as his head fell back with a groan. She could feel his release fill her, scalding, primal, satisfying.

After a long, low groan, Dax fell on top of her, winding his arms around her and holding her tight. "Love you so much."

And then he fell right back to sleep, his breathing deep and even as he cuddled her.

This time she let his warmth seep into her skin. She would make things right between them. She had to. There was no other choice because she couldn't give this man up and she wouldn't let anyone take him from her.

NINE

Dax looked at the ring. The gorgeous emerald-cut two-carat yellow diamond would look so damn beautiful on his girl's finger. No. Not his girl. His wife.

He was going to ask Holland to marry him.

"You're sure it's not too soon?" His mother had given her blessing when she'd given him the ring that had been in the Spencer family for generations. She'd never worn it herself since his grandmother had been alive when his parents married, but she'd left it for Dax to give his wife.

"It feels like I've waited forever." *And I won't wait anymore,* he thought as he slid the ring into his pocket. He'd gotten here just in time from the looks of his mother's suitcases. She was heading to D.C. to help Gus find a new apartment.

Gus didn't need any help, but his sister knew their mom loved nothing more than decorating a new space, so Gus had invited her up for the week.

With a sigh, his mother peered up at him. "Then you shouldn't wait anymore. I love Holland like she's my daughter already."

"I'm leaving the Navy, Momma."

That startled her. "Are you certain? I thought you wanted a career like your . . ."

"Like Dad's? His didn't end well. I think I'll try something different."

The ills between his parents stemmed from spending too much time apart. If they'd been a typical suburban commuter couple, his father probably wouldn't have taken mistresses. He also wouldn't have been near a fifteen-year-old prostitute or left himself open to everyone believing the lies about him. Dax grimaced at the thought.

Tears sheened his mother's eyes. "I'm so glad. And you'll stop this investigation into your father's death? You need to focus on the future, son. Not the past. It's over and done."

"I have a few questions left, but I promise I'll be careful." He was leaving Holland out of his visit to Sue Carlyle. He'd pulled some strings so he could meet her next week. He'd also hired a PI to talk to two of the women she'd been incarcerated with who had since been released. He was expecting a report in the next few days.

The Carlyle woman was a key witness. Somewhere in her drug-addled mind likely lay the secrets to what happened with his father. It was a gut instinct and he intended to follow it. But after seeing how going to the prison had affected Holland, he couldn't ask her to go back. When he had all the reports and information, he would show them to her so they could discuss the next steps.

Until then, he would concentrate on his proposal.

"How do you intend to ask her, Dax?" His mother settled into her big rocker on the front porch with a smile. He hadn't seen her look so happy in what seemed like forever.

"I've got a plane taking us to Vegas. I know it may not sound romantic, but she's never been and we've only got a few days off. So I've got something special planned. Mad keeps a crazy lush penthouse there complete with a butler and private chef. I want to treat her right. On the last night, I'm going to ask her to marry me."

And she would say yes. Another gut instinct he was going to go with.

His mother sent him a sharp stare. "Don't you tell me you're getting married there."

"No. No eloping allowed. I'm only going to do this once so I intend to do it right. You and Gus and Holland can go big. I want a white wedding shebang, everything Holland has ever wanted."

"I'm so happy for you, son. I'm happy for all of us. It's past time we had good news in this family. Augustine is starting her new job. You're getting married." She squeezed his hand. "It really is time to move on."

"Mom, do you miss him?"

She sighed and sat back, resting in the big rocker. "Often. I miss the man I thought he was, but I'm going to move on now, too. I'm going to get out more often, resume my charity work. I've certainly missed that. I was asked to head the planning committee for the annual charity ball."

Those nasty bitches had turned their backs on his mother when the scandal broke, but he knew she missed her place in society. The gossip seemed to have cooled enough to allow her to live something close to normally again.

Guilt made his stomach turn at the thought that he could undo her social progress. He might not care, but being included in the community was something his mother lived for. It would kill her to go through it all again.

Was she right? Should he concentrate on the future? Holland could get dragged into the scandal. Gus as well.

No. He took a deep breath. He had to do this. He would have to be careful so he didn't upset her new status quo. He would keep his investigation quiet until he'd proven his father was innocent. Once he had, she'd never have to worry about her place in society again. And they could all truly put the past behind them.

His cell trilled as a text came through. He smiled. Gabe.

Just heard the news. Congrats and good luck! I'll give you an
early wedding present by keeping Mad away from Vegas
while you're there.

He smiled. Perfect. He texted back his thanks and glanced at the
time. He needed to head out. Holland's shift would be over and she
had no idea he'd arranged for her to take some time off. He'd contacted her superior the day before, requesting some of her vacation
time as a surprise. Her boss had been happy to give it to him. Dax was
fairly certain the man had thought he was calling to rail about his
father's case again. He'd been obviously relieved.

"I love you, Mom. I'll call you when we get to Vegas tonight. I've
got to get back to the apartment so I can whisk her away. Mad is sending the plane as we speak. We'll leave late, but it's Vegas, so everything
will still be open when we get there." And he would enjoy a night flight
with his almost fiancée. He intended to show her just how depraved
he could be at thirty thousand feet.

"You're a nice boy when you want to be but I know you've got a very
bad side." His mother winked his way, then rose as a black sedan
pulled up. "There's my car. Gus sent it, along with that fine young
driver."

Dear god. The man was in a suit, but he looked like he was built to
strip. Yeah, that was exactly what Gus would look for in a driver for
their widowed, sixty-something mother.

He helped get her into the car and waved as she drove off for what
looked like a fun trip.

His mother finally seemed ready to move on. For months he'd been
worried about her and now it was as if the clouds were shifting and the
sun was shining in his mother's life again.

Was he doing the right thing by poking into his father's death? Or
just dredging everything painful back up?

He would talk to Sue Carlyle's cellmates and decide from there. If
it really was a dead end, he would put the past behind him and con-

centrate on the present, on marrying Holland and starting a new chapter of his life.

He pocketed the ring and started toward the streetcar station. He had a week's worth of leave and he wasn't about to waste a minute of it.

His cell trilled again. Roman this time. He swiped his finger across the screen to accept what would likely be some hearty congratulations. "It's a good day, my man."

"Hey, Dax."

Dax stopped because that didn't sound like a congratulatory voice. The last time he'd heard that gritty tone to Roman's voice, his friend had been calling to tell him what had happened to his father. So he got right to the point now. "What's happened?"

"I need to talk to you about a story that the *Times-Picayune* was going to run tomorrow morning."

"Was?"

"I think Gus effectively quashed it." Roman sounded so grim.

"Gus?"

"It's part of what she does for Liz. Of course Liz runs the press office, but Gus is like her enforcer. She heard about the story first. It's why she thought it best to bring your mother here to D.C. In case the paper decided to print this shit anyway, she wanted your mother here with us where we can insulate her a bit. But I want to assure you that when Gus says something's dead, it usually is."

"What is the story about?"

"Pictures of your father have surfaced."

"All right. There were pictures when the scandal first broke." Of his father entering the seedy motel with the girl. "What's different about these?"

Roman paused for a moment. "He's in bed with the teenage prostitute, the one from the video. They're . . . explicit."

Dax's stomach took a nosedive. Lousiest fucking timing.

"And there's more. Someone is planning an exposé on your family. Do you know anything about your father having multiple affairs?"

"Yes, but only because my mother told me." What the hell was going on?

"Someone else knows about it. Someone is shopping a book deal airing all of your family's dirty laundry and naturally they found a publisher to bite."

Dax could feel his whole body tense. "Goddamn it. I do not need this. My mother doesn't need this."

"I know. Unfortunately, I'm not done yet," Roman continued. "Gus has been asking a few questions and poking around. She thinks she's found the source for this sudden story. There's been a leak. Those photos were kept in lockup at NOLA PD. Recently, another investigator got hold of them. This particular investigator had a hundred thousand dollars deposited into her account from an offshore bank yesterday. Not sure why she chose to do it that way. She should have gotten an offshore account herself. It took Gus all of five minutes to figure it out."

His stomach was still sinking. Only one investigator would have gone after those files. "Are you saying Holland sold pictures of my father and this teenage prostitute to the press?"

"It looks that way."

"It's not possible." Holland would never do such a thing. Someone had to be framing her.

"Look, I'm not going to tell you how to play this and I've got Gus on a leash for now. I can't begin to tell you what she wanted to do. Your sister is very creative with revenge. This is your girl and you have to figure out how to handle this. As for the scandal, it's done. There won't be a book."

God, what had they done to get that tell-all book quashed? "How did you manage that?"

"The publisher is part of a media conglomerate. Zack agreed to give their news arm an interview about Joy's death."

"No." He couldn't let Zack do it. He was one of the most private human beings Dax had ever met, and talking about something as personal as the death of his wife would crush him. "Tell him I said I'll find another way."

"He knew you would, which is why he's already made the deal. It's done. There's no backing out now." Roman paused. "Dax, he needs to do this for you. Let him, so he can feel as if he's done one damn good thing to help."

Because his job seemed so very large there was nothing he could contribute. "All right, but I can never repay him for this."

God, what had happened? How had it come to this and who was fucking with Holland? There was zero chance she had chosen to sell him out. Something was going on and his need to see her skyrocketed.

She could be in danger. This whole situation had suddenly gotten so out of hand.

"He doesn't want repayment. He wants you and your family safe." There was a pause over the line. "Dax, I know how you feel about your father, but I need you to think of Gus now."

"What do you mean?"

"I mean if this story blows up again, she'll be directly in the line of fire. She'll be all over the papers and a good amount of her credibility could come into question. We put out this fire today, but you reopening this investigation will likely cost Gus her career. I hate that. I hate even saying it, but image is everything here. Zack can keep her on, but if these photos of your father get out, Gus goes from having a tragic background to pictures of her father abusing young women being the top story every time someone Googles her."

"Gus would disagree with you," he said, though Roman's words were making him think.

"Yes, she would, but I'm worried about her. I'm worried about your mother. Gus would want you to soldier on. She's a tough lady, but this is a world where a person's career can be ended with a single news story. The only reason I brought Gus on for such a high-profile job in the first place was that the media had died down and most people have forgotten."

"Why didn't you hire her because she was good?" Anger was starting to thrum through his system.

Roman paused. "I know you probably think I'm being ruthless, but I really am thinking about Gus. And quite frankly, those pictures . . . Dax, I don't want to believe it, either. Not about your dad, but I saw them. I can't unsee them."

Dax shook his head. "I can't talk about this right now. I need to go."

"All right." Roman sighed heavily. "Just think about what I said. And I'm sorry about Holland, Dax. We've all been there. We've all been duped by someone we care about. It's heartbreaking."

"My heart is not broken, damn it. Holland didn't do this. I'm going over to see her right now and we'll get this sorted out. I'll call you soon." He hung up and practically ran to get to the streetcar that would take him closer to Holland.

Hello?"

"Good afternoon, Special Agent Kirk."

Holland's blood nearly froze in her veins. She knew that voice. How could she possibly forget it? She'd heard that voice in her nightmares for the last few nights. She heard him talking and then she would see Dax's body cold and still on the streets.

She had to wonder now if the theft of her laptop had been random. It hadn't been hard to replace, but they could potentially have found out how far she'd gotten in the investigation. They'd obviously known she'd been looking into the situation. They likely had someone on the inside who fed them information.

She intended to find that person. Quietly. She might not be able to take on the *Bratva* singlehandedly, but she could find the backstabbing mole.

"What do you want?" There was no need for professional politeness with this asshole.

"I want what I've always wanted, Special Agent Kirk. Peace and quiet. My job is infinitely easier when I have those things."

"I've dropped the investigation."

She'd been a good girl these past couple of days. Oh, she'd told Dax she was continuing, but she'd kept to her own cases, her own desk. She wasn't going to give that man any reason to send someone else after him. And each night, she'd lied to Dax about her progress. The guilt was starting to eat at her. She would lie in his arms and the feeling of contentment she normally had with him washed away the second she remembered she would have to crush his need to see his father exonerated soon.

Somehow, she had to tell him she was quitting the investigation. She would have to convince him his father wasn't worth the trouble.

"You might have dropped the investigation," the man said grimly, "but your boyfriend seems to have picked it right up where you left off."

"What are you talking about?"

"Captain Spencer pulled a few strings and learned the names of Sue Carlyle's former cellmates. Additionally, he's scheduled a meeting with the drug addict herself next week. You didn't do what you promised."

Her heart did a flip in her chest. "He did what?"

He'd mentioned absolutely nothing about it. Not one word. As far as she'd known, he'd been trying to wrap up the training protocols with Courtney. She'd dreaded that since it meant he would be leaving soon, but it would also take him out of the reach of the man on the phone.

"You heard me. I've had to take extra measures. I had two choices, Special Agent. I could do what I've done or I could have eliminated the problem."

Terror sparked through her. "If you touch him in any way, I swear I won't ever stop hunting you down."

"I rather thought that would be your reaction, so I chose Door Number Two. I had to sell it to my boss. The next time he'll do what he wants to do. You won't like his choices, Special Agent."

Her hand clenched around the phone. "What have you done?"

"I've ensured that the problem goes away. Unfortunately, you're part of the problem. Spencer is here in New Orleans for you as much as his investigation. I've ensured he won't want to be around you again. He needs a distraction, and a little betrayal will do wonders for his focus. Once he gets back on his ship, he won't have time for things like investigations. Hell, he won't have time to communicate with the outside world and that's how we like it."

Yes, she could see where focusing Dax on something besides his father's death would be helpful. "Where do I come into it?"

"You'll find your bank account is much healthier than once it was. I hope you enjoy the hundred grand. It's yours to keep from my gracious employer. Consider it a fair exchange for your relationship."

"For my relationship? Why would me breaking up with Dax cause him to stop investigating his father's death?"

A chuckle came over the line. "I'm sure he won't, though he'll likely take his time getting back to it. But he won't have NCIS access. He won't have a law enforcement professional smoothing the way for him."

"He could have the damn president smoothing the way for him." Did they forget who Dax was?

"Your captain would never drag his friends into this," the man replied smoothly. "If that were true, he already would have. He can't go to a reporter because that would hurt his mother and sister. His only real option is you. If he can no longer trust you, he'll have nothing but hired hands to turn to."

She shivered. "And hired hands can be bought."

"Everyone can be bought, with the exception of a woman in love. I don't trust you, dear. I think the captain might get on his boat and you could rethink everything, decide that maybe you can find the answers he seeks. You're dangerous together so I'll tear you apart one way or another."

Her blood chilled. "And you think a hundred thousand dollars can tear us apart?"

"Yes, I do. I believe this will work and even when Spencer comes home after his next six months at sea, we'll have had time to fix any leaks we might have. He won't find the same information again. He can look, but we'll have done a better job this time."

"Why not just show him those damn pictures?" She wouldn't be able to. Just the sight of them had made her sick, but she was so confused.

"I would in a heartbeat if I thought it would truly change things. No. I think I've chosen the right set of moves. It's like chess, you know. In a few moments Captain Spencer will be confronted with your betrayal. He'll also have to think about the ramifications of the case being opened again. He thought he could do it quietly. I've shown him that's not likely. Even now someone will probably be calling him and throwing around words like *scandal* and *exposure* and *optics*. Of all the men in the world, politicians and their ilk are really the most predictable. He'll go to his boat and lick his wounds and decide that perhaps his sister and his mother and his friends are worth more than a dead man's memory. The scandal will fade again. The Hayes administration can stay on task instead of answering questions about their employee's family. And my boss gets to stay out of the spotlight as well. We're all happier with the investigation closed. Even the captain, as he never has to see those photos. Everyone is better off. Well, except you."

It could work. She still didn't know what was going on, but Dax might shut down the investigation if he thought it could hurt his sister. "I'll talk to him about it. I'll get him to see reason."

Dax would put his family first. Surely. She could make him see it was their only choice.

"I doubt that," came the reply. "When the captain comes to confront you, I hope you'll remember that old saying: sometimes you have to be cruel to be kind. Good-bye, Special Agent. This is the last time we'll speak. The next time, I'll use more than words to deal with the situation."

She'd never felt more helpless than she did when she heard that line go dead.

What the hell had that man done? It couldn't be good. Her stomach clenched, tears starting to pierce her eyes.

A hundred thousand. Someone had paid a whole lot to set her up. But set her up for what?

The door opened and Dax stormed in. His normally perfect hair was slightly disheveled and his eyes wide. "Holland!"

She moved into his line of sight. "I'm here."

He sighed and stepped toward her, pulling her close. "I was so worried about you."

"Worried? Why?" She clutched him close for a long moment, breathing him in. She had a sudden feeling that this embrace might be their last.

"Sweetheart, I need you to go and look at your bank account. I think someone's fucking with us, and we need to figure out who it is. I'm going to tell you something disturbing, but I want you to stay calm. I need you to understand that I'm going to make everything right. I'm not going to let anything happen to you."

She had to force herself to breathe. Not playing along with the mobster's scheme meant something terrible would happen to him.

She stepped back, her heart in her throat. "What are you talking about?"

She was fairly certain she didn't want to know.

"Someone wants me to believe that you're trying to sell photos of my father and Amber Taylor together in bed," he explained, his mouth a flat line.

"The girl he was accused of raping?" She could still see those photos. The hollow look in the girl's eyes would haunt her for the rest of her days. Dax thought he'd known his dad, but those pictures reminded her that no matter how well she thought she knew someone, she could never know the depths of their darkness.

If they got out into the public, the Spencer family might never recover.

A single brow rose over his left eye as he took another step back. "The girl he was accused of sleeping with, yes. Apparently someone stole the pictures and whoever wanted to destroy my father is now threatening to release them and blame you."

God, her mystery mobster had released the original blackmail photos and set her up to take the fall, hoping that Dax would be so overwhelmed by her betrayal he would walk away from the investigation. They hadn't sent them to Dax himself. Dax had made it plain that he was investigating what he believed was his father's murder. The potential belief that his father was guilty of the crime hadn't thrown Dax off.

But the idea of those photos being out in the world might. The idea that the woman he loved had betrayed him utterly could derail him and send him right back to his ship where he couldn't cause trouble. Not any the mob couldn't control. If he sent private investigators, they would be bought off or blackmailed. They'd proven there were very few people they couldn't get to.

They'd put her in a horrible position. She'd meant to put him on a boat in a week and then she would have had six months to figure out how to handle the situation. She would have come up with something, some way to gently turn his mind away or to try to prove to him his father really had killed himself.

Now she had nothing. If she defended herself, he could die.

"Where are they releasing the photos?"

Dax shook his head and headed for the bar. She had a decent bottle of bourbon there and he poured out two glasses. "They'd intended to go to the papers with the pictures. And the reporter who was going to break the story was finalizing a publishing deal. Apparently they can't take down my family with a single story. They needed a whole book."

"Was finalizing a deal?" How far had they gone?

Dax handed her one before taking a good swig of his own. "Yes. My friends found out about the deal and it's dead now."

How would her man with no name take that? Would he be angry?

Or could she satisfy him by throwing Dax off the investigation? Panic warred with anger inside her. She didn't want to lose Dax but Holland was furious that she didn't see a way out. Or had that all been part of their plan in the first place? They had to know Dax's friends could kill that deal. This was all about making her look bad. The "deal" would get quashed so the rumors and investigations wouldn't be public again, but one person would have to take the fall. Her. "How did they do that?"

"Zack handled it."

When one of your best friends was the president of the United States, she supposed one could accomplish a lot with a minimal amount of red tape. "What are you going to do?"

Not that she could believe him. He hadn't mentioned that he'd made plans to go to the prison. Unless the man on the phone had been lying to her?

"I'm going to find out who's setting you up and I'm going to make them pay. I'm not an idiot, Holland. I know you wouldn't betray me like this. Someone wants me to think you would. They're trying to drive a wedge between us, and I won't let it happen."

She fought back tears because how many men in his position would believe her? None that she knew of. He loved her. It was the only reason he could possibly look at all the evidence and still come to the conclusion that she was innocent.

It was sweet and touching . . . and heartbreaking. Clearly, he wouldn't stop trying to vindicate his father or her. Never. He would be a dog with a bone, and the mob would take him down eventually. They would call it an accident, a tragedy. No one would be able to prove anything, but Dax Spencer would cease to be.

She was the only one who could possibly stop it. She had to make him believe his father was guilty. It was the only way to end this. That was her real job in all this chaos.

"He was guilty." The words dropped from her mouth like a boulder that was suddenly too heavy for her to bear.

"Connor is overseas right now, I suspect. I never really know where the man is." Dax continued on like she hadn't said a thing. "I'll leave him a message, but as soon as I can I'll talk to him about delving into your banking records. We have to be able to figure out who sent you that money."

"He was guilty, Dax." She had to make him understand. "Your father committed statutory rape and he killed himself because of the repercussions."

He stared at her for a moment, his eyes not quite focused. "I'm sorry, sweetheart. I don't understand. What are you saying to me?"

This was going to be so much harder than she could have imagined. Dax wasn't going to simply accept that his father had possessed a dark side and move on, but then that was the mobsters' plan. The man on the phone had been explicit. He wanted Dax Spencer back at his Naval post and without resources here at home. He wanted her separated from Dax. He hadn't counted on Dax believing she was innocent.

She needed the man she loved to think she was the bad guy. Holland didn't see another way to make this work. If she told Dax the whole truth, he'd only fight harder and bring his friends into this danger. No, she had to sacrifice their relationship to save his life.

She thought for a moment, trying to figure a way out. Maybe she could tell him the truth and that he needed to leave her, get on his boat and they could try again, more quietly this time. He could leave her here and let her try to bring the mob down.

Yes, he would just quietly get on that boat and leave her. Not in a million years. He would never leave her behind. He would go straight to the Navy and open another investigation—this one into the threats against her.

They had no idea who the mob had on the inside. Of the cops. Of NCIS. Of the Navy.

The only way to save Dax was to hide the truth and get him on that damn boat.

Holland turned her back on Dax and wrapped her arms around herself. God, she'd love to hold him one last time . . . but that wouldn't convince him that she'd sold him out.

Instead, she drew in a deep breath and forced herself to go cold as she turned to face him.

In a few months, maybe a year, perhaps she could try to talk to him again. Perhaps they could meet secretly and she could explain, but now there was no way except to make him hate her.

"You heard what I said, Dax. I've spent the last several weeks investigating this case. I've put my life on hold for it and I've come to one and only one conclusion. Your dad raped that girl. I've seen the photos. In fact, I was the one who found them."

The blood leeched from his face, leaving him pale. He chugged back another long drink before looking up at her. "When did you find the photos? And where are they? I want to see them."

She shook her head. "I don't have them anymore."

She placed careful emphasis on the "anymore," praying he would come to the proper conclusions. She couldn't handle a nasty, prolonged fight. At some point she would break down because what she needed more than anything was for him to pull her into his arms, to hold her close and promise everything would be all right. She needed it more than anything and it was the one thing she might never have again. After today, he might well hate her for the rest of their lives.

And she would love him forever.

His lips thinned to an angry line. "What are you saying, Holland?"

"I think you know. Who called you? Was it Zack himself?"

He shook his head. "Roman."

Of course. Roman did Zack's dirty work. Always had. "Did Roman tell you it was my fault?"

"Of course he did. Though you should know it was Gus who found it."

Holland's knees nearly buckled. God, she hadn't thought about the fact that she was going to lose them all. Gus would never forgive her.

Sure, Gus seemed like a happy, fun party girl who guarded her friends and family like a momma bear. But once she'd been branded guilty, Gus wouldn't speak to her again, wouldn't call and force her to go to lunch or to parties. Holland knew damn well Gus wouldn't ever allow her to see Judith Spencer again.

God, she was going to miss them. But every single one of them would be alive. That's what mattered most.

"I should have guessed. She's a smart cookie. I thought I could get away with it." She forced her voice to sound arctic cold. Inside, she desperately wanted to cry, but she couldn't give him a hint that she wasn't anything but a mercenary bitch.

Dax stood, staring for a shocked moment. "I don't understand. Tell me what you did. Tell me in plain English."

He wasn't about to make this easy for her. He never did. She was going to have to sell it. "When I realized you were completely wrong about your father, I had a decision to make. I'm not going to ruin my career for you. I'm not about to be the idiot agent who let some man drag her down. I'm smarter than that. Besides, any woman you end up with is going to be a cipher, Dax. She won't exist except as an appendage to you. Same with any of your friends. Do you think I've forgotten how Joy was treated? She was my best friend and when she died, all anyone could talk about was how her murder affected Zack's fucking campaign. No one cared that she was gone as long as he won the damn election."

Sometimes it was easiest to tinge the lie with a bit of truth. She really had felt that way about Joy's death. No one had celebrated her sweet friend's life or really even mourned her death. They'd simply talked about how her assassination had been a mistake since they'd obviously wanted to kill the senator and wasn't it a shame. But hey, three days later, the senator had become the president. Then no one had given a damn about Joy Hayes anymore.

Yes, she was still angry about that. She could use it.

Dax paled. "That is blatantly untrue. Something in Zack died when

Joy did. We all loved her. We all still grieve for her. Don't pretend we didn't care about her."

"It doesn't matter." It really wouldn't. No one would care what she thought after Dax believed the worst of her. "Whatever. The thing is, you can't expect that I would stay with you long-term. I explained this to you years ago. I'm not going to be tied to someone with the paparazzi following him around for the rest of our lives. I don't want that lifestyle."

Again, a little bit of truth. That possibility had always scared her.

"I'm more than a damn lifestyle, Holland. I'm a man. I thought you realized that."

Now she had him. She'd hit him where it hurt and it was working. "Lately, I've been thinking that the apple never falls far from the tree. You're the son of a pedophile. I tried . . . but I can't get past that." She shrugged like it didn't matter, as if her whole world wasn't crumbling with every word. "Since I don't think I can build a future with that sort of man, I decided to get something out of it and make you my paycheck." She gave him a slightly apologetic glance. "I hope you understand. I just don't think I can love you."

His face flooded with red. "What did you say to me?"

"You heard me." She couldn't say it again. It had hurt too much the first time. "I sold those pictures because the public needs to know the truth about your father. These stupid conspiracy theories need to be put to bed. Your father did everything he was accused of. That includes his suicide."

"Why are you doing this?"

"I explained, Dax. Look, it's been fun and I like you, but I can't damage my career so you can pursue some stupid fantasy that your daddy wasn't a criminal. I would love to spend more time with you in bed. You're spectacular, but I don't think you can be more than that to me. Besides, if I go public as your girlfriend, no one will take me seriously as an investigator anymore. I'll be just another dumb bimbo, one who quite frankly couldn't do her job properly."

"Meaning?" he bit out.

"I investigated. I found the truth. Let it go. This case is closed and it won't be opened again. Period."

That was as baldly as she could put it. She wasn't going to risk Dax's life so he could vindicate his father, because according to those photos, the admiral had been guilty as sin.

"So you didn't want to go public as my girlfriend? Oh, sweetheart, you don't give me enough credit. I'm so much stupider than that." A nasty grin twisted his lips up. He reached into his pocket and came back with a glittery engagement ring. Her heart nearly stopped. "I wanted to be your husband. I meant to propose with my grand-mother's ring, but obviously that's never going to happen. I thought I could convince you to come away with me tonight. I was going to get out of the Navy in six months and take a job with Zack so we could be together all the time. I wanted to have children with you, to raise a family and have a life with you. What a fucking fool I was."

He'd planned to propose? The news battered her chest until it felt as if she'd implode. She would have said yes in a heartbeat. Now that he'd revealed the future he sought with her, so full of infinite possibil-ities, she knew what she hadn't before. She would have married him and never looked back. She'd always been afraid of her deep, abiding feelings for Dax, but her fear was nothing in the face of his love.

Unfortunately, her sacrifice had to take precedence and none of that beautiful future would ever come to pass. She couldn't love him if he was dead, and Holland found she was willing to do anything to ensure he was breathing tomorrow.

Once Dax had left her behind, she would very quietly try to figure out who these fuckers were and find a way to take them down if it was the last thing she did. And she would do it alone so she didn't risk any life but her own. But she would have her revenge on the men who had cost her the love of her life and their future together.

Now that she knew they were watching, she would be more careful and hey, the way she felt right then, if they came after her, it wouldn't fucking matter. In that moment, she really didn't care.

She sighed long and hard, as though the conversation bored her, trying to sound as if she wasn't dying inside. "Like I said, Dax. The sex was great but I don't see sharing more with you."

"You said you love me."

She shrugged. "I love what you do to me. I love how you make me feel in bed. It doesn't go any further than that. A long time ago, I told you I knew the kiss would be amazing and I would still walk away. This time I'm walking away with a whole lot of money."

"How much would you have gotten if the publishing deal had gone through?"

"Enough to set me up for life comfortably. Enough to ensure I don't have to marry someone like you for money."

It was a calculated play. If he thought about it for two seconds, he would see the obvious flaws in her logic. She wouldn't marry him but she would betray him for money? Marrying him would bring her so much more money and position, but she was counting on the fact that he wouldn't see past her betrayal and the emotion of the moment. After all, it had happened to him before. It had happened to all of his friends before. They were American royalty. They'd been betrayed for money and fame, and wanted for everything but the men they were.

Brave. Loyal. Wild and true. Most women couldn't see past the facades to their hearts.

Why do I love Zack? I don't know. It's funny, but once I saw him with his friends, I knew he was the kind of man I could build a life with. He's real. They all are. Look past the glamour. Look to their hearts. You'll find what I did, Holland. You'll find a family.

She missed Joy. The loss of her friend still made Holland actually ache. If Joy had been here, she would have called the woman, asked for advice, listened. Joy had been the sister she'd never had.

And she'd been a member of a family Holland never would be part of, because she'd made her choice. Dax would live. One day in the future she would look at the paper or the web and see that he was marrying someone he loved and she would be happy for him. She would know that ripping her own heart out had been worth all the terrible pain.

Dax stood so still she wasn't certain he would move again. "I don't believe you."

He had to believe her. Everything—including his life—depended on it. "Then you're a fool. I don't love you. I won't ever marry you. Go away, Dax. I'm over it. Do you understand?"

Her whole body trembled. She felt weak. Tears pressed against her eyes, stinging. She blinked them away and forced herself to stand strong.

"Yeah, I think I do. And you know what? I won't ever forgive you. Not for a second. You're not the woman who's had to be strong for others and hid her heart to protect herself. I'd convinced myself that you needed love and coaxing. But you're just a cold bitch, aren't you?"

She wanted to throw herself at Dax, vow that her heart was his. She was so in love with him. "No, I'm a smart bitch."

"Well, at least we agree that you're a bitch." He shoved the ring back in his pocket and strode toward the door, fury sharpening his every move. She could practically feel his volcanic rage. "Don't call me again. Don't call my sister or my mother. I'll make sure they know exactly what you are."

He slammed the door and her world felt like it had disintegrated under her feet. She felt as if her life was over.

She crashed to her knees and lowered her face to her hands. The tears fell like rain.

Dax scrubbed a hand down his face. He'd been wrong. So fucking wrong. Wrong about everything.

"Another?" The bartender frowned like that wasn't the best idea in the world.

The bartender hadn't gotten his soul ripped from his body and pissed on by the woman he loved. "Yes. Make it a double."

The bartender took a deep breath and then poured the bourbon. His friends preferred Scotch, but Dax liked the nasty shit. He liked the burn. It shouldn't be easy and smooth. Liquor should hurt.

What was he doing? What had he been doing? He'd kicked up a hornet's nest and it had bitten him. He felt an actual ache in his bones.

He took a long drink and ignored his trilling cell phone. It would be his sister or one of his friends calling to make sure he was all right.

He wasn't fucking all right. He would never be all right again.

As he'd been sitting here he'd had to ask himself the question he'd been avoiding for a long time. He'd been so sure that he could find justice for his dad. At first he'd intended to clear his father's name. Now, according to Roman—and his own mother—his father really had been involved with other women. There were pictures of him hurting a girl. And because he'd gone to Holland, they'd almost gotten out and ruined Gus's career and his mother's life all over again.

Had he known his father at all? He sure as hell hadn't known Holland.

What would his father want? If he'd been half a man he would want his family safe. He would want them to heal and go on living, even if it meant he never got justice.

Maybe it was time for Dax to start thinking about moving on, too. He would cancel his appointments at the prison. He would walk away and maybe this wouldn't touch his family again. Maybe.

He glanced down at his watch. Mad's plane was picking him up in an hour. Not that he had any reason to go to Vegas now.

Or should he? Maybe he should head to Vegas and fuck as many pretty girls as he could handle before he reported back to base and his ship.

He would be out to sea for six months. It might be enough time to forget how she smelled, how her arms had felt around him.

"Hey, you." A feminine voice pulled him from his reverie. Courtney. She was wearing a short skirt and a too-tight blouse, her raven hair flowing around her shoulders. She was about as far from Holland

Kirk as a woman could get in every way. Courtney didn't give a real shit about her career. It was a way station between college and getting married. She certainly wasn't calculating enough to set him up for a payday.

Courtney liked him. She'd made no qualms about it. The moment he'd met her he'd known he could have her if he wanted. She was sweet and had always looked at him like he was ten feet tall. And she was Holland's best friend.

He looked over at her as she eased onto the barstool next to him. Yeah, maybe she was exactly what he needed.

"Hi." He poured the rest of the whiskey down his throat. Nothing mattered now, and a really bad idea took root in his brain. Well, his dick really. "Hey, how do you feel about Vegas, baby?"

When her eyes went wide, he knew he had her.

PART TWO

NOW

TEN

Holland watched the video in utter dismay. How could one computer bring such terrible memories? It unfolded a bit like a horror movie. It started out with a lovely day and ended in someone's heart getting ripped out of his body.

In the footage, the sun was shining on the Quarter. The camera was perfectly placed to capture every single moment. Then the flash mob took shape and started dancing as one. A man on a mission emerged at the front. He was a stunningly gorgeous male, could have made a fortune with those piercing blue eyes and sharp cheekbones.

All of his friends—and they were numerous—danced along to a song about love and commitment and he strode up with a black velvet box in his hand. He wore a tux and was so beautiful it hurt to look at him. Then he dropped to one knee.

It was every woman's dream proposal, but the woman in the video stepped back and shook her head, the denial on her face making it clear that she wanted to be doing anything but listening to him ask for her hand in marriage.

Unfortunately, that woman was Holland Kirk and the title of the viral video was "Nasty Woman Turns Down Amazing Man." And it had traveled the globe in less than two weeks.

Yep. She was the nasty woman and she'd turned down the most amazing man because he hadn't been Dax Spencer. Captain Awesome.

She hit the pause button on the video and cursed under her breath. More like Captain Asshole.

How long had it taken him to get over her? Maybe fifteen minutes. It couldn't have been much more since he'd been married to her so-called best friend the day after he'd walked away from her.

Holland took a deep breath and tried to relax the fists she'd clenched at her sides. She had to forget Dax Spencer. He didn't mean anything to her anymore. Since she'd severed their relationship, he'd moved up in rank again and gotten a bigger boat with more staff and responsibility. At least he was alive and she'd made that happen. Not that he'd thank her.

Asshole. Apparently, his "love" had meant next to nothing. She'd sacrificed her future and her heart for him, and he'd married her best friend at the time not twenty-fours later just to stab her in the back.

Three years later, her thoughts still circled right back to Dax. She should be focused on what the hell to do about this video and the man whose feelings she'd hurt. But no.

It had taken Holland a good year, but she'd finally started dating again. When Detective Chad Michaels had asked her out at her uncle's yearly crawfish boil, she'd agreed since she'd had nothing better to do. She'd kind of fallen into the relationship because it had been easy. They'd been friends, and he was nice. Then one night she'd been so desperate to wipe Dax from her mind that she'd found herself in bed with Chad. She'd cried afterward but marched forward because she needed to move on. Fourteen months later, she'd had to deal with the consequences.

"You're watching that thing again?" Her new partner's hazel eyes went wide. Gemma White was a tall woman with icy blond hair and a ready smile who could kick more ass than Holland had ever dreamed of. Gemma was the real shit—a former Naval officer who had spent a little time with the FBI before coming home. "You come off like a total bitch, you know."

She was also opinionated and so honest it hurt sometimes.

Holland felt that way when she saw the video. "Thanks for pointing that out."

Gemma shrugged. "I do what I can." She leaned over and pressed the button that started the whole thing over again. "This is my favorite part. Look at that. Everyone looks all shiny and happy. Oh, there. He brought his grandma out of the nursing home for the occasion."

Holland felt her whole body flush. "Yes. And then she had to go to the ER because she complained of heart palpitations."

Holland wasn't entirely sure the woman hadn't done it so she could sue.

"I have a screenshot of that moment when you say no." Gemma's lips curved up as the camera centered on Chad's handsome face and a light seemed to die in his eyes. "Yeah, right there. I made it my screen saver."

Mortification rolled over her. "You have to take that down."

"No can do, partner. I want it to serve as a sign for you. I was right. He's a dick. Yo, Johnson. What did you think of Kirk's old boyfriend?"

A younger agent popped up, a smile on his face. He was dressed casually, having just come from a nasty crime scene. "He was amazing. He was only around for a few weeks, but he's a damn legend around here. He sent us all barbecue one day. I guess that's why they call him Captain Awesome."

Gemma shook her head. "No. The more recent old one."

Johnson's face fell and the kid practically snarled. "He's a total dick. You were right to dump his ass. Me and some of the guys have a drinking game based on that video. We take a shot every time the douche bag checks himself in a mirror. I got trashed on Tuesday. Yeah, I probably shouldn't have done that right before I had to process a multiple homicide." He shrugged. "Live and learn."

All around her she could hear her colleagues agreeing that Chad Michaels was an asswipe of the highest order.

"There was a reason he didn't invite any of us to his little proposal, and it wasn't all because Jim can't dance to save his life," Gemma explained.

"Hey," Jim yelled over his cubicle wall. "I'm a fine dancer. Ask anyone who saw me last Christmas." He stood up and got serious. "And you were right to turn that kid down. I'm not as fond of Captain Awesome as nitwit Johnson, but that man was madly in love with you. Officer Michaels is looking to move up and thought you would be the perfect wife."

She frowned. She'd never once felt as if Chad was using her. Quite the opposite, in fact. And Holland had always felt guilty. "Chad was fun to date. And might I point out that Captain Spencer couldn't have been too madly in love since he got married the day after he dumped me."

"He dumped you? That's not how I heard it, Kirk. The story circulating was that you'd devastated the man and the idiot got shitfaced, then found himself in a bad situation," Jim shot back. "Since I've been married four times, I sympathize with the guy. Never got the one woman I loved so I kept trying to make it work with someone else. Like I said, you were right to turn down Detective Michaels, for more than one reason."

"Are we having some kind of therapy session here?" Her boss, Bill Edmonds, was a fit man, having spent over twenty years in the Army. Now, at sixty, he headed her unit. "Because if we are, I'm running the other way."

"We're discussing Kirk's love life," Jim pointed out to his former partner.

Bill nodded. "Yeah, that's been a fucked-up mess since she dumped Captain Awesome. You don't come back from that, Kirk. Give it up. Be a nun. Or find a boy toy like White here and pump out a couple of babies."

Gemma shot their boss the finger. It was that kind of workplace.

"My Frasier is a beautiful man and he gave me three gorgeous babies. Kirk would be so lucky."

Frasier White was a skinny little academic teaching comparative literature at Tulane. He weighed at least twenty pounds less than his wife and had about a quarter of her muscle tone, but she lit up every time she saw him.

Yeah, she could be so lucky. Only one man had ever made her light up, and he was lost to her forever.

"I need reports in thirty minutes on all open cases, people. Sort out your love life later, Kirk." Bill stopped at her desk. "Though if you give a damn about my opinion, you did the right thing. Michaels wasn't good enough for you."

Bill nodded and moved on.

Holland flipped her laptop closed, unable to look at the screen a second more. "Well, at least we have a consensus."

Gemma leaned on the desk. "You have to let him go."

Holland gestured to her laptop. "Oh, I think I did that already."

"Nope. I wasn't talking about the replacement. I was talking about the real thing. Spencer. You know, when I transferred here two years ago and got assigned to you, Jim and Bill told me that you'd gotten involved in a little side research that meant something to someone you loved and it went bad. They said you'd never gotten over it. You still haven't, honey. It's time."

She'd moved on . . . mostly. She'd known three years ago that she was giving up Dax and his warm, loving family. She hadn't realized how much it would hurt the first time she'd seen Judith Spencer and the woman had turned away from her, her aristocratic head held high and tears in her eyes.

She'd kept up with Gus. Her crazy friend was doing so well in D.C. Every now and then she caught sight of Gus following after Roman and Zack and her direct boss, Liz Matthews, as they all got out of Marine One or Air Force One or whatever amazing transportation they happened to be taking.

Not that she answered Gus's phone calls. They had been numerous that first year. Gus had left message after message complaining about a lack of information from Holland's side. She'd told Holland she wanted the truth. Holland couldn't give it to her so she'd ignored her friend.

It had worked. After about a year, Gus had stopped calling.

She didn't have Courtney anymore, either. It was funny. She hated the woman and missed her at the same time. Once Courtney had eloped with Dax, Holland hadn't had a friend to talk to. Maybe it hadn't mattered. After her split with Dax, she'd gone into her shell and hadn't come out. Not even for Chad. Oh, she'd gone through the motions, tried to wear a brave face, but she'd held herself back from everyone and everything that happened around her. She'd done her job, gotten through the days, and tried hard to convince herself she was falling in love.

Why hadn't she simply said yes to Chad? She wasn't going to get a better offer. At least she could have had a life with him. Now she was a walking cliché—well over thirty, sad, and never been married. Maybe she ought to get a passel of cats and start hoarding.

"I've got to go get ready for that meeting. I'll present for both of us. Why don't you take an early lunch," Gemma said with a pat on her back. "No one will mind. And hey, come out to the house this weekend. We'll barbecue and relax with my monsters by the pool."

Gemma winked, then strode to her desk to gather her files.

One by one, all of her coworkers left the room to join the meeting. Every single agent who walked by sent her a sympathetic glance or smile. Within moments, she was all alone and everything seemed far too quiet.

This was the way her life would be from now on. Quiet. Uneventful. She could see it so clearly. Despite what the others had said, Chad had been a nice guy. Maybe he had been looking to further his career. Who wasn't? But she couldn't believe the man would have married her simply to gain favor with her uncle. No one attached themselves for life to another person for the sake of a few rungs on the career ladder.

She flipped open her laptop again and the video began to play. Everyone looked so happy—except her. God, was this clawing emptiness all she could expect in life? She'd thought it would fade over time but no. Would she live the rest of her days unable to accept love or joy because it hadn't come from one man?

"You know, I think I should start a support group for men who've been turned down by Holland Kirk. It's getting to be a sizeable group, so we could have meetings and form our own twelve-step program."

Holland froze in her chair, her stomach knotting. She'd know that sexy, gravelly voice anywhere. Had she hallucinated that voice in a desperate attempt to maintain some connection to the man she'd loved and lost?

Please let that be it. Because she was going to be mortified if Captain Dax Spencer was actually standing behind her, watching her complete and utter humiliation play out on the web.

"This is my favorite part," his voice whispered. "Right there. That's when that guy's soul kind of died. You can see it. Hey, at least I didn't get all dressed up for my big moment. You look nice, though. Somehow you manage to look gorgeous even when you're breaking a man's heart."

She thought about not turning around. All she had to do was stand up and walk away. She never had to look at his face. She would go to the meeting room. Her boss would deal with him. Hell, she could send Gemma out and see how Dax dealt with Xena: Warrior Princess.

Or she could be an adult.

She sucked in a bracing breath, then turned to him. Dax lounged against her desk with a smirk, looking like a decadent god. He wasn't dressed in his normal neat khakis, but well-fitting jeans and a white T-shirt that hugged his muscular torso. He held a helmet in one powerful hand and his hair was longer than it had been before. He looked slightly older, a little harder, and so beautiful it hurt to look at him.

"Maybe you can recommend eloping with my best friend to all my sad-sack men?" Okay, maybe she wasn't capable of acting like an adult in front of him.

"Well, sweetheart, your best friend wasn't a betraying bitch who accepted money in return for torching my family." His lips had curled up in a nasty smile. "And she was way better in bed than you ever thought of being."

God, where had her sweet man gone? Dax hadn't been capable of this kind of nastiness before. That was precisely why she'd never been able to truly turn him down. He hadn't been ruthless or capable of throwing someone under a bus to get a little farther down the road. He'd certainly never been capable of being so mean.

"Well, I was very sorry to hear about your divorce. Really, after how much time you put into the relationship beforehand, I would have expected you to last a whole extra day or so." She'd always been capable of being mean, especially after circumstances had forced her to tear out her own heart. The anger she'd felt afterward festered and brewed under her surface, but she tamped it down. Usually.

Her words didn't seem to affect him. If anything, he smiled a little more brightly. "Well, we did our best. It looks like you moved on to the next idiot. Tell me something. How much money did you make off this asshole? Like the tux, by the way. He really went out of his way."

She was done with this conversation. "Is there something I can do for you, Captain Spencer? If not, I'd like you to leave the premises. I don't invade your workspace and I expect that you won't enter mine again. Get back to the base. I'm sure there's some bright-eyed civilian waiting to be your next drunken conquest."

"I don't need to get a girl drunk to get her in bed, sweetheart. You should know that."

"No, she just needs to be drunk to marry you."

He froze for a moment and she wished she could take the words back. "Well, now that is true, but that's what happens when your life gets dragged through the mud and predatory insects spend all their time using you. Did that little boy know that you enjoy fucking for cash? I swear, Holland, if I'd known all you really wanted was a little profit, we could have worked something out. Hell, I'd have paid a lot to fuck your ass."

One minute she was listening to him and the next she was barreling down on him, her hand arcing through the air and connecting with his cheek. The sound flashed through the quiet room like a crack of thunder.

His eyes flared and he leaned in, looking ready to reach for her. Then suddenly, he shook it off. Disappointment wound through Holland, though she did get some small satisfaction from seeing her handprint on his face. It wouldn't be there long. In fact, it was already fading, but at least he'd feel it for a few moments.

How the hell had they gotten here? She'd loved this man with all her heart. She'd given everything to save him. And he'd called her a whore. It really was time to move on. She'd let him go to protect him. She realized now she'd always believed—and hoped—that one day he would stand in front of her again so they could start over because they were meant to be.

It hit her with the impact of a two-by-four to the chest there was no "meant to be" in life. Was she really still five fucking years old and waiting for her prince to come? Her daddy. Yeah. She was still waiting for her father to come home and treat her like a princess, to see everything her mother had sacrificed. The truth was her mother had died broken and alone and waiting. Not long after that, her father had remarried and shipped his daughter off to New Orleans so she wouldn't cause trouble with the new wife. So she could be forgotten.

Holland was suddenly so tired.

"Believe it or not I didn't come here to insult you," Dax said after a moment.

"It doesn't matter." It really didn't anymore. This man who stood in front of her now wasn't the same man she'd fallen in love with. Maybe that man hadn't existed in the first place. Maybe she'd merely made him up in her head. "If you're looking for someone in particular,

I suggest you speak with the receptionist. Everyone's in a meeting right now. They should be out in an hour or so."

She picked up her purse. Screw lunch. She would take the afternoon off. Everyone would know why when they saw who was here.

Holland frowned. In fact . . . why was he here if it wasn't to make her miserable? She supposed there could be any number of reasons and not one of them concerned her.

"Take care," she murmured, then started to go, but he reached out, grabbing her arm.

"Wait. I came to see you, but not about us. Obviously. Neither one of us wants to dredge up old wounds. I came here because there's been a break in my father's case and I expect you to do what you didn't do last time—your job. I guess you like to make your money the old-fashioned way—by selling out your lovers—but this time I need you to be a cop."

She stared at him for a moment, feeling her jaw drop. He was back here to look into his father's case? And he was still calling her a whore. Everything she'd done, she'd done to protect him, but he was too stupid to see it.

She was done playing his games. She was stepping out of the middle of this shit for good. If he wanted to risk himself and the people in his life, that was his call. She was done.

Holland twisted her arm away and tossed her purse down, then turned back to her computer. The case files were still there. She hadn't deleted or altered a thing. In fact, she'd spent the last three years quietly searching for the man who'd casually ruined her life. She'd been smart about it this time around since she'd known someone would be watching her. She'd kept up her life at NCIS and found ways to mine information on the deep web where no one could track her. That man on the phone had proven elusive, but she'd found him. Apparently his usefulness had come to an end six months before because they'd found a John Doe in New York City who matched her man's description. She'd recognized him from the photos in NYPD files, but no one knew his name, only that he'd had connections to the *Bratva*.

Without another word, she e-mailed the entire file to Dax. As soon as she got home, she would delete every shred of her investigation. She would burn the hard copy she had and start life over again. Without him. Without any expectation of him.

"There. I just sent you my whole file, including all my case notes and everything I've discovered in the last three years. Think before you look at some of those photos. They'll make you look at your father in a different light, but that's your call now. If you tell my superiors I sent you that file, you'll surely get me fired. I'm certain that will make your day. Don't ever call or contact me again, and I would absolutely get bodyguards on your loved ones if you really give a damn about them. Once the Russian mob knows that you're looking into this again, they'll come after your mother and sister."

The hard look left his eyes, and just for a second he looked like her Dax again. "What are you talking about? Holland, what do you mean you've been investigating for the last three years? And the Russian mob? That's the lead I have."

She inched away from him. She wasn't going to fall into the snare of that gorgeous male face or those chocolate eyes. She needed to get out of this building because she wasn't going to let anyone see her cry over this asshole ever again, least of all him. "Yes. They called me three years ago, just before we split up, and told me if I didn't drop the investigation and persuade you to do the same, they would kill you and your family. I made the decision to save you. It's all in there. You'll see the details when you read my files. Good-bye, Dax."

She turned and walked out, her head held high.

They were finally over, that chapter of her life closed for good. Somehow it wasn't the relief she'd thought it would be.

Dax stared after her. What the hell had just happened?

He was stuck, unable to move, unable to do anything but stare after her. Even when she walked out, he still stared.

He hadn't meant to say any of those things to her. He'd meant to be civil, polite. Cold, yes, because she wasn't a friend and apparently never had been. She'd been a bitch out for money and fame, like the rest of them, but he'd gotten past it. Despite what he'd said to Connor, he was over Holland Kirk.

Hell, he'd even tried to make his marriage to Courtney work. He'd woken up the day after with a hangover from hell and a marriage certificate and decided that if he couldn't have Holland, he'd do his best with Courtney.

She'd been sweet and she'd tried, too. More than he had. He'd been happy to ship off for six months and to ignore the leave he was offered. He'd chosen to re-up his commission and gone back to sea. When the divorce papers had shown up along with a note that she'd fallen for someone else, he'd written her a healthy check and wished her well.

Courtney had cheated on him and the last time he'd seen her, he'd given her a big hug and asked about her new husband. He'd felt absolutely no rage toward her.

The minute he got in the same room with Holland, he called her a whore.

His cheek still hurt and he'd deserved it.

What the hell did she know about the Russian mob? He pulled his phone out of his pocket and checked his e-mail. Sure enough, there was a massive file from Holland he'd received minutes before. Too big to open on his phone. He would have to wait.

Had she lied to protect him? Or was she lying again?

"Holy shit. Are you Spencer?"

He glanced up and there was a tall woman who looked like she could take him in a fight. She had platinum hair cut in a fashionable bob, but somehow it didn't soften her. "I'm Captain Spencer. I was here to meet with Special Agent Kirk."

The woman's lips curled up. "I gotta teach that girl how to fight. She should have punched you. Maybe she could have broken your jaw. An openhanded slap reminds me of all those bitchy housewives on TV, and that handprint shows. Real women punch. Or kick. You deserve a good kick to the gnads, Captain. We'll see how awesome you are when your testicles hit your abdominal cavity."

"You're very specific in your threats, Special Agent . . . ?" He needed a name to call her besides Ball Buster.

"Gemma White. I'm Holland's new partner. I say new, but we've been working together for almost two years now. That's new in law enforcement since our partnerships tend to be long-term. Unlike you Navy boys we don't change out crew every year. We know how to watch each other's backs. And how to take out the trash when we need to."

So she was a fan. "I didn't come here to cause trouble."

"Good, because I have zero intention of allowing you to. You want to explain why you're here?"

"My father's case."

She shook her head, sending him a glare that told him she thought he was a flaming idiot. "Your father's case was closed a long time ago. He was guilty. End of story."

It still got his back up. "He was not and I have some proof now."

"Care to show it to me?"

"I think I'll keep it to myself for now." He had zero idea who this woman was. Given all the danger he'd endured with Gabe and then Connor, he wasn't going to simply trust anyone around him because their badge said they were law enforcement.

Gabe, Connor, Roman, and Zack. They were the only ones he would trust with this information. Mad was dead because he'd stumbled into a sliver of it.

Had Holland been warned off? Had she known something about this conspiracy years before? Been threatened by it?

"You broke her heart."

"Yeah, well, she broke mine, too." Did it really matter if she'd been doing it to save him? It only proved that she didn't trust him. If she had, she would have divulged everything, given him the chance to decide with her.

He needed to read her documents, see the files for himself and make a decision. The last thing he should do was what his every instinct screamed at him—chase after Holland and get her under him. Make her beg for his forgiveness. And maybe, just maybe, he would fuck her until he got her out of his system.

If he even could.

"I couldn't have broken her heart too badly. She seems to have moved on, according to the Internet. If that police officer was proposing, they've probably been together for a while." Although he'd been ready to marry her a couple of weeks after they'd gotten together. Hell, he'd been thinking about it the first time he'd slept with her.

Shame twisted his gut when he remembered what he'd said to her, especially that Courtney had been better in bed. He couldn't even remember most of the sex he'd had with the woman he'd married. He could count on one hand the times he'd actually slept with her, and every time he'd been thinking of Holland.

He joked with his friends about picking up women, but the truth of the matter was he hadn't slept with anyone since his divorce. He couldn't. It wasn't fair to any woman since they would simply be a stand-in for the one he wanted. The one he loved. The one he fucking hated.

Holland. Holland was it for him and had been from the moment he'd met her.

"That?" Special Agent White said with a cocked brow. "That was her attempt at trying to find something normal again. I knew it wouldn't work. He was an asshole behind her back. You're the better kind. You're an asshole to her face or she wouldn't have smacked you. What are you really here for?"

"I told you." He wasn't going to lie. If anyone was watching and intended to off him for investigating his father's death, then bring them on. These people hid in the shadows and he so wanted to drag them into the light. They'd taken his friend, and now he was almost certain they'd taken his father and Zack's mother as well.

And Joy. Joy's name had been on that kill list. Now they knew that

Joy hadn't been the victim of a rogue shot intended for Zack. Her murder hadn't been an accident. No. She'd been the target all along.

So bring them all on. It was long past time to meet these fuckers who'd had a stranglehold on his life for years.

"If you're interested in a closed case, maybe you should contact our supervisor." Special Agent White's eyes narrowed as she looked at him. "I can go and get him for you."

There was no way he was sitting here and getting lectured for hours. And he wasn't about to out Holland to anyone, not even her partner. "I was just feeling her out. I've recently heard a few rumors that my father's aide left the service. I'd like to talk to him, but I can't find the man."

It was true. His father's aide, Peter Morgan, had left the Navy eighteen months before and then seemingly fallen off the face of the earth. Connor's main job at this point was to find the man who had turned his father in. Dax had a few questions for him.

"That's not our problem, Captain Spencer, as your father's case is not open. It's closed and the ruling on his death isn't going to change, so unless you have evidence you're willing to share, I would appreciate it if you would stay away from my partner."

"I'll see what I can do." He turned because further baiting Holland's partner wasn't going to advance his cause. He needed to regroup and figure out what the hell was going on. Nothing today had turned out as expected. He'd thought he'd walk in and see Holland again and realize he was truly over her. He would see that she wasn't as beautiful and vibrant as he'd remembered.

All he'd felt was a terrible urge to hold her and a massive wave of jealousy at the thought of some dickhead proposing to her. The same dickhead who'd likely been in her bed. He knew he was a hypocrite, but the idea of her sleeping with another man had made him mean as shit.

So mean he'd deserved that smack.

He hopped back on his bike and headed for home, determined to figure out what the hell was going on.

ELEVEN

D ax looked up from his computer and all the printed pages that had overtaken his father's desk.

"I thought you might like some tea." His mother set the teacup on a mostly uncluttered corner. It rattled slightly against the saucer, a sure sign that she was tired.

He glanced at the window. The afternoon had gotten away from him and now waves of orange light streamed in, the final vestige of the dying day.

He wasn't sure if this was one of the worst days of his life or the best.

"I was wrong about Holland."

His mother eased herself gingerly into the chair across from him as though she wasn't certain she really wanted to. It made Dax wonder exactly how much time she'd spent in this room since his father's death. He'd only camped in here because Gus had set up the printer at the back of the office so she had a place to work when she visited home. Somehow the pictures of Gus and her friends that now dotted the desk alongside their father's old pictures made the place seem cheerier, as though the living were taking back the space in a slow and inevitable march of time.

His gaze caught an image on the far side of the desk. Three lovely women stood arm in arm, all smiles. Joy Hayes stood in the middle, beaming in her lovely white wedding dress as she clutched her closest friends, Gus and Holland.

Now that he'd looked at all the evidence she'd accumulated and thought about what she'd said, he realized that Holland had given up everything for him. He'd selfishly thought only about their relationship and how much losing her had hurt, but Holland had been woven into the thread of his family for years. She had so little of her own that she'd become a sister to Gus, an extra daughter to his mother.

And when he'd left in a tantrum and taken Courtney, Holland had been alone.

"What's this about Holland? I thought that relationship was over." Her mouth firmed as though even saying Holland's name had been difficult for her. "Son, I understand that male affection often comes from sexual impulses, but I really think you need to remember what that woman did to us. Almost did to us. If Zachary hadn't intervened, well, we would have been ruined all over again. I know your sister thinks we should give Holland the benefit of the doubt, but I can't see much doubt in what Roman said."

He found it interesting that his sister was still championing Holland. God, she was going to kick his ass when he inevitably had to tell her she'd been right all along. "Roman didn't know everything. Roman had no idea that Holland had been threatened by a member of the *Bratva*."

"The brat what?"

He was going to have to explain this to her. "*Bratva*. It's Russian for *brotherhood*. It's their mafia. Apparently Dad got in their way somehow. But this isn't all about Dad. It's bigger than Dad. That's the only reason I would bring it back up. This is affecting all of us and it won't stop because I don't look into it. I'm going to need you to be very careful for a while. I'm hiring security for the house and a bodyguard for you."

His mother waved her hand. "Bah, I don't need that."

"You do and you will take it. Otherwise I'll ship you off to D.C. to spend time with Gus."

She shook her head. "I'm not an old woman. Well, I am, but I don't appreciate being treated like one, Daxton. If your father got in someone's way, I want to help find out who."

She might be helpful. She might remember things he hadn't been here to witness. He needed to look into his father's past, and no one knew that the way his mother did. "If I let you help, you have to agree to the bodyguard."

A single shoulder shrugged up in weary acceptance. "Fine, but Gus gets to pick him. I want one of those D.C. boys. I like their accents and they have the best stories."

Awesome. His mom wanted a boy toy to watch over her. "I'll get her on it immediately. I'll have someone here before I go out tonight, and I expect you to call me if you see anything odd or even if you don't feel safe."

She stood and strode to his father's closet, opening it easily and coming back with a nicely kept shotgun. "Gus has one of those handgun things, but I'm really better with this."

He stared at her, his eyes wide at the sight of his genteel mother with a full-blown double-barrel in her hands. "I think you should leave that to the bodyguard."

She shook her head. "Just make sure he knows I can use this. I wasn't always a debutante, Dax. You know that prissy Clementine Gray-Jones is supposed to call on me tomorrow. I'll bet I can get her to piss herself if I take careful aim." She smiled. "This is going to be fun, son. Let me know how else I can help. I do believe I'm going to arm the maid. Rosalie's good with knives but she's an excellent shot with a sniper rifle. Have Gus send us pictures of the proposed bodyguards. Rosalie and I will pick a handsome one. Let me know if you're staying for supper."

What the hell had he done? Next she would be telling him the gardener was laying landmines in the front lawn.

His cell phone rang and he answered, knowing exactly who was calling. He'd sent all the information to Connor hours before. He couldn't imagine his best friend hadn't already plowed through it. "Hey, buddy."

"You fucked up."

Didn't he know it? "You can confirm what she's got?"

He wasn't sure which way he wanted this to go. Well, he was, but the tiniest part of him wanted to believe he wouldn't be such an idiot as to have left her here all alone after she'd sacrificed everything.

"I can verify most of it. I've also got an ID on the body she tracked down to New York. I'll send you his file, but he was a well-known *Bratva* lawyer. His death was covered up by the FBI because he'd been trying to inform on his bosses at the time. The feds can't let it out that they know who he is or the agents they have undercover could be at risk. Your girl was on the right track. She simply didn't have the clearance to know it."

"So all these years, she thought she was protecting me?"

There was a slight pause on the other end of the line. "No, Dax. All these years she *was* protecting you."

He shook his head. "I can protect myself, Connor. If she'd told me, I could have brought you into it. I could have brought everyone into it. God, have you even thought about it? Have you thought about what we might have been able to prevent?"

That possibility had been like a lodestone dragging him down.

"Maybe if we'd known, Mad would still be alive," Connor said gravelly. "Yeah, I've thought of it, but I've thought of other things, too. We had zero idea there was any kind of conspiracy at that point. If I'd looked at the same evidence Holland had, I would have made the same call. I wasn't in the country at the time, Dax. I was out of touch for six months. I can't tell you what I was working on, but it was important. Zack was struggling to get his administration going. Mad and Gabe, for all their smarts, aren't investigators or security specialists. If I'd seen those photos, I would have tried to sway you away from investigating further, too."

"I don't believe them." They'd made him sick, but he still didn't believe. "Yeah, they look incriminating at first glance. But his eyes aren't open in any image. I think he's drugged."

"Maybe. I've got Lara trying to reach a friend of hers. I'd like to get hold of the original photos and let him take a look. Also, I'd like to look at that videotape again. Not me, really. That's not my specialty, but Freddy's a genius when it comes to exposing a cover-up."

Dax groaned. Freddy. Dear god. The last time he'd tangled with that freak, he'd nearly had his head taken off by a swinging axe. Freddy might be brilliant at debunking or proving conspiracy theories, but he was also pretty inventive with home security. "I thought he went underground preparing for the apocalypse or something."

Freddy had taken off when he'd figured out Connor was CIA. Lara's friend did not like government agents. Of course, he'd also been the one to figure out that Joy Hayes's murder hadn't been an accident. They all owed the man.

"According to my wife, he's got several hidey-holes, as he likes to call them, and Lara has a way to reach him," Connor explained. "She takes out an ad in some weird newspaper asking for parts for her SETI machine. Apparently, the search for extraterrestrial life is code for *call me.*"

Dax snorted. "ET phone home."

Sometimes he loved Connor's new geek wife.

"That's horrible, but yeah, it fits. We'll try to bring him in and get him to take a look at the material. Until then, Gus has a new bodyguard and we're sending two out your way. I would prefer you use one of them."

He wasn't keen on that idea. "What the fuck do I do about Holland? How do I ever make this up to her?"

"You don't. You try to find someone new. Look, she won't expect you to make it up to her. She knew what she was sacrificing and she did it to protect you. In her head it's over and there's no going back. Are you angry with her for lying to you? Do you blame her for Mad's death? Because that, my friend, is not logical. I can't imagine you wouldn't do the exact same thing she did. You're pissed because you're the man and you don't need protection. Well, get your panties out of a wad. She's a law enforcement agent and you captain a boat. If she needs to be protected from missiles or submarines, you're the go-to guy. She knows more about this than you do. If she made this call it was because she loved you enough to give up everything to protect you."

It burned through him. "I'm not mad. And you're right. If she'd told us back then, we wouldn't have understood even the small piece of the puzzle we do now. I can't look back."

"She won't be mad because you bought what she sold you. She wanted you to. Mission accomplished." He paused. "Courtney is another thing altogether."

How the hell did he make her understand why he'd done what he had? He couldn't justify it in his own head. She'd been sacrificing and he'd done her best friend. And then bragged about it earlier today. "She'll never forgive me."

"Probably not. Look, she thinks she's done with this mess, but we both know otherwise."

He'd made her a target just by walking through her door. "I'll come back to D.C and hire a private investigator, do things as quietly as I can. If I don't see Holland again, maybe the *Bratva* won't come after her. You said the original man who made the threats is dead, right?"

"Yes, but they would have hired someone new immediately. They don't let things like this get pushed aside or forgotten. I would assume the minute Mad started looking into the diary they assigned someone to watch all of us. And if what happened three years ago has anything to do with what's happening now, they'll come after Holland."

What had he done? Had he really put her in danger all over again? "But she's not connected to us any longer."

"So what? She knows something." He scoffed. "More than any of us, really. She'll be an asset to us, so a target to them. I'm going to ship this intelligence to Roman and Zack. I'll call in a bodyguard for Holland."

"She won't accept it." Dax's stomach turned, knowing a lifelong criminal was likely already watching her. "She'll tell us all to go to hell and go about her normal life."

And then someone would kill her.

"So what do you suggest?"

Dax sighed. "I suggest I get used to begging, Connor. Because I can't let her go. She's mine. She's always been mine. I shouldn't have left her back then. I should have stayed and fought it out with her. I won't make the same mistake."

Connor whistled. "Just remember this is a woman who knows her way around firearms."

"Yeah, there's a lot of that going around these days." How was he even going to get Holland to trust him again, much less protect her? She'd rather shoot him. Unless . . . "Hey, can you get Zack on the line for me? I need him to do me a small favor."

Holland sniffled and wished she'd thought of stopping for a bottle of wine. Or whiskey. Maybe that would be better. Which one went with mourning and ice cream? Unfortunately, she didn't know of a website that gave recommendations on the best way to drown one's sorrows when the one who got away returned to town.

Dax wasn't a fish. Nope. He was a nasty shark and he'd taken a chunk out of her hide. She'd let him off the hook, and if she was smart, she'd keep it that way.

Why couldn't she get him out of her head? Why did she now feel like shit that she'd given him that damn file of information? She also hadn't deleted her copy. Oh, no. She was sitting at her kitchen table studying it. She'd been ready to hit the delete key. For some reason, she simply couldn't.

This information was her last tie to him. Well, to the him he used to be. She had to view it that way. That Dax Spencer was gone. Maybe he'd always been an illusion since he'd turned on her the minute he could.

She slammed the stupid laptop lid shut because now she was lying to herself. He hadn't. He'd seen that money trail and he'd believed her. If she'd given him a hint that she hadn't been guilty, he would have trusted her word over all the proof in the world. She couldn't fault him for that.

But then he'd gone right out and married her best friend. He'd had a ring for her, his grandmother's. He'd been planning that trip for them and he'd replaced her as if she'd meant nothing, as if she were interchangeable.

Now Courtney was married again, from what she'd heard. She was also pregnant and happy. Dax had bought her a house to celebrate their divorce. She'd cheated on him while he'd been away at war and Dax had all but rewarded her.

He hadn't even called tonight. Somehow she'd thought he would call. She'd expected it all afternoon. She'd sat and watched the phone, waiting for the moment when he realized he'd been terribly wrong about her.

But nothing.

He'd grown cold. Had she done that to him? Or had other forces combined to change him? Had losing Mad been the thing to push him over the edge from happy boy to bitter man?

He hadn't seen her at Crawford's funeral. She'd slipped into New York and attended with the thousand or so mourners because Mad had meant something to her, too. Even if all the Perfect Gentlemen hated her now, at one point, she'd been friends with them.

It was hard to believe that Mad was dead and Gabe Bond was getting married. Zack had settled well into his presidency, while Roman still ate their opponents for breakfast. And Connor . . . his activities were probably top secret. But they'd all moved on while she was stuck here.

Those tears she'd been so good about not shedding now rolled from her eyes, making the world a watery mess and scalding her cheeks. So much time wasted. All gone and all for nothing. Dax was back on the case. She should have known she couldn't derail him forever. She'd merely bought him a few more years.

Damn it, she'd cut her heart out and forfeited her future so he could have a good life.

A loud knock on her door jerked Holland from her thoughts. She swiped at her tears and glanced at the clock. Seven thirty. It seemed later. She had to wonder which of her coworkers had come by to check on her. She'd gotten a call from Gemma earlier. It looked as if everyone knew Dax was back in town. The receptionist hadn't been able to keep it under wraps. The minute they'd gotten out of their meeting, she'd told everyone she could about Captain Awesome's return, followed quickly by Holland hightailing it out the door.

She thought seriously about not answering the knock, but if she didn't it was entirely possible that Gemma would simply break in. Her partner wasn't good at letting things slide.

Holland opened the door and then wished she'd cleaned up.

Dax stood there with a bottle of wine in one hand and a pizza in the other. What looked to be a bouquet of flowers was clutched under his right arm. Lilies. His face softened as he looked at her. "Hey."

She slammed the door and locked it. Damn him. He'd caught her crying. At the office, she'd managed to keep her dignity and leave before he'd seen her tears. Now he'd messed it all up.

He knocked again, the sound softer this time. She stared at the door like it was a snake ready to bite her. She hated this feeling. She wasn't a teenage girl, but she was crying like one.

"Holland, sweetheart? I'm going to leave the flowers and the wine and pizza here, all right? I'm going to go, but I wanted you to know how sorry I am for what happened. I know you can't forgive me, but I just wanted . . ." He sighed. "Damn it, I wanted to give you something even if it's nothing more than dinner and flowers."

He sounded like the old Dax. Kinder. His voice again held that hint of Southern accent no amount of prep school had been able to completely destroy. It was the way he'd talked to her when he'd loved her.

Said he'd loved her. No man who loved a woman could possibly marry her best friend the very next day.

She wasn't going to engage him. She would ignore him and move on with her life.

His boots thudded as he went down the stairs. She felt like an idiot, but she stared through the peephole and watched as he retreated, the door that led out to the street opening and closing.

She had to change the code on that door. She hadn't thought to before since Dax had been gone. Besides him, only Gemma and a few coworkers had the digits that would get them up the stairs to her front door. Over the years she'd had some coworkers get her mail and water her plants while she was away. The security company forced her to change her door code once a year, but no one cared that she was lazy with the building code.

Well, that changed tomorrow. She would make sure no one could get in. And then what? She would never leave the city again? Or get rid of the plants? Maybe. It wasn't like they loved her back.

But she couldn't exactly leave the stuff Dax had brought with him out there. It wasn't sanitary.

She opened the door and quickly gathered his blood offering, her stomach rumbling and reminding her she'd had nothing to eat since a very dry piece of toast and some eggs this morning. The pizza smelled heavenly, but the wine was what she really wanted.

She locked the door and tried to put a good face on the situation. He was gone and she wouldn't have to see him again. It was over.

He would go back to wherever he'd come from with his new data. It didn't matter if he understood what she'd done now. It was over.

And somewhere down the line she'd find out he'd been murdered by the Russian mob.

The idea made her stomach turn. She slammed the pizza down and thought seriously about tossing the flowers, but they hadn't done anything wrong to her. Neither had the pizza. Or the wine. Definitely not the wine. It would be wrong to waste it. All right. Being honest, she needed a damn drink.

Why had he come back to New Orleans? Why couldn't he leave well enough alone? Nothing he uncovered would bring his father back.

She found the corkscrew and had just uncorked the wine when the door to the balcony came open. She went for her gun but stopped short when she realized who stood there.

Dax ran a hand over his slightly shaggy hair. He'd let the military cut grow out an inch or two, and it just made him all the sexier. "Sorry. I think I broke the lock on your balcony door, but then you really need to upgrade your security system. I think you need an entire new rig and I want to rethink these windows. They're pretty but anyone from the other side of the street can see in."

Her stomach knotted. "What the hell are you doing here? You said you'd go away."

He shook his head. "No, I said I would leave. I left the front door and climbed up your balcony trellis, but only after I got the voodoo shop owner to promise she wouldn't call the police. Or stick pins into a little doll of me. Luckily, she's a romantic."

She was going to have a long talk with her downstairs neighbor in the morning. And she might look into a little voodoo herself. "You can leave the same way you came in."

"I understand that you're angry with me, Holland. You have every right to be, but we have to talk, so pour me a glass of that wine. Let's sit and be rational. I haven't been rational in three years, so it should be an interesting new experience for me."

She hated how calm he sounded when everything inside her felt so chaotic. "We don't have anything to talk about. I gave you the information you requested. I'm no longer involved. And you gave me the wine. I'm not giving it back."

His lips curled up a little, reminding her of how sexy he could be when he smiled. "You won't even share a tiny bit with me?"

"No."

He reached into the messenger bag that crossed his chest and came out with a small bottle. "Good thing I brought the whiskey. I remember how greedy you can be with the wine. You should remember, though, that if you don't feed me, I get a little testy. So let's pop that pizza open and see if I can brush the mushrooms off my half."

He hated mushrooms, but she loved them, so he always ordered them and then he would carefully pull his off and double them up on her slices. It was a silly, but at the time it made her feel cared for.

Chad didn't eat pizza. No carbs of any kind after noon. So when she ate pasta for dinner, he shook his head as though he could see her fattening up right in front of him.

Dax pulled his bag over his head and set it down. "If you're still hungry afterward, I'll run out and find us some bread pudding. Lots of caramel, the way you like it."

The deep timbre of his voice went straight to her girl parts, bringing them flaring back to life. She might have hardened her soul against this man, but all her reproductive organs were traitors willing to lay down arms the minute the hot guy with the really talented penis walked in the room again. She wasn't falling for it. "Why don't you go get some now?"

"So you can find a way to lock me out?"

"Yes." She had zero reason to lie to him.

He sobered, his smile fading. "Thank you for trying to protect me. I should have followed my first instinct. I knew you weren't capable of that kind of betrayal. Even after I'd gone, I kept thinking that you'd always been the kind of woman to refuse me to my face, not stab me in the back. You're a very good actress, Holland. But then the stakes were pretty high for you. You were protecting the man you loved."

Her stomach rolled and she knew she wouldn't be touching that pizza. "That's enough, Dax."

She turned away, but she could feel him moving behind her.

"I don't think so. You sacrificed yourself to save me and I acted like a complete idiot. Holland, after you convinced me you had sold out my family, I went crazy."

She wasn't listening to this. She turned on him. "I don't care. What happened between you and Courtney is your business. She was your wife. You made the decision to marry her."

"Bourbon with a tequila chaser kind of made the decision for me, but I was the one who drowned in booze. Please, sweetheart. Let me explain what happened, how I felt."

He'd felt horny and his plans for the weekend had disappeared. She knew the story. Captain Awesome didn't go without for long. "No. Leave now or I'll call the police and have them remove you."

His disappointment tugged at her. "I understand why you feel that way, but there's more at stake than simply the two of us. Mad's death had something to do with my father's."

She stopped, his words hitting her like a bucket of ice water. "What do you mean? I thought it was ruled an accident."

"We're keeping the truth quiet for now, but we have conclusive proof that Mad was killed because he got involved in some sort of plot by the *Bratva* that goes back years. He was searching for a woman named Natalia Kuilikov. She was Zack's nanny in Moscow when he was a young boy. She wrote a diary that people have died and killed for. Her writings aren't specific but we know the group that sent her to work for the Hayes family had big plans of some kind. She immigrated to the U.S. later and disappeared. Connor and his new wife tracked her down a few weeks ago. As they were talking to her, she was murdered in front of them."

That rattled Holland. Another murder? The string of them was getting long. "Wow."

Dax nodded. "It gets worse. They managed to find what Natalia had been trying to hide. A list of people targeted for assassination by the *Bratva*."

She shivered but took a step back as she really thought about everything he was saying to her. "No. It can't be connected. You read my report. What happened with your father was a blackmail scheme gone wrong."

"That's how it was made to look so there would be a simple, clean explanation for his death. But my father knew something that could stop whatever the group is planning. I don't know what that was yet. I'm still digging. But all roads in this case lead to Zack." His voice softened. "My father's name was on that dead pool, Holland. So was Joy's. Her death wasn't an accident. We believe it was meant to move the polls in Zack's favor, to ensure that he won the presidency."

She had to hold on to the bar or she would have fallen. "No. I was sure. I was stopping this thing in its tracks, Dax. I was doing something good."

"Yes, I know." He moved in as though ready to catch her. "You thought you were saving me and my mother and Gus. You thought you were doing the right thing. I'm humbled by everything you did for us."

But she couldn't escape. She'd kept quiet. She'd kept the secret she'd been given. To no avail. It had all been a setup. And she'd been stupid enough to believe it. Unfortunately, she hadn't been the only one to pay the price. "Mad's dead because of me."

Instantly, Dax shook his head and wound his arms around her. Suddenly she didn't have the will to fight him.

"It wasn't your fault, sweetheart. I've been through this endlessly. Connor and I talked. Even if you had told me everything at the time, there's no way we would have figured out the scope of this plot. We still don't understand it completely. At the time, I would have come to the same conclusion you did. I could have decided to protect my mom and sister and given it up."

No. She knew Dax. He would have found another way. "I was so stupid."

He tucked her close to his body, and Holland closed her eyes, not wanting to think about how good it felt to be in his arms. But she couldn't ignore the profoundly right feeling.

"No," he assured. "You didn't have all the facts. I looked at those photos today. They made me sick. If I didn't know there was a massive conspiracy involved, I would likely see what they want me to see. They wanted you to believe my father didn't deserve justice, that a monster had died and should be forgotten, because that's how these conspirators stay in the shadows."

"I'm a fucking cop, Dax."

"Yes, and you've seen enough to know that most men in this situation are guilty as sin. You made the call to protect the innocent. I don't put the blame on you, sweetheart. None of us does. We do need your help, though. This is growing and getting bigger every day."

She wasn't sure she would ever forgive herself, but she sank into his embrace and reveled in being this close to him again. So perfect and right. It was like she'd been in the cold shadows for so long and was finally seeing sunlight again, illuminating her path home.

His kindness and coaxing were an illusion like everything else. He needed her for now. Maybe he was even thinking that since she wasn't guilty, she would make a good sexual companion. Dax didn't go for long without getting some. If he was going to be in New Orleans, he would want someone in his bed. They'd been good together. She would do.

And that's bad, why?

Holland slammed the lid on that line of thinking. He'd seen her cry enough. He wasn't going to see her beg.

She forced herself to step out of the comfort of his arms. "I'm so sorry about Maddox. No matter what you say, I'll always blame myself. But I'm off this case now. I'm not involved and that's for the best. I wish you all the luck in the world, Dax, but I'm not going to work with you on this. It's best if we go our separate ways."

His jaw hardened and for a moment she thought he was going to grab her and haul her into his arms again. He took a careful step back. "I'm afraid that's not an option, Special Agent Kirk. You've got a new assignment. You'll be working with a Naval officer on a special case."

She shook her head. "No. I've received no notification of that. That lie won't work, Dax."

Her cell phone started to vibrate on the bar, the sound jarring.

Dax strolled into her kitchen, helping himself to a glass and pouring a couple of fingers of whiskey. "You should get that. It's important and he doesn't like to be kept waiting."

She looked down at the number. UNKNOWN.

With trembling fingers, she pressed the button to answer the phone. What had Dax done to her now? "This is Special Agent Kirk."

"Please hold for the president of the United States," a competent female voice said.

Shit.

Dax gave her a grin and poured her a glass of wine. "You're going to need this."

Yes. Yes, she was.

TWELVE

Sometimes having the president of the United States on his side was a definite advantage.

Dax watched as Holland brought out a set of sheets and what looked to be her lumpiest pillow. The blanket she'd brought him was superthin and she seemed to have turned the air conditioner to an arctic setting.

She dumped it all on the couch, then turned to him, her glance challenging him to say a word. Yes, that was one pissed-off female.

Since the moment Zack had explained that she was now on special assignment and under the charge of Captain Dax Spencer, Holland had frozen up. She'd downed a glass of wine, but then corked the bottle, claiming she didn't drink on the job.

When he'd explained they didn't have to be on the clock tonight, she'd pointed to the door. Dax had promptly gone back on the clock. Luckily for him, he didn't have her very prim views about imbibing while working, because he'd definitely needed that whiskey.

She'd fought like hell, even calling her supervisor, who explained that yes, indeed, the president could in fact do this to her and the only way to refuse the assignment was to quit NCIS.

He had her backed in a corner and she was furious about it.

He'd rather go back to that moment when she'd held on to him like he was a life raft. For just a moment, he felt as if they had reconnected. And Dax had recalled all over again what he'd truly missed during this dark period. It hadn't been support, because he'd always had that from his friends and family.

He'd missed *her*. So very badly.

All the anger he'd carried like a weight on his chest was gone. She'd truly believed she had done the right thing. He would likely have made the same choice in her shoes. She was a warrior, his woman. She didn't back down from a fight and she protected the people she loved.

She'd loved him. She'd sacrificed for him. Could she ever forgive him?

One thing he knew for sure, she wasn't ready to forgive him tonight.

He also wasn't giving her any reason to kick him out. He was exactly where he needed to be. "Why yes, Holland, I'll make up the couch myself. I know just how I like it."

Her eyes narrowed. "There is zero reason for you to sleep here tonight."

He bit back a groan because they'd already been over this a few times. "There's every reason and you know it. They'll have had someone watching you. Even after all this time, the Russian mob knows what you're doing. They'll know you saw me today. Hell, they may even know I'm here now. There's no reason to believe they won't come after you again."

"That's where your logic sucks, Spencer. They didn't come after me in the first place. They came after you. You're endangering me by being here. Don't you have a megamansion in the Garden District to go home to?" She gasped. "Your mother. Dax, your mother is there all alone."

Before she could start for the door, he stood. "No, my mother is being protected by two bodyguards, and I'm fairly certain one of them moonlights as a male model. She and the housekeeper are also taking turns in sniper positions around the house. God save me from Southern women."

Holland calmed a bit. "Good. Gus is being protected at the White House?"

"Yes, she's got Secret Service and security around her pretty much twenty-four seven. I'm not worried about Gus." Roman had promised he would watch over her. He'd also had to promise that their mother would mind the guards or Gus would have been on the first plane back, cracking open the gun case alongside their momma.

"But you haven't explained why you think I'm a target and in need of protection," she replied. "Like I said, they were after you and the people you love."

"Oh, that's an easy one, but you're not at all ready to hear the answer, sweetheart." He'd never loved anyone the way he loved Holland. The deep, sure feeling had flooded back the minute he had realized she'd lied to him three years ago. Even when he'd been at his most angry and disillusioned, his devotion had never really gone away. He'd just done his stubborn best to banish it.

She shook her head, her mouth a flat line. "Don't even say it. I told you. I'll talk about the case. I'll talk about what's going on with your friends. Hell, I'll talk about the weather if you want me to, boss. But the minute you try to make this personal, I'll complain to anyone who will listen to me. The White House doesn't want a sexual harassment complaint."

He sighed. Naturally she would go there. "Yeah, you're definitely not ready. But the answer to your question is easy. If the *Bratva* thinks for a second that you're helping me, they'll eliminate you. Especially if they think you're vulnerable."

She brushed back her blond hair. "I've been vulnerable for years, Dax. They haven't come after me yet. They've had three years to take care of me. They could have arranged for a convenient accident. I'm a single woman who lives alone."

"But you haven't been single. You've been dating that cop, right? What's his name? Charles? Chazz?"

She rolled her eyes. "Yes, his name is Chazz. A very traditional New Orleans name."

So he wasn't going to fool her. "Fine. Chad. I know his name. I've memorized a whole lot of things about that asshole."

"Why would you know anything about him?"

Confession time . . . "Because I've watched you ever since I woke up in a Vegas hotel room and realized I'd made the biggest mistake of my life. I've kept up with your social media."

She huffed, sounding shocked. "I unfriended your ass."

"Yeah, well, I might or might not have made up another identity." It wasn't something he was proud of.

"Stalker." She crossed her arms over her chest.

"Yeah, I thought you would view it that way, but I needed to know you were all right." He wasn't telling her the whole truth. In the beginning, he'd wanted to see if she was as miserable as he'd been. He'd been desperate to know that he wasn't alone in his agony. "I didn't talk to you or anything, just sent you a friend request as a second cousin on your mother's side."

She looked at him like he'd lost his damn mind. "You're Sissie Mae who raises labradoodles? You send out an awful lot of cat videos, too."

Damn his friends. "Yeah, Mad set that sucker up. I was back on my boat and it was easier for him to do it. I asked him to make me a male cousin. Someone with a job. Naturally, I become Sissie Mae, lover of all animals and reader of cat mysteries. Did you know there's such a thing as cat mysteries? It's apparently a whole genre. I haven't figured out if the cat solves the mystery or is the mystery. Mad had a weird sense of humor."

"Unbelievable," she breathed. "You know I could accuse you of stalking me and ruin your career."

She could, but he knew her. She wouldn't. "Like I said. I never contacted you personally after the initial friend request. I just wanted to see what you were up to."

"Or you wanted to monitor me to make sure I didn't come after your family again."

How long would it be before she stopped putting the worst spin on his every move? "Maybe in the beginning, but you made me believe that. You painted yourself as someone who would ruin everyone I cared about. You can't blame me for that. I even argued with you. I told you I thought you were innocent."

For a moment she looked as if she might snap out a rebuttal, but she heaved a long sigh. "I know I did. You're right. I can't blame you for that. But I need you to keep some distance from me now, Spencer. I admit that I want to catch these guys, too. I want to see how deep the rabbit hole goes, but I don't think it's a good idea for me to be around you."

All he wanted was a chance. "We start over again."

"I can't do it," she said, her voice small.

He wanted to haul her close but maintained his distance. "Holland, at one point in time we were friends. Pretty good friends. And you trusted me. Can we forget about what happened this afternoon? I was bitter and angry and I lashed out at the one person I should never hurt. Let's try again. Hey, Holland. How have you been?"

She laughed, though he couldn't call it a happy sound. "That is never going to work, but you're not going to give up, are you?"

It was so funny that he'd come to New Orleans thinking that he could get back at her. Now he only wanted to get her back. "I can't. It's too important. But if it makes you feel better, I'll concentrate on the case. I'll sleep out here on the couch like a good boy, but I'm not leaving you alone. Tomorrow, we sit down and figure out where to go from here. I'll give you access to everything I've learned and you now have clearance that would make your boss's head spin."

That finally got her to smile. "Okay, that does sound kind of fun, but no funny business, Spencer."

He held his hands up in a likely useless gesture of innocence. "Promise. It's nothing but business from here on out. I will warn you, though, that at some point we're probably going to have to meet up with a . . . what should I call Freddy? A conspiracy enthusiast? A doomsday prepper? Mostly he's a complete lunatic who thinks nothing of nearly deballing a simple intruder, but apparently he's really handy at uncovering whether a piece of film is authentic or faked. Connor wants him to take a look at the video from the motel and the pictures in your uncle's file. And speaking of your uncle . . ."

Dax didn't want to get into this with her, but he didn't see a way to avoid it.

She shook her head. "He wasn't the only one with access to the file. Most of it can be found in the police records. He kept the photos out of the press. He didn't have to use them since there wasn't going to be a prosecution."

"Was he the only one who knew about them?"

"Not at all. He wasn't even the one who originally discovered the photos. Sue Carlyle brought them in. She was the one who figured out there was a camera on her daughter's purse. She simply didn't know how to get them off the drive. The pictures themselves were wirelessly pulled from the small camera that was really a microcomputer. Once Sue realized what it was, she thought the police would give her money for the camera. She was deeply disappointed, to say the least."

He was still interested in her uncle. Someone had tipped off the Russians that she'd obtained the file and seen the images. "Where did you go after you visited your uncle that day?"

She frowned. "You think someone in my uncle's office could have known? You're looking for a mole."

"Yes. Someone tipped off your dead *Bratva* lawyer."

She was quiet for a moment, seeming to think. "He didn't have to know I had the photos. All he had to do was plant them with the press or put the idea out there."

"No, he actually gave a reporter the photos and they appeared to have come from you. We've tracked down this lead." He briefly went over what Roman and Connor had discovered. "The reporter received information about the photos from an e-mail account set up in your name. It originated from a computer at a public library in New Orleans. As soon as the photos-for-cash deal was sealed, the account was shut down. Same with the book deal. The publishing house received a proposal for a tell-all book about the scandal and my family from that same e-mail account. They made sure all roads led back to you. But what I find interesting is that you actually had the photos they said you did."

He didn't believe in coincidences anymore. She'd had the photos, and someone had known it.

"All right. I'll ask my uncle if he told anyone," she conceded. "Obviously everyone saw me go in that day. After I went back to my office, I studied the file at my desk."

"Did you leave it there for any reason?"

She nodded. "I got upset. I went to the bathroom for a few minutes to calm down because I saw those pictures. It was on my desk, but you can't think one of my coworkers is a plant for the Russian mob."

He didn't like to think about what she'd gone through that day. "Not a plant, but the government pays crap. An unscrupulous someone could have made a little money on the side. I'll have Connor scope that out."

Her cheeks flushed, her shoulders straightening. Her mouth flattened into a stubborn line. She was ready to do battle. "Don't mess with my coworkers."

The time had come for Dax to explain just how the situation had changed, because apparently she hadn't internalized it yet. "Special Agent, they are no longer your coworkers. For the rest of this assignment you work for the White House and the White House alone. This is no longer about someone coming after my family. Someone is coming after my president. I took an oath a long time ago to defend this country from all invaders foreign and domestic, and if that includes one of your former coworkers, then you better believe I will take them down with extreme prejudice. If your loyalty is deeper to the people you once shared an office with than to your country, then let me know because you're not the woman I thought you were."

Her jaw tightened and she held up her hands in obvious capitulation. "All right. Check into their backgrounds. Please do it quietly. I have to work there after you're gone. Those people are the only friends I have left. And if you're also going to look into the NOLA PD, dear god, don't let anyone know. They get touchy."

He would look into her uncle, but he was also interested in her boyfriend. Detective Chad Michaels was her uncle's right-hand man, looking to move up in the ranks from what Dax had heard. It was shockingly easy to find information on the man, but something about his astringently clean record made Dax suspicious.

Everyone was a little dirty. Not criminally so, but there wasn't a person he knew who didn't have some breath of scandal in their past . . . except Detective Chad.

"I'll be very discreet."

"Sure you will." She crossed her arms over her chest. "Don't think because you've put me in a corner professionally that you can get anything personal out of this, Spencer."

What he wouldn't give to hear her call him Dax again. "I wouldn't dream of it, Holland."

"All right. In the morning, we need to come up with a plan of action. I think we should go back out to the prison, but this time we don't call ahead. I don't think we should give anyone time to plan for our visit. Do you have all the video we need? It should be easy enough to get. I can requisition the original if you like."

He shook his head. "I've got everything we need."

She was still for a moment. "You really think they're after Zack."

He nodded. "I can feel it in my gut. This is bigger than we ever dreamed and we've already lost so much. Zack's mom. My dad. Joy. Mad. We can't let them take anyone else in our family."

"What does the Russian mob want from him?"

That was the billion-dollar question. "It could be anything, but I suspect this all revolves around money and power. Nefarious shit usually does. We're wondering if Zack's father made some deal with the

Bratva when he was stationed in Moscow and they're now coming to collect. Roman is making a list of all the major contracts coming up, but Zack doesn't approve those."

Holland frowned. "Why would they have waited so long to make their move?"

Again, he had no idea. "It's possible Frank Hayes promised the Russians something when Zack became president, so they've bided their time. But the old man has dementia now, so if they're waiting for him to strong-arm Zack into something, they're doomed to disappointment. He mostly shuffles around the residence and hums a lot. Sometimes he thinks it's the sixties again. Zack tried finding a memory care facility for him, but he got so violent the press reported on it. He's calm when he knows Zack's close by. Hopefully, if we figure out why they killed my father, we'll figure out what they want and we'll stop them. My father must have known something. That's why they silenced him. I need to find his old aide-de-camp, Peter Morgan. He's the key."

"And naturally he's off the grid and his whereabouts are unknown."

"We'll find him. His family was from New Orleans. I'll stay up for a bit and do a little research. You should get some sleep," Dax murmured, wishing he could take her in his arms.

It had been a rough day for her. When she'd opened the door earlier, the sight of her tears had kicked him in the gut. Holland was always strong, and the idea that seeing him again had undone her, even temporarily, made him feel about two feet tall.

"Fine." She turned and started to walk away. When she reached the hall to her bedroom, she stopped, her spine ramrod straight, head held high. She didn't face him. "Did you ever love her?"

His heart clenched for a second. Easiest answer he'd given her all day. "No."

"That makes it worse, Dax." She walked away and closed the door quietly.

His heart sank. He'd lashed out and made that stupid-ass mistake when he'd been angry and in pain. It had affected them deeply, but then they'd both screwed up. She should have trusted him with the truth. She had to have known he'd never put his mother and sister in danger. That he'd move heaven and earth to keep Holland safe.

Still, someone had to give in, and his mistake had been far worse. He'd make the first gesture. Maybe he could finally win her once and for all. This was his first night back in her life and he was already sleeping on her couch. He remembered where that had led the last time.

And she'd called him Dax.

He sat down in front of his computer and started his search, more hopeful than he'd been in years.

Holland pressed the button on the coffeemaker and sighed as she looked around her kitchen. Her houseguest was far too used to a maid apparently. Or having a whole boat of underlings eager to curry favor and clean up after the boss. She knew he'd been on leave for a while, and it seemed to have played hell with his normal cleanliness.

The half-empty pizza box still sat out on the bar. The wine bottle was corked but his whiskey sat open, tempting her. The only thing he'd cleaned up was the couch. She saw no sign that he'd slept there at all. She'd glanced into the hall closet and noted he'd neatly folded and stacked his sheets, along with the crappiest blanket and pillow she owned. This morning she felt vaguely guilty for what must have been an uncomfortable night.

Around her, the scene looked as if she'd enjoyed a nice date the night before. Or a work-related evening. It certainly hadn't been a date. Papers and pictures from the case files littered her dining room table. His laptop still sat there and she wondered how late he'd stayed up.

She tried not to think about the fact that she'd slept well for once. And dreamed about him. It wasn't like she didn't do that often. It was simply that this time the dream hadn't morphed into something terrible. This time, he'd held her and made love to her and begged her forgiveness. His hands had moved over her body, offering repentance with every hungry stroke.

Nope. She wasn't going to think about that.

She poured herself a cup of coffee and wondered how long he'd been in the shower. She could hear it running in the guest bathroom. He was in the bathroom—naked. Had his body changed? His heart? What had happened during the years they'd spent apart? She'd studied him the night before and beyond the change in his hair length, she'd seen a few small lines around his eyes that betrayed the three years that had passed.

She caught a glimpse of herself in the mirror on the wall of her living room. What did Dax see? Had she changed in the three years since she'd pushed him away? She saw a woman dressed in pajama bottoms and a T-shirt that covered her properly. No more sexy things for Holland. She'd thrown them all out.

She'd also thrown out so much of her sexuality the minute she'd lost Dax. Was that why it hadn't worked with any other man? Had she been part of the problem because she lacked some sensual quality? Or was she a sad sack who had given her heart once and her body had followed?

When Dax touched her the night before, her skin had come alive again. She hadn't felt as if she'd truly been living for three long years.

The shower turned off and she could picture him stepping out, his body glistening with moisture. Once, she'd loved to shower with him. Silly thing. She'd been with the man for such a short time and yet they'd made their own rituals, which she missed to this day. She used to hop in the shower to get ready for work and Dax would inevitably follow. Often they stayed there entwined until the water went cold.

How could she miss something she'd never really had? She'd dated Chad for so much longer. Yet with the exception of the humiliating Internet video, she couldn't single out a memorable moment they'd shared. Being alone again had been a guilty relief.

Despite the fourteen months she'd spent with Chad, they'd never gotten around to moving in together. Never even talked about it. Dax had practically moved in the night he'd returned to her.

She had to wonder if he wasn't re-creating the damn scenario. He'd fallen asleep that first night on her couch and the night before he'd positioned himself right back there again.

How long would she really be able to hold out when she already wanted him so badly?

She heard a knock on her door. Muttering a little curse, she swore once again she would change the downstairs code. This time she looked through the peephole, anticipating that Gemma or someone else from work had come to ask why the holy hell she was now on a presidential task force of two.

Nope. It was so much worse.

With a long sigh, she opened the door. "Hello, Chad."

Chad Michaels stood in her doorway, his suit pressed to perfection. Somehow he managed to look neat even in the heat of a New Orleans morning. Her hair was already curling, but his blond perfection was ruthlessly gelled back in a sleek do. "Holland. I've heard some very distressing rumors and I wanted to stop by to check in on you."

He stepped into her apartment without an invitation.

"This is really not a good time." She wasn't sure how the hell she was going to explain the man in the bathroom. Unfortunately, unlike Chad, Dax's grooming routine didn't take an hour. Dax pretty much showered and brushed his teeth and called it good. Chad could spend hours on his man moisturizer and plucking invisible hairs from his brows.

Why had she slept with him?

He smiled down at her and she could smell his powerful cologne. "You didn't change the code to the stairway. Someone's having second thoughts, I think."

"Yes, I am definitely having second thoughts about changing the code." She would do it the minute she got rid of him.

He chuckled. "I pushed you too hard. It was too fast. Everyone knows I go after what I want. That works for me most of the time. I didn't mean to upset you. I think we should talk. We both said a few things we didn't mean last week."

She couldn't think of a single thing she hadn't meant. "I only said no. I meant that, Chad. Look, I'm so sorry I turned you down in such a public manner. I would never have willingly humiliated you. But you didn't exactly consult me beforehand. I never gave you any indication that I wanted to marry you."

She'd been floored, utterly caught off guard that he'd been even thinking about a long-term future. Holland had barely considered where they would go for their next date night.

"You're not ready to get married," he allowed. "I talked to Dr. Jansen about my feelings and I really worked some things out. It took a while. I've been in session every day since you turned me down. It's cost me a lot, but it's brought me here. Holland, I forgive you."

"That's awesome." The dude spent entirely too much time with his overpriced therapist. How did Chad even afford him? "But I think we should end things here, on a positive note. Forgiveness is good. It's time for both of us to move on. Thanks for stopping by."

Any minute, Dax would step out and this would blow up in her face if she couldn't convince Chad to go.

Despite the fact that she'd opened the door, Chad didn't move an inch. "According to Dr. Jansen, your fear of intimacy and your inability to commit stem from your childhood experiences. I understand that now. Let's start over. I've made an appointment with Dr. Jansen for you this afternoon. Even your uncle agrees that you should see someone."

She felt her jaw drop and slammed the door. "You talked to my uncle about this?"

He watched her with a sickening sympathy on his face. "Your uncle understands that I'm good for you. Your refusal last week was part of a need to play out your own mother's unhappiness. It was an irrational decision and one you should explore in therapy. I think once you acknowledge that you're allowing your past to hamstring you, we can get back on track."

"Let me tell you something, buddy. If I wanted to play out my mother's unhappiness, I would find the nearest superhot, emotionally unavailable Naval officer and go to town." Yes, now she was remembering all the reasons she and Chad weren't compatible. He could be a sanctimonious douche nozzle.

"I understand your reluctance." He frowned as he paced deeper into her apartment and glanced at the bar. "Really? Wine and hard liquor? Have you been doing this all week? And pizza? You know what carbs after noon can do to you. This is more self-destructive behavior."

"Ah, the whiskey is mine and I helped her on the pizza. I actually encouraged her to eat. She's getting a little skinny," a familiar voice said.

Damn it to hell. Holland shook her head and turned, praying the situation didn't look as bad as she feared. Nope. It was so much worse. Dax stood there wearing nothing but a towel wrapped around his lean waist, his chest all muscled and perfect. He carried a second towel, which he rubbed over his wet head.

"Captain, why don't you go and get dressed?" She managed to bite the words out, her whole body flaming with embarrassment.

Dax grinned and winked her way. "Sorry, sweetheart. I thought we were alone."

"Well, you can see now that we're not," she shot back. "So clothes would really be appropriate here."

"All right, then. I suppose I could get dressed after our lazy morning." He grabbed his bag and turned to the bathroom. Just when she thought she was home free, he whirled back, his eyes narrowing on Chad. "You look familiar, kid. Maybe I saw you on YouTube or someplace. And just so you know, Holland, I'm completely emotionally available, so don't you go thinking you can use me for some psychosexual therapy thing. I am available to you in every way a man can be to his woman, darlin'."

She sighed as he strode off and closed the door behind him.

"Is that who I think it is?" Chad had turned a perfect shade of red.

Even his angry flush looked as if someone had painted it on his skin. He didn't go blotchy the way she did.

How had she ended up dating a man prettier than her? "It depends. Who do you think he is?"

"Captain Daxton Spencer, one of the president's closest friends, but more important, the man who dumped you for your best friend."

"I didn't dump her. She dumped me and I ended up in a drunken marriage," Dax yelled from the bathroom, proving that while she couldn't hear anything outside her apartment, the walls were super-thin inside. "So really when you think about it, it's all Holland's fault. Did she send me a happy divorce present? Nope. Not even a card."

She had something she could send him. Holland yanked a pillow off the sofa and threw it at the door, wishing it had been Dax's head. "You jerk."

Chad ignored their byplay. He turned her around, hands tight on her shoulders. "That man used you and made you look like a fool. Everyone knows it."

"Really?" She wasn't able to keep the bitterness from her tone. "Everyone? I think there are some people who don't know. Maybe in Antarctica. And it's none of your business."

"Of course it's my business. I love you, Holland. I'm the man who stayed with you, the one who watched out for you. Not him."

She let go of her anger. It was misplaced. "You've misunderstood the situation, Chad. Captain Spencer and I are working together on a project. That's all. We worked late and he ended up sleeping on the couch. But the truth of the matter is, my love life is no longer your concern. I appreciate that you came here to check on me, but it's not necessary."

He strode to her dining room, looking to the whiteboard she'd set up and the documents they'd printed out and pinned there. Despite the fact that they each had a laptop, it was simply easier for them to look at everything together on a whiteboard. She preferred it because it often gave her an overview she didn't have when she looked at pieces of evidence separately.

His eyes flared as he turned to her. "Do you know what kind of trouble you could get into for giving that man access to those documents? Did you even run it by your supervisor? Some of these are NOLA PD documents. Did you get them transferred to you through proper channels?"

Chad was big on proper channels. "My uncle gave them to me. You can ask him yourself."

"If he did, it wasn't so you could call up that manwhore and lure him back into your life. This case is closed. It's been closed for years. If Captain Spencer wants to stir up trouble again, let him do it on his own time."

"Would love to, but apparently I'm now on a presidential task force and Dax is my boss."

Chad stopped. "What is that supposed to mean?"

"It means she can't talk about it." Dax strode back into the room. At least this time he was wearing a pair of jeans. He seemed to have forgotten his shirt again. "This case is classified. I'll let you know if we need the help of the New Orleans PD." He turned her way. "Sweetheart, do you still like your eggs over medium?"

"I like my eggs alone. They're so much happier that way." When had she completely lost control of the situation? This scene was like something out of a terrible comedy of errors, especially when Dax walked into the kitchen and proceeded to prove he knew exactly where she kept everything. How did he remember where she stored her skillet after three years?

Chad frowned and took her by the elbow, hauling her back. "You need to explain to me what's going on right now. Why is that man here?"

"You need to get your hands off her," Dax said, following them. He looked awfully masculine for a man with a cast-iron skillet and spatula in his hands. Somehow he made both ordinary kitchen tools look like the weapons of a predator.

"I can handle Chad, Captain Spencer."

"Yes, Captain Spencer." Chad curled one arm around her shoulders in a possessive move. "This is between me and my fiancée. So back off. I'll put my hands on her whenever I like."

Dax started to puff up in that caveman way that shouldn't be so damn sexy. But it was. Still, as interesting as it might be to see him take Chad down, she could do it herself.

Holland grabbed Chad's wrist to prod him to let her go. When he tightened his hold instead, she flipped him neatly onto his back, his weight hitting her floor with a loud bang that hopefully didn't upset Madame Delphine in the unit beneath her.

Chad leapt to his feet faster than she would have liked, his face now a florid red. "You're going to regret this, Holland. When he fucks you over again, you're going to wish you had chosen differently. You're going to look back and regret ever leaving me."

He stormed out of the apartment.

Dax grinned her way. "Or would you rather have an omelet?"

She barely managed not to scream.

THIRTEEN

Dax couldn't help it. He knew a smug grin sat plastered on his face since he was still standing inside Holland's apartment and that dumbass was currently running away with his overly stylized tail between his legs. "Is your uncle recruiting officers at Abercrombie and Fitch these days?"

She locked the door and took a deep breath before she turned around, a warning glare in her eyes. "Don't even start. What the hell was all that preening peacock routine, Spencer?"

Ah, they were back to Spencer. So she'd regrouped during the night. "I was just getting clean, partner. I intend to be a very good coworker to you, and part of that is keeping a good grooming ritual. And if you need any help at all with yours, I am here for you. I seem to remember there's a place right at the small of your back that you struggle to reach. I can help."

She flushed and he was almost certain that pink color wasn't all about anger. "I can handle it, Captain. After all, I've been handling it on my own for the last three years. Did you help your wife bathe?"

She knew exactly where to stick the knife. "Do you want to talk about Courtney?"

"No. I told you. I don't care about your marriage or your divorce. Or anything but the case." She huffed, a frustrated sound. "I'm going to get dressed and then we can start working. The faster we solve this thing, the quicker you'll be out of my life."

She turned on her heel and stomped away.

For a woman who didn't want to talk about his marriage, she brought it up an awful lot. He sighed and went to her fridge to figure out what to make for breakfast. Maybe she would be in a better mood if he fed her.

Dax really wished he'd punched that asshole. Carbs after noon? Was he fucking serious? Had he made Holland feel bad about her curves? She was a gorgeous woman, and he adored every inch of her. No one should ever make her feel like she wasn't perfect.

Though he did intend to get her to eat more.

He opened the fridge and realized he would have to actually buy her some food to accomplish that. There was nothing in the fridge except a bagged salad, some condiments, and a small container of milk.

What the hell? He put the pan down. He wouldn't be showing off his culinary skills today. They were going to the damn grocery store, because he couldn't survive on rabbit food.

His cell phone rang. He'd already spoken with his mother, so it was likely either one of his friends or . . . "Hello, Gus. Are you doing all right?"

"I'm great. I got to eat reporter for dinner last night. Dumbass kid thought he could sneak into a press conference on his boss's credentials. Have I ever properly explained how much I enjoy ruining the lives of the completely stupid?"

His sister was a pistol. "I know it's a hobby of yours. Now ask me what you know you want to ask me."

She let loose a long sigh. "Fine. How is she?"

Gus had missed Holland and had given him holy hell for their breakup and his impulsive marriage. "She's Holland. She's strong, but I hurt her."

"Asshole, you practically eviscerated her."

"You know at the time I thought she'd betrayed me in the worst way possible." They'd been over this before, but he still felt the need to defend himself.

"At the time, I believe I told you there was something fishy going on, but does anyone listen to me? You all think I'm just a gorgeous warrior woman, but I have deep feelings, too. Well, not really, but I appreciate it when others have them. And I know when someone is hiding something, which Holland definitely was. Women like Holland don't change, not for money or sex or fame. So you need to get on your knees and beg like a good man should."

"Do you think I wouldn't try that? She won't listen to a word I say whether I'm on my knees or not."

His sister scoffed and he could practically see her rolling her eyes. "I wasn't talking about words, silly. I was talking about oral sex. You need to get down there and not let up until she's had so many orgasms she's too exhausted to fight you anymore. Trust me. This is a tried-and-true technique. I had to deal with a very obnoxious foreign ambassador last week. No one thought I could get him to move on trade concessions. But three hours later and the U.S. of A. had the deal of a lifetime."

Dax's ears burned. "Are you kidding me?"

"I'm a motherfucking patriot, brother. So I know of what I speak. Get on your knees and beg properly or I'll come down there and make the noogie incident of eighty-nine look like a walk in the park. I want Holland as my sister-in-law."

Damn, Gus really was mean. "And I want to give her to you, though for my own selfish reasons. But I don't think she's going to give in so easily. I really hurt her."

"And she hurt you." His sister's voice softened. "Don't give up. She loved you enough to let you go. You need to remind her that she loved you. She turned down that super cheesy engagement for a reason. Most women wouldn't. That ring alone would have swayed the majority of women, but Holland didn't even look at it. She just shook her head the whole time. You still have a shot with her."

Did he? He couldn't stand the thought that he didn't. "I'll try."

"Don't try. Do. You're a damn Spencer, Dax. It's time you started acting like one. We don't back away from the things we've done wrong. We fix them. You've spent the last three years of your life hiding and let everything slip away. I want my brother back."

Damn, Gus was right. He had hidden away and licked his wounds and tried to forget.

He'd been an idiot. He should have stood strong, dug deeper, and figured the situation out. He should have been right back on her doorstep. He loved her. He'd never stopped loving her. If she'd kept up the ruse that she'd betrayed him, he should have made it plain that was unacceptable behavior and dealt with it. He should never have run.

Dumbass.

He'd left Holland all alone, abandoned. He'd left everyone who mattered to him when he really thought about it. And he'd done his father a grave disservice. Gus was right. Spencers didn't shrink back when they'd done wrong. They faced it. Like his father would have faced a trial and fought like hell to reclaim his name and reputation. "Have you seen the pictures?"

He'd sent them to Connor and Roman the night before.

"Oh, yes. Roman tried to pretend they weren't there. I guess he wanted to protect my delicate disposition." She laughed. "But I know his passwords."

"Augustine!" a masculine voice shouted.

So she was hanging out with Roman. Her voice went low. "You know the man has a weird *Magnum P.I.* fixation. So yes, I've seen them and I don't believe them. They're doctored in some way or he was drugged. Look at the sheets and the bedding. Do those look like they belong at a cheap motel?"

He strode to the table and pulled out the file. In seconds, he located the printed pictures, blown up to reveal the image's finer details. He hadn't paid any attention to the actual furnishings or appointments, only the two people. "I don't know a lot about sheets, Gus."

"Well, I do. Do you see how the sheet has a bit of a gloss to it?"

"Like it's satin or something? You don't think the motel had satin sheets?"

She made a gagging sound. "No one has satin sheets, brother. Seriously, leave the seventies behind. I'm saying that the sheets have a nice thread count. Higher than the crap they would have at a no-tell motel. Beyond that, I examined the corner of the third photo."

He flipped through until he found the image she referred to. It was a picture with the sheets gathered around the couple on the bed. All of the photos had been taken from a single location in the room and captured the same general view. In this one, his father seemed to be on top of the young girl, his body pinning her to the bed. There was no way to miss the scar on his back. He'd taken fire once and the shrapnel left a silvery section of scars on his back, winding around to his chest. For a moment that was all he could see—the seeming proof that his father had been unfaithful and criminal. "I'm looking at it."

"First off, this photo doesn't look very active. Stop looking at it like a son and put your thinking cap on. I'm putting you on speaker because Roman's poking me."

"Hey, first off, I did not put her up to that crap with the Brazilian ambassador. I knew nothing," Roman said quickly. "Secondly, I think she's right about this picture. If these two are engaged in sex, why are his muscles so slack? She's the only one who seems to have any motion in these photos. Hell, she's the only one who looks coherent."

Dax put his cell on speaker and laid out the photos. He'd spent so much time focused on that scar that identified his father. He'd seen these pictures through the eyes of a son betrayed and hadn't truly studied them as an investigator. He forced himself to pull back.

The muscles of his father's back were completely at rest. In every photo. The only movement he could discern was the girl's. She pushed at him as though trying to fight off an attack. But Dax wasn't convinced that one had actually happened.

"He's drugged," Dax said.

"We can't know that beyond all doubt, but the lax state of the musculature leads me to believe that your father wasn't as engaged physically as the people who sent these photos want us to think," Roman said.

"Let me translate the lawyer speak for you," Gus offered. "These pictures are complete bullshit."

Roman sighed. "She's probably right."

"Of course I am. And I'm also right about the hotel," Gus insisted.

"What about the motel?" Dax couldn't think of what she was talking about.

"No. Not motel. That's the whole point." His sister was like a dog with a bone, but she seemed to be thinking without all the anger and disillusionment he had been.

"You think these photos were taken somewhere else?"

Dax turned because the voice had come from behind him. Holland stepped in, looking down at the photos.

"Holland? Hey, girl. You understand that you have to fucking answer my fucking calls now or I swear to god I'll send you a strip-o-gram an hour until you do," Gus vowed.

Roman cleared his throat over the speaker. "She really will do that. I thought she was kidding. Imagine having to explain to White House security why ten strippers were requesting access to my office."

Holland sniffled a little, and he could have sworn tears had welled in her eyes. "Hey, Gus." She turned her attention right back to the task at hand. "What were you saying about the motel?" She touched one of the photos. "Oh, I see what you mean. Look at the clock. That's not a cheap piece of crap. That's a docking station."

"Yes, it is," Gus replied.

"Hell, I missed that," Roman said, disgust in his voice. "I had one of those a few years back. They get outdated pretty quickly, but for the time it wasn't cheap. I think one of the big luxury chains used to have those in every room."

"The same one that uses Italian-made sheets." Gus's tone rang with triumph. "Look at the corner of the photo. There's a tag hanging off. It's hard to see but if you look through a magnifying glass that's the logo of a very expensive Italian sheet maker. The sheets themselves are made of expensive percale. Hence the pretty sheen."

Holland whistled. "She's right. I splurged on some myself. They're pricey. A seedy motel would never have the budget for these. The pictures must have been taken elsewhere."

Dax thought back. He'd gone over his father's every move a thousand times. "He'd been in London the week before."

"You're right," Gus agreed. "He told me he'd been feeling really run-down while he was there, like he'd been on the verge of getting the flu or something. But what he'd been was drugged, and that's when all of this went down. He'd been at a conference. Let's check into that, see if we can find out anything."

"No, Gus. There's no point." He hated to have to disillusion her. "I've already checked into the timeline."

"There was no conference," Holland said.

Dax speared Holland with a surprised glance.

She shrugged. "I made a timeline, too. I have notes on everywhere your father went for the six weeks preceding his death."

"No conference?" Gus asked. "You think he was meeting one of his mistresses? If so, I can try to find out. I don't recall him having one in Europe, at least not one that Mom knew about. But it's possible."

"Or he was there for another reason entirely and that's what got him killed," Dax said with finality. The truth seemed right at his fingertips. That trip to England must play into this.

Holland nodded his way, giving him support. "I know he stayed at a Gately Resort Hotel. They use the same sheets and bedding worldwide. Only the colors change. Roman, I'm going to bet you have some killer MI5 contacts."

"I'll get on it," he replied. MI5 was England's version of the FBI. "It's been years, though. I don't know what they'll have. CCTV feeds are only kept for so long."

"Try anything." This was the first real lead they'd had in so long, and Dax meant to follow it as far as he could. "We'll pull all his credit card records and try to figure out where he went while he was there. You two let me know what you discover."

"Will do," Gus said. "And you should really work on that other project we discussed."

"Five hundred bucks says Dax is shit out of luck," Roman offered.

Great words of encouragement from one of his best friends. Good to know he had support.

"Oh, I will take all of your money, Calder," Gus shot back. "Bye, Holland. Have a good time with Dax. I'm coming to see you in a few weeks. Plan something fun."

The line went dead.

He turned and Holland was still looking at that phone wistfully, as if she hadn't wanted the call to end.

She'd cut herself off from everyone to save him. He had to find a way to give it back to her. Maybe Gus was right. Maybe charm would work. And oral sex. He was willing to give it one hell of a shot.

Holland stared at the screen, her mind wandering.

"Did you find anything?"

She shook her head as Dax brought her out of her thoughts. She'd been remembering those days three years earlier when she and Dax had finally come together and everything seemed possible. Today he'd lingered in her space. She sat at her laptop, running through reports and looking at his father's credit card receipts from the London trip. Dax hovered right behind her, crowding her. She could smell the soap he'd used earlier, feel the heat of his body. Every now and then he brushed against her, skin to skin, and she remembered exactly how long it had been since she'd felt real lust.

Hours had passed, and now the day was sinking into night again. Dax was still here and he showed not a single sign of leaving.

"I have receipts for fuel," Holland replied. "I found a rental car agreement, too. He bought gas twice. My question is why would he need a car in London? It's so much easier to use public transit. Even getting to and from other major cities in England is easier to do on trains. So I think he was heading somewhere off the beaten path."

Dax nodded. "Where did he purchase the fuel?"

She winced. "Just outside of London. It looks like he filled up the tank both times at a petrol station on the M25, the highway that runs around London. From there he could have gone anywhere, though I suspect he was heading north from the placement of the station."

She wished she had better news. Hell, she wished she could simply solve the whole thing so he could go on his merry way and not sit across the table, tempting her with what could no longer be.

He'd behaved perfectly all day. He'd even brought takeout back for lunch so they didn't have to pause long. He'd brought exactly what she'd asked for. A spinach salad. The bastard had also brought a muffuletta sandwich and a dozen macaroons from the bakery down the street. And pralines. He'd claimed they were a late afternoon snack. He'd even made her a cup of tea to go with it.

Damn man. Somehow her appetite had come roaring back, too.

She was already wondering if she could sneak in a glass of that stupidly excellent wine with whatever dinner Dax cooked up. He'd brought a sack of groceries in earlier with their lunch, claiming she needed a proper meal.

She'd really been skimping on her calories lately. Somehow she'd let Chad the Ass convince her she was carrying a bit too much weight. It had been a subtle thing, really. He'd mentioned his own diet and then somehow she'd started falling in line.

The realization was maddening because she wasn't the sort to change for a man. And she was only eating the stupid pralines now because they tasted good.

Dax sighed. "That led us nowhere. And he didn't use his credit card for anything but the gas and hotel."

"He withdrew a thousand pounds sterling at Heathrow, so he probably used cash for everything else."

"Damn it. What was he doing over there?" Dax sounded as frustrated as she felt.

Her cell phone rang. Holland looked down, saw who it was, and sent his ass straight to voice mail.

Dax speared her with a glance. "Should I have a talk with your erstwhile suitor?"

"He'll eventually go away." She was fairly certain of that. It was her uncle who wouldn't leave her in peace. He'd left a single stern message asking her to call him because he'd heard that she was in serious trouble.

She was in serious trouble because she was already softening toward Dax. At one point she'd actually found herself nearly touching him like old times. She'd stopped short, before she'd lost her head in all his warmth and muscled goodness.

"How did you get involved with him?"

"How did you end up married to a woman you never even dated?" She sounded like such a freaking shrew. The words just popped out, bubbling up and exploding like a nasty volcano of jealousy.

He sank into the seat beside her. "I was stupid and foolish and so angry I couldn't see straight, so I got drunk as shit. I make lousy decisions when I'm drunk as shit, sweetheart."

She stood up. "I'm not talking about this."

"We have to."

They did not. She shook her head and strode away, escaping onto the balcony for some fresh air. Her body felt tight, every muscle as taut as a bowstring. How would she survive being locked in with him for days? Weeks?

Fresh air didn't help. The humid air dripped moisture. And being out on the balcony only reminded her of the way he'd once touched her out here. In fact, she couldn't forget what it felt like to have his hands on her. Dax was a furnace in bed. He gave off so much heat she didn't need a blanket, only his body wrapped around hers. She didn't remember a time she'd felt so safe. So loved.

She rubbed at a spot just above her chest. It felt tight. The ache just wouldn't go away.

"Holland, we can't ignore it forever."

Naturally, he wouldn't give her a second alone. "Watch me."

"You were always stubborn."

"Tell me something, Dax. Would you have come back if you hadn't found that lead on your father's case?" She knew the answer, but she wanted to hear it from him. He would never have come back. He wouldn't have spoken to her again.

He moved beside her, leaning against the wrought-iron balcony. "Eventually. Maybe not so soon, but yeah. I would have come back."

"Liar. You never would have forgiven me."

"I was angry, I'll admit. But even when I was pissed as hell at you, I still knew that you were the center of my world. You have been since the day I met you. You were my dream girl back then. When I thought you betrayed me, you became my nightmare. But I was focused on you. Loving you, hating you, it didn't change the fact that you were and always will be everything to me."

Holland closed her eyes. Sweet words . . . but she wasn't sure she believed them. "It doesn't matter. I moved on. I knew when I let you go that it was the end of any relationship we had."

"Did you?" He turned to her, looming over her in the late afternoon light. "Really?"

She forced herself to face him. "Yes, Dax. I knew it the minute I got that call."

"So why did you get involved with a boy you knew you could never love or marry if you had truly moved on from me?"

She'd asked herself that question a lot, but she wasn't about to admit that to him. "I liked Chad. We move in the same world."

"Law enforcement." Dax scoffed. "That means nothing. If that pretty boy cares more about his arrest record than his hair gel, I'll eat my khakis for dinner. I know his type. We have them in the Navy. They want to be officers for the privilege it affords them. They view it like a corporate job and start climbing the ladder."

"And you don't, Captain?"

"I work my ass off for my country and my men. I'm not stupid. I'm not going to move much above where I am now. I might get a better ship because I'm damn good at my job, but after the scandal with my father my name is crap."

Thereby proving her point. "Hence we're working to clear your name so you can achieve your destiny, Admiral Spencer. I've always known that's where you were headed."

"You know so much about me, huh? Did you know I was ready to leave the Navy that day?"

"Bullshit. I know you said that, but I doubt you really would have done it." He couldn't have been serious.

He simply nodded. "I'd made the decision that having a family with you was more important than my career. I'd decided to call Zack and ask for a job since you could easily transfer to D.C. I didn't want to end up like our parents. We need to be together every day, every night."

Had he really decided that? Or was this little speech something he'd dreamed up to appeal to the romantic in her so he could insinuate himself back into her life? She couldn't go down this road with him again. The last time had hurt too much.

She'd been right to fear the power he could wield over her. Growing up, she'd feared being like her lonely, heartsick mother who had waited her entire adult life for a man. After Dax had left New Orleans, Holland had become that woman. He alone could twist her inside and out.

"It doesn't matter anymore," she insisted.

"Yes, it does. I want you to tell me what you really saw in Chad

Michaels." He gritted the words out between his teeth as he moved in, invading her space. "Why did you date him?"

"I was attracted to him."

"That's a lie." He moved in, forcing her to take a step back. "I know the kind of guy you're attracted to, and it's not a metrosexual boy posing as a man. Try again."

She didn't want to play this game with him and yet she couldn't force herself to move away. If she wasn't careful, something would give way between them. Holland felt helpless to stop it. Her rational side seemed to have shut down. Her softer side was more than willing to play the antelope to Dax's prowling lion. "I was lonely."

He shook his head as he moved in again. "You've never minded that before."

He was going to make her admit it. Out loud. She suspected this was Dax's version of therapy. Chad would have hauled her into an expensive shrink's office where she would have discussed her feelings for fifty minutes at a time. Dax's therapy would involve something more physical.

Somehow, she thought Dax's methodology would be way more helpful.

Maybe he was right. Maybe they needed to have it out. Maybe they needed to be honest with each other once and for all.

"I dated him because I didn't give a shit, Dax." She retreated again until her back hit the wall and she had nowhere else to escape.

He didn't stop coming for her. He moved in until mere inches sat between them. His chest almost brushed her breasts. When they did, would he be able to feel how hard her nipples were? When his hips locked against hers, would he feel her heat and know she was wet and ready for him simply because he was close?

She knew she should, but she couldn't force herself to push him away anymore.

He was wrong. She had been lonely. Chad had taught her that no one could fill the void but Dax.

"Finally, we're getting somewhere." He lifted his hand, fingers brushing back her hair. "You knew you couldn't love him. Tell me how you knew."

She looked into his eyes, nearly getting lost in the depths. She'd been cold for so long. But not today. Not right now.

Between dealing with Chad, being so close to Dax, and talking to Gus for the first time in years, she teetered on an emotional edge. Just a little shove would send her over. Then she could let go of the terrible past and dismal future. She could forget sorrow and heartbreak and what might have been for a few hours in Dax's embrace. She could sink into him. Of course it wasn't forever. She knew how this would end, but maybe if she went into it with her eyes open this time, maybe she could preserve a piece of her heart.

"You know why."

He lowered his head down, their foreheads touching. "I need to hear it."

"You're a bastard." She wanted him to kiss her so she didn't have to admit it. If he took her lips with his, pressed their bodies together, she could forget everything except how good it felt to be with him.

"Yes, I am. But that doesn't change anything. I need to hear the words from you."

She shouldn't give a damn about his needs, but she wasn't sure she could go another second without his kiss. Her desperation underscored all the reasons she should run as fast as she could. She simply couldn't deny him. "I knew I couldn't love him because he wasn't you."

Relief and triumph consumed his expression. He cupped her face as if she was something infinitely precious and breakable. "That's how I feel, too. For me, it's always been you. It always will be you."

He leaned in, his mouth descending on hers. For the first time in years her body sprang to life. She couldn't wait to wrap her arms around his lean waist and tug the T-shirt from his jeans. Not to get it off his body. That could wait, but she needed to feel his skin under her palms, warm and alive.

She'd dreamed of him dead so often. After those nightmares, she'd closed her eyes, hating the fact that he was still miles from her, despising the fact that she couldn't touch him and assure herself that he was still somewhere out there. Their breakup had been like a death, killing something deep in her soul that she'd thought gone forever. Touching him now felt like a reawakening. Holland knew from experience that the love she gave to him could be filled with such beauty and pleasure. It could also cause immeasurable pain.

She shoved the thought aside. She would have time to decide her future later. For now, all she wanted was to revel in how right it felt to be pressed against him, open to his touch.

He deepened the kiss, his tongue sliding along her lower lip and begging for entry. She parted her lips for him. Yes, the case would eventually end and she would be alone again. But for a few weeks, she could be his lover, gorge herself on the pleasure he could give her.

She let her hands slide along the strong muscles of his back, and he groaned against her mouth. He pressed deeper, letting her feel every bit of his passion. He'd never held back or pretended with her. He'd always let her know how much power she had over his body.

"God, I've missed you, sweetheart. I've missed everything about you. I want to touch you everywhere, remind myself of just how beautiful you are." He whispered the words across her skin. "I want to taste you again. You can't possibly taste as good as I remember."

Her body moved with his instinctively, as though they'd never been apart. He slid his hands down to cup her backside. She arched closer.

"Let me take you to bed," he offered. "I swear everything will make sense in the morning. You'll see."

She wasn't sure about that, but she also knew she didn't have the fortitude to turn him down.

Holland peered up at him, fearing she'd regret this. But she no longer cared. She nestled her body against his and nodded.

"Down!" another voice screamed. "Shooter! Three o'clock."

Her eyes widened as a shot cracked through the air.

FOURTEEN

Dax moved the minute he heard the voice. *Down! Shooter! Three o'clock.*

On his right.

He tightened his arms around Holland and shoved her down, to his left, just as the bullet whizzed past them.

Someone was shooting at them from the rooftop across the street, and he'd gotten caught without his gun. Since realizing that his dad's death had been part of a larger plot, he hadn't been without a weapon of some kind on his body. He was always ready to defend not only himself, but his friends and family. But when he was with Holland, he forgot about everything but her.

"Are you all right?" He covered her body with his.

Dax had tried to take the brunt of the fall, but he was sure she was scraped up.

She nodded. "But we need to get inside. We don't have much cover here."

He'd rolled her to the back of the balcony where it would be harder for the gunman to spot them, but she was right.

Another volley of gunfire sounded, and he turned them again, exposing his back and using his body to protect her. Dax tensed, waiting for the feeling of the bullet piercing him.

"We need to move," she whispered. "I hear two types of fire. One is from a handgun and the other a rifle. I think whoever has the handgun is giving us some cover. But we need to get inside and now."

She was right. There were definitely two shooters, and one had tipped them off. Good to know they didn't have two armed bastards with murder on their minds after them.

He rose to his knees. "You stay close to the wall. We'll move as quickly as we can. When you get inside, stay down and away from the windows."

"My gun is on the bar. I can get to it with minimal exposure. You find your phone and call the police," she said calmly.

His girl was good under fire. "I don't think getting the cops here will be a problem."

Tourists screamed on the streets below as they realized people were exchanging gunfire. The Quarter would be a chaotic mess in minutes, making it very simple for the assassin to slip into the crowd and fade away.

Dax crept across the rest of the balcony and let Holland in first. He could still hear screaming and intermittent gunfire, but now the sweet sound of sirens joined the mix.

He shoved the balcony door open and forced his way through. By the time it slammed behind him Holland had already retrieved her SIG and was easing toward the front door.

"I don't think that's a great idea, sweetheart." He knew she wanted to get out there and search for the person who'd shot at them, but they had no idea who they were looking for.

Holland paused at the door, glaring. "You can't expect me to sit on my hands. I need to figure out where the asshole was perched. He might have left something behind."

"I think we should figure out who warned us first." The voice had been deep but he would bet anything it had come from a woman. "Besides, the police are on their way. We'll have to give a statement."

Suddenly, he heard a crashing sound. Glass shattered all around them. Dax whipped around to the balcony windows. As the curtains caught fire, horror dawned. Someone had tossed a Molotov cocktail through the window.

"The files," Holland said, her eyes widening.

Already Dax could feel the heat as her thin curtains flamed and the carpet caught fire. He ran for the files as another bottle sailed onto the balcony and added to the flames. He could hear more gunfire but it didn't matter—nothing did except getting Holland out. He grabbed one of the laptops and the file folder, leaving everything else behind.

"Go," he ordered, aware they had to escape onto the street to avoid the blaze . . . where they would have nowhere to hide.

Holland snatched up his bag from the couch and slung it over her shoulder. It would give them an extra weapon. He would take it.

He took her hand and threaded their fingers together. No way he was losing her.

"The door in the back leads out to the streets. Unless they have someone on the top of the building or waiting for us, we should be able to slip out and take one of the side streets away from the Quarter. We can get in touch with the police from there."

He already had his cell in hand. One of the great things about dating Holland Kirk was that when assholes tried to assassinate them, he could divert his attention enough to call for help because his woman knew what she was doing. She took the lead, making sure the hall and stairway were empty as they began their descent.

He called the cavalry. It only took a single ring for Connor to answer.

"What's happening, brother? Is Holland proving to be stubborn? I hope so because Lara and I have a bet riding on this. Actually, I have a bet. She told me it was nasty and inhumane to bet on a friend's love life."

Good for Lara. "No time. Someone just took a shot at us and torched Holland's apartment. I need a safe house. We're heading out of the city and I'll call when it's safe. Make transportation arrangements for us, too." He disconnected the call and slid the phone in his pocket.

"We should make our way to the police station," Holland said.

"I'm rethinking NOLA PD involvement, sweetheart. Only two groups know I'm in town—the cops and your team."

Her jaw tightened as they made it to her building's back door. "You think someone on one of the teams is working for the mob and you're probably right. Both teams also knew I had the photos. One of them has to be responsible for this."

As he poked his head outside, he cursed. "Damn it. You take the nine and I'll take the three."

She nodded, and they both burst through, him veering left and ensuring no one shot them from that direction, and her preventing the same on the right. When their surroundings looked clear, he took her hand again.

"Let's head toward Canal Street. We can find a bar and wait until Connor calls."

She gritted her teeth, as though the idea of running upset her. But she slid her gun into the back of her jeans and hid it with her shirt, nodding. "All right. I need to text my uncle though, otherwise he'll put a BOLO on my ass."

The last thing they needed was the police hunting them. Oh, someone on the force might be, but they didn't need it to be official. "All right. Let's go."

He squeezed her hand and they lost themselves in the crowds as sirens filled the air.

As they crept out of the Quarter, Dax had to wonder about that woman who'd screamed a warning for them to move.

Her identity was a mystery, but one he intended to solve.

H olland frowned at the text as Dax turned off the highway and
straight into bayou country.

Worried about you. Call me when you can. And watch your
back. Trouble is following your old boyfriend everywhere.
He's not to be trusted.

Her uncle. She'd managed to convince him not to send a SWAT
team her way, but he wasn't convinced she was safe. Of course, since
it looked as if she was headed into *Deliverance* territory, she wasn't
certain, either.

"Do you know where you're going? Are you sure this is where Connor told us to hide out?" Because she'd just seen an alligator lazing on
the roadside and that didn't give her a warm fuzzy.

Dax grinned as though this was all just one big adventure. "What's
wrong, city girl? Can't handle a few critters? I thought you were raised
in New Orleans."

"Exactly. New Orleans. I was raised in the city, not the swamp. My
aunt always told me the swamp was for gators, tourists who wanted to
get eaten by gators, and criminals who knew no one wanted to hang
out with gators. Which of those categories does your friend fall into?"

If anything, his lips tugged up higher. "He falls into the crazy
motherfucker category."

"You're awfully happy for a man on the run."

He turned back to the road with a shrug. "I wouldn't say I'm happy.
I'm just content that we're going to solve this thing. Now that we're on
our own, we're going to focus."

"Focus? You think I haven't been focused? I've spent years trying
to figure this damn mystery out."

"How about this, then?" he said. "I'm optimistic because we're together. We're a good team. The last time we worked a case together we were so damn good the Russian mob came after us."

"And that was such a plus." He was infuriating and yet she found herself smiling at him.

"Call it what you like, but we're perfect together."

He focused on the road again and she fell silent. She should probably disagree . . . but she didn't.

The minutes rolled by as she looked out on the moonlit bayou. Silvery beams illuminated the still waters of the swamp. Every now and then it reflected off the light from creatures' eyes. She shuddered.

"Can we talk about us now?" Dax asked softly.

She wasn't ready, though she'd started to believe that at some point she might be able to discuss that with something other than sarcasm and cynicism. "Not yet."

He was quiet for a moment, the only sound between them the pounding of the Jeep against the pavement. "All right. Let's talk about the fact that someone warned us today. Any idea who?"

She'd heard the same thing he had. "It was a woman. I don't know. It was chaotic and she didn't yell out after that. From what I can tell, they were both across the street from my building."

"Why would they have two agents across the street from us and why would one sell the other out?"

It was a question she'd been asking herself. "I don't think they were together. One of the buildings across the street is a good two stories taller than the other. Whoever called out to us must have had the better vantage point. I suspect she'd positioned herself on that taller building. She took multiple shots at him, I'll bet with the handgun. The guy with the rifle was directly across the street from us, so his perch was closer to my window. That's why he had an easy time throwing those Molotov cocktails into my place. The competing gunfire had ceased by then."

"She obviously wasn't there to kill us."

"Agreed. I wish I'd gotten a look at her. Unfortunately, that whole running-for-our-lives thing got in the way. That really rankles."

It did. It made her restless that she'd been so vulnerable, that not one but two people had been watching them. If Dax hadn't been there, she would have hauled off in hot pursuit. With him by her side, she'd had more than herself and her pride to think of.

She'd sat quietly in the bar of one of the larger hotels while texting her uncle and trying to figure out who would have warned them. While they'd waited for the Jeep Connor had arranged she'd come to terms with the fact that her only real concern in that moment hadn't been herself or her apartment or even the files.

It had been Dax.

At the end of the day it didn't matter how tough she was. She was a stupid girl at heart. She was still foolishly pining for a boy. No, a man. She could trust him with her life, just not with her heart.

"According to the directions, we're not far now," Dax said as he turned again, this time onto a one-lane dirt road so narrow that trees brushed the sides of the Jeep as though reaching out to pull them into the thick gloom of the swamp. Wherever they were headed, it was isolated.

"Did your uncle mention how much of the building was lost?" Dax asked.

"The good news is the fire department got there quickly. Uncle Beau thinks there's no real structural damage. He was there when the fire department arrived, and he signed all the paperwork for me. He's going to send in an engineer to make sure. He'll keep in touch by e-mail, but at some point he's going to want to see me."

"Let's give it a day or two."

"How's your mom?" It was so much easier to talk about family than the elephant in the Jeep. They hadn't talked about that kiss yet or the fact that if some asshole hadn't started shooting, she very likely would have surrendered to Dax on the balcony. She would have spread her legs wide without a word of protest and welcomed him inside because she hadn't cared about anything in that moment except being close to him.

"So far, so good. I tried to get her to go to D.C., but she's being stubborn."

All the Spencers were stubborn. It seemed to be bred into their DNA.

Finally, a building came into view, illuminated in the twin lights of the Jeep. She couldn't make out many details in the surrounding dark, but at least it wasn't one of the small fishing camps that dotted the bayou. It looked like a cabin big enough to actually live in. The door opened and out stepped someone she hadn't seen in years.

"Is that Connor?"

Dax stopped the Jeep and killed the engine with a smile on his face. "Asshole didn't tell me he was already here."

"Maybe he came out this afternoon."

Dax shook his head. "Nah. He's probably been here since I hit New Orleans, waiting for the minute I needed backup."

He hopped out of the Jeep. In the moonlight, she watched Dax point a finger at his friend, stalking closer. Then the two men did that manly hug, beat-on-each-other's-back thing.

Connor had come all this way because he wouldn't leave Dax without backup. When was the last time she'd had a friend like that? Probably Joy.

Or had she pushed away another true friend because the woman happened to be Dax's sister? She brushed the thought aside and exited the Jeep. With Connor here, she was firmly in Dax's world again and she would have to remember that they weren't really alone. Only she was. He was surrounded by people who loved him. She'd lost those a long time ago.

Even as she hopped out of the vehicle, she saw Connor size her up. Dax's best friend had always been a deep one, the dark to his light. Dax always seemed so sunny while Connor obviously preferred the shadows. Sometimes she thought it would have been easier if she'd fallen for Connor. That man would never have pushed her for more than a good time in bed.

She wondered what his wife was like. It was hard to imagine him married. Likely she was as dark and emotionless as Connor appeared.

"Holland," he said, nodding her way.

"Hello, Connor." Yes, it was going to be an awkward reunion all the way around, but then what did she expect? Dax's friends had spent years hating her for the way she'd hurt him. Just because she'd had good reasons didn't mean they would stop. "If you've set aside a room for me, I'll just go and get comfortable while you two catch up."

A faint hint of a smile creased Connor's mouth. "That will have to wait. My wife decided to cook dinner. I'm so sorry, man. I hope you ate earlier."

His wife was here? So she would have to put up with some cold-as-ice chick who had likely been taught to hate her on sight. Awesome.

"It's not that bad," Dax said. "It's just very vegan."

The door opened and a slight figure stepped out. Lara Sparks was wearing a bright sundress, her dark hair piled in a messy, ten-pound updo of curls on her head. Even in the dim light, she could see the woman had huge blue eyes.

"Holland!" Petite Lara came at her with a smile and pulled Holland into an embrace, her head resting on Holland's shoulder. "It's so good to meet you. You're like the missing piece of the family."

Holland looked to Connor, utterly surprised by his affectionate, vegan bride.

He simply shrugged. "Yeah, let her get it out of her system. She's a hugger."

Lara's head snapped up and she turned her husband's way. "Human beings need physical affection, and after everything Holland's been through, she likely needs a good hug, especially since she's been exiled for so long for a crime she didn't commit."

"She was in New Orleans. No one sent her away," Connor pointed out.

Lara stepped back. "She's Dax's one true love."

"Oh, I wouldn't say that." Holland didn't want to mislead Lara.

"She's right," Dax said with a nod. "I've learned that Lara has a deep understanding of the people around her. I think because of all the yoga she does."

Lara glanced between Holland and Connor with a frown. "Connor, don't you want to give Holland a hug to welcome her back into the family?"

Holland shook her head. "He's already said hello. We're cool."

Connor's face broke into the most open smile she'd ever seen on the man. He stepped forward, and before Holland could protest, he'd put his arms around her. "I never argue with my wife. I'm sorry it's been so long, Holland. But you're a dumbass who should have asked for help three years ago."

"Connor!" Lara protested.

Holland laughed and hugged him back, feeling better than she had in forever. "You're the dumbass, Sparks."

He nodded and stepped back. "Maybe. I definitely shouldn't have listened to his drunk ass when he claimed you were the devil. Come on in, Kirk. I brought along some Scotch. Let's all sit down and have a drink and figure out what the hell we're going to do. Oh, and you can meet Freddy."

Lara nodded. "Give me a minute. I need to make sure he's not in firing position." She jogged back into the cabin. "Freddy, it's all right. They're not feds. Or aliens. Just Dax and his one true love." A low, masculine voice rumbled before Lara spoke again. "Okay, so she's kind of a fed, but the good kind. Yes, there is a good kind, mister. There is good in everyone, damn it. Well, all right, you have a point. There's no good in Reticulan Grays."

Connor sighed. "Sorry, we let Freddy watch a documentary on ancient aliens. He's all about abductions now. You'll have to forgive him. He's actually quite brilliant."

"He's a fucking maniac," Dax said. "And I'm having a talk with him about his paranoia."

Holland lingered outside with Connor. "Will he really shoot at me? Because I've already had that happen once today."

"Freddy, no. I'm not going to, either. I'm sorry, Holland. I should have followed my instincts."

"Your instincts?"

"When Dax told me what you had done, my first thought was fuck no. I should have followed that thought through, but I was scared to."

"Scared?" Was Connor afraid of anything?

"Because Dax was already married." He took a long breath and stared out over the water. The cabin was roughly twenty feet from the bayou. She could see what looked like a pier and a boat at the end of it. "I worried that if I discovered I was right, I would have to tell him he'd fucked up his whole life. And yours."

"I'm good, Sparks," she lied. "I did what I had to do, and I've made my peace with it."

Connor scoffed. "You're so full of shit. He won't give up, you know. He's missed you."

"He was married to Courtney for two years, so I question that assessment."

That truth was the hardest pill to swallow. Dax hadn't woken up, realized he'd made a colossal mistake, and gotten a quickie divorce. He'd stayed married to Courtney until the woman had left him.

"He was embarrassed. His decision to stay with her was more about you than anything else. He didn't want to look foolish or like he couldn't move on. Deep down I think he decided if he couldn't have the woman he wanted, he might as well give it a try with someone else."

If Holland could have removed herself from the scenario, Dax's actions made sense. But she couldn't. "It doesn't matter anymore."

"It does. I would have agreed with you on this a few months ago. I would have told Dax to move on and find someone else if he absolutely had to get married and do the family thing. But I figured something out."

"What's that?"

"People aren't interchangeable. There's only one Lara in the entire world. She's the only one who could . . . I don't know." He shrugged. "Complete me. Just saying that makes me feel as if I have a discernable estrogen level, but it's true. Dax can't move on because you're the one woman in the world for him. You have been for a very long time. I remember the day he met you. He called me and told me he'd met the future Mrs. Spencer. I told him he was insane. But he was right."

"I seriously doubt I'm the one woman for him, Sparks. He's just feeling guilty about not fighting harder three years ago. But I didn't want him to fight. He did exactly what I intended him to and I don't regret it." Even as she said the words, Holland knew she was lying to herself, but she couldn't lay her feelings bare to Connor or Dax or anyone. She couldn't tell anyone how she'd mourned him. "We weren't together very long. It was brief and intense, and at the end of the day, it was a good thing we broke up because it wouldn't have worked."

Except he'd said he was going to leave the Navy for her. She would have happily moved to D.C. if he'd been there.

But he wasn't and the time had passed. Now she knew what it meant to be without him, and she couldn't let herself fall in love with him again.

"If you say so. But you should know that Dax is pretty good at getting what he wants, and there's no doubt he wants you."

"And what if I told you I'm just going to use him? I'm going to sleep with him and get him out of my system. And at the end of all this, I'm going to walk away." She'd thought about it the whole drive out here. She wasn't sure she could stay away from Dax physically. The heat between them was far too strong. Maybe if she gave in, she would realize that her memory was faulty. They couldn't be as good together as she remembered.

It would help her if Connor told Dax to stay away from her. Dax might actually listen to his best friend.

Connor grinned. "I'm going with my gut this time, Kirk. You can talk all the smack you want, but you loved him then. You can tell yourself that you're getting him out of your system, but you love him now. That's all that matters. You're the type of woman who gives her heart away once. It won't ever happen again. Oh, you might fool yourself into believing you could be content with someone else. You might be able to date another guy and sleep beside him, but when it comes down to really committing, you won't be able to. You'll always say no because deep down, you will always be waiting for Dax. Like that cop found out. Bet he wants to strangle whoever uploaded that sucker to YouTube. Let's get inside and see what fresh horror my wife has created with tofu."

Holland watched as Connor ducked inside, worried that his words would prove all too true.

FIFTEEN

Dax sat back as Freddy pointed to a whiteboard. Apparently one of the first things Lara had done when Connor had secured this place a few days back was to set up a conspiracy room. The cabin belonged to a wealthy businessman who had donated heavily to Zack's campaign, and he'd been eager to allow any of Zack's friends to use his little cabin on the bayou, as Connor had explained. Dax had to wonder if the dude would be so eager if he could see the way his den was being used.

There were whiteboards, sticky notes, and taped-up papers covering what used to be a lovely room. Everywhere Dax looked along the far wall was some note or thought of Freddy's.

"So you believe Joy was killed in order to ensure that Zack won the election." Holland sat on the floor, her legs crossed and her blond hair held up by a pencil she'd poked through her bun.

He supposed it was practical, but all it did was make him want to touch the soft skin at the nape of her neck. He could run his nose over it, filling his lungs with her scent before he kissed her. She would shiver and then he could haul her close.

He was so damn horny. He couldn't even concentrate on the case because all he could focus on was the fact that they would have to share a room. The cabin only had two bedrooms and one couch. Freddy had explained he rarely slept in a bed anyway, so he was happy to take the sofa.

"Yes, I believe that's why Joy Hayes was eliminated. I've theorized a number of reasons the same people would want to kill the admiral as well," Freddy explained.

In the last few months, the dude had put on some muscle. Apparently fleeing from government agents and losing himself deep in the Appalachian wilderness had done wonders for Freddy's physique. He looked like a Special Forces soldier, with the single exception of the long hair he kept in a queue.

Was Holland staring at Freddy because the dude was crazy, or did she think he was hot?

Because Dax was pretty sure he was hotter than Freddy. And sane. Mostly.

"We think he knew something," Holland said with a smile the paranoid guy's way.

Lara nodded and stood beside Freddy. "Absolutely. The only question is, what? Dax, are you aware that your father had several articles concerning Joy Hayes's death on his person at the time of his arrest?"

That made Dax sit up straight and focus on something other than his jealousy. "No."

"It's in the police report," Freddy said.

Holland frowned. "I remember that when they arrested your dad, they logged the contents of his briefcase when he went through processing. According to that report he had ten pages of *New York Times* and *Washington Post* articles inside, dated a few days prior. How can you be sure the articles were about Joy?"

"The page counts match up with what he would have torn out of the paper. I reconstructed the main articles, pieced them together, and came up with a theory. It's conjecture, but I feel strongly about it," Freddy said with a nod.

"So you think the Russian mob learned about this trip and set him up?" During dinner, they'd gone over what they'd found out the day before.

Freddy had confirmed the pictures had not been taken at the same place or time the police believed. He'd also scanned one of the pictures into the computer and managed to isolate the numbers on a glowing clock far in the background. According to Amber Taylor's police statement, the incident with the admiral had occurred between seven and ten p.m., while the clock in the pictures displayed a time of two twelve in the morning.

Dax had handed the rest of the photographs to Freddy. Lara's former neighbor might be crazy but damn he was good.

"Not necessarily," Connor said. "It may simply have been the easiest place to drug your father and set up the situation. I need to know why he was in London before I can really decide."

"I'll sneak back into town tomorrow and talk to my mother." He would have to. His mother was the only one who might remember.

"Good. Ask her if she knows anything about a connection between your father and Zack's mom," Lara said.

"Constance Hayes?" Holland asked, obviously surprised. She turned to Dax. "They knew each other, right? You guys went to school together for years."

Dax chuckled. How little she understood about their lives. "Zack's mom wasn't exactly the type to show up for parents' weekend. Half the time his dad didn't make it, either."

"And when summer break rolled around, they would either put Zack in some summer academic program or leave him with a nanny. Excuse me, I believe they called her a companion. Most of the time they hired grandmotherly types, but I remember that summer we were all sixteen, someone fucked up and hired an undergrad." Connor nodded Dax's way. "Ah, the great cover-up. I was staying with Dax and we convinced his parents that we were going to spend a week in New York with Gabe and Mad."

Holland smiled. "Who I'm sure decided to tell their parents that they were spending it with you guys. And Roman?"

"He was supposed to be interning at Crawford legal," Dax admitted. "We all went out to the beach and convinced the undergrad to bring some friends. Good times, man. Well, for everyone else." He was suddenly aware that he shouldn't tell those stories with such relish anymore. "I was just there for the beer."

"Me, too." Connor gave him a thumbs-up. "But the other guys had an orgy."

Lara groaned and threw a pillow at her husband's head. "Such a manwhore. I'm going to bed, where we're not having sex. Maybe ever."

Connor's lips curled up in a wolfish grin. "Want to bet?"

Lara's cheeks heated. "No. You cheat."

"Damn straight I do." He followed his wife when she ran off to the bedroom. "See you guys in the morning."

Freddy sighed. "So ask your mother about any connections between your father and Constance Hayes."

Dax could barely remember a time the two had been in the same room . . . except when they'd interrupted his first kiss with Holland. "Any particular reason why?"

Holland scooted up and onto the couch beside him. It took everything he had not to pull her closer. "Do you think he was in England because of her?"

"Zack's mom had been dead for something like five years by then." It suddenly hit him. "Shit. But she died in England. And her name was on that list. I wonder if my dad knew about the dead pool? Have you made heads or tails of the other names on there?"

Freddy set down his marker and stretched. "I'm working on it. A few of the names are Russian nationals, and one or two died right around the time Natalia went to work for the Hayes family. It's not easy to get almost-forty-year-old Soviet documents. It could take me a couple of days, if they even exist anymore. I have a network in place. It's a matter of running them down. The Russian I know is a little touchy. Last I heard he thought Putin was after him, so he's probably hiding in Siberia."

"Isn't Siberia where they send dissidents?" Holland asked.

"Yeah, hide in plain sight, man. That's Oleg's way. That and drinking a lot of vodka. I'm going to pop into town and pick up a few things. There's an all-night Walmart about ten miles away. I need tinfoil. Who doesn't have tinfoil? It makes me wonder about the guy who owns this cabin. Can I take your Jeep? I walked in."

Dax tossed him the keys because he wasn't certain if Freddy had walked in from the bus stop or whatever transportation he'd chosen, or if he meant he'd literally walked from the East Coast. "Sure, man."

"I'll be back. Oh, and I might have put some traps around the house. You really shouldn't go too far. Night."

Dear god. Dax prayed Freddy hadn't put in land mines. But he wouldn't put it past the crazy bastard.

The door closed, and suddenly he was alone with Holland and about a thousand questions. Literally. They were surrounded by whiteboards covered in questions. But the one he most wanted answered wasn't anywhere on the wall.

"Do you think you'll ever forgive me?"

She stood abruptly. "I already have. There's nothing to forgive, not really."

"I married Courtney."

"We weren't together at the time. You were perfectly free to marry anyone you chose."

That had to be her pride talking. And her fear.

"I chose you. Damn it, Holland. I chose you, not her. It was a horrible mistake and one I regretted the minute I sobered up." He couldn't explain to her how hollow he'd felt when he realized what he'd done.

"You must have decided it wasn't such a terrible mistake since you didn't divorce her right away."

At least they were talking about it. "Courtney and I discussed it. I wanted to, but the press had caught the story and I didn't want to embarrass my family any more. It was stupid, but pride was all I had at the time. And I had to protect Mom and Gus. So Courtney and I stayed married. I shipped out a week later. You were lost to me. And I was so angry."

It had been the worst time of his life. After losing his father and believing the worst about him, Holland had seemingly betrayed him. He hadn't been able to fill the hole in his heart until he'd recently realized that she'd never meant to hurt him.

"I might be able to buy that for six months, not two years," Holland pointed out.

"And I was at sea almost every one of those days. It was easy to forget that I was married. I gave her money and let her get an apartment that I spent exactly two nights in. Did I try to make it work? Not really. I might have thought I was at the time, but I was fooling myself. I knew it wouldn't work for the same reason you knew it wouldn't work with Chad. She wasn't you."

She shook her head, biting her lip as her gaze slid away. "I don't think we can go back."

"Then let's move forward." He closed the distance between them, unwilling to be parted from her a minute more. "What happened is in the past. It doesn't define us. I only know how damn much I need you now. I can't breathe I want you so much. The only question is do you want me, too?"

Her head snapped up. She met his stare, both uncertainty and heat flaring in her eyes. "I've always wanted you. No one has ever made me feel the way you do, Dax. In bed. Out of bed. Good and bad. It's always you."

Bitterness rang in her tone, but he ignored it and chose to focus on the positive. If he could get her into bed, get her underneath him, he could remind her just how good he could make her feel. He could also show her how much he cared. She wouldn't be able to turn away from him then. Once he was back in her bed, he would bind her to him and never let her go.

He sank his fingers into the silk of her hair. "I need you, Holland. My life has been a wreck without you in it."

She shook her head but didn't attempt to wriggle free. "I want you, too. I can't seem to help it. The minute you walk in a room, my body comes alive. But that doesn't change anything between us. It doesn't fix anything."

She was the one fooling herself if she thought making love again wouldn't right a few wrongs between them. He'd take that bet. It would change everything for him, and he suspected it would do the same for her.

He lowered his head down and layered his lips over hers.

Sweet perfection. Kissing Holland was more intimate than sex with all the other women combined. When he kissed Holland, he could feel them aligning, communicating on a level he knew he never would with anyone else.

Her arms wound around him, and Dax knew he had her. Now there would be no flying bullets, no interruptions. He had the night with her and he intended to make it count.

Over and over he kissed her, reminding himself of her taste and the sweet way she fit against his body. He would learn her all over again.

With a little whimper, she gave in and tugged at his T-shirt with a desperation that sent his blood racing. He pulled it over his head, tossing it to the side. Holland flattened her palms against his skin and he could see the sleepy expression of desire in her eyes as she looked him over. She caressed his chest slowly, as if assuring herself that he was real. He forced himself to remain still but he couldn't stop the groan that escaped his chest. It had been so damn long since he'd felt her skin against his. He closed his eyes and let the sensation take over.

Holland brushed warm palms over his shoulders and pecs, tracing the lines of his muscles down to his abs. She spread her hands apart, continuing her exploration a bit lower.

Her shocked gasp forced him to open his eyes. She'd found his latest scar.

"That's a bullet wound." She touched the puckered scar on his left side, right above his hipbone.

Naturally, she would know exactly what had caused the scar. He would be able to shrug and tell any other woman that it was an unfortunate cigar burn or something, but not a woman who had been around guns all her life. "We ran into a small incident back a few months ago. Connor, Gabe, and I had a little run-in with our Russian friends. The good news is, they're dead and I'm alive."

"Just an inch or two either way and . . ."

He forced her to look up at him. "There's no point in wondering about what could have happened, sweetheart. I lived. I managed to give Everly, who is now Gabe's fiancée, enough time to save him while Connor did the heavy lifting. But it's good you saw this. You should know the shit storm you're getting into if you continue investigating. They're not playing around. This is damn real."

Was he doing the right thing, dragging Holland into this? Dax couldn't treat her like some fainting flower who needed protection day and night. Maybe he should send her into hiding with his mother.

"You're not getting rid of me that easily." She narrowed her eyes at him. "Tell me you didn't just think about shipping me off to your mom's."

Sometimes she could practically read his damn mind. "Never. You're an asset. You're smart and capable and you know this case. I need you with me, but I wonder if I'm being selfish. If anything happened to you, I don't know how I'd live with myself."

Her fingers brushed the scar one more time, but when she looked up, her jaw had taken on that stubborn line he knew so well. "I'm not going anywhere. This is my case, too. I started it and I'm going to finish it. And you're right. We can't think about what could have happened. We need to live in the here and now. It's all we've really got."

He could have argued that they had a future, but she rose up on her toes and pressed her mouth to his, her tongue boldly sliding against his own. She plastered her body to his, letting him feel the soft fabric of her blouse, the pebbling of her nipples. He needed more from her, wanted her warmth against him, but he couldn't do it here and he needed to make things plain.

"I want to make love to you, Holland."

"I can't seem to say no tonight."

"Perfect." He lifted her into his arms and strode toward the bedroom.

SIXTEEN

Holland was past logical thought. She didn't care right now what had happened in the past. Not tonight. She could reconstruct the walls around her heart tomorrow, but tonight she intended to take everything he gave her. She didn't have the strength to fight him—and herself—anymore.

Any encounters she'd had while apart from Dax had been forgettable and unsatisfying. Only one man knew how to handle her. He was dangerous to her peace of mind, her soul, but if she played this right she might get what she needed without getting too burned.

He lifted her into his arms as if she weighed nothing at all. When she was with Dax, she could indulge her feminine side. So often she had to be tough and physical. She had to prove she could carry her own weight. Not with Dax. She never felt more feminine and delicate than when he picked her up and then laid her down on the bed they would share.

It was funny. She would never extend another man this kind of physical trust. She feared anyone else would drop her, but the thought never entered her mind with Dax. He wouldn't let her fall. Not ever.

Punishing him for his marriage was unfair. Deep down she knew it, but she couldn't seem to let it go. He'd entered into the most sacred institution between two people with another woman. She'd mourned him while he'd been saying I do.

"Don't." He stopped outside the bedroom door. "Don't go there. Stay with me tonight."

A sound from the bedroom down the hall caught her attention. She heard a low growl, followed by a feminine laugh before the obvious sounds of bedsprings squeaking.

"You'll have to excuse them. They're trying to conceive a baby." Dax's face softened.

"They're in love. It's natural. I would never have thought Connor could love any woman."

"Only the right one," Dax whispered. "It's that way with all of us. We'll play and fuck and party until we meet the right woman—and then we're done. Holland, let me take you to bed. Let me show you."

Her body reacted to the sounds of lovemaking that filled the house. She wouldn't be able to sleep next to Dax and not be with him. She'd been foolish to ever think she could be in the same room with that man and not touch him.

She nodded and tried not to think about the past.

Dax opened the door and tossed her on the bed, following her down onto the sea of soft bedding and fluffy pillows. He raised up enough to work open the fly of her jeans. The hiss of her zipper still lingered in the air when he dragged the denim over her hips. "Do you know how long I've been dying to see you like this?"

No matter what they did, the past was always there. "About two days?"

He shook his head as he unbuttoned her blouse and pulled the halves apart. He stared at her for a suspended moment before he palmed the lacy cup surrounding her breast with a reverence that brought tears to her eyes. "Always. Even when I was so mad I couldn't see straight, I wanted you right here. I wanted you naked and spread out for me. I wanted to look down and know that this gorgeous body belonged to me."

"You hated me." She still couldn't stand the thought. Yes, she'd planned it that way, pushing him to see her in a bad light. Sometimes she still pushed, trying to gauge the extent of the damage between them.

So far it all seemed one-sided on her part, and Holland wasn't sure what to make of that.

He flicked the center clasp of her bra. A lone light shined in the room from a small table lamp and it cast shadows around them, making Dax's body appear even more heavily muscled and predatory than usual. He settled himself on top of her, still wearing his jeans while he'd stripped her down to nothing but a bra and a filmy pair of panties. His every muscle seemed taut and there was a lean, hungry look in his eyes.

"Maybe." He drew the cups of her bra to the side, freeing her breasts, exposing her peaked nipples. "I still wanted you. I wanted to fuck you until you couldn't muster the energy to betray me again. On those long nights at sea, I would close my eyes and there you would be, spread out underneath me. You would beg me to take you back and offer me your body. And, oh, I would accept. I would brand you with my skin and you would never be able to leave my side again because everyone would know you were mine. In those dark hours, nothing mattered but making you pay and, sweetheart, I was definitely interested in my pound of flesh."

Somehow he made the nastiest things sound so sexy. "Tonight isn't about revenge."

He cupped one breast. "No. It isn't, but I still want to fuck you so long and hard that you can't even think of another man again. I want to be the only man in your mind, your body, and your heart."

She couldn't tell him that he'd already achieved his goal. Even when she'd dated another man, she hadn't forgotten Dax. No one would ever match him. "Touch me. No one touches me the way you do."

He palmed the other breast. "No one cares about you the way I do, Holland."

It was true. She could pretend that her desire stemmed simply from the fact that he was so damn good in bed. But she'd learned that his passion and skill in bed meant nothing without the emotional connection they'd found.

Maybe it had been severed when they parted. Maybe it wouldn't come back.

He leaned in and his naked chest met her breasts. "You're everything to me. When I was bleeding in the Crawford building after being shot, the only thing I could think about was you. I couldn't imagine dying without seeing you one last time."

The idea of a world without Dax filled her with complete denial and terror.

Holland clung to him tightly as his mouth descended on hers. She let go of her reservations, her barriers. No more talk of the past or the future. She couldn't handle it tonight.

Instead, she looped her arms around his back to find the smooth skin there. She traced the long line of his spine as she kissed him back with everything she had. Their tongues tangled as her nipples hardened, begging for his attention. "Please, Dax."

He nipped at her ear, the sensation flaring along her skin. "Please what?"

"Kiss me all over. It's been so long."

"How long? Never mind. I don't care. What you did with that asshole doesn't matter to me. I only care that you're with me now." He kissed the shell of her ear, dragging his tongue over the sensitive flesh there.

She shivered. He was right. All that mattered was the here and now.

She had to stop thinking about anything except how good it felt to be in his arms in this moment.

He kissed his way down her neck, leaving a trail of heat wherever he touched her. He forced her legs apart, making a place for himself between her thighs. The roughness of his denim rubbed against her damp folds. Only those thin panties shielded her and they did nothing to disguise his thick erection jutting against her.

"It feels so good to be here with you." His low voice rumbled over her breast as the heat of his mouth caressed the skin around her peak. "Like finally, finally coming home."

Holland concentrated on sensation as his tongue laved her nipple and tried not to think about his words. They were too sweet and they dragged her from the now into insane thoughts about the future.

She rolled her hips, needing the friction to take her higher. The frenzy she always felt when he touched her, took her, was already starting. The desperate need to feel him inside seized her.

But he seemed determined to take his time. He pinned her down, his body pressing her deliciously into the comforter. "Are you going to go wild for me?"

"I already am." She couldn't play coy or pretend.

Now that she'd made the decision to give him her all, she couldn't stop touching him. She hated the scant clothing still between them. It felt wrong. Nothing should come between them when they were alone together. They should spend hours naked and entwined.

"You're going to have to wait until I'm ready."

"Dax." She pressed her hips up, grinding against his hard erection. "You feel ready."

"Not even close." He sucked her nipple into his mouth as he forced her back down.

He tormented the tips of her breasts, his body infuriatingly still. Tingles brewed between her legs. As he brushed her hair from her face and murmured her name, Holland felt dangerously adored. Dax must know it, but he just piled on the torture, licking and sucking, moving between her nipples until she wanted to scream out her need. Every time she skidded toward the edge, he pulled back, contenting himself with a kiss, a caress, a sweet nip on her aching buds.

"Please, Dax," she panted, feeling feverish and restless. "I can't take it anymore."

He lifted his head, lips curling in an arrogant grin. "What do you want from me?"

"You know what I want." She clawed at his back.

"I want to hear you say it."

Of course he did. And in that moment, she wasn't too proud to let him hear it. "Fuck me."

He shook his head. "Can't yet. I need to taste you again. All over again. It's been so long. I can't move on until I remember just how sweet you are on my tongue."

She wanted to scream in frustration, but Dax was already sliding down her body, leading with his mouth, kissing his way over her breasts and to her belly. His tongue delved into her navel briefly before he licked his way to the elastic edge of the panties clinging to her hips.

She peered down the length of her body. He stared back up, those chocolate orbs meltingly intense. Their eyes met. The connection flowing between them jolted her.

"I've never gotten the taste of you out of my mouth." He dipped his fingers under the waistband of her panties, tugging them down. When they wouldn't move any farther, he simply ripped them off.

"Damn it, Dax. Those were my only pair of undies."

"You don't need them when you're with me. I want to keep you just like this. Open, ready for me. God, you smell so good." He nestled his nose right in her pussy, breathing deeply.

If anyone else had done that, she'd likely squirm and try to wriggle free or distract him. Not Dax. With him, her hips moved of their own accord, lifting to offer him everything. It wasn't wrong for him to bury his nose there. Nothing was too intimate between them.

Holland tossed her head back. She wanted this, ached for his mouth on her. Needed him so desperately. She could feel how wet she was. Her pussy pulsed in anticipation, and he was the only one who could send her hurtling into screaming ecstasy. He was the only one who could make her heart ache.

He pressed her thighs apart. "If I had my way, you would never wear panties again. You wouldn't ever leave this damn bed again. I would keep you right here, always ready for me. Always sweet for me to taste you. You're my favorite treat."

As he breathed, his hot exhalations spread over her pussy. She fisted the comforter, trying to hold in a whimper. But it was impossible. She begged without a word, her whole being focused on his generous mouth. He had full, sensual lips that shouldn't belong on a man. They, along with the rest of the package, made him far too sexy to deny.

He was also a man who liked to hear her talk dirty. She was willing to do it for his pleasure.

"Please, Dax. Please put your mouth on me. Lick me. Make me scream."

"Oh, sweetheart," he said, his Southern drawl arousing her even more, "I can do that."

He lowered his head and his tongue into her vulva, dragging up toward her clitoris. He stopped just shy, pausing to exhale his hot breath over her again. Holland bit back a scream. But he wouldn't give in or be rushed. He was far too stubborn and determined to make her pay. He clearly intended to extract his pound of flesh, waging a sweet war by using her own body against her.

He wouldn't let her up until he was satisfied. And unless she was willing to fight with him, she could do nothing but give in and let him have his way.

Finally, Dax dragged his tongue over her clitoris, warm and soft, and she couldn't muster the strength to fight him a second longer. She liked being helpless and at his mercy. She had to stop trying to control things between them and simply let them be for as long as they remained together.

Holland relaxed as his fingers parted her slick flesh, allowing him full access to her feminine core. His tongue pierced her. So good. The intimacy, the sensations, felt beyond anything she'd remembered. How had she forgotten for a second what this man could make her feel? So far beyond mere pleasure, being with Dax hit her square in the chest, right in the heart. Had she ever really been out of love with him?

She was so cold and intellectual most of the time. Given her occupation, she had to be. But with Dax, she couldn't seem to take a mental step back. He made her feel like the center of the world, like she was the only one who mattered to him. When she was with him, no one else mattered to her.

Dangerous thoughts, but she was past caring.

His thumb found her clit and he started to rub in sweet circles. "I want you to come for me. I've never been able to forget your flavor when you do."

He pressed down as his tongue thrust deep inside her. Ecstasy spiked and bliss rolled through Holland as she gave herself over to the orgasm. The tidal wave of pleasure racked her body and shook her deeper, leaving her stripped before Dax and so very vulnerable.

Even as she floated down from the high from her climax, Dax doffed his jeans and returned, a condom in hand. She watched as he rolled the latex over his cock and climbed between her thighs.

"I never feel more like a man than when I'm in bed with you." He fitted his cock to her opening and started to press inside. "Hell, I never feel more like me than when I'm with you, sweetheart. Missed you so much." He moved in, filling her in one long thrust.

Holland clung to him and gasped, feeling so full. God, she'd been empty for too long. Now she not only felt full . . . but complete.

She brought him closer because he was still too far away. "Kiss me. Please, Dax."

"There's nothing I love more than that." He gave her his weight, his body pressed to hers as she wrapped her legs around his lean waist.

She needed more of him. She plunged her fingers into his hair and drew him as close as two people could possibly be. Mouths fused together, breasts to chest, his cock deep inside her.

It didn't matter that she'd just come. Holland felt the urge building again, the need ratcheting up with every deep, rhythmic slide inside her until she clawed at him. He kissed her as his hips worked, grinding and thrusting. She rocked with him, following his every motion with ease.

Everything about this moment with him took her breath away. It was as if they'd never ended the relationship and never stopped making love. In this, they were still one.

He grabbed her hips and captured her mouth again as he thrust up hard. Holland went flying all over again, clinging to him and calling out his name. He lost control, plunging inside her again and again until he finally stiffened and roared out his own pleasure.

As they came down from the euphoric high in a tangle of breaths and sweat-dampened limbs, he sighed in satisfaction against her skin. "I've needed that for three years."

She held him close but said nothing because she was fairly certain she'd need him for the rest of her life.

Despite the pleasure still humming through her, she was afraid.

Dax woke up with a smile on his face.

Was there anything a night of amazing lovemaking couldn't cure? He was fairly certain there wasn't. He hadn't merely had sex with Holland or simply fucked her. They'd made love—three times, in fact, before she'd fallen into an exhausted sleep.

He turned on his side, careful not to wake her. She was deep in slumber, her body nestled against him. He wondered if she knew how much she resembled a soft little kitten when she slept.

Here, when she was most vulnerable, she trusted him. What would it take for him to win that trust back all the time?

"Are you watching me sleep?" she murmured with her eyes closed.

He couldn't help but smile. They were in the middle of a damn murder investigation, trying to unravel a conspiracy that might reach all the way to the White House, but he was grinning like a loon. "Yes."

"Weirdo."

Maybe, but he was her weirdo.

Dax sighed. They could stay in bed longer. Whatever was going on in the outside world could wait another thirty minutes. Besides, Connor would knock if something really craptastic had happened. Hell, Connor was probably finding delicious ways to wake up his own wife.

Wife. He meant to marry Holland, and they would do it right. No more quickie-Vegas shit. He and Holland would have a real wedding. He would wear his dress whites and she would find some gorgeous bridal gown. Gus would likely be the maid of honor and sleep with every groomsman she could.

"What are you laughing about?" She stared at him suspiciously with one eye open.

He sighed and settled against her, kissing her shoulder. "I was just thinking that Gus is going to be an interesting maid of honor."

Holland went still beside him. "Maid of honor? Who's getting married?"

Damn it. Would he ever get this right with her? He rolled over, his head propped on his hand. "Us."

"Us?" She sat up, tugging the covers around her body.

Which left him naked. Luckily, he didn't mind and it wasn't exactly chilly. He'd been warm lounging against her, and his cock was already straining. "Eventually. Sorry, I know that wasn't exactly romantic, so forget I said anything. Come back to bed."

"You're thinking about marriage."

"Of course I am, Holland. I never stopped wanting to marry you.

That can't be a secret, so what's wrong? Like I said, I know I'm not very romantic, but you don't want me to do the whole crazy dancing thing in the middle of the Quarter."

She stiffened, then stood and turned to him. "I never asked for marriage, Spencer."

Shit. They were back to Spencer. "I think asking is traditionally the man's role."

"I never asked you to ask me." She flushed, her skin going a lovely shade of pink as she glanced down at his erection. "Can't you do something about that?"

He grinned. "I certainly can if you'll come back to bed."

"Be serious for a minute, Dax. You just talked about marriage. I thought I made myself clear last night."

He didn't like the way this conversation was going. He sat up, trying to ignore his still-hard cock. "Yes, we were clearly together. Last night meant everything to me. It was a promise between lovers."

"It was inevitable because we are really good in bed together. We've always had combustible chemistry, but I'm not ready to marry you for it."

His first impulse was to lash out at her for rejecting him. The pain felt too familiar. Was this her form of revenge against him for marrying Courtney? She'd been the one to break faith with him, shove him aside. She hadn't trusted him.

Why was she making him into the bad guy?

He jumped to his feet and grabbed his pants, beyond ready to have it out with her. After last night, after all they'd been through, she thought she could dismiss him?

Then he looked at her—*really* looked at her. She stood there so proud and tall, chin lifted, shoulders straight. If he simply took her at face value, she seemed cold. But he knew better.

He'd once made the mistake of hearing her words but not really listening to her. It had cost them three years.

He refused to make the same mistake again.

"Coward."

She frowned. "Don't be ridiculous. I'm not afraid of you. I'm simply not interested in a long-term thing. Not with you. Not with anyone."

He was going to have to be patient with her, but that didn't mean he wasn't going to call her out. If he let her, she would hide forever. He didn't have that long. "Anyone? Sweetheart, this is about us. It's all about me and how I hurt you. I could go into the ways you hurt me, too, but that would be counterproductive."

"No, please tell me all the ways I hurt you."

He didn't bother with his pants. He wouldn't need them. This wasn't going to end the way she thought it would. He had zero intention of giving up. "You left me. Being apart from you hurt me deeply."

"Forgive me if I doubt that. You were married twenty-four hours later." She clutched the sheet like a shield. "It doesn't matter anymore."

"Oh, it matters." He stalked toward her. "A great deal. To both of us."

She took a step back, her eyes taking on a wary cast, as though she realized he intended to meet this problem head-on and demolish this barrier between them.

He stalked closer, need and instinct thrumming through his blood. Oh, he was about to teach her that he wouldn't fight fair. This was the most important battle of his life and he had no problem playing dirty.

"What are you doing, Dax?"

"What I should have done that day. I should have listened to my gut, Holland. You stood there and explained all the ways you'd betrayed me. Do you know what my instincts said to do?"

She stepped back again and gripped the sheet she'd wrapped around herself. Her response came out in a sweet, breathy gasp. "No. I don't."

She could stand tall all she liked. The truth was in her tone. Slightly breathless. Trembling. And her eyes. The windows to her soul looked open and vulnerable.

"My every instinct told me to get you into bed. You can't lie to me in bed."

"I'm not lying to you." She edged back again and she hit the door. Now he had her cornered. She had nowhere left to run. "I'm not ready to think about a future with you. Not now. Maybe not ever."

The words hurt, but he knew where they were coming from. He had to view this through her eyes, because his point of view wasn't the only one.

A realization struck him with a forcible whack upside the head. If he intended to love Holland, really love her the way she deserved to be loved, he had to bend and compromise. Gabe and Connor had already been through this. They'd learned to force their own needs and fears aside to deal with their women.

In the past, he would have stormed out of the room, hurt and aching and in search of a bottle. Now he simply eased closer to her because distance between them didn't solve anything. He didn't leave her any space, simply pressed his body against hers until the only thing separating them was that silly sheet she thought was protecting her.

She would never need protecting from him but Dax understood why she thought she did. He'd savaged her before. He'd taken everything meaningful and tossed it aside. She'd had a hand in it, too, but he'd committed the real crime.

"I'm not going anywhere, sweetheart," he vowed, sliding his hand along the nape of her neck. "Not ever again, so you don't have to worry about that. I'm going to be here today and tomorrow and all the tomorrows after that. The future is going to take care of itself. And I'm going to take care of you."

"It won't work. I've always known it can't." Tears sheened her eyes when she shook her head. "I wish it could."

He pulled her close, offering her the comfort of his body. "Then we'll live in the moment. If it doesn't work, we'll have had this time together."

"You don't mean that," she accused, but she let go of the sheet and wrapped her arms around his waist. "You're telling me what you think I want to hear."

He chuckled because she really did know him. "I am indeed. I'm telling you that because you're scared, but I know that I'm going to love you forever. I'm never going to leave again."

She lifted her chin. Light slanted in, illuminating the sadness in her eyes. "But I will. Do you remember that day? Joy's wedding. You said if I could kiss you and still walk away, you would let me go. I'm going to walk away at the end of this, Dax. I can't do this with you again. I know you think you can promise me the world, but I don't trust anything anymore."

Then he would make her believe. But now there was no point in arguing—at least not with his words.

He kissed her. "If all we have is the next few days or weeks, I'm not going to waste them."

He cupped her breast, his cock lengthening against the soft curve of her belly. She sighed, her head falling forward onto his shoulder.

"I won't fight you. As long as we're working together, I'll be in your bed. I don't want to fight about that. But I will walk away. I don't want to hurt you, but when this is over so are we."

He would see about that. He had days to convince her and he knew one surefire way how.

He took her mouth in a long, luxurious kiss. He would never let her go. When this mission was over, he would still be by her side. She would want him there. He would make sure of it.

"I made that deal with you a long time ago," he whispered against her lips. "I was a different man then. You should know I'll fight dirty this time. I'll fight for us, Holland."

He picked her up and carried her back to bed.

"There's no fighting," she said as he laid her down. "I told you, I'll be your lover while this lasts."

She was so stubborn and she would try to hold out until the very end. Dax intended to make that utterly impossible.

"Then I think I should get my way, don't you? If I've got so little time, I should definitely have you any way I want you. Get on your hands and knees, sweetheart." He moved to the bedside table where he'd tucked the condoms in the drawer.

"What are you doing?" Hesitation halted her voice, but she obediently turned over and rose to her hands and knees, leaving that glorious backside in the air.

So fucking pretty. He ran a hand over her cheeks and down to her pussy. She was already warm and wet for him. He tested her, sliding a single finger through her labia. "I'm going to make you scream for me. Look at that. You're already ripe and ready."

"How do you do this to me?" She bowed her head, blond hair brushing the mattress, in a sign of surrender.

"The same way you do it to me. Do you honestly believe I walk around with an erection all the time? Not even when I was a kid." He found her clitoris with lazy fingers and circled it, watching the way she arched and squirmed. "Only one woman can get me hard and ready just by walking in a room. The right woman. You."

Holland moved her hips in time with his rhythm, mewling like a pretty little cat in heat. "It feels so good. I know I shouldn't give in, but I can't help it."

And that was exactly what she was afraid of. She wasn't in control with him. He had to teach her that was all right. He wasn't in control with her, either, but she was a safe place. They didn't need control with each other. They needed to let go and simply be.

"Do you want to come, sweetheart?"

"Yes," she whimpered. "I need it."

"And I need to watch you. I love watching you climax. I love the way it feels when you're wrapped around my cock and you finally let go. Don't come yet. Not without me." He aligned his stiff flesh with her slick opening and pressed in with slow, short thrusts.

He loved how tight she was, how right she felt. No matter how many times he had her, he always had to fight his way inside. But once he did . . . they always fit together perfectly.

Holland's breathing turned shallow. She cried out his name as she shoved her hips up in silent entreaty, offering herself to him.

He gripped her hips and gave her what she wanted, sinking a bit deeper with each little move. She felt different from this angle and he loved that he could see how he affected her through the way she clutched the railing of the headboard, arched her spine to take more of him, and tossed her head in pleasure. Her whole body was taut and wanting. She wasn't thinking about all the ways he'd hurt her now. She was simply lost in the moment with him.

He would change her mind. He had to. He couldn't live without this woman.

I love you. He said it silently because he hadn't earned the right to say it out loud yet.

He used her hips to pull her back as he began to fuck her in earnest. She wouldn't accept words of love from him so he let his body do the talking. He worshipped her, caressing her softly, bending to press a kiss to her back, whisper words against her neck. More than once, he took them both to the edge of climax and then dragged them back because he wanted this to last. He never wanted his time with her to end.

She rocked with him, shoving her hips back and taking him as deeply as she could. She fought for her pleasure, and it excited him like nothing else could. Somewhere deep down, like that heart she didn't want to acknowledge, she wanted him, too.

When he couldn't hold out a second more, he reached around and found her clitoris again, giving it a firm rub as he delved even deeper inside her.

Holland gasped and pushed back against him, the muscles inside her core tightening deliciously.

He couldn't stop the freight train of desire. A tingle began at the base of his spine, then shot through his body. Dax could have sworn he exploded with pleasure. As climax hit, she turned him inside out and flattened him. With a long groan, he gave her everything, gritting his teeth with the effort to hold himself deep and stay inside her as long as possible.

When he had nothing left, he fell on top of her, not even thinking to keep his weight from her. They landed in a tangle of arms and legs. It was exactly where he wanted to be.

And where he intended to be when everything was over—right here with her.

SEVENTEEN

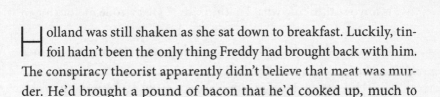

Holland was still shaken as she sat down to breakfast. Luckily, tinfoil hadn't been the only thing Freddy had brought back with him. The conspiracy theorist apparently didn't believe that meat was murder. He'd brought a pound of bacon that he'd cooked up, much to Lara's displeasure.

Connor had been sneaking pieces of bacon all morning.

And all she'd been able to dwell on was the fact that Dax had mentioned marriage.

She shouldn't let herself even think about it, much less hope again. How was she supposed to trust him? He said all the right things, but the minute the chips were down would he turn to the nearest available woman and run off to Vegas again?

She'd told him she could forgive him, but was she fooling herself? She didn't want to be Dax Spencer's second wife when he'd gone into his first marriage with such a cavalier attitude. What did marriage really mean to a man who could do that?

"So we've had some overnight developments. Mostly because Freddy doesn't sleep," Connor said, pouring her another cup of coffee.

She was so ready to focus on anything besides her love life. "You don't sleep?"

Freddy shrugged. "Not much. That whole eight-hours-of-sleep thing is a myth perpetrated by the mattress companies and big pharma."

"Freddy's very wary of big pharma," Lara acknowledged. "But he's also really good at digging up stuff other people can't find."

"Like records of Admiral Spencer visiting a psychiatric hospital in the English countryside. He requested records there," Connor added.

That had her sitting up straight. "Records for who?"

"A patient named Jane Downing," Freddy explained. "But I highly suspect that's an alias. The hospital is known for being a hideout for the wealthy and insane. It's small, with a high employee-to-patient ratio. They employ a gourmet chef."

"Is anyone thinking what I'm thinking?" Dax strode in, tucking in his shirt. His hair was still wet from his shower.

"If you're wondering if Jane Downing was actually Constance Hayes, then yes," Holland replied.

She didn't like to think about how close she'd come to climbing into that shower with him just to feel him wrap his arms around her again. The impulse had been there. She'd thought about inviting him into hers. Instead, she'd locked the door. She'd needed time, a little space.

"We've put a call into Zack," Lara explained. "And we've got Everly trying to check some other rehab centers or mental hospitals to see if that alias comes up. We know she went on a couple of 'vacations' that were actually stays in a place like this. Not that any of them took."

"Everly?" The name suddenly rang a bell. "Gabe's fiancée? Sorry, I'm still getting used to the guys actually having women attached to them for more than a night or two."

Lara smiled. "Everly is wonderful and she's really good at getting inside computer systems . . ." She cleared her throat. "I mean at investigating."

So Gabe was marrying a hacker. "As long as she's not hacking the military, it's not my jurisdiction. Besides, sometimes you've got to break a few rules to find justice. Every good cop knows that."

Lara sighed. "Thank god."

"She says that because she hasn't always been on the up-and-up, have you?" Connor eyed his wife with a ghost of a smile on his lips. "Little criminal."

"I have not. Anything I ever did was to expose criminal activity," Lara replied primly.

"She's scared that because you're a fed, you'll arrest her," Freddy said with a grin. "I think she was right the first time around. You're a Mulder."

"I'm a what?"

Lara waved it off. "Freddy has this idea in his head that all government employees are either Mulders or Smoking Men. He's watched way too much *X-Files*. Mulder was the one after justice, you see. He was the one who believed. And the Cigarette Smoking Man was evil, always involved in lots of bad things. So him calling you a Mulder means he likes you."

Awesome. She gave him a smile because he was actually kind of interesting, in a weird way. "Thanks. I'm glad you don't think I'm the other sort. So what are we doing while we wait for Zack to call back? I have some ideas about how to track down Peter Morgan."

Dax sat down across from her. "My father's aide-de-camp? I thought everything surrounding him was classified. We're not hacking Navy personnel files. I've got Roman looking into it. They can't find his current address."

"I know, but I found out that his mother is in a nursing home not two miles outside of New Orleans." She'd made a few phone calls, talked to some staff. They'd been more than happy to tell a "social worker" that Peter Morgan's mother got a weekly visitor without fail. "I think he's seeing her. The nurses at the home say it's her nephew who stops in, but his mother was an only child. Needless to say, I think he's visiting his momma and he usually does it at the same time every week. Which happens to be this afternoon."

Lara clapped her hands. "We're staking out a nursing home." She stopped suddenly and frowned. "Wait. The last time we did that someone died horribly."

"Yeah, how about you stay here and hold down the bayou with Freddy." Connor patted his wife's hand. "Holland and I will stake out the old folks' home and figure out where Peter's hidey-hole is. I don't want to spook the man, at least not until we're ready and know everything we want to ask him."

Dax frowned. "I'll go with Holland."

She shook her head. "You have to talk to your mother, find out if there's any connection at all between your father and Zack's mom."

"There's this little invention I call a cell phone," Dax offered.

"I think you should see her." Holland didn't like the idea of Judith rattling around that big house with only bodyguards and her housekeeper for company. "After we nearly got burned alive last night, you should check on her. Talk to her. Pick her brain. Search your father's office. It might spur something. I know it's been years. Maybe something was overlooked."

"By NCIS? I doubt it," Dax replied, then sighed. "But I should make sure all is well and no one has come near my mother."

"Besides, she needs to lay eyes on you. I'm sure she's heard about the fire." Holland would be worried out of her mind if she were Judith. She would want to see Dax, reassure herself that her baby boy was all right. She wouldn't be able to sleep otherwise. "Did you even call her to tell her you're okay?"

His face turned a dull red. "Fine. I'll visit her, but I'm going in quietly. I don't want anyone to follow me back here. I know an indirect route in. As a teenager, Gus was really good at sneaking in and out of the house. She taught me well. Connor, take care of my girl."

He was gone before she could protest that she wasn't his girl.

He would probably just argue anyway.

"So we're staking out an old folks' home. That sounds like a blast."

She'd be alone in a car with Connor for hours. Yeah, nothing could possibly go wrong.

Connor sat back. "We should definitely get there soon. You know, I could tell you some stories about Dax on the way. That will be entertaining."

Holland suspected that was Connor code for *I'm going to ask you a bunch of questions you don't want to answer.* She sighed. It was going to be a long afternoon.

D ax eased into the house, the bodyguard at the backdoor nodding his way.

"Hello, sir."

Dax held out a hand and shook the other man's. He was a big guy dressed in an impeccable if nondescript suit, despite the fact that he would spend almost all day indoors. But that was how the Secret Service tended to roll. Dax had pegged the agent the minute he saw the guy. Gus hadn't sent out mere paid guards. She'd talked Zack into sending the big guns.

"How have things been around here?" he asked.

"Quiet, sir. Though your mother took me and Bentley for fifty bucks apiece when we played cards last night."

"Oh, don't be silly. That was fake money. I never play for real money. Buying shoes is what real money is for," his mother said as she walked into the kitchen, her arms wide. "You come here, boy. If you weren't too big I would turn you over my knee for scaring me like that."

So Holland had been right. His mom had heard about the torch and burn at Holland's place. "I'm sorry I didn't call. Obviously we escaped but things were a little crazy. I didn't realize you would know that Holland and I were involved. They didn't mention names on the news."

"Holland's uncle called looking for you. He was worried about his niece. I had to tell him I had no idea where you were. It's not the same thing as when you're deployed, Daxton. You have to call."

He stepped toward his mother, pulling her slender frame in for a hug. "Sorry. I promise. Can we talk for a few minutes? I have to get back out to Holland, but you should know we're not alone. Connor is with us."

She patted his back. "Well, that makes me feel better. He's a good man. Shall we go to the parlor?"

"Dad's office is more appropriate."

Her face tightened. "Oh. This isn't a social call."

He hated having to grill her, but she was the only one still alive who could talk—and he wanted to keep it that way. "No, Mom."

She nodded and turned, her shoulders squared, a true Southern belle about to do her duty. He loved his mom. Holland reminded him of his mother at times. She had that same steel in her spine.

She was silent as she walked into his father's office. The shades were drawn and she drifted to the windows as if to open them, but stopped with a shake of her head.

Instead, she sat in the seat across from the desk, her hands in her lap. "What do you need to know?"

He hated the fact that she couldn't open the blinds. She couldn't let sunlight into this room. When this was over, he was hiring someone to redecorate, to make this into a room his mother could love again. "Dad took a trip to London shortly before the scandal broke out. Do you know anything about it?"

"It was a conference of some kind."

He shook his head, hating that he had to tarnish his father's memory more and further disillusion his mother. "He didn't actually attend a conference. We think he went overseas for personal reasons. Have you ever heard of an institution called Homewood? It's a small hospital in the English countryside."

She frowned. "Was your father hurt?"

"No. He went there to request the records of a patient named Jane Downing."

"I know that name." She put a hand to her forehead as though trying to recall where she'd heard it. "Downing was a family name. Oh, why can't I remember? Hayes. Downing was Constance Hayes's mother's maiden name. They were a very genteel family. From Sussex, I believe."

His mother had an interest in genealogy. "Was there a family member named Jane?"

"Oh, I did Zack's genealogy for him back when you were in college. Such an interesting family. I don't recall a Jane in the last few generations, though if memory serves, it was Constance's middle name. I've got the family tree here somewhere."

"No need, Mother. I think that answers the question." She'd gone into the hospital under an alias. "Did Dad have some kind of connection with Constance Hayes?"

"Are you asking me if your father had an affair with her?" His mother waved a hand in utter dismissal. "Not a chance. Your father liked them younger and far less troubled than Constance. That woman was a mess. I don't think I ever encountered her when she wasn't drinking. She had a serious problem. And lord, she could talk your ear off. About the strangest things, too. Never made any sense. I wasn't surprised to find out she was intoxicated when she died in that car accident."

The hair on the back of his neck was prickling his skin. Constance Hayes's name had been on Natalia's list. People who talked got silenced in this world. Had her fatal wreck really been an accident? Probably not. So what had Constance known? "What kinds of things?"

"I don't recall specifics."

"I need them, Mother."

She frowned. "What does this have to do with your father's case?"

He had to tell her. He hated dragging her back in before they knew all the facts, but he couldn't keep it from her. "I think Dad was drugged when he was in bed with Amber Taylor."

"Why would you imagine that?"

"The police had actual photos of him in bed with her, but he appears to be drugged. He's not actively participating and those photos weren't taken at the motel in which he supposedly assaulted the girl. I think they were taken in England and used later to frame Dad because he was investigating something dangerous." He quickly gave her a rundown of what they'd uncovered.

"A list? And everyone on the list is dead?"

He nodded. "At least all the people I recognize. I think Dad must have suspected that Constance hadn't died because she'd been driving drunk. When he began digging into her life and her death, they invented dirt on him. When he refused to be blackmailed, they killed him. I don't believe he committed suicide, Mom. Not for a second. Neither does Gus."

Tears pooled in his mother's eyes. "You really think he didn't sleep with that child?"

At least he could give her some comfort. "No. And I think I can prove it. The entire incident was staged to strip him of credibility and give him something else to focus on."

His mom drew in a shuddering breath, seeming to steady herself. "Constance would talk sometimes. Mostly gibberish. We didn't see them very often, you know, but she seemed to gravitate toward your father when we got together. I thought it was because he was so handsome, but maybe she had another reason. Do you remember Zack's wedding day?"

"Vividly. I remember I had to help Dad get Mrs. Hayes out of the sight of reporters and cameras because she was so wasted."

"Yes, but you didn't sit with her. Your father and I did until her husband arrived. I do believe she was afraid of him. At the time, we decided not to interfere. She was so out of sorts that it was impossible to know which of her fears were real and which were in her head."

"Did she talk about anything specific? I know it was a long time ago, but anything at all could help."

"She talked about Joy. Constance was worried about her. At first I thought she was distraught about the marriage, as though she thought Joy wasn't good enough for Zack. Then she said something puzzling about Joy finding out. I wasn't sure what she meant precisely. She wasn't always coherent. But it sounded as if something happened in Russia. She said that if Joy found out about Moscow, they would kill her. No idea what that meant. She also talked about Zack being a baby and how difficult it was. Was he a cranky child? Constance didn't say more and I didn't really understand. But I do remember that your father was disturbed by something she said to him in private."

"What was that?"

"He said that Constance asked him to protect her. She said, 'One day they won't need me and they'll kill me.' So you really think her accident wasn't an accident at all?"

He shook his head. "I'm beginning to suspect someone has gone to a great deal of trouble to hide something that's deeper and goes back further than we ever imagined."

"Your father didn't really hurt that child? I'm sorry. I need to say it out loud."

He crossed the floor to his mother, sinking to one knee in front of her and taking her hand. "He might have been guilty of a lot of things, but not this."

"And you really think he didn't kill himself?"

"No, Mom. That was a setup, too."

Her hands tightened on her lap. "I was going to divorce him. I was so angry. I didn't know how he could possibly be the man I'd married and had two children with. I thought . . ."

"You must have never known him? You did." All these years and she'd been drowning in unanswered questions and guilt? "He was going to fight. He told me that in a letter he never mailed. He wrote that no matter what happened he would fight to clear his name and save his family. He didn't kill himself to escape his shame or guilt or his marriage. He was going to fight for you."

She squeezed his hand. "I loved him. I truly did."

"He loved you, too. I know he didn't always show it. He did things that hurt you, but I truly believe he loved you." Dax couldn't find it in his heart to judge his parents any longer. Their marriage had blossomed in a different time, and its inner workings would always be a mystery to him. The fact that his father could dishonor his vows and his wife with another woman still pissed him off, but anger served no purpose. There were always two sides to every marriage. The best any son could do was to love his parents.

Dax vowed to work as hard as he could for his own marriage and treat it with the sanctity it deserved.

After a moment's tears, his mother reached for a tissue and dried her eyes. "But if he didn't hurt that girl, then why did he walk into the motel with her?"

That was a very good question. "You know, we never see his face in that video."

"It was his uniform. I know because I'd had to patch it. He'd torn the sleeve and they were getting him a new one, but he was stuck wearing the two jackets he had until they replaced it. I don't know why he chose to wear the one that needed to be fixed, but I recognized it."

"Did you ever ask why the hell he would wear a uniform to the scene of a crime at all? I know you were angry with him, but give him some credit. He wasn't a foolish man."

"He was drunk that night. He did stupid things when he'd had too much Scotch."

He couldn't argue with her on that. "Did they leave you a copy of that video? I know Dad's attorney got a copy of it. You don't happen to still have one, do you?"

She sighed. "The lawyer left a box with me. I'm sure it's in there, along with all the legal filings. I have a copy of everything, though I've never really looked through it. Dax, if your father was innocent, we have to clear his name."

He cupped his mother's shoulder. "That's exactly what I intend to do."

EIGHTEEN

Holland got out of the car, stretching after hours of being cooped up and listening to Connor tell stories of how amazing Dax Spencer was. According to Connor, Dax had singlehandedly helped him pass algebra, saved him from drowning once, and given Zack the idea to run for office. Holland wasn't sure when he'd had time to do those things since apparently young Dax had spent a whole lot of time helping the poor and guiding old ladies across the road. Oh, and Connor had worked in a story about Dax saving a dog, too.

"You know, if your back's giving you trouble, you should really see Dax."

She rolled her eyes. "Give you a lot of back massages, did he?"

Connor grinned. "Overplayed my hand?"

For a former CIA operative, he wasn't very smooth when it came to building up his friend as a potential mate. "A long time back, Sparks." She sighed as she closed the car door. It looked like Dax was already back at the remote fishing camp and waiting inside. "I'm not so sure we shouldn't have confronted Peter Morgan. He could easily disappear again."

"I don't think so," Connor replied. "He seems pretty settled into his house. It's off the beaten trail. He thinks he's pulled himself off the grid. I can promise you, he didn't catch me tailing him. We know where he is. When Dax is ready, we confront him. But we need to know what we're going to ask him first."

"We should ask him why he turned in an innocent man." It seemed pretty simple. If it had been up to her, she would have hauled him in and questioned the little bastard until he gave everything up.

Connor shut his door. "I want Dax there. He deserves to be involved in whatever goes on. You know he took a bullet to save Gabe's fiancée a few months ago."

"Yes. I saw the scar."

Connor's jaw tightened before he spoke. "I know you think you have to push him away, but don't throw something good out because it might go bad someday. I thought I needed to do that but it's better on this side, Kirk. It may sound stupid, but it's true. Take a leap. You'll see. And if you don't, well, if you ever need anything, you come to me because whether you're brave enough or not, he'll always love you and that means I'll always help you."

Holland blinked, stared. She had zero idea how to handle that.

Connor turned toward the house. "Don't stay out here too long. We need to catch up with Dax, see what he might have learned and decide how we want to proceed. We can't hide out here forever."

No. They couldn't, which meant she would have to decide what to do about Dax soon. She'd walk away. Wasn't that decision already made?

The cell in her pocket chirped and she was happy for the distraction. Her uncle. Yeah, her happiness faded somewhat. She answered anyway. "Hello, Uncle Beau."

"Holland, I'm glad you decided to pick up the phone. I think we should talk."

"I don't have a ton of time, but you should know that I'm safe. I'm with a couple of very well-trained men."

"If you're with who I think you're with, you could be in serious trouble." Her uncle's deep voice rumbled over the line. "I looked into this situation and it's bad. Come in and let me put you in protective custody."

Like she was going to let that happen. "I'm fine. The last thing I need to do is sit in a cheap motel eating takeout. I'm good."

"Have you wondered why the only times your life gets really dangerous is when that man is in it? I'm not saying he means to put you at risk, but he's involved in something none of you can handle."

"What have you found out?"

"The bullets match a very specific gun. We found three casings on the assassin's perch across from your building. And yes, I said assassin because those casings were specially made and matched casings found at three other crime scenes. Apparently they're this bastard's calling card. He's some kind of European hit man. Holland, someone is trying very hard to kill Dax Spencer and this killer won't care that you're in the way."

That was interesting news. "Is he Russian?"

Beau paused. She could hear her uncle shuffling paperwork. "Um, they think he's Russian because he does a lot of work for one particular syndicate. Have you ever heard of someone named Ivan Krylov? I fucking hate these foreigners."

She'd read all of Connor's documentation about the events in New York a few months ago. A lieutenant with the Krylov syndicate had shot Dax. The same group had also been involved in Maddox Crawford's murder. She held her tongue, though, because that information was classified—not in any formal way, but Connor and Dax didn't want it leaking. "I'll check into it."

"Damn it, Holland. We're all worried about you. I know you put in a request to visit the prison so you can interrogate Sue Carlyle again."

She'd had to. Unfortunately, one didn't simply walk into a prison and visit without paperwork. "It's not really an interrogation. I just have some follow-up questions."

"She's dead," he said, his tone flat. "She was found in her cell hanging from her bed sheets a few weeks ago. She didn't leave a note."

It wasn't a stretch to imagine a mad woman becoming suicidal but . . . damn it. "Can I read the reports of her death? I presume there was an autopsy?"

"Sure. Come into the office and I'll let you read everything I've got."

So he could put her in protective custody? No thanks. "Just e-mail me the report, please."

He sighed. "Haven't you noticed that people around Captain Spencer and his friends die? His buddy Connor was visiting a woman at a nursing home a few weeks ago when this same assassin apparently murdered the woman he was talking to."

Natalia Kuilikov. "I wasn't aware it was the same assassin who's after Dax. Of course, I didn't know any assassin was after Dax. I can tell you're worried, but I can't let this go. Maybe the heat would be off Dax if the NOLA PD would officially open an investigation into the admiral's death. If we start shining a light on this, the vermin will run back to the shadows."

"Or you'll get my men killed."

She was so frustrated with him. "I let you talk me out of this once, but I have to ask . . . Why the hell did you become a cop? To walk away the minute an investigation gets dangerous? That's the nature of our job. We take those chances so everyday citizens don't have to. Protect and serve, Uncle Beau. It's what we're trained to do and you're telling me to do neither."

"I'm telling you to grow up and stop being so fucking naive," he growled. "Do you know why I became a cop? Because it was that or getting my ass shot off in the goddamn military. I'm not about to get me or my men killed because your boyfriend stuck his nose in where it doesn't belong. Tell him to get out of my town and go back to D.C.

where he belongs. You know what? I'll tell him myself. And, Holland, you better rethink your position, because he's going to get you killed."

The line cut off abruptly and she stared at her phone. Her uncle had never spoken to her like that. Never.

"You all right?" Dax stood not ten feet away from her, his big body illuminated by the afternoon sun.

She slipped her cell in her pocket. "I'm all right. We can cancel our trip to the prison."

His eyes closed briefly. "Sue Carlyle's dead, then. Suicide?"

"By all appearances." The time had come to choose a side and make it known. "Likely the Krylov syndicate arranged the scene, just as they did with your father. They killed your father and now they're trying to kill you."

He stepped closer, and when he put his arms around her, she didn't push him away. "I'm sorry this is causing trouble between you and your family."

"It's all right. All that matters is figuring out what happened and what these criminals want." She let herself soak in the warmth of his body.

He stepped back, taking her hand. "I'm glad you said that, because I think Freddy found a clue."

"Good." She turned to follow him, when something caught her eye. She stopped, staring for a moment at the dirt nearby. It had rained earlier, making a single footprint on the far side of the dirt road they'd driven up visible. "Has anyone been out here?"

She crept closer to inspect. Connor had parked close to the tree line in order to give Dax room on the narrow road in case he needed to leave in the Jeep.

Maybe it wasn't a print. Damn rain. It could be anything. She was being paranoid.

"I think we've all been outside." Dax looked down to the spot she examined. "Sweetheart, that's so muddy I'm not sure what it is. Do you want to have Freddy look at it?"

"No. We just need to be careful. And maybe we should get inside." She took his hand, leading him toward the cabin. Suddenly, being out in the open made her feel exposed. "Did everyone turn the locator off their phones?"

"Yes. Freddy made sure. The truth is someone who really wants to trace a call can get it to the nearest cell tower, but then they'd still have a search on their hands. Camps like this are all along the bayou."

"Yeah, we tracked your father's aide to one earlier, though it's not nearly as nice as this one." She glanced around as they entered. "Have I thanked you for not insisting we hide out in a hovel?"

"Yeah, we may be the target of the Russian mob, but never say we don't lay low in style," Dax said with a wink as he escorted her in. "I was talking to Connor about everything. After we have a discussion with Peter, it might be time to head to London. We need to go to that hospital and figure out if Constance Hayes really was there and why."

"How is Zack handling it?"

"In his usual Zack way. He does that thing where he's silent for a moment. Then he thanks me for the info. Roman isn't much better. I tried to leave Gus out of it, but apparently she listens in a lot. One of these days Roman is going to fire her."

Holland had to laugh at that. "No, he's not. He will never, never fire Gus. Not when he's done so much to keep her close."

Dax stopped and stared. "What do you mean?"

Maybe she shouldn't have said anything. After all, she merely had a theory. The truth was she hadn't seen Gus or Roman in three years. "Nothing."

"Are you talking about the way Roman acts kind of like a big brother around Gus and pokes at her, all while watching her like a hungry lion who wants to pounce on an antelope?" Lara asked, looking up from her laptop.

Connor frowned, looking down at his wife. "That's ridiculous. Roman and Gus had a thing like a million years ago. She's so not his type. And who's the antelope in that pairing? It's sure as fuck not Gus. She's a predator."

Dax sent his friend a stare that could have stripped paint off a wall. "Hey, that's my sister!"

At least someone was willing to stand up for Gus.

"You see Roman with her long-term?" Connor shot back. "Roman, who likes his women demure and genteel?"

"No, but she's not a predator. I'll admit she's got claws, but she's not looking to take Roman down." He went pale as he looked back at Holland. "Is she? Please tell me she's not, because she'll be doomed to disappointment. Roman really is looking for his Jackie Kennedy."

She shrugged a little. "I haven't seen them together for years. I could totally be wrong, but the air used to crackle around them whenever they stood in the same room."

"He might think he wants a Jackie, but damn, he sure looks at the Marilyn a lot," Lara said. "I just think you two are too close to him to see it. I know he thought he was in love with Joy, but I don't see it from what I know about her."

"Roman was in love with Joy?" That floored Holland. "Did they have an affair? No. No. Joy would never have cheated on Zack."

Dax looked straight at her. "And neither would Roman. He put her on a pedestal as an example of his perfect woman. She was kind to him. Gus isn't always kind."

"No, but Roman would have walked all over Joy. She couldn't have handled his ruthless side. Gus would find it hot." The more Holland thought about it, the more she felt sure she was right. "Joy would have bored Roman to death. Two years, maybe less, then he would have moved on. But it sounds like he's still circling—and still interested in Gus." Holland smiled at the thought. "Zack was definitely more Joy's speed."

"Did she love Zack?" Dax asked.

"Yes, but then Joy tended to love everyone. I know they didn't have the most passionate marriage. I adored Joy, but she was very quiet. She preferred to stay in the background. Her father approved of the marriage and that was that. But I'll be honest, I worried Zack would break her heart because of his press secretary. I always feared he would have an affair with her because he obviously wanted her."

"Liz." Connor sighed. "Yeah, we don't have to worry about that now. Zack hasn't touched Liz, by the way. He's still faithful to Joy, so don't think too poorly of him."

"I wasn't. I simply worried about Joy, but she's gone. Why wouldn't Zack pursue the woman he so obviously wanted?" The answer hit her. "He thinks the Russians will use her against him."

Dax nodded. "Yes. Which is why we need to deal with the situation here ASAP so we can end the rest of this mess. If Peter can't tell us the whos and whys, we'll need to go to England and start working it from that angle. It's the only other lead we've got."

"We might think about going to the source," Holland urged. "The Krylov syndicate. Yesterday my uncle found evidence that our would-be assassin was a known Krylov associate. He said the bullet casings matched the murder of a woman Connor was visiting at a nursing home."

"Shit. So we've got a pro after us," Dax said under his breath. "After me."

She knew that expression. It was his "protective man" look, and she wasn't letting it go any further. "Don't you dare even think about leaving me behind. My uncle already tried to talk me into protective custody. I'm not doing it. I might have a uterus but it doesn't mean I'm not damn good at my job. If you don't want me with you, I'll investigate on my own, but I have a stake in this and I'm the only one here with anything close to real jurisdiction."

"I have presidential authority," Dax pointed out.

"You captain a boat for your commander in chief. You don't investigate murder and mafia. I'm the law enforcement officer. Let me do my job, Dax."

He held up a hand, obviously giving in. "I will, since you have a stake in this."

He was deliberately misunderstanding her. "Like I said, I'm NCIS and this crime involved a Naval officer."

Dax sighed. "Of course. I didn't expect you to give a shit about anything else."

She was being stubborn. "These bastards fucked me over and fucked over my friends, and I'm not going to stand by and allow it to happen."

"Then come with me and we'll show you what we have," Dax promised.

Connor stepped aside. "I'm actually going to go look into something else. You didn't happen to get the police report on the shooting yesterday, did you?"

She nearly growled her frustration. "No, my uncle told me the only way he would give it to me is if I came in. We all know where that would lead."

"I have some friends. I'll see what I can do." Connor left the room, striding down the hall.

"By friends he means hackers," Lara offered with a smile. "Come on. Freddy is using the same techniques he used to bust that new Sasquatch video that came out. He's up on all the latest ways to forge a video."

Freddy looked up from his laptop. "There are lots of software programs that can change the appearance of frames or sequences. Hollywood has some great special effects, and now any kid with a tablet can use most of them, but I don't think they used software to fix the problems with this. They went low tech, which is actually surprisingly effective."

"What do you mean?"

"Watch the video of the admiral supposedly entering the hotel room with Amber Taylor. He never turns his head," Freddy pointed out.

"Yes, so there's no positive identification except the desk clerk who checked him in." It had always nagged at her. This video had been shown all over the news. It was much less damning than the photographs, yet this was the evidence they'd released. Had they known the still photos of the two of them supposedly in bed wouldn't stand up to real scrutiny? If they'd sent those pictures to the press, they would have been analyzed to death and someone probably would have found out the issue with time and place.

"Eyewitness testimony can be faulty," Freddy said as he typed, and a new screen came up. "Sometimes the mind simply can't remember all the details. And . . . then other times people are just assholes who can be bought. I would bet that's the case with this guy, Anson King."

"Where is he now?" Dax asked.

"Conveniently died of cancer about six months after your father." Freddy sent him an acidic scowl. "I'm sure his family got a windfall for his assistance. He was a perfect choice. Because of the media circus and high-profile attention, the statutory rape trial against your father would likely have taken longer than King's six months. The guy could have signed an affidavit, or been questioned by the police or attorneys, but he didn't. Either would have been admissible in court. But even if the judge had elected to throw out King's eyewitness account because he couldn't be cross-examined, everyone on the jury would still have heard his version of events. Unless the judge was dirty. Who knows? I'll give it to these Russians. They are very thorough."

"They are," Dax agreed with a sigh.

"But I'm smarter." Freddy never took his eyes off the keyboard. "And I understand little concepts like math."

"He also wrapped his sleeping bag in tinfoil," Lara said, patting his head like she would a Labrador retriever.

"It keeps the aliens from getting into my dreams. They do that, you know. Especially to creative people."

If Holland didn't get them back on task, Freddy might give them a lecture on ancient aliens and the dream world. "How does math help us here?"

"Look, I want this tape to be wrong, too. But my mother told me she was certain this was my father. She said she recognized the uniform jacket." Dax pointed to the screen. "See. It's hard to tell, but if you look closely there's a patch on the left shoulder. Dad tore it walking through a construction zone while getting a tour of a new facility. Is there any way he's drugged in this video? They did it once. They could do it again."

"Absolutely not." Freddy touched the keyboard and suddenly a bunch of lines and numbers appeared. "How tall was your father?"

"Six foot two. A couple of inches shorter than me."

"Yes, that's what I put him at, too," Freddy replied. "I pulled up photographs of him from the Internet. This particular software can mathematically examine a photograph."

"It looks at spatial relations and assigns height and sometimes weight to an object," Lara explained. "Even humans. See the lines? It takes measurements of objects, compares them to relative objects, and uses that to determine the size of the people and items around it."

"I've seen this before." Holland leaned over, examining the screen. It was really simple geometry, but it could explain so much that the human eye couldn't understand. "Don't you need a fixed, known point?"

"Yes." Freddy's finger touched the soda machine to the right of the couple. "That is a standard machine. They all have the same dimensions. Lara called the company and got the specs for the machine. They haven't changed in five years."

"This particular machine was installed about three months before this picture was taken." Lara looked down at her notes. "That fall the owner signed the contract. So we know for certain what the height and width of that piece of equipment is."

"According to the math, this man is exactly six foot two," Freddy said with a smile.

Holland felt her gut roll. "Just like the admiral."

"I don't understand. If this was a setup . . ." Dax's whole body had gone stiff.

She touched a hand to his back and felt him sigh into her touch. "You're going to explain how this is a good thing. Right, Freddy?"

"Tell them about the torso-to-leg ratio," Lara encouraged.

He swiped at the keyboard again and a picture of his father appeared, dressed head-to-toe in slacks and a button-down shirt, with a belt around his waist. He'd been snapshotted smiling and waving. "I got this off social media. Okay, so when I measure from your father's waist to shoulders I calculate about thirty-five-and-a-half inches from waist to the top of his head. Your father had slightly longer legs than torso. His legs were roughly thirty-nine. He's wearing loafers, so I think I'm close."

"All right," Dax allowed.

She could hear the tension in his voice and rubbed her hand down his spine in a soothing gesture. He leaned into her, obviously needing the affection, then slid his arm around her waist.

"Let's do the same thing with a screenshot from the video." Freddy pulled up a still photo. The admiral was almost out of range, his full body in the shot. "So we know your father's measurements. When I put them in here though, the torso-to-leg ratio is off. Do you see where the natural waist falls? This man's legs are nearly six inches longer than his torso."

"That's not my father," Dax said with a huff.

"No." Lara's voice got higher as she seemed to get excited. "And we have even more proof. Once we realized we could prove it with math, we went a little further. Freddy isolated the hand on Amber Taylor's shoulder." She held up a printed shot of the enlarged digits. "Do you see it?"

Holland stared at the image of a man's hand on the girl's lower back. They'd enlarged it and focused on the fingers. Left hand. She realized what was missing. "There's no ring."

"Sweetheart, I don't think my father would wear his ring if he was cheating," Dax pointed out.

Lara held up her hand, slipping the wedding ring off her finger. "I've only had it for a few weeks. It leaves an indentation. Your father wore that ring for decades. This hand has never worn one."

They were right.

Admiral Harold Spencer was innocent. She'd known it, but seeing the visible proof made her eyes water, her emotions swell. Dax could finally find some closure and peace. So could his mother and Gus.

"Thank you, Freddy." Dax held out a hand.

Freddy nodded. "You're welcome. This is a really fascinating conspiracy. I haven't figured it out yet, but I have some theories. I think the next few weeks will be interesting."

"What do you know about the Krylov syndicate?" Holland asked. If Freddy was this good with research, maybe they should set him to work.

"I can start on it. It's not really any different than the way the Reticulan Grays organize." Freddy pulled up a notebook. "I've got a friend in Interpol who can help."

"I need to know if there's a man named Sergei involved in that crime organization," Dax said. "If you come across anyone by that name, flag it."

Lara had gone still. "I have a theory."

"Who is Sergei?" Holland asked.

"That's what we all want to know." Dax took a step back and Holland was surprised at the loss she felt. "We first heard his name when Mad asked Gabe about it just before he died. Then a Russian who worked for the syndicate not only confirmed that Sergei existed but this mystery guy was closer than we thought."

"And Natalia talked about him, too. Well, she did before she was murdered horribly." Lara shuddered. "She loved him. We don't know if he was a husband, brother, lover, son . . . My bet is that she had a love child with Zack's dad while he was living in Moscow and she was hired at the embassy while she was Frank Hayes's mistress. I think Sergei is Zack's half brother."

Holland groaned. Having a half brother in the *Bratva* could be a political killer for Zack. "You think they're going to disrupt the upcoming elections? Why wouldn't they have done it the first time he was trying to get elected?"

"Because they want Zack to be president. My guess is that they want him to expend his political capital doing something for them while he has power," Dax explained. "And the second time around, he'll be a lame-duck president. Because he can't run again, he can do whatever the hell he pleases. It makes sense. The Russians want some political favor. Maybe this is how they intend to blackmail Zack into giving it to them."

"Like you said, he doesn't have to run. He can make an announcement tomorrow that he won't seek reelection and then no one has anything on him," Holland pointed out.

"But a Russian-mob bastard brother could ruin his legacy. And he does care about that. These people probably know it. They will make a move in the next few months, as the election cycle is in full swing—if we don't find a way to hit them first."

She finally got the complexity of this insidious scheme. "We have to unweave whatever web they've got Zack caught in."

"Yes, and it's about forty years' worth of conspiracy. If I'm right, Sergei didn't start this. His parents did." Lara sat. "We have to figure out a way to stop them. To do that, we have to reach them."

"We start with Peter Morgan. He knows someone involved with the Russians." Holland would bet on that. "How long was he your father's aide?" Something about the whole uniform thing bugged her. If the admiral hadn't been the man in the video, then who and how had he gotten hold of the admiral's jacket?

"Four years, but they were friends before that. My father trusted him implicitly," Dax explained. "I'm not convinced he's worthy of that trust, but I also haven't been able to look through his records. They were classified when he took that new assignment after my father's death."

"Could Zack find them? No one has better clearance than the president," Holland reasoned.

Even Lara laughed at that. "Zack has to be careful. If he starts putting his fingers in Navy affairs, he could stir up serious trouble. It would be even worse since everyone knows he's close to Dax."

"It could look like he was trying to find a way to cover up my father's crimes," Dax finished. "We have to protect Zack."

They also had to find justice. "Zack isn't the only one involved in this."

Dax reached for her hand. "Zack is like my brother. I loved my dad. I love my mother and my sister and Zack means as much to me as they do. He's my family, Holland. He's gotten my ass out of hot water more times than I can count and he'll be beside me to my dying day, so don't ask me to hurt him in any way."

"Not even if it meant justice for your father?"

Dax grew grim. "No."

She'd always known he was loyal to his friends. Still, his willingness to sacrifice amazed her. "All right. Then we figure this out without Zack's power."

"I didn't say that," Dax replied. "I merely said we leave him out as much as possible. Connor said you figured out where Peter Morgan is living these days."

Freddy was back to staring at his screen. "And if anyone is wondering, Peter Morgan totally fits the torso-to-leg ratio of the man in the video if he was wearing lifts. Which I think he was in order to appear as tall as the admiral. He would have had access to the jacket, and he's never been married. I take tips, if anyone wants to leave one. Or tinfoil. Either works."

"We're going to find that little shit and I'm going to make him talk."
Dax took Holland's hand again. "Let's end this."

Her heart sank because once this was finished, so were they.

Dax pulled up the narrow drive that led to Peter Morgan's bayou
home. He'd killed the lights and had to go very slowly because the
foggy gloom made it tough to see the crappy dirt road.

"It's a little farther up," Holland said. "He really decided to go off
the beaten path. I think he wanted to be as far from New Orleans as
he could without leaving his mother. I'm sure once she's gone, he'll
completely disappear."

"Yeah, we got lucky." Dax wasn't feeling lucky. He was feeling shitty
because he needed more time with Holland. If Peter gave them the
answers they needed, she could walk out of his life as soon as tomorrow. She would file all her paperwork, kiss him good-bye, and walk off
to find her happy life without him.

He couldn't let that happen.

"It's nice to know that even bad guys love their moms," Lara said
from the backseat.

"Yes, though it's not going to save him," Connor muttered beside
his wife, pounding on a laptop. "I've completely lost my signal. Why
can't these assholes hide out in urban environments? I really need the
Internet right now."

"Save him?" Lara asked. "Save him from what? Connor, I expect
you to follow the Geneva Conventions rules about treatment of pris-
oners."

Holland snorted beside Dax, something she did when she was
caught off guard and thought something was humorous. "Um, I don't
think Sparks got that memo."

"I'm sure that Connor is very thorough yet gentle with his interro-
gations," Lara said primly. "He understands that you catch more flies
with honey than vinegar."

"And we catch more criminals with waterboarding," Dax muttered.

Connor groaned. "Don't get her started on Gitmo. Please. I promise to very nicely question the man who might be aiding the Russian mafia in trying to blackmail the president of the United States. There. See, you could have stayed with Freddy."

"Uh huh, and that's when you waterboard the man. I'm naive, my love, not stupid. I'm here merely as an observer," Lara explained. "Why didn't you stay behind if you need that file you're trying to retrieve so badly?"

"What file are you waiting on?" Holland asked.

Connor's gaze flashed up, meeting Dax's in the rearview mirror as a rare patch of moonlight beamed into the vehicle. "The Natalia Kuilikov file."

"Why do you need that?" She frowned.

"I want to check something." Connor's gaze skidded back to the road.

That sounded like his best friend's "I know something and don't want to tell" voice. It made Dax edgy, but he wasn't going to interrogate Connor now. "Tell me when I should park. We'll walk the rest of the way."

"Don't worry about Morgan," Holland said. "I watched him earlier. He's in no shape to run. He's in poor health himself. He's hiding out here so he doesn't have to run. When we cased the place earlier, I didn't see a boat dock. He's on the water, but I seriously doubt the dude is going to swim for it."

"In these waters? Not unless he's suicidal." Out this far, the bayou had plenty of critters that didn't mind a little human feast. "I don't want him escaping. We need answers."

"We'll get them," Connor promised. "At least we'll get whatever this guy knows. I doubt he knows everything. But he can point us in the right direction."

"I want to know who killed my father." A burning urge to right the wrongs done to his father had settled inside him that moment Freddy had given him true, hold-up-in-court proof that his father hadn't been the man leading a teenage girl to a scuzzy motel room so that he could rape her. Deep down, Dax had always known it, but seeing proof centered him in a way he hadn't been for years.

Now he could turn his gut-wrenching anxiety on the woman he loved and wondering whether she would leave him for good after tonight.

Up ahead, he saw the house his father's aide-de-camp was living in these days. Peter Morgan had retired from the Navy recently, but it looked as if he hadn't saved up much. The "house" was more like a shack. A glow emanated from one of the windows, so at least the place had some kind of power. Dax remembered Peter Morgan as a smart man, ambitious and friendly. He'd thought Morgan was not only his father's man, but also his friend.

He'd been very wrong and now he was finally going to learn some hows and whys.

He parked the car and let the women slip out. They shut their doors quietly. Before Connor had the chance to move, Dax turned to his best friend. "What are you not saying?"

"I'm checking on something. Don't worry about it. I'm crossing all my *t*'s and dotting the *i*'s on this one," Connor informed him. "I put a call in to Roman before we headed out here. He knows where we're going and when to expect us back. If we don't call him within an hour, he's going to come looking for us."

"You think we're being followed?" Dax hadn't seen anyone on the road, but he trusted Connor's gut.

"I'm just being cautious."

Holland tapped on his window and he opened the door. "Is there something I should know?"

He eased out and tried to reassure her. "Connor's just being paranoid."

Holland narrowed her eyes as Connor closed up his laptop, shoved it in its bag, and emerged from the car. "I think we're being watched.

I can't say why except that I can feel it in my gut. Someone's following us."

Connor nodded. "They're good. I didn't actually see anyone on the road, but I think they're here, too."

"We should leave, then," Dax said.

"And give up what might be our one chance?" Holland asked. "If we walk away now, Peter Morgan will suffer a timely accident. Unless someone here thinks he's a bigger part of this conspiracy than we ever dreamed."

Dax had to shake his head. "No. He's a pawn. But I don't want to risk you or Lara."

Connor sent him a meaningful stare. "You know I can hold my own."

No arguing with that. Dax had seen the aftermath of Connor's "work" in the Crawford building the night he'd been shot. It had been a surgical slaughter of enemies. Lara was a question mark but Connor would never let anything happen to her. "Yeah."

Holland frowned and she eased the SIG from its place in her holster. "I'll watch your back, Captain. When was the last time you were in a close-quarter fight?"

Sometimes he understood why Roman wanted a quiet, demure woman. "Not lately. Thanks for the reminder, sweetheart."

"Well, when I need someone to direct operations on a battleship, I'll give you a call. Now it's time for you to let me do my job." She eased into his space.

Fuck. No sweet, demure woman would ever get his motor running the way this one did. He'd take his slightly crazy female any day of the week. He brushed his lips over hers. "All right, then. Keep an eye on Lara, too. She's a pacifist."

"Yeah, not so much since what happened a few weeks back," Lara admitted. "I've decided that fighting for one's life is a natural response. Not that I brought a weapon. I'm really bad with guns, so if the bullets start flying, I'm supposed to hide behind Connor."

"You will keep your head down and wait for my instructions," Connor reinforced in a low voice.

Lara rolled her eyes. "He's so bossy."

And it was obvious she loved him that way. She tangled her fingers with Connor's, of course on his left side. His firing hand had to be free.

Holland holstered her weapon, and Dax relaxed a little when she stepped beside him. "It's going to be okay. Whoever is on our tail . . . we need to figure out how they tracked us down. I'm fairly certain we weren't followed earlier."

Dax bet he knew. "Someone was watching my mother's house. I tried to get in and out without being seen, but if anyone was watching closely, they could have seen me and followed me back. I thought Freddy had traps."

"It's a lot of ground to cover and we haven't had time to set up cameras," Connor admitted. "Again, this is where an urban environment would help."

They made it to the front door. "We'll call Freddy when we get a cell signal again. We tell him to clear out and we won't go back."

"We head straight for D.C.," Connor agreed. "It's time to get out of New Orleans."

He knocked on Morgan's front door before Holland could put in her two cents. He was fairly certain he would get an earful about her job with NCIS and that New Orleans was her home. Screw that. Dax intended to be ruthless this time. He would use the whole presidential-task-force thing to keep her by his side. Just because one part of the case was over didn't mean she got to quit. Uncovering all the pieces and players could take a while. They needed to go to London. He would use that, too. He would keep her close and before she knew it she would find herself with a ring on her finger.

Maybe he should get her a little drunk. Hell, it had worked on him.

A quiet fell around them as they waited. Not silence. There was never silence on the bayou, but he could still hear the floorboards creak as the man inside the house moved.

The door opened and a weary face looked out from behind the screen. Peter Morgan was dressed in his pajamas and a robe, glasses sitting on his face. He'd aged ten years in the three since Dax had seen him last. He'd lost weight. That kind of gauntness bespoke disease.

"I always wondered if you would find me, Captain."

He didn't need to kill Peter Morgan. It looked like life was doing a good job of that. "I have some questions."

Morgan hesitated but then finally nodded. "Of course. Come in. You'll have to excuse the place. It's not what you're used to, of course. Mr. Sparks, I presume. And Ms. Kirk." He looked Lara's way. "I'm sorry, dear, I don't know what part you play in this game."

Connor's bride smiled as though she was being invited in for tea. "Lara Sparks. I'm married to the big guy who will not be torturing you this evening. Consider me an investigative journalist."

"Ah, they brought a weak link. I was hoping for one." Morgan shut the door behind them.

"Lara's not weak," Dax shot back. He glanced around the room. Despite its dilapidated nature, it was neat and tidy. Austere. Morgan wasn't one for knickknacks. There was a sofa and lounge chair, two bookshelves, and a few lamps. He didn't see a television, but a neat stack of newspapers and magazines took up a corner of the small dining room table.

"I didn't mean that in a moral or physical sense," Morgan clarified, gesturing for them to sit. "I meant I can appeal to her softer sensibilities in a way I cannot with you. You blame me for what happened to your father. Ms. Kirk is law enforcement. She won't see past justice to compassion, and Sparks . . . well, from what I know, you have no compassion."

"None." Connor's smile would have made anyone squirm.

Lara frowned as she sat down on the couch. "He does. But we're not here to hurt you. We simply have a few questions."

Connor walked around the room, his eyes seeking the corners. "Many questions."

"I'm not a threat, Mr. Sparks," Morgan said wearily, sinking onto the lounge chair. "There are no traps. I never was a violent man. I always thought it amusing I ended up in the Navy. After I left Admiral Spencer's command, I found work in intelligence. I was much happier there. It was a good fit for me. I was safe there, too."

It didn't look like anyone nefarious would jump out and murder them, but Dax was on guard anyway. He didn't like the slow way Connor was prowling around the cabin. Something had his friend on high alert, and he trusted Connor's gut.

The faster they got what they needed, the better.

"Why do you need to be safe?" Dax asked.

Morgan sat back. "Because of what I did. I assume you're here because you've finally figured out what I did to your father."

Holland had her cop face on. She pressed a button on her phone and set it down on the coffee table. "I'm going to tape this interview, if you don't mind."

Morgan waved a hand. "Only if the sweet one promises to look in on my mother from time to time. The nursing home is all right, but they don't always change her sheets regularly. I pay extra to ensure her comfort."

Lara's eyes had gone a little misty. "I promise. Do you think you're going to jail?"

He shook his head. "Not at all. I'm going to die. If not tonight, then soon. The cancer is everywhere. So it doesn't matter anymore if I talk or not. I'm miserable. Judith is miserable. I fought all these years to live and now I don't really care if I die, because there are worse things than death."

"Like betrayal?" Dax snarled. He didn't like the fact that this man had even mentioned his mother's name. "My father helped you."

"But he also cheated on your mother. She's an amazing woman. He was never worthy of her. When they offered me a way to show her the man he truly was, I took it."

Dax tried to reconcile Morgan's words. "Are you telling me you set him up to expose him? Or for revenge?"

"It wasn't really revenge. I meant to scare him. Your father always had everything so easy. He got away with murder half the time because he was rich and connected." Bitterness poured from Morgan's mouth. "I was smarter than him. I got better grades. I was well behaved. Life still handed him everything on a silver platter. He got promoted up the ranks. He had your mother. Even when she learned what sort of man he was, she still picked him over me."

Morgan had utterly ruined his family over jealousy? "I remember you through most of my adolescence. You came to the house for dinner. You were my father's friend. How could you do this to him? To us? You called the Navy and sent in the fake video."

His head shook vigorously. "I did not. Like I said, to me the scheme was merely blackmail. I wanted my cut. I was hidden in your father's shadow for decades. Most of my life had been about making his easier. How do you think I felt when I should have been in a place of power and all your father offered me was the position of a glorified secretary? He owed me."

Dax thought seriously about throttling the man, but he was so pathetic Dax simply sat beside Holland and stared. She took his hand in hers, grounding him. "I don't understand how you thought blackmailing my father would teach him a lesson."

Morgan coughed, a rattling sound in his chest. "I knew the minute Hayes won the election that Hal would crow to everyone about the fact that he knew the president."

"Zack is one of my best friends. A *loyal* friend," Dax shot back.

"Your dad talked about all you boys over the years. It's one reason Constance Hayes's death concerned him."

Now they were getting somewhere. "He took a trip a few weeks before he died. He said he was going to a conference."

Morgan's head shook. "Yes, but he went to the UK because he thought the president's mother had been murdered. After Joy Hayes was killed, he said Constance had told him years ago that anyone who knew would die."

"Knew what?" Holland asked.

"I don't know. I guess that's why I'm still alive." He rocked back in his lounger. "Originally, I assumed he was flying to London to meet one of his sluts and he didn't want me to know because he thought I would tell Judith."

"Would you?" Lara asked.

"No. She already knew," Morgan replied. "She was too much of a lady to divorce Hal. We're not like young people today. We have morals. But I finally saw my opportunity to ensure he never became one of the Joint Chiefs of Staff—his dream job. He was so close and he knew it. I wish I could have seen the look on his face when he realized he would never be appointed."

Holland squeezed Dax's hand as though she knew he was close to losing control.

Morgan never noticed. He just smiled, his lips curling in a nasty snarl. "God, he wanted that position. He told me I could come with him to D.C. After holding me back all these years, he acted as if he was doing me a favor. You don't know what it's like to always be in someone's shadow, to never get to step into the light."

Dax thanked god for the friends he had. They would never bow to petty jealousy or betray him the way this piece of shit had betrayed his father. "Who approached you about blackmailing my father?"

"I guess there's no point in concealing the truth now, is there? I can tell you because I'm already dead. You know the funny thing? I hated Hal and I loved him. I still miss him. It was never supposed to end this way. I just wanted to win at least once." Morgan coughed again.

"Who contacted you?" Dax asked, his words clipped.

"A man. I didn't really understand who he was until later, and then it was far too late to back out. The man who initially contacted me was American, but I found out later he worked for a Russian. Weird name. Kuilly-something."

Connor went still. "Kuilikov?"

Morgan pointed while fighting off another coughing fit. "That's it. That's him. He was a big, scary fellow."

This was the closest they'd gotten. "Sergei? Was that his first name? How old was he?"

"No, his name was Boris. He was an old guy. Probably a couple years older than me."

Lara leaned over. "Boris Kuilikov is a name we've heard before. We don't know exactly who he is. Natalia's brother maybe. We've suspected he had something to do with the Russian mob, but we don't know how he's connected to the people who killed Natalia."

"I didn't understand right away that Boris was with the Russian mob. I thought he wanted to make some money, like I did. They called me for help setting up the blackmail scheme and I agreed. But I didn't send that tape to the Navy, Dax." Morgan leaned forward. "I know I'm a bitter old fuck, but I wouldn't have done that. I didn't want Hal publicly humiliated or dead. He was my friend."

The man sitting in front of him didn't know a thing about friendship. "So you agreed to do what?"

"I agreed to work with the girl they had hired. I snatched your father's uniform, set myself up as him, and allowed the cameras at a motel to film what appeared to be your father walking in with the teen prostitute. Once they'd successfully blackmailed him, I was just supposed to get a cut of the money. But I knew your father. He would have paid the money the first time, then turned down the Joint Chiefs position so he couldn't be blackmailed again. That's it. I celebrated that he wouldn't have been able to achieve his damn dream and he would finally know how it felt to be like the rest of us."

Again, Holland squeezed Dax's hand as though she knew he needed it, reminding him that now wasn't the time or place to lose it. He would deal with Morgan later, after they had the truth.

"When did you realize they meant to kill him?" Dax demanded.

Morgan fell quiet for a moment. "They called the night before the

story broke. They told me I had sent a letter to the secretary of the
Navy, exposing my boss as a pedophile. They told me if I denied that
I'd written the letter, they would kill my mother. I believed them. That
was my first inkling of just how ruthless they were and their true
intentions."

"That man in the prison parking lot told me they had no intention
of killing the admiral," Holland said. "He told me Morgan here
screwed it up. Why would that man have lied? Why did they want me
to break up with you so badly?"

"To refocus Dax and derail the investigation. They wanted to avoid
killing a second member of the admiral's family," Connor explained.
"One could be ruled a suicide. Dax's death would have been more
difficult to explain away. He was close to the president. His death
would have incurred even more media attention than his father's. They
wanted to stay in the shadows. I would have done the same thing in
their shoes."

So they believed Morgan's version. After all, a dying man had nothing to lose and no reason to lie. "Why would Boris Kuilikov kill Natalia, one of his own relatives? It's not like the guy found out forty years
later that she'd been screwing the ambassador. He must have known."

"That's conjecture," Lara reminded.

"But it makes sense. Hell, he probably set her up to have a fling with
Frank Hayes. Maybe she was a spy," Holland mused.

"The Russians seem to avoid killing anyone they don't have to, so
why wait decades to kill Natalia?" Lara asked, her voice tight. "Connor? Did I hear a car coming up the road?"

Connor looked out the window. "I can't tell. If someone's driving out
there, they've killed the lights, because it's too dark to see anything."

A minute later, a banging on the door resounded through the
room. Everyone stopped, turning toward the intrusion. No one made
a sound.

Connor put up his left hand, pulling his gun out with his right.
"Don't move. Kirk, get my six."

Dax stared at his friend. "Are you serious?"

Connor shrugged. "She's logged way more time on the gun range than you and she wasn't recently shot."

Holland stood, moving in behind Connor. She winked Dax's way. "I got this, babe."

Okay, the "babe" part made him feel a tiny bit less emasculated. "I'm going to remember this the next time I'm called on to play limo driver or to be the dipshit who has to invade Freddy's home."

Lara patted his knee. "It'll all work out."

He wished he were as optimistic as Lara.

Connor opened the door and immediately shoved his SIG in the newcomer's face. Gemma White was ready, with a stony expression and her gun pointed right at Connor.

NINETEEN

Holland felt her eyes widen as her partner stood in the doorway, gripping her SIG Sauer and aiming it at Connor Sparks.

"Stand down, Special Agent," Connor growled.

Her warrior-queen partner didn't look like she wanted to comply. Her arms never wavered as she stared at him. "You stand down, whoever you are. Holland, I need to talk to you."

"When you put the fucking gun down, maybe we can chat," Connor spat back.

"Maybe after we chat, I'll put the fucking gun down," Gemma replied.

Holland knew Gemma could argue all day. "What are you doing here?"

Her partner's intent stare never wavered from Connor. "I've been following you and I'm not the only one. You have incoming. NOLA PD is about to surround the place. I think you can use an extra gun."

"Why would you follow me?" Holland moved behind Connor.

"I took this assignment because Augustine Spencer asked me to. I'm Secret Service, but she wanted someone to watch over you. She told

me if we were ever in this position to tell you something that would
prove who I work for."

"What's that?"

"She said to tell you that she doesn't give up on her friends. Even
when her friends are being call-dodging assholes."

Connor lowered his gun. "Yeah, that's Gus."

"You were the one who shouted out the warning before the shooting started at my apartment." It must have been Gemma.

She strode through the door and slammed it shut. "Yes. Since Captain Awesome came back, I stepped up my surveillance, and you're
lucky I did. Nice job on the balcony there, Romeo."

Dax stood up. "My sister sent you?"

"Your sister is smarter than the rest of you. She figured out something was wrong the minute blondie here decided to turn twelve kinds
of bitch." Gemma moved, looking out the blinds. "We need to get out
of here."

"So you moved your whole family here because Gus asked you to?"
Her brain was still reeling.

"My husband and kids are actually my brother, my niece, and two
nephews. They're good cover. Their mom walked out and I stepped up
to help. Now let's go. The NOLA PD is coming. I think they've had this
place staked out for weeks."

Holland frowned. "Why would they come here? We're out of their
jurisdiction."

And why did her uncle care enough to have Morgan's cabin watched?

A few items that hadn't made sense previously slid into place.

Her uncle had called and told her the bullet casing matched
another crime. He'd known within hours when that kind of thing
could take days. He'd also known the assassin was Russian. Again,
something that could take much longer to confirm. But he hadn't
known a name? Bullshit.

"Why were you trying to pull up the police reports on Natalia Kuilikov's death?" she asked Connor.

His face went stony. "I wanted to see if they'd found bullet casings at the nursing home. As far as I remember, there were none."

Connor Sparks wouldn't make a mistake like that.

"Holland? Are you all right? You've gone white." Dax was suddenly in her space, his hands supporting her waist.

"You think my uncle had something to do with this." Though she felt Dax's hold, she couldn't lean into him.

Connor's jaw tightened. "How else would he know? Who convinced you to betray Dax? Was it really the man representing the Russian mob?"

After seeing that man in the prison parking lot, she'd driven straight to her uncle's and he'd had the file ready and waiting for her. He'd had those damning photos sitting right there. Why would he have kept them in his office, right at his fingertips?

She forced herself to think, to shove aside the emotion and look at the evidence. But all she could surmise was that her uncle had been involved with the initial investigation.

She looked over at Peter Morgan, who had struggled to his feet. "After the call girl tipped off the police— Wait. That wasn't planned?"

Morgan shook his head. "No. Suddenly the NOLA PD was involved and simple blackmail was no longer an option. I started panicking then but played along, identifying Hal in the video. I wasn't sure what else to do when the cops showed up at my door and started asking questions."

"Who interviewed you when you talked to the civilian police?"

She believed him now. Everything was making sense. After all, he'd be out money if his blackmail scheme got exposed to authorities and then the press.

Morgan's eyes had widened. "A big man showed up. Kirk. Are you related?" He took a step back. "You're here to kill us all, aren't you?"

She held up a hand. "I'm not." Then she turned to the man she'd once loved. "Dax, I'm so sorry."

His jaw had tightened. "Your uncle? He killed my father?"

"I don't know, but I think he was somehow involved. And he's on his way." She reached for her phone and turned the recorder off, handing it to Lara. "You have to get this out of here. Connor, take your wife and Dax and run. I'll handle my uncle."

Lara clutched the phone. "I don't know which way to go. Point me in the right direction and I'll get this back to the city, but I think Connor should stay and back you up."

"No one is going anywhere," Connor said. "Let's find a place to hide you and Morgan."

"How long do we have, Special Agent?" Dax asked, his hand on his gun.

Holland tried not to think about the fact that he could barely look at her.

Gemma shook her head. "Not long. The good news is he's only bringing two squad cars, but every one of those men will be his. You've got another two minutes or less."

Connor nodded. "Do they know I'm here?"

"If he had someone staking out this place, the most they could have reported were that two men and two women entered the premises, but it may have been too dark for that. The windows on your SUV are tinted right? Maybe they couldn't see anything."

Holland nodded. So they'd have to take their chances that the NOLA PD didn't know who was here and what they were up against.

"Once they arrive, I can guess where they'll take cover," Gemma continued. "If that helps."

It was the only chance they had.

"Lara should hide," Holland said. "Connor, can you find a sniper position somewhere?"

They all looked at Morgan.

"Head out the back door," he said. "You'll have to follow the path around the swamp. It will take a few minutes, but you'll be right behind them. They'll never see you coming. If you simply walk out the front, they'll make you for sure."

"On it." Connor gripped the knob of the back door. "Keep the cops out of the house. I won't be able to see them in here. Use the dark. My night vision is excellent. And whatever you do, don't let them know anyone is here but you and Dax. You're not suspicious of him at all."

Dax nodded. "We got here and Morgan was gone."

"Right. Take care of Lara." Connor gave his friend one last look and disappeared.

"She should hide in the closet," Morgan said, nodding toward the only room with a door. "It's back there. I'll show you the way. I don't have any weapons. I always knew if they found me, I would die. I really don't care anymore except it will hurt my mother. She's all I have left. I lost Judith when Hal died. So many friends gone. That was the horrible part. I found out everything was meaningless without him."

Morgan might lose his mind before his life.

Holland heard a car pulling up, saw red and blue lights stream in through the thin curtains.

Her uncle. It hurt more than she could process now, but she couldn't explain away the evidence. She should have seen it so much sooner and she could have saved Dax heartache.

"They'll see my car. I couldn't hide it. I didn't have time once I realized they were on their way. I'm assisting you in this investigation and trying to cover NCIS's ass," Gemma said. "Your uncle will understand that."

When a hard knock sounded on the door, Holland realized her time had run out.

"New Orleans PD. Open up." Her uncle's voice resonated through the portal.

She certainly wasn't going to hide. She would talk to him, get him to go away, and begin to build her case against him.

Holland opened the door before Dax could stop her. "Uncle Beau? I'm surprised to see you out here. Are you looking for Peter Morgan?"

Her uncle stood there, his big body illuminated in the porch light. Behind him she could see he'd brought along Chad and three other cops, all familiar.

This was her uncle's pack, the ones who would know where the bodies were buried because he'd ordered these men to do the burying. They were mutually complicit, and it made her sick.

"I was looking for you, Holland," her uncle replied. "And Dax Spencer. He's wanted for questioning down at the station."

Was that how he intended to play this, all aboveboard so he could separate the two of them and later inform her of Dax's untimely but shocking accidental death or some such nonsense? Her heart sped up because this tactic made everything more dangerous—and difficult.

Keep the cops out of the house. That was what Connor had said. Was he close to making his way around the swamp so he could circle around and position himself behind the cops?

That was when she remembered the camera. Peter Morgan didn't keep a gun around, but he had a camera on the front door that her uncle had either not seen or thought he could handle.

"Questioning about what?" Holland stood her ground, not giving her uncle an inch.

Beau's eyes narrowed. "I have enough evidence to prove he hired the assassin who tried to kill you. I've seen his bank transactions. Very damning. You know I told you that boy was trouble. He's going to use your death to shine a light on his father's death and get NCIS to reopen the case. That family is ruthless."

"He doesn't have to do that. I've already reopened it." She glanced over to the left, where Dax had his back to the wall, just out of her uncle's line of sight.

Connor might have joked about Dax and the gun range, but he handled his sidepiece like a pro. He might not do this kind of thing every day, but he would be competent. He wouldn't waver. Gemma moved behind her.

"Lieutenant," Gemma said with a nod. "What seems to be the problem? My partner and I are working a case. We came out here to speak to a witness."

Her uncle's head tilted as though he was trying to see inside. "You're here to talk to Morgan?"

He must be desperate, because he'd forgotten he wasn't supposed to know where Morgan lived. It was time to get him talking.

"He's not here." Holland frowned, pretending confusion. "How long have you been working for the *Bratva*?"

Beside her, Dax closed his eyes. When he opened them she saw how furious he was.

Holland had to keep him talking, had to keep that camera rolling. If she let her uncle take Dax in, he would very likely be thrown into a cell where some paid asshole waited to take him out. And her uncle would get to keep his hands completely clean.

She couldn't let that happen. That meant getting her uncle to talk so when Connor found a position and made his move, he didn't get charged with murdering a police officer.

Because there was no way this wouldn't get bloody.

"What are you talking about?" Her uncle crossed his arms over his chest and towered over her. "Holland, everything I've done is to protect you. That boy has been dragging you down for years. Now he's using you to prove something when he should just have accepted his father's crimes. You can't trust these rich boys. They'll do whatever they need to when it comes to protecting their money."

He didn't know Dax at all. He wasn't a typical rich boy. Yes, he'd been wild, but he'd always been a faithful friend, loyal and kind. He wasn't shedding light on his father's death for money or glory or so he could move up the ranks. All that mattered to him was the truth and honoring a father he loved, despite his faults.

Dax was the kind of man who loved with his whole heart.

"How did you know this is Peter Morgan's place? The deed isn't registered in his name," she pointed out. She kept her eyes on the men behind her uncle. One of them was edging toward the porch.

Chad. Naturally Chad was her uncle's man. It made her wonder if

Beau had ordered Chad to date and sleep with her so he could keep an eye on her, to make sure she didn't uncover anything she shouldn't.

"Holland, it's time to stop thinking with your libido," Chad said. He'd removed his jacket, showing her the big pistol in his holster. "It's time for you to pick family rather than some guy who screwed you over as he fucked you."

"No," she disagreed. "It's time for me to figure out exactly how involved my family was in taking down Admiral Spencer."

Gemma moved beside her. "I think we might need to interview your uncle. I'd like to know where he was the day of Admiral Spencer's death."

"That is none of your business," Beau spat. "Now turn over Dax Spencer."

"If you want to talk to Captain Spencer, you can do it at NCIS headquarters." Maybe she could get him to back off. In her office, she could control the situation. She might even do some questioning of her own.

"Don't pull jurisdiction with me. I'm sick of the way the Navy thinks they're better than the rest of us," Chad snarled.

Most PDs were more than happy to hand off to NCIS. This had nothing to do with protecting turf and everything to do with Chad's wounded ego. She could do without it. She needed to focus on getting information out of her uncle.

And keeping him from getting his hands on Dax.

She knew it was killing Dax to not face them, but she was the only one who could confront them. She would do this for Dax and right the wrong she'd done him three years ago.

"I am going to need to know where you were on the day of the admiral's death." She couldn't back down from that.

"I believe I was working that day. I'm sure I was. Holland, you don't want to do this. Don't push me to do something I've tried to avoid." Her uncle stared at her, stony eyed. "Let me see if I can break this down. You're lying about Peter Morgan. He's in there and you've talked to him. He told you that I was the one he dealt with at the beginning of the investigation."

"Was there really an investigation?"

"Gotta make these things look good, sweetheart," he admitted.

Outside, in the distance, she saw a hint of movement. Connor. He must have dashed around the swamp and was now settling into position in case this blew up.

"Why would you do this? Why? You knew I was friends with that family." The betrayal was an actual ache in her body.

If her uncle was worried, he didn't show it. He put a hand on the wall and leaned in. "That family means nothing to me. Do you know what I get paid to put my ass on the line every day? Next to nothing. So when the big boys offer me money to take down some rich asshole, I take it. This is the way the world works. We can't fight organized crime. All we can do is take a little piece of the pie. That's what a smart man does."

"Holland, you're going to get us all killed. They won't stop. They've been careful, but they won't let you uncover the hows and whys of their plans," Chad argued.

"Why did they want the admiral dead?" Gemma asked. Holland could feel how tense her partner was, but her voice was calm.

"It doesn't matter to me," Uncle Beau said. "Way I heard it, he was putting his nose where it didn't belong. Morgan got twitchy and turned snitch. The admiral wouldn't bend to their demands and the big boys decided to pull the plug on him." Her uncle tried to look inside the house. "You hear that, Spencer? You want to know who killed your daddy? You come out here and I'll tell you."

"Or are you going to let your girlfriend do all the dirty work?" Chad taunted.

"He's not here," Holland explained. "I left him behind because he can't stay calm and let me do my job. It's just me and Gemma. Are you really going to take us on? Are you ready to kill a fellow officer?"

"I don't want to, but I'm certainly not going to jail," her uncle vowed. "Of course, I'm also ready to turn this all around. You see, you've been acting oddly lately. Hasn't she, Chad?"

"Very odd. She used to be so sweet. I'm pretty sure those were drugs I found at her apartment the other day." Chad sighed. "We put them in evidence. Oh, I was almost certain they belonged to the captain, but I can always change that theory. You might have been trying to harm yourself. After all, you've been spiraling."

How obvious. "So you're going to put me on a seventy-two-hour psych hold? Really? How will you deal with everyone else?"

"That's simple," her uncle said with a smile. "I'll kill 'em. Starting with your partner."

He had his gun out before Holland could think. Gemma shoved her out of the way and slammed the door shut as the first bullet went flying.

She felt something heavy hit her. Dax had thrown himself over her body.

The door exploded inward and she heard another volley of shots.

"I'm giving you one last chance, Holland," Chad shouted. "Come out and we'll talk, but you have to give the rest of them up. That's the only way this ends."

She heard a shout and another shot.

"Or Connor can handle them," Dax growled, jumping to his feet.

"There's still three of them and they're armed to the teeth," Holland whispered. "But I think I've documented enough. He fired first. The tape will show that."

"Sweetheart, I got an audio of the conversation in case Morgan's video doesn't capture voices. I've got his confession on my phone," Dax replied. "Gemma, are they coming in?"

Gemma had taken up a position behind the couch. "Not yet. But I can't really see much."

"He'll try to wait us out or smoke us out," Holland said a moment before her uncle proved her right by shoving the door open and rolling in a canister of tear gas.

"Damn it." Dax pulled his shirt over his mouth and held a hand out to her. "I'm going out first."

Her eyes were already starting to burn. Lara and Morgan would have some time, but if she didn't finish this, those two would be trapped and unprotected.

She looked back through the smoke at Gemma, gesturing to the back door. Gemma nodded and silently started moving toward the rear of the house to retrieve Lara and Morgan.

In the distance, she heard gunfire again.

"Let's go. That's Connor giving us some chaos to escape in. Sweetheart, I know you don't want to, but please let me go first," he practically begged as he coughed.

But he didn't understand. "They'll be reluctant to kill me. I'm going out with my hands up. You come behind me. Then you can save me."

If he walked through that door alone, they would immediately kill him. She could distract Beau, Chad, and the others. She could give him a chance. Between Connor, who was firing enough to start his own war, and Gemma, who would return after setting Lara and Morgan on the path around the swamp to provide another distraction, Dax had a shot at survival. Lara would make a clean getaway and meet up with Connor in front of the house, probably when the rain of gunfire ended.

Honestly, she didn't give a shit if Morgan died. He was an ass.

"Sweetheart, I can't lose you." Dax squeezed her hand.

Despite the gas that was making her eyes tear, she kissed him. "Then don't."

There was no more time then to figure out their relationship or decide what she should do. There was only the here and now and she loved him. She couldn't let him walk out there first because he would die and her life would be over.

Even if she never touched the man again, she couldn't live in a world that didn't have Dax Spencer in it.

She dropped her gun and darted out the door, holding her hands up high. Holland hoped her leap of faith, that her uncle and Chad wouldn't simply shoot her, paid off. She had to take the chance so Dax could live.

As soon as she emerged, fresh air hit her eyes. Tears flowed freely down her face, but she could sort of breathe again. She dragged air into her burning lungs as she took in the scene in front of her. A body lay strewn on the ground about ten feet away. Another was laid out to her left. Chad and her uncle were back to back, looking for the sniper.

Her uncle stopped, training his gun on her. "Stay right where you are. Where's Spencer?"

"I told you. He's not here." She needed him to believe that now . . . but Dax couldn't linger in the noxious house too long. "I told you, I left him behind. He's too reckless."

"Who's out there shooting?" Chad demanded.

"Gemma's fast." She wasn't revealing Connor's presence. "But I'll play along with your plan. Take me in. Just don't shoot me."

She only needed them to believe her surrender for a minute or two, just until Connor could get a clean shot at Chad, then the others could back her up to take her uncle in.

But she feared Dax wouldn't stay in the background.

In fact, she knew he would come for her. Always. He could be angry with her, feel betrayed by her. It wouldn't matter. He would come for her.

She wasn't a woman who needed saving, but Dax would still be there, supporting her.

"Go and get in the car, Holland," her uncle insisted.

"Do it!" Chad yelled.

She nodded, stepping off the porch and into the yard. "I will."

Smoke poured out behind her and she moved slowly, not really having to pretend distress and disorientation.

"In the *back* of the car," her uncle yelled, his finger on the trigger.

He followed directly behind her. Holland's heart pounded furiously. She hoped like hell her calculated risk hadn't been a mistake. She'd had to leave her gun behind and had zero way to defend herself. She was trusting that blood meant something to this man who'd already ruined her life and Dax's.

So many things could go wrong. But she prayed that Dax would be all right.

She pretended to hobble down the porch steps, hands still raised. When she looked back, she saw Dax emerge from the house. Instantly, she hit the ground.

"Twelve o'clock," she yelled. He wouldn't be able to see well. She needed to give him some point of reference.

Gunfire cracked all around her. She tried to see what was happening, hoping Dax wouldn't be mowed down in a hail fire of bullets. She couldn't lose him. She'd been so scared of what would happen between them, but she knew that losing Dax would ruin her life. She would never love another man.

The mist of gas began to clear. Tears still poured from her eyes, the burning painful, but she had to be Dax's eyes now.

Then the world exploded with gunfire again. Nearby, she heard a thud. Her uncle tensed and grunted. She dragged a hand across her eyes, trying to focus.

When she stared at Beau, he clutched his chest and coughed, spitting blood from his mouth as his weapon fell from his hands. He'd been shot—and it looked bad.

"You chose the wrong side, girl."

She wasn't listening. Despite all the terrible things he'd done, she couldn't simply let the man who had half raised her die. She knelt and held his jacket over his open wound to stem the bleeding. "Don't talk."

He pushed her hand away. "Listen to me. If you ever loved me, let me die. I can't go to prison." He sputtered and gasped. "Hear what I'm saying while I can still talk. Stop looking for answers or they'll take you all down. They won't stop. This game has been going on for decades."

Dax darted to her side, kicking Beau's gun away. Vaguely she noted that Gemma had a weapon trained on Chad, who had fallen to his knees, hands in the air.

"What game?" She leaned over to try to hear her uncle's words.

"Sergei's game. That's what the old man told me. He said Sergei will burn everything down. He'll burn you, too." He coughed again just before a terrible blankness entered his eyes.

Holland couldn't spare a moment for grief now. Maybe later, but at the moment she was simply glad to be alive and have Dax beside her.

He wrapped his arms around her. "You're safe now. Gemma is arresting Chad. Connor and I took out everyone else and he's taking Lara and Morgan to safety now. Sweetheart, I'm so sorry."

She looked down at her uncle and her tears weren't just about chemicals now. He'd been such a big part of her childhood. He'd been the reason she'd gone into law enforcement. He'd been a lie, but she'd loved and idolized him as a girl.

"I'm sorry for all he did to you."

"You had nothing to do with that. It's going to be all right." Dax held her tight.

They'd done their job. The scandal surrounding the admiral's death had been exposed as a hoax and the investigation was over. But not only was someone still after the president, her whole world had changed. Nothing could ever be the same again.

TWENTY

Washington, D.C.
Twenty-four hours later

Dax wanted to reach for Holland, but she seemed so damn far away.
From the moment they'd boarded the private jet to the White
House with Lara, Connor, and Gemma, she'd been distant. She'd sat
with Gemma, writing up a joint report to satisfy the White House,
NCIS, and the New Orleans Police Department.

The night before she'd slept on a couch at NCIS, napping in
between interview sessions.

He'd sat and stared at her and wondered if she would ever let him
touch her again.

Now he walked into the residential wing of the White House, wishing he could hold her hand.

"Oh my god!" a familiar voice said. Gus was standing in the hallway, dressed to the nines in a cocktail gown and sky-high heels. They
clacked along the marble as she ran toward him.

He braced himself for an armful of sister. "Hey, Gus."

She slammed into him and that was when he noticed Roman behind her. He wore a tux, his hair slicked back. How long had Roman been shadowing his sister? Now that he thought about it, Roman had been lingering around Gus for a really long time.

"I was so worried. When Gemma called and said you were all out in the bayou about to be horribly murdered, I freaked out," Gus said, stepping back and looking him over. "You look all right. Better than you did after New York."

"Yeah, well, I only got gassed this time. I avoided a bullet," he admitted. Actually, the last few months of leave had been way more dangerous to his well-being than being on his boat.

"I'm glad to hear it." Roman held out a hand. "Sorry, we were at a party for some diplomats. Zack is on his way. You guys got here quick. I'm glad to see you're all right. Holland, I'm so sorry about the last few years."

Holland was dealing with Gus, who wasn't taking no for an answer on the hugs. She'd wrapped herself around her friend. "Holland sucks. Stupid girl. You should have called me when you found out the Russian mob was after you."

Holland smiled and squeezed her back. "They weren't after me, silly. They were after you and Dax."

"I still would have taken them down," Gus promised. "I missed you, sister."

Holland's eyes suddenly had a sheen to them. "You have no idea how I've missed you, Gus. The world is not as bright without you."

Gus kissed her cheek and then reached out to shake Gemma White's hand. "Special Agent, thank you. Any assignment you want. You tell me and I'll force Roman to make it happen."

Roman's head shook. "You're going to kill me one of these days, Gus." He turned to Dax. "Your sister is a menace. I have absolutely zero idea why I don't fire her ten goddamn times a day."

Connor looked at Dax and smiled. "I'm sure you're just lazy, Roman. That's the only explanation."

How had he not seen it? There was a crackling energy between Roman and Gus. He probably hadn't acknowledged it because he hadn't wanted to know one of his best friends had fallen for his sister. Did Roman know she'd slept with Mad a few years back?

Probably. Gus didn't hide her past. She didn't apologize and she had no reason to. She was a force of nature. If Roman couldn't see how amazing his sister was, then Roman didn't deserve her.

And that was his great loss.

Roman put a hand on his arm. "Come on, buddy. I've got some ridiculously good Scotch waiting for us. I think we all could use it. Zack brought a date to the ball tonight. A very pretty lawyer."

Shit. When they'd realized how dangerous his situation could be, Zack had decided to pull away from Liz. The White House Press Secretary had been the woman in his life for years, but he'd never made a move. Liz had been his wife in every way except the bedroom. Dax was fairly certain Zack was in love with the woman, and dating someone else was a sacrifice.

"A total bimbo law whore," Gus hissed. "You tell Zack he can bite my ass and he's lucky, and I mean lucky, that he got Liz to sign that contract or he would be looking at a complete turnover in the press office because he sucks. He's the president of sucking." Gus grabbed Holland's hand. "Come on, girls. We're not drinking with the boys this evening. Liz is really excited to see you again, Holland."

Holland gave Dax a glance before she followed after his sister.

"Well, we know which side Gus is on," Connor said acerbically as he waved good-bye to his wife.

Roman frowned as he watched the women move down the hall. "The wives won't tell Gus about why Zack is suddenly dating someone he doesn't love, right? Because Gus can't keep a secret to save her life."

Gus could keep a secret. She'd done it for years but he plainly saw that she was still in love with Roman. But Dax knew Roman was right in one way. She wouldn't keep any secret about Zack's feelings for Liz. Under her shark exterior, she was a romantic. "Holland won't tell."

"Neither will Lara," Connor said. "They both know what this game is. If Zack wants it quiet, they'll stay quiet."

Roman was watching the women as they moved down the hall. "Good, because she is a pain in my ass. If she understood what was really going on, I wouldn't be able to stop her."

Dax couldn't help but note that Roman watched Gus until she turned and disappeared. Then his friend shook it off.

"Come on. Zack will join us when he can. I want to know everything you found out," Roman said. "I'm going to London in a few weeks. Zack has a summit with the prime minister. I'll contact the hospital and start looking into Constance's death. I also have some contacts there with Interpol who can brief me on the Krylov syndicate."

"Good," Dax said. "I think I might back you up."

Roman slid him a long look as they started down the hall. "Really? Because I thought you would be busy with your new girlfriend. I snuck a peek at Gemma White's reports once I realized what Gus had done. Have I mentioned what trouble your sister can cause? Gemma was one of our best agents. I thought we lost her over pay."

His sister was a schemer. She'd also watched over Holland when he'd been too stupid to. "I don't think she's my girlfriend. She told me she would walk away at the end of this."

They headed past uniformed guards and into the president's personal apartments.

"You should really make sure she doesn't do that," Zack said as they entered. He had a crystal decanter in his hand and he poured out what looked like a couple of fingers of Scotch.

Gabe Bond, who had been sitting on the sofa, stood and crossed the space between them. "Dax, I'm so glad you're alive. I thought you were going to get eaten by a reptile."

Such a city boy. "Yeah, the gators aren't so bad."

Gabe shook his head. "I was talking about the cops in New Orleans."

Funny, some of them had turned out pretty good. They'd taken

Chad into custody and promised a full investigation. He believed
them. They would get to the bottom of what had gone wrong with their
department. Unfortunately, even the good guys sometimes went bad.

"We survived. I wish we'd taken Beau Kirk alive, though."

Zack passed him a glass. "All that matters is you're safe, Dax. Let
Roman and me take it from here."

Connor snorted. "Hell, no. I promised Lara a London honeymoon."

"Already bought my tickets," Gabe agreed. "Everly is very interested in seeing the local sights."

"I wouldn't miss it for the world." It wasn't like he would have anything better to do. "After all, who's going to chauffeur all you taken
men around?"

"Don't mind him," Connor said, going for the Scotch. "He's being
a horrible pessimist. I thought that was my job. Twenty years' worth
of being the dude who can't see a silver lining and I end up as the Suzy
Sunshine of our duo."

Dax flipped his best friend off. "Screw you, Sparks. I can handle my
own love life."

Zack slipped his tuxedo jacket off. "It sounds like you can't. Dax,
you've been crazy about that girl since Joy introduced you to her. You
can't let her go."

"I don't know that I have a choice." He'd thought about this the
whole way from Louisiana to D.C. "Do I even have the right to bring
her into our collective nightmare? You're not bringing Liz in. I heard
you had a date tonight."

Zack's jaw tightened. "Yes. I'll have another in a few days. I have
an entire 'romantic' calendar planned. All anyone will be able to talk
about is the playboy president, and they'll forget the rumors that I was
ever in love with my press secretary. Holland is a trained agent. Liz
has no idea how to handle this. She would get hurt. She would do what
she always does, throw herself into solving the problem. And she
would end up dead. Holland knows what she's doing. So do Everly and
Lara. We're keeping the truth from Liz and Augustine."

Roman started to pace. "I don't even like to think about what would happen with Gus. She plots behind all our backs. She would try to take over."

Dax didn't miss the way Zack bit back a smile.

"We all know Gus would immediately inform Liz and then unionize the women against us," Zack said with a shake of his head. "We'll keep this quiet. As far as Liz and Gus know, Roman and I are going to London for meetings and they don't need to attend. Connor, if you wouldn't mind being pressed into security duty, I would appreciate you looking out for Roman."

"I don't need anyone to look out for me," Roman complained. "I'm perfectly good at protecting myself."

Gabe laughed. "Yeah, buddy. You don't even know which way to point the gun. Let's be democratic. All for Connor being in charge of security say aye. Aye."

They'd instituted democratic voting over crazy shit at Creighton, often when they ganged up on one another—especially when it was in the best interests of the ganged-up-on party.

Roman rolled his eyes as the rest of the group issued their ayes. "You know I miss the shit out of Mad because at least I could count on him to dissent."

Mad often dissented just for kicks. Dax missed him, too. "We've got your back, one way or another. I spent too much time today with a man who didn't understand the meaning of friendship."

Peter Morgan was alive and talking. So was Chad, though it appeared he didn't know as much as Beau Kirk had. He'd simply done what his superior demanded.

One thing was certain. They had a whole name—Boris Kuilikov. And a bit of direction about who he was and what might be his game.

Zack walked up and put a hand on his arm. "I do understand. You have no idea what it means to have you four around me. I know Mad would be here if he could. The five of you . . . well, you made my life bearable then. You do the same now. My brothers. So understand when I tell you, don't let that woman go."

Gabe joined them. "You've been in love with her forever. You made a mistake. Don't make another one."

"But we get invited to this wedding, damn it," Roman insisted.

Connor stepped in. "She loves you, too. There's no doubt in my mind. But you fucked up when you pulled that shit in Vegas. Have you apologized?"

Did Connor think he was a moron? "Of course. I said it was a mistake."

"It was more than a mistake," Connor said. "Look, I get this shit from my wife, but Lara is actually very good at figuring emotional stuff out. You've been circling this woman for what? Ten years?"

"Just about," he allowed.

"And she's been circling you. You took something from her. While she was sacrificing for you, you married someone who didn't matter to you," Connor pointed out. "Holland will always be a second wife. That's meaningful for women. A lot of them believe that the first wife is the true love. You need to make her believe she's not second."

"How do I do that?" She'd never been second for him.

Connor sighed. "No idea, man. But I do know you can't do it if you're on separate continents. Fix this or go back to New Orleans and you don't leave until she agrees that you're an idiot and she was always the one for you."

"Women like to think they're the one." Gabe tipped his glass up and took a swallow of Scotch. "In my case, it was true."

"Me, too," Connor agreed.

"First wives aren't always the only woman you ever love," Zack murmured.

"Yeah, well sometimes a man wants to believe he's the only one, too." Roman held out his glass.

Did Holland think that marriage didn't matter to him because he'd done it stupidly once? Had he made her believe it didn't have to be forever because he'd once treated the institution with so little respect?

He'd apologized, but had he explained why he wanted to marry her? Or had he left it as an abstract concept—an idea that simply made sense because she was female and he enjoyed having sex with her? Because they were so familiar?

He could clear up all of those misconceptions very quickly.

"What bedroom did you put her in?" Dax asked.

Zack looked up from pouring Roman's drink and smiled.

Holland opened the door to the bedroom she'd been assigned to with a long sigh. Her one piece of luggage would have been moved in and she assumed her closet would have the necessary items. She'd spent the last twenty-four hours cleaning up the mess her uncle had left in New Orleans. She hadn't had time to do more than throw an overnight bag together. On the flight over, she'd called and explained what she needed. The White House was thorough. Gus made sure of it. As far as she could tell, everyone was terrified of Gus, with the exception of her friends.

Liz Matthews had put on a good face, but it had been obvious she was on the brink of tears all evening. Gus had explained that Liz and the president had been very close until recently. So close there'd been speculation about an affair. Liz had basically been the stand-in for Zack's first lady. But earlier this evening, the commander in chief had shown up with a bimbo on his arm. It didn't seem to matter to Gus that said bimbo had a law degree from Harvard. She was slutastic and every woman in the room agreed.

God, Holland had missed colorful Gus and her straightforward honesty.

She was going to miss Dax forever.

Back in the bedroom she'd been assigned, Holland closed the door behind her and turned the lock. Habit. Almost nowhere in the U.S. was more secure, but she probably wouldn't sleep if she couldn't lock the door. Hell, her own uncle had turned out to be a damn mob plant. Who the hell could she trust?

She didn't bother turning on the light. She didn't need to see how empty her room was. She didn't need to wonder where Dax was. He was likely still drinking with his friends since they had the freaking White House as their man cave. Most likely, it wouldn't be long before Dax found another willing woman, like pretty, sweet, and laughs-at-everyone's-jokes Courtney. He would find a woman who would cower prettily behind him when the bad guys showed up and let him be the man. Despite what he'd said, he would move on.

And Holland would think about him every day for the rest of her life.

Was she making a horrible mistake by insisting they go their separate ways now? Maybe the wine was talking for her. Or the tequila shots, since Gus had brought out the big guns. Either way, the liquor was making her sentimental, but she wondered if she shouldn't sneak into Dax's room for one last night.

If you're leaving, then go. You've already decided to be a coward and let some other chick have him, so stop being such a wishy-washy bitch. Let the man of your dreams have his silly little never-shot-a-criminal-before woman.

Or you could claim his ass and defend him against all invaders cute and cuddly and with fake breasts.

Holland groaned. She might be an idiot, but she had to talk to him. She hoped they could find a way to work this out.

She stroked on some lip gloss because she was fairly certain she looked horrible. She groped the wall, looking for a light switch and hoping to find a mirror to prove herself wrong. Her fingers latched on to their prize and she flipped it up.

And she nearly screamed.

"Don't shoot me," Dax said from the bed in front of her.

She stopped and caught her breath because under the sheet covering his lower half, she didn't think he was wearing a stitch of clothing. He'd covered the bed in rose petals.

"What are you doing here?" she breathed.

His sexy smile caught her off guard. "Waiting on you."

And he looked so good. Yummy and male and ridiculously hot. "Why are you here?"

He pushed the sheet aside and proved he wasn't, in fact, wearing anything. He stood, his body looking like nothing less than sheer perfection. "Holland, I'm not letting you walk away."

He could say whatever he liked, but he'd let her go once before. Less than twenty-four hours later, he'd married someone else. He'd never apologized for what he'd truly done to hurt her. Yes, he'd said he was sorry for getting drunk, but that didn't heal the heart of her pain.

"So you want a few more weeks in bed? It won't matter."

He remained near the bed, giving her space. "Because I married Courtney?"

"It's not just that."

"You're right. I was making it too simple. I took something from us that should have been sacred and tossed it in the trash. I love you, Holland. You should have been my only wife. 'Til death do us part and long after because I'll love you until I die. Hell, I'll love you as long as this soul exists. That's why we should get married. And why it will mean everything. I never wanted to marry Courtney. I wanted to prove that I could . . . forget you, I suppose. But I couldn't. No other woman in the world is like you. So you can walk away, but I'll be right behind you, praying that you change your mind, because I can't be whole without you."

Tears welled in her eyes hard and fast. She knew she should stop this conversation or she'd soon be sobbing, but she couldn't. They had to talk this out. "Even years later, I couldn't marry anyone else."

He crossed the room to her and cupped her shoulders. "I know, sweetheart. You were faithful in a way I wasn't, and all I can do is beg your forgiveness and promise that our marriage will be forever. I'll put my heart and soul into us. You're everything I've ever wanted. I'm leaving the Navy. I'll live wherever you want. I'll be patient if you can't forgive me yet, but don't shut me out."

Her tears flowed freely. She hadn't really mourned three years ago, she realized. She'd shoved her pain down and tried to act as if his marriage didn't matter. Even after pictures of Dax and Courtney had appeared in magazines, she'd shrugged and shoved her hurt deep down.

"You gave her my ring." She'd hated that.

He stopped and shook his head. "No. I did not. Holland, sweetheart, why would you think that?"

"You had it in your pocket when you left that day."

He dragged her into his arms, his warm skin surrounding her. "And it stayed there. Even when I was drunk off my ass, I was smart enough to stop at a jeweler and buy her ring because the family ring was meant for you, not anyone else. Look at the nightstand."

She glanced over his shoulder and there sat a red velvet box. Her ring. "You brought it."

"Yes," he whispered into her ear. "I'll carry it around until you say yes and let me slide it on your finger, which is where it has always belonged."

She breathed him in and made her choice. She couldn't make any other choice. He was the love of her life.

"Make love to me, Dax."

"I will never refuse that command. Holland, are you on the pill? Because if you aren't, I'm going to have to sneak out and scrounge up some condoms from god knows where."

She had to laugh at the idea of Dax running to the Secret Service to ask for condoms. It would be a very Perfect Gentlemen thing to do. Her body heated at the thought of not wearing any protection beyond her four-times-a-year shot. "We're covered. I also had a checkup and I'm perfectly clean."

She let her hands roam over his skin. There was something sexy about him being naked while she was clothed. He was here for her pleasure. Her comfort and protection, too, but tonight was definitely going to be about pleasure.

"I haven't had sex with anyone else in a year," he admitted. "I'm clean. Can I take you, sweetheart? Nothing between us. I'll be faithful to you. For the rest of my life. I don't want another woman. Only you."

"A year?" It was inconceivable. Dax had a crazy sex drive. He would be on her at least twice a day. He was always trying to get inside her.

"Yes. After we split up, I only slept with one woman and only a handful of times."

"Courtney." It was easier to say her name now. They would never be friends again, but some of the toxic feelings had faded. That was a relief, because there had been pain on all sides.

"Yes."

"You didn't cheat on her?"

"No. I was cheating on you. That's the hard truth. I know that's my true sin."

She forgave him, finally and fully. "Don't do it again."

His eyes were solemn as he lowered his head. "Never. I'm yours. Everything I am and everything I have is all for you."

She bridged the slight distance between them, rising up on her toes to press her mouth to his. Passion flared, hot and quick. But it had always been that way between them. All she had to do was think about him and her body softened for him.

She kissed him, covering his mouth and tangling her tongue with his. He granted entry, pulling her against the hard length of his body. He was so warm, her man. It was right this time and she intended to stay with him for the rest of her life.

Their tongues played, gliding along each other in a silky slide. Her hands explored the strong muscles of his back. She let them slide down to his backside and cupped him, rubbing her body against his. His cock reacted, twitching between them.

"You're going to kill me tonight, aren't you?" Dax smiled as he kissed her nose and cheeks.

"I'm going to take what's mine." He was her man and she would have him any way she wanted him.

They would always have this push and pull. Giving and taking. When he needed control, she would yield to him, but on nights like this, she would take him and show him what it meant to be her man.

He shuddered. "I'm yours. You should definitely claim me. Otherwise, I'm going to be very lonely. I'll sit outside your door just wearing nothing. It could cause a scandal."

She couldn't have that. "Get on the bed, Captain."

He stepped back, giving her a spectacular view of his sculpted chest, not to mention that monster cock that stood at attention. "Your wish, my command."

His stare never wavered as he spread his big body across the mattress. All that delicious, gorgeous man was laid out for her delectation.

This was the rest of her life. All she had to do was say yes and they could love and live and play together. They could have a family. They could have a whole life of adventure.

She watched him as she unbuttoned her blouse and let it fall to the side. "I love you, Dax. It's always been you. I was afraid. I still am, but I'm not going to walk away this time."

"You've got nothing to be afraid of." He held out a hand as she slipped out of her shoes and slid her slacks to the floor. "I'm going to spend the rest of my life making sure you're safe and happy. It's all I want."

"All?" She had to ask because one specific part of him looked as if he wanted more.

"Semantics," he replied. "Love and happiness is what I want to share with you. And that gorgeous body on top of mine? Yes, I want that from you, too. God, you're beautiful."

Somehow he made her feel that way. She glanced at him, at everything he had to offer her. She shook her head. He was the beautiful one. She ran her hand over his chest, soft silky skin covering his rock-hard muscles. Down to his rigid abs and past that part of him that seemed so determined. She would get to that, but first, she intended to explore.

He groaned as her hand moved down his thigh. "You're going to kill me."

Only with pleasure. It would be a good way to go. "I'm just exploring."

"Take off that bra, Holland. Please."

She liked to hear him beg. She supposed since he was being so patient, she could give him that. She climbed on the bed between his spread legs and got to her knees. She would never call herself a sensual woman. She didn't tease her lovers, but it was different with Dax. His stare fused to her chest, waiting for the moment she revealed herself to him. She found herself moving slowly, deliberately drawing the moment out. She twisted the front clasp of her bra, but held it for a moment, locking gazes with him. She eased the cups almost to her nipples, enjoying how still he'd become, how intent.

She eased the bra off. Then his hands covered her, palming her. Cool air was replaced with the warmth of his callused hands moving on her.

"I'll never want to stop touching you," he said, his thumbs moving over her nipples.

Her skin flared to life, nipples becoming hard pebbles under his hands. Her blood started to thrum through her in a pleasant pulse. After all the stress of the day, this was what she'd needed—to be alone with him, intimate with him. She needed to lock the world out and be the Holland she was only with him.

"Let me touch you, Dax. Let me taste you." She eased back, her skin crying at the loss of his touch, but she wanted a deeper connection. She moved between his legs, lowering herself down so she had access to his cock.

It pulsed under her lips as she gently covered it in kisses and little licks. She loved running her tongue over the spot where the head sloped down to his thick stalk. She definitely loved lapping up the head.

His body shuddered under her, but he let her have her way. He raised his hand and tangled it in her hair. "Please put your mouth on me."

She had to admit, she liked torturing him. She pressed a peck on his flesh. "It is on you."

He laughed, though she heard a frustrated hiss behind it. "Suck me. Please suck my cock, Holland. I'll die if you don't."

She couldn't have that. She gently eased the head of his cock into her mouth, sucking lightly and enjoying the way he tasted, salty and sweet and masculine as hell.

Dax groaned as she began to take him deeper. She ran her tongue over his velvety flesh, drawing him into her mouth. He was so big, but she could handle him. One hand cupped his heavy testicles, rolling them and making him squirm and beg for more.

She took her time, making the moment last. Dragging her tongue over and around, she didn't want to miss an inch. She worked him inside, opening herself bit by bit as he murmured to her. He told her how much he loved her, how happy he was, how she would someday agree to marry him.

She had news for him. Someday was sooner than he would think.

"I don't want to come in your mouth, Holland." His hand tugged on her hair. "You keep doing what you're doing and I'll take over."

There was only so much he could take before he gave into his alpha-male instincts. She would try to remember that because she wanted to be on top this time. She gave him one last lick before she sat up. When she started to tug at her undies, he stopped her.

"Let me help." He reached for the sides of her lacy panties and ripped them apart before tossing them off the bed. "See. That was easy."

He was hell on her lingerie, but she had to admit, it made what she was about to do so much easier.

She straddled him, sliding her aching folds over his cock. She was so wet she didn't need any more play. She just wanted Dax inside her, connected to her. The day without him had been too long. She needed the reminder of where she belonged. With him. Always with him.

He gripped her hips and began guiding her down. As he filled her, she leaned in and kissed him. Their bodies entwined and she moved with him.

Together, they found a rhythm. She took him deep. His hands moved over her body, taking and giving. His hips thrust up, sending him deeper and deeper, and they got lost in their connection. She rode his cock, their eyes locked. He'd told her he loved her, couldn't want anyone else, and finally she was able to give the words back to him.

When his finger found her clitoris and pressed down, she rode that wild wave of pleasure only he could give her. She felt him stiffen under her, the hot wash of his own pleasure sending her spiraling again.

Finally she sank onto his body, curling herself around him. As the blood pounded through her she knew she would never leave him again.

"I think I'm ready for that ring now."

Dax jerked up on his elbow, staring down at her, gaze searching. "Are you serious? Be sure, Holland, because this is forever."

"I'm sure. But we are not going to Vegas." She wouldn't be swayed on that.

He reached over and grabbed the box. He had that ring on her finger before she could take another breath. "No Vegas. I love you. We can go anywhere you like."

She had a plan. "I've heard there's a lovely rose garden here."

It would be the perfect place to start their lives together.

TWENTY-ONE

Roman adjusted his chair, scanning the area for one of his aides. Air Force Two was brimming with White House staff on their way to London. They would set up everything for the president, who would come on his own in about a week.

He glanced out the window as they jetted farther and farther from D.C.

"You want a drink?" Connor asked, sliding into the seat across from him.

"I probably had enough at the wedding," he admitted.

Earlier in the afternoon, Dax and Holland had said their vows in the Rose Garden, a small ceremony capped off with a party thrown by the president. About fifty people had attended, but naturally Roman only had eyes for one.

Augustine Spencer had been Holland's maid of honor. The bride hadn't stuffed her lone attendant in some nasty pastel gown. Oh no. Not Augustine Spencer. She'd worn an emerald green sheath that hugged her every curve and a plunging neckline that caught the eye of every man in the room.

She was the sexiest thing alive and she knew it.

"You know we could have waited until tomorrow," Connor said. "I was surprised you decided to head out tonight."

If he hadn't, he would have been forced to deal with Gus, who thought she belonged on this trip. He'd explained that she could come out with Liz and Zack next week. He'd sprung it on her when she'd been too tied up to work her magic.

For once, he'd managed to put one over on her.

"Yes, well, if I'd waited we wouldn't be alone. Gus would be here and then we would have to deal with her sticking her nose in our business."

A smile curled up Connor's lips. "So this was your way of sneaking out on your work wife?"

Maybe he would have another drink after all. "I wouldn't put it like that."

He didn't put the words "wife" and "Gus" in the same sentence—ever. When he finally married, it wouldn't be to a mouthy, brazen sex bomb. Gus tied his stomach in knots. Gus made him crazy.

No, he'd choose someone who calmed and soothed him. Like Joy. Though she'd been Zack's, Joy was exactly what Roman sought in a wife. Faithful, kind, even-tempered, demure. If she'd lived, Joy would have been a wonderful mother. She would have given Zack a serene home to return to every night.

That was what Roman craved. Simple, blessed peace. He'd seen too much so-called passion from his parents. His childhood had been marked by their fights and their constant making up and breaking up. The upheavals had been chaos, and he refused to go through it again.

It was precisely why he'd broken it off with her back in college. He'd known it couldn't work. So why couldn't he get his mind off Gus even decades later? Why had he watched her dancing with another man and wanted to rip her out of the asshole's arms?

She turned him into a caveman and he wouldn't have it. He was doing the right thing in leaving Gus behind, and when he returned from this trip, maybe he'd put some real distance between them once and for all.

Because working with her every day and not touching her was slowly driving him mad.

"Have we found the mysterious Sergei? Do we have any idea how he's connected to Boris?" He needed to focus on something else, like the mysterious man coming after Zack.

Finally, they had a name and a trail. So he and some of the others were heading to England to investigate Constance Hayes's death. Maybe they'd finally uncover the secrets she'd been hiding and who killed her for them.

"I've got a PI in Russia running them both down for me. Do you really think Sergei could be Zack's half brother?" Connor asked.

It was the only explanation that made sense, given what they knew. "If they're coming after Zack to blackmail him, it's a good play. He's going into another election. Our enemies would never let anyone forget that the president is related to a Russian mobster. Let me know the minute you find out anything about that man."

"You got it." Connor nodded.

"What man?" a familiar voice asked. "Are we plotting? The great Roman Calder loves a good plot."

Roman froze, then cursed under his breath.

Gus slid into the seat beside him and crossed those long legs of hers that made him think of sin. She'd changed into a skirt and silky blouse that couldn't quite hide the fact that she was cold. Her nipples were nearly visible.

Just like that his cock hardened.

Connor sent him a shit-eating grin. "I should have mentioned that we had a last-minute addition."

"Lucky for you, I pack fast, Calder." She sat back, her lips curling up like a cat who'd stolen the cream.

"I will have that drink after all, Connor." It looked like he was going to need it.

Roman, Augustine, and all the
Perfect Gentlemen will return in

SMOKE AND SIN

And if you can't wait for more perfectly
seductive romance don't miss . . .

SHAYLA BLACK'S
FALLING IN DEEPER

A Wicked Lovers Novel coming July 2016 from Berkley!

AND

LEXI BLAKE'S
RUTHLESS

A Lawless Novel coming August 2016 from Berkley!

Shayla Black is the *New York Times* bestselling author of nearly fifty books, including the Wicked Lovers novels (*Wicked for You, His to Take, Theirs to Cherish, Ours to Love,* and many more). She lives in Texas with her family.

Lexi Blake is the *New York Times* bestselling author of the Masters and Mercenaries series, including *You Only Love Twice, Cherished,* and *A View to a Thrill.* She lives in North Texas with her family.